PULSE

Books by Rodman Philbrick

Slow Dancer
Brothers and Sinners

J.D. Hawkins Mystery Series
Shadow Kills
Ice for the Eskimo
Paint it Black
Walk On the Water

T.D. Stash Mystery Series
The Neon Flamingo
The Crystal Blue Persuasion
Tough Enough

PULSE

Rodman Philbrick

SPEAKING VOLUMES, LLC

NAPLES, FLORIDA

2012

PULSE

ISBN 978-1-61232-853-9

For Lynn Harnett, with love

PROLOGUE

Sunday, January 4
Sprauken, Maine

12:25 A.M.

It was cold enough to freeze blood. The heater in the hearse was out of order, so Quentin drove with his mittens on. His breath crystallized on the windshield. He had to keep scraping at it, trying to maintain a little circle clear enough to see through. Luckily there was no one else on the road. A few small, hard flakes of snow drifted into the headlight beams as he turned into the dead-end street.

"Never shoulda stopped," Quentin said, his teeth clicking.

He was talking to himself. There was no one else in the hearse. A man in his profession had to learn to keep himself company, especially on an out-of-town job.

"You shoulda eaten later, Quen," he said. "Finished up here before the snow started spittin'."

He had started the job at six, then decided to drive to the commissary for a quick burger. The idea was to chow down, then return to finish the job. The burger had been followed by several beers—unintentional beers, really. What happened was, a group of workers from the plant had come in after their shift and they were drinking and throwing darts, and Quentin had sort of blended into the crowd. None of the plant workers knew what he did for a living, or why he'd come to the village, and Quentin had been careful not to clue them in. They were a pretty friendly bunch, open to a stranger in their midst, and Quentin knew a little something about darts. He was a success, in a quiet way.

Then suddenly it was midnight and the bartender was announcing last call, and Quentin had to get back and finish up his client.

"You'll never learn, Quen," he said, giggling to himself. He wasn't fond of out-of-town assignments, but this one paid very well and he couldn't afford to screw up and lose any future trade.

A low, shed-style building came into the headlight beams at the end of the cul-de-sac. He slowed carefully, steering into a section of the parking lot that had been plowed earlier in the day. The fat hearse tires made sighing noises in the snow as he came to a stop.

Quentin got out, slapping his mittens together and shivering. Cold as a bastard. He located the key in his overcoat pocket. It wouldn't do to drop it, not when it was this late, or this dark, not when his head was still a little fuzzy with beer. He trudged to the shed building. It was a storage facility, a row of bays, each with an overhead garage door and a regular access door beside it. The bay he used for the occasional client in Sprauken was on the far left side at the north corner of the building.

The lock was frozen.

Quentin had to warm the key with his breath before the tumblers would move. When he finally got the door open he reached quickly inside and clicked on the lights. The fluorescent tubes sputtered, brightened. He pulled the door shut behind him and took off his mittens. It was cool inside, but bearable. An electric space heater kept the temperature well above freezing.

"Coffee, Quen," he said. "Have a cup to warm your guts."

He kept a hot plate on the workbench, and fixings for instant coffee, right next to the kit of Restoration Wax, Weldit Lip, Eye Sealer, and a gallon container of Blossom-brand embalming fluid, guaranteed to return a "glow of life" to the client. Quentin always said "client." It was really a much nicer word than "deceased." He was just setting the pan on the burner when he happened to glimpse something out of the corner of his eye. The gurney.

He turned and stared, squinting slightly.

"Shit," he said.

The gurney was empty. The sheet that had covered the client lay on the concrete floor of the storage bay. Quentin felt a kind of fluttery, empty feeling in the pit of his stomach. He glanced to each corner of the bay. Nothing but bare walls.

"You son of a bitch," he said.

Quentin didn't have a particular son of a bitch in mind. Just whoever the prankster was who'd removed the client from the temporary mortuary before the job was done.

He went to the gurney and stared at it, as if he might will the client back in place. There were stains on the plastic cover where he'd been a little sloppy with the arterial drain, and a few stray hairs where the client's head had lain. The unsettled feeling slowly congealed to anger. Someone was playing a joke.

Then Quentin noticed the side door. It was a fire exit triggered by a push bar, and he had never had any reason to open it. Now he noticed a vertical slice of dark shadow at the edge of the door. The exit had been breached. And there was something about the impenetrable darkness of that narrow shadow that made Quentin afraid.

"You're spooked, Quen," he whispered. "Ain't nothin' out there can hurt you."

Gathering his nerve—and his was a profession that required considerable nerve—Quentin strode to the side door and flung it open. The light behind him spilled out into the blankness of the bleak winter night. As his eyes readjusted he could just make out the stark, snow-covered hills in the distance, lying along the edge of the valley like a sleeping, animate form.

The shape of the distant hills didn't bother him, though. What bothered him was the single track of fresh, naked footprints leading away from the door, out into the inhuman coldness of the night.

1:35 A.M.

He never saw the patch of black ice. The traction on the main access road had been good, and Dr. Thomas Weston hadn't bothered to put his brand new Jeep Wagoneer into four-wheel drive. The carelessness may have been the result of the nightcap bourbon he'd been finishing just before his beeper went off, or his irritation as he listened in disbelief to the disjointed call from Trevor McNeil, the male night-duty nurse.

"It's walking, Doc," McNeil had said, his voice tight with panic. "The freaking thing is back alive. Or something."

Quite a statement. It made him wonder what McNeil was smoking.

The Jeep had been a Christmas present to himself, a less-than-successful effort to overcome the holiday blues that centered on how much he still missed Jeannie. He knew his late wife would have been amused by the vehicle and all the crazy options he'd ordered. The oversized tires, the roll bar, the special padded upholstery, and a stereo system that threatened to shatter the windows, if not his eardrums. Jeannie had been a classical music freak, with a low opinion of rock, but Dr. Weston had a Rolling Stones greatest hits CD in the player when the accident happened. Blame it on Mick Jagger.

It was a bitch of a night, cold beyond reason, and the patch of black ice had a super-slipperiness he wasn't expecting. The Jeep simply drifted out of control. Weston wrenched the wheel ineffectively. He continued to slide backward, piling rear-end-first deep into a snow bank on the south end of the lot. The bumper connected with something solid and the Jeep shuddered and jerked to a stop.

Dr. Weston couldn't get the Jeep door open. By now his momentary fear had given way to a nervous good humor—how could he have been so dumb? He rolled down the window and wedged himself backward out into the cold, crisp snow.

The stereo was still blaring "Let it Bleed" when he managed to free himself from the snowdrift.

*   *   *

The ER nurse was startled to see a tall, white-shrouded figure stamping clumsily through the automatic doors. It staggered inside, arms akimbo. It sneezed and white frosting disappeared from a rusty brown mustache. Handsome, watery blue eyes blinked, shedding snowflakes.

"Dr. Weston!" the nurse exclaimed, coming out from behind the reception desk. "What happened?"

Weston continued stamping his feet until he was relatively free of snow. He then peeled off his down parka and tossed it on an empty chair in the small waiting room. "Nothing happened," he said. "I'm sure it's McNeil's idea of a practical joke."

"Oh," the nurse said. After retrieving his parka she dusted it off and spread it out on the back of the chair to dry. She had no idea what Dr. Weston was talking about. So far as she was aware there were no emergency cases requiring his presence at the clinic, but she knew better than to question the Chief of Medicine when he stumbled in at nearly two in the morning, smelling faintly of bourbon.

The surge of adrenaline was starting to ebb when Weston pushed his way through the swinging doors into 144-B, the basement room that served as a temporary morgue for the clinic. Inside there was a strong smell of phenolic disinfectant, the musty scent of death and decay, and, oddly, the sharp odor of urine. Part of the room had been divided off by a light-blue curtain. The work, Weston surmised, of the county medical examiner, who had undertaken a postmortem on Saturday. The other thing he noticed was cigarette smoke. He noticed this not because he really cared about the clinic's no-smoking policy, or who might violate it, but because he had recently given up smoking as a New Year's resolution. After four days the desire for nicotine was still very strong.

Fuck it, he thought. Out loud Dr. Weston said, "McNeil, you wiseass Irish bastard, you got me down here, the least you can do is give me a cigarette."

There was no response. Weston went to the curtain and pulled it back. McNeil, a normally unflappable R.N. with a rangy athletic build and ten years' supervisory experience, was braced against an empty gurney. Holding it in a defensive posture, apparently. He was staring at something in the corner of the room. A cigarette dangled from between grayish lips. He flicked a glance at Dr. Weston and said, "I'm not an Irish bastard, I'm a Scottish bastard."

He tossed a pack of cigarettes to the doctor, who decided he didn't want a smoke bad enough to endure menthols. "What the hell's going on here, Trevor?" Weston asked in a joking manner. "Have you been snorting nitrous oxide again, or what?"

"See for yourself," McNeil said, jerking his chin at the corner.

Dr. Weston looked at the mess on the floor and shook his head. "What I see, buster, is a pretty pathetic attempt at a practical joke. Who put you up to this? Was it Dr. Nash?"

Alvin Nash was the clinic OB-GYN. He and Weston were close friends, having together endured the rigors of internship at the Mary Hitchcock Medical Center in Hanover, New Hampshire. Nash had a notoriously twisted sense of humor and Weston half expected to find him lurking somewhere in the temporary morgue, directing the R.N.'s performance.

McNeil ignored the jibe. "I think it's over," he said, indicating the cadaver that lay awkwardly sprawled against the wall. "It started to slow down right after I called you."

"Come on, Trevor. I'm not buying it."

McNeil backed away from the gurney. He pointed to the front of his white uniform trousers, which were soaking wet. "Dr. Weston, before I signed on here I was senior R.N. on the Mass. General ER Trauma Team. We got vehicular victims, knife assault, gunshot, fire, you name it. I saw just about every gruesome sight there was to see, Doc, but I never before pissed my pants."

Weston dropped the cigarettes on the gurney and studied McNeil. If the R.N. was acting he was doing one hell of a good job staying in character. His complexion was splotchy, pallorous, and the color had drained from his lips. There was a sheen of cooling sweat on his forehead. He looked like he'd been badly frightened. Weston glanced at the cadaver sprawled in the corner, noted the broad stitches of the autopsy, and said, "Okay, tell me exactly what happened."

BOOK I

The Phenomena

"When you have eliminated the
impossible, whatever remains,
however improbable, .
must be the truth."

Sir Arthur Conan Doyle

Tuesday, January 6

10:15 A.M.

Light snow was falling from a slate-gray sky over the Portland International Jetport. The young man leaning against the green stretch Mercedes stuck out his tongue and waited for a flake to dissolve there. Expecting, from the look of the stuff, that it would taste like cotton candy. He smacked his lips shut and grimaced. Iron filings was more like it. All the crap they put in the air, even here in Vacationland.

On the airfield Piedmont Flight 214 was deplaning directly to the tarmac. The passengers came off the stairs and moved in a slow rhumba line, like maybe they thought they could dodge the snow. Welcome to beautiful downtown Maine, he thought, grinning. He opened the limousine door and retrieved the piece of posterboard that had been hand lettered with the name "Dr. Cullen, Sprauken International." He held it over his head and kept grinning, because he'd been told the gap in his front teeth made him look like David Letterman. It didn't, but the grin was friendly enough.

A slim girl with short, strawberry-blond hair veered toward him. She was wearing a leather flight jacket, a pair of tight, acid-washed jeans, and brushed suede boots. Snowflakes had caught on her long eyelashes. She looked at the Mercedes limo, then at him, and said, "Going my way?"

What a line. He grinned until his face hurt. "'Hey, I'd

love to, honey. Only I gotta wait for this guy,'' he said, rattling the sign over his head.

The girl blinked the snowflakes from her pale green eyes.

''That's me.''

''Huh?''

''I'm Dr. Cullen.''

''You're shitting me,'' he said, and then winced. ''I mean welcome to Maine, Dr. Cullen.''

As the limousine cruised north on the turnpike, Dr. Susan Cullen settled herself into the lush passenger compartment, suppressing a desire to giggle. It never failed—she still got a kick out of riding in limousines, just as she enjoyed the shock of uncertainty that had flashed in the driver's eyes when he realized his mistake. Susan had recently turned thirty-three. The fact that she easily passed for ten years younger was due, she knew, to the luck of the genetic draw. She was blessed with a flawless, radiant complexion that kept her looking remarkably youthful. For years, especially during her residency, she had endeavored to make herself look more mature. Choosing clothes and hairstyles and makeup that made her appear somber and serious, if not really older. Now, having established herself as one of the leading specialists in her field, she no longer had to play that game.

There was freshly brewed coffee in the limo's minibar, and two morning newspapers. Susan scanned the *New York Times* and then leafed through the local *Portland Press Herald*. Neither paper mentioned any unusual incidents in Sprauken, Maine. No surprise there. As a major defense contractor, Sprauken International was security sensitive, sometimes maddeningly so. The story would leak eventually, Dr. Cullen assumed, but not before she had a chance to investigate and provide, it was hoped, a reasonable explanation for the phenomenon.

If, in fact, it had occurred.

As she watched the whitened landscape unfurl around her, the limousine left the turnpike and headed away from the coast, into a wilderness of frozen lakes and stark, uninhabited mountains.

"How far is the village?" Susan asked.

The driver showed his gap-toothed smile. "As far as you can get. Sprauken is where the road ends. And if you don't mind me sayin' so, Doc, they don't like you should call it a village. They got a population of seventy-five hundred now, since the new contracts came through. In Maine that's big enough to be a city, almost."

"Thanks," she said. "There is a ski resort nearby, have I got that right?"

"Yeah," the driver said. "Ice Valley. 'Bout an hour drive to the west, if the road's clear. You a skier, Doc?"

She smiled. "Never had the time to learn," she said. "I have friend who's an avid skier, though."

The grin faded. "Boyfriend, huh?"

"Sort of," Susan replied, staring at the bleak, frozen landscape.

The luncheon specials at the Employee Health Clinic cafeteria included *scalloppine alla Zingara* and steak *au poivre*.

"Truffles in Maine?" Susan asked Dr. Weston, who had insisted on lunch before giving her the grand tour of the facility. "I expected lobsters, maybe. Not truffles."

Weston laughed as he carried the tray back to his office. He had decided on the privacy of his office rather than the cafeteria dining room not only because the young pathologist was attractive, but because he wanted to confound the clinic rumor mill as much as possible.

"When we were drawing up the subcontract for the medical facility I insisted we get the same menu as the management dining room at the plant," he said. "I guess Kenneth Goddard and his staff must like truffles. Never touch the stuff myself."

Dr. Weston would have liked to decant a good white wine, but Dr. Cullen had requested plain soda water and he had no intention of drinking alone. He put the tray on the conference table and set out the covered dishes and the cutlery wrapped in linen napkins that were, typically, embossed with the company logo. Usually the conference table was littered with files, but he'd been notified of Dr. Cullen's pending arrival and consequently had had his office straightened out at the last minute.

"We didn't think you'd get here until tomorrow at the soonest, Dr. Cullen," he said, taking his place on the opposite side of the table.

"This is an informal visit."

Weston relaxed a little. A tall, confident man with hawkish good looks and a ruddy, fresh-air complexion, he was used to having the final word at the clinic. The idea of a top-notch medical troubleshooter intruding on his territory was disturbing. He was aware that Dr. Cullen had frequently published in the new field of biohazards. Her state-of-the-art roving lab had been the subject of a feature article in *Newsweek*. Impressive stuff. Weston had been expecting a high-powered, monomaniacal scientist, a type he detested.

Susan Cullen didn't fit the picture, or act it. So far so good.

"Call me Tom," he said, toasting her with a glass of soda.

She laughed. "Are you serious?"

"I guess you better call me Dr. Weston," he replied with a shrug, thinking maybe he'd have to reevaluate his impression of Dr. Susan Cullen.

"Sorry," Susan said. "It's just I never knew a Chief of Medicine who wanted to be called by his first name."

He shrugged. "Well, in my case 'Chief of Medicine' is something I got stuck with because the company likes titles, as I'm sure you're aware. My real role is to keep the wheels greased here at the clinic and to act as resident internist," Weston explained as he cut up his steak. "Actually the clinic is really too small to require a Chief of Medicine. We ordinarily have, at most, a dozen beds occupied. Half for maternity. If you go by titles, in addition to being Director and Chief of Medicine I'm also the Chief of Surgery, which means I arrange for gypsy surgeons to come in for routine procedures. Sometimes I even scrub for the op, if the cutter isn't too much of a martinet."

"Sounds like you've got a nice setup."

"You bet," he said. "We keep the people healthy, wealthy,

and not too wise. And there's plenty of time left over to enjoy the good life.''

"Such as?''

He ticked off the options. "Hunting, fishing, water sports, bird-watching, skiing—whatever turns you on. I'm a mean man with a fly rod, Dr. Cullen.''

"Susan.''

"Right.''

The rest of the meal was devoted to small talk, concentrating on the vagaries of local weather, ski conditions, and the peculiarities of living within a community that was designed, built, and owned by a security-conscious defense company.

"This reminds me of Colorado,'' Susan said at one point, referring to another Sprauken community where she'd been involved in detecting a leak of toxic gas. "Mountains, snow, and a hundred miles from nowhere.''

Weston was amused by the comparison. "Apples and oranges,'' he said. "Except we've got the same brand name. Actually this part of Maine is a hell of a lot more remote than Sprauken, Colorado. Before the company bought up the area the only outposts of civilization were a few hunting camps.''

After the meal was over they had coffee at Weston's desk while he laid out the available data on what he preferred to call the "unexplained events.''

"The first occurrence—at least the first I knew of—was early Sunday morning in the makeshift morgue we have in the basement here,'' he began, pausing to sip his coffee. "The cadaver was that of one Robert J. Simpson, fifty-eight, electrical engineer in the Guidance Systems Division. Domestic accident. Fell from a ladder while changing a light bulb. Spinal injury, followed by cardiac arrest. The company usually requests an autopsy in instances like that, for liability purposes. Could the death be job-related, et cetera. Autopsy was performed by Dr. Pendergast, the county medical examiner. His notes are here. You can listen to the cassette later, if you like.''

"I'd like,'' Susan said.

"Fine. Seemed normal enough, from what I can tell. Being just a humble and simple internist. The brain had been sliced and examined for any obvious tumors or hematomic infarctions. None found. The slides are here if you want to view them."

"I'll do that," Susan said, smiling.

Weston grinned right back at her. "You're already way ahead of me, right?" he asked.

"Not at all," Susan said. "Please go on. We'll run full-scale tissue and neuropathic tests as soon as the lab arrives. The semi truck that hauls it got held up in a snowstorm, or it would have been here already."

"Okay, I'll skip the postmortem gibberish and just tell you what happened. Or what McNeil said happened. He was the R.N. who observed the, ah, event. Or claims to."

"You don't believe him?"

Weston shrugged and made a face. "I don't know what I believe. At first I thought it was a practical joke. Morgue humor. But McNeil sticks to his version, so far. And then there was the other event, which appears to have taken place at about the same time. I think they've both been faked, of course, but it's no joking matter now. Not that I have any theory on *how* they were faked. Especially the other event. That's a real puzzler."

Susan nodded, scanning the files. As she had expected they were incomplete. The medical examiner's notes were virtually illegible. From what she could make out he was a cut-'em-up-and-weigh-'em man from the old school, trained in forensics, not clinical pathology.

"The second cadaver," Susan said. "Was it autopsied also?"

Weston shook his head. "Nope. Had been partially prepared by an undertaker, though."

Susan looked up from the files. "Is this McNeil person around? I'd like to hear it from the horse's mouth, if you don't mind."

"Hey, be my guest. If I know Trevor McNeil, he'll appreciate the attention."

At his request the senior R.N. had been shuttled off the night shift. He was located in the staff lounge. Cigarette smoke hung like a bank of blue fog from the ceiling, almost obscuring the prominently displayed No Smoking signs. McNeil's mood had been such that not even the more militant of the staff nonsmokers had cared to apply the rule to him.

Susan's first impression, after the R.N. shook hands, was that the man had a drug abuse problem. His pupils were slightly enlarged and the way he kept licking his lips and smacking his tongue indicated chronic dry mouth. Weston, sensing her diagnosis, explained that McNeil had been taking medication only for the past forty-eight hours.

"Valium. Right, Trevor?"

McNeil nodded. "I don't much like the side effects, but it helps with that out-of-breath feeling. If I get some sleep tonight I'll shitcan the pills tomorrow."

Susan nodded and said, "Do you mind if we pay a visit to the room where the incident took place?"

Clearly McNeil did mind, but he assented readily enough. The elevator dropped them to the basement level. McNeil attempted to sublimate his tension by rapid clenching of his jaw muscles, Susan noted.

"You probably think I'm crazy," the nurse said without meeting her eyes.

"Not at all," Susan said soothingly.

"Like I told Dr. Weston, I'm willing to take a lie detector test."

Susan couldn't dismiss the offer out of hand, although like most M.D.s she had grave misgivings about the effectiveness of the so-called polygraph devices. But she was well aware that the Security Division had a firm pro-polygraph policy. Plant employees at almost every level were tested as an integral part of the counterespionage program. By contract the questions posed were supposed to be confined to security-related matters. In practice the method was intrusive and demeaning.

As they approached 144-B Nurse McNeil's legs seemed to stiffen, as if he had to force himself to keep walking. Susan was disturbed. Since her medical investigations usually involved company personel and how they were affected by a work environment, she had had to develop her powers of psychological observation. Was an employee faking an unexplained neurological disorder to get a disability settlement? Had a worker exaggerated respiratory distress? Were the symptoms real or psychosomatic? The result of an undetected biohazard or just imagination? In effect she had to function as her own lie detector, and it was now telling her, in no uncertain terms, that Nurse McNeil suffered from very real stress that intensified in direct proportion to his proximity to room 144-B.

Dr. Weston paused outside the door and cleared his throat. "I, uh, had the heat shut off in there," he explained. "We're not equipped to store cadavers for any length of time, but I assumed your lab would want tissue samples before the, ah, deceased is cremated."

"Absolutely," she said. "We'll be running the full range."

The room, as they entered, was indeed cold. It was also dark. The cool air was laden with the sharp odor of phenolic disinfectant and Formalin. Weston snapped a light switch. Fluorescent light tubes flickered and began to glow. Susan shivered. The room was above freezing, but not by much. McNeil hung back, as if ready to bolt at the least provocation.

Weston drew back a curtain. The cadaver lay on a gurney, covered with a white sheet. Susan lifted the sheet and gave the body a cursory visual examination. She saw nothing unusual. The mortal remains of the late Mr. Robert J. Simpson, electrical engineer, showed evidence of the early stages of putrefaction. The lowered room temperature would help slow down the inevitable process of decay, but she would have to take tissue samples soon, or risk having test results skewed by bacterial infections.

"Dr. Pendergast preserved organ samples. Brain, liver, spleen," Weston said, indicating the Formalin-filled jars arranged on a nearby work counter. "What he didn't choose to sample he returned to the abdomen before closing the incision."

Susan glanced at the sample jars and then noticed that the nurse was trembling. She said, "Nurse McNeil, would you prefer to sit down?"

McNeil shook his head and remained standing close to the

door. Despite the chilling air there was sweat visible on his forehead. During the brief examination of the cadaver he had kept his eyes leveled at the floor. Now he seemed to find comfort in staring at the fluorescent lights.

"Nurse McNeil, please tell us what happened here on Sunday morning."

He nodded, sighed, and closed his eyes. "We had a cardiac patient on a mild Lidocaine drip, awaiting transportation to Maine Medical in Portland. I came down to the storeroom to sign out a Lidocaine bag. I heard a lot of noise. Trash cans rattling, glass breaking, like that. Coming from this room."

Susan stopped him to interject a question. "Did you know the cadaver was being temporarily stored in this room?"

"Sure," McNeil said. A cigarette appeared in his fingers. He shoved it into the corner of his mouth as if plugging a hole in a dike. "Of course. The information was on my chart when I came on shift. I already knew an autopsy had been scheduled."

"What did you think when you heard noise coming from this room? Were you frightened?"

McNeil lit the cigarette and inhaled. "Doc, give me a break, huh? It was no big deal we had a deceased on the premises. It happens, okay? What I thought when I heard all the ruckus, I assumed a raccoon had got into the room."

Susan smiled. "A raccoon?"

"Sure. A 'coon will make a hell of a racket. That's what I was expecting to find, or anyhow some small animal. Skunk maybe. Driven inside by the cold weather. All I did, I opened the door and turned on the lights. The screen was pulled across. I went behind it and . . ." McNeil's voice trailed off and he concentrated on the cigarette, as if determined to absorb every milligram of nicotine.

"What did you see?" Susan said firmly.

He sighed, exhaling. "What I told Dr. Weston when I called him. The deceased was moving."

Susan said, "Can you be more specific?"

"Yeah, sure," McNeil said. "The thing was trying to walk, okay? It had tipped over a trash barrel and some other stuff and there it was, right up against the wall, trying to walk forward. At first I thought it was a patient had got in here somehow and was having a seizure. Then I saw the autopsy stitches. It was the deceased, no doubt about it. Dead as a doornail except the legs were thrashing."

Weston caught Susan's eye. He shrugged as if to say, *What do you think?*

Susan ignored him and said, "How long did the phenomenon last, Nurse McNeil?"

"Pardon?"

"How long did the legs thrash?"

McNeil thought about it. "I wasn't looking at my watch, Doctor. I called Dr. Weston from the phone right here in the room. He told me he'd be right down. The thing stopped moving a few minutes before he got here."

Susan turned to Weston and raised her eyebrows.

"Should have been ten minutes," he said. "It was more like twenty. I got stuck in a snowbank."

Susan nodded and turned back to McNeil. "So would fifteen minutes be a fair estimate?"

The nurse shrugged. "Beats me," he said. "It seemed like forever."

3:15 P.M.

The panic seemed to center in her throat, like a tiny fist. Ruthann had trouble breathing. She had to force herself to inhale, exhale. Steering the car, something she usually did without thinking, became a task of mind-boggling difficulty. Tears blurred her eyes.

This was so dumb! You were supposed to call an ambulance and wait, not go charging off to the clinic on your lonesome. The panic had fogged her thinking. Pete would be angry—he was just as excited about having the baby as she was, maybe more so. Now something had gone wrong, badly wrong, and it was all her fault.

Suddenly the ER entrance was looming before her. Ruthann turned off the ignition and tried to get out from behind the wheel. It was no use, she was going to faint. She leaned on the horn.

Two orderlies appeared almost instantly. Charging behind them was the portly Dr. Nash, whose office Ruthann had called just before leaving the house. Dr. Nash was at her side as the orderlies lifted her from the car and placed her gently on the lowered gurney.

Ruthann looked at him imploringly. "Save it," she begged him. "Save my baby."

"Relax," he said, stroking her forehead. "You'll both be fine."

Dr. Nash was almost as baffled and upset as the would-be mother. Ruthann was young, healthy, and halfway through her second trimester. As of the last examination, the fetus was likewise normal and healthy. Ruthann was past the stage where he might have expected a spontaneous miscarriage. The event was abnormal in the extreme.

"Please," the young woman whispered as she was wheeled into surgery.

Alvin Nash made more soothing noises, but, as he quickly determined, the baby was beyond saving. He eased the premature labor contractions with an injection, but the uterus was already partially dilated and the fetus was positioned in the birth canal. Lividity revealed that the fetus had expired; there was no heartbeat. Probably the death of the fetus had triggered off the premature labor, causing the miscarriage. Uterine bleeding was severe—more severe than he would have expected.

Dr. Nash ordered up a unit of whole blood. The fetus was gone. Now his problem was to insure that the mother survived.

The hemorrhaging was unabated when he completed dilation of the cervix. Nash took great care as he performed a curettage; the placental tissue had to be cleared away from the endometrium, but he did not want to aggravate the uterine bleeding. The D and C procedure took less than five minutes. It was another forty minutes before the hemorrhaging was brought under control. By the time the bleeding had stopped Ruthann had gotten two units of whole blood and she *still* looked pale as a ghost.

"What happened?" she asked weakly. "What went wrong?"
He had no ready answer.

It was the damndest thing, Dr. Nash reflected, stealing time for a few quick puffs on a cigarette before he went back to break the bad news to the husband, a technician from the MGS Division. Ruthann's was the second spontaneous miscarriage in less than five days and this time with complications that were more suggestive of a hemophiliac than a young woman with perfectly normal blood chemistry.

He exhaled, staring moodily at the gray smoke, and then crushed the cigarette butt under his heel. He wanted to go back in there and tell Ruthann and her husband not to worry, that the miscarriage was just one of those things. The "blessing in disguise" routine. His heart wasn't in it, though. He was not at all sure that the young woman should attempt pregnancy again, not until he had ordered a full barrage of blood tests.

Something was out of whack. He couldn't make a diagnosis until he saw test results, but medical intuition told him that something had gone seriously wrong.

4:05 P.M.

Before taking her to the site of the second phenomenon, Dr. Weston suggested a short ride through the valley, to help orient Susan to the town layout. She agreed it would be a good idea.

"You'll want something warmer than that leather jacket," he advised. "It gets bitter cold as the sun goes down."

"My personal effects are with the lab," she explained, turning up the collar of her jacket. "All I brought with me is what I could jam into a garment bag. If you'll take me 'round to the PX I'll pick up a winter coat."

"Fine," he said, opening the door of the unlocked Jeep. Susan noticed the missing bumper and the broken taillight but refrained from commenting on his driving skills, or lack of them. "You'll want a down windbreaker. With a hood," he said, glancing at her thin suede boots as she slid into the passenger seat. "Insulated boots might be a good idea. We treat a lot of frostbite at the clinic."

Susan grinned. "Whatever you say, uh, Tom."

He smiled back at her and started up the engine. For some reason the expression on her face made him giggle. The sight of the rugged guy giggling was too much for Susan, and she joined in, unable to hold it back. She laughed until tears ran from her eyes.

When Tom Weston finally got control of himself his face was crimson. He handed her a Kleenex to wipe away her tears and said, "Nervous reaction. You listen to McNeil tell that whacked-out story of his, you don't know whether to laugh or cry."

"That's it," Susan agreed.

"Nerves," Weston said, as if repetition could make it true.

"Right."

He put the Jeep in gear and they exited the parking lot in silence. The town had been laid out in a rough crescent on the valley floor, with the inner curve roughly parallel to a medium-sized lake, now frozen and crusted with snow. The housing was arranged in ten-unit clusters around a variety of short streets and cul-de-sacs. The cluster roofs were steeply pitched to shed snow. The siding was cedar shingles stained in various earth tones. Plumes of wood smoke rose from a few of the shingle-covered chimneys. Susan commented that from the air the town would blend into its gray-and-white environment. Weston agreed.

"The high fliers wouldn't know we were here," he said. "Who knows, maybe that's what the architects had in mind. When you work for an outfit like Sprauken International, you get used to the paranoid view. Especially with Kenneth Goddard in charge."

"What do you mean by that?" Susan asked. "I heard Goddard was some kind of genius."

Weston shrugged. "Oh, nothing. Just a personal opinion."

They cruised slowly around the outskirts of the town. The streets were quiet, almost serene.

"In the fall it gets real pretty for about three weeks," he

said. "The trees are mostly maple and birch, so we get lots of brilliant reds and bright yellows."

The plant facility covered more than a hundred acres of hillside behind the residential crescent. Although none of the numerous industrial buildings were more than five stories in height, the hillside elevation had the effect of making it appear to loom above the town.

"The majority work in the MGS Division," Weston said, pointing out the largest cluster of buildings. "They build missile guidance systems. The Experimental Division is smaller but more elite, with a slightly higher pay scale."

"And that's Goddard's division?" Susan asked. She was curious about the powerful, reclusive executive. At this point she'd never met the man; he was just a famous name from the old days of the Apollo program, a former astronaut with a doctorate in electrical engineering.

"Well, he's in charge of both divisions, but he and the Whiz Kids spend most of their time at Experimental."

"Whiz Kids?"

"Local slang for the young engineers he has on his staff," Weston said. "I don't see much of that crowd. Most of the work-related injuries we treat are from MGS. Hardware assembly. Welding burns, metal chips embedded in the cornea, acid burns, that sort of thing. Basically a pretty low per-man-hour injury rate. Way better than the OSHA guidelines. If everybody wore protective eyegear at all times they'd put us out of business. From what I gather, the Experimental Division is heavy into research. More a think tank. From there we get mostly ulcers and hypertension."

"Any nonspecific infections or symptoms?"

Weston gave her a quizzical look. "Just the flu," he said. "What do you mean, like Legionnaires' disease?"

"Just anything out of the ordinary. Unexplained rashes, that sort of thing."

Weston grinned. "Well, last summer we had this young guy come in with a walloping case of poison ivy on his pubes. That's about it for unexplained rashes."

Now it was Susan's turn to blush. It had the effect of heightening the green in her eyes.

"Hey, 'scuse me for being a wise guy," Weston said, obviously not at all sorry, "but what's with the 'infectious' line of inquiry? Is there a type of microorganism that can actually stimulate muscle contractions in a cadaver?"

"Not that I know of," Susan said. "Look, it's part of my job to ask a lot of questions. Don't take it personally."

Weston turned the wheel and slowed as he entered a residential cul-de-sac. "Go on, fire away," he said affably. "I am yours to command."

"Why are we stopping?"

"My place," he said. "Don't move an inch. I'll be right out."

The Jeep door slammed with a thud. Weston jogged up to a cedar-shingled building. Susan amused herself by checking out his CD collection, stored in a rack under the dash. When he returned she was happily tapping her feet to a Talking Heads tune. Weston opened her door, catching her slightly off balance.

"Oops," he said. "Here, try this on for size."

He held out a green, down-filled parka with a detachable hood. Susan got out of the Jeep and shivered as she slipped off her leather jacket and tried on the parka. It was a little long in the sleeves but otherwise fit perfectly. Weston handed her a pair of down-insulated boots. "Seven and a half," he said. "Close?"

"Close enough," she said, getting back into the Jeep. "What's the story, you keep an array of women's clothing on hand?"

Weston got in and kept his eyes glued to the mirror as he backed up. "Something like that," he said.

The way he said it closed off further inquiry.

They drove to the outskirts of town.

"Everyone here is from somewhere else," Weston said, pulling up to a remotely situated storage facility. "Most people want to be buried back home, wherever that happens to be, so we don't require the services of a full-time funeral director. If no other arrangements have been made, as was the case here, a service is conducted at the nondenominational chapel. Interment is in the company plot, up on a pretty little hillside overlooking the lake,'' he added, sounding almost wistful.

Susan got out of the Jeep. It was getting colder, as Weston had promised, and she was glad to have the parka and the boots. A white Saab pulled into an adjacent slot. A Sprauken Security emblem was emblazoned on the side. A broad-shouldered, big-gutted man of about sixty got out from behind the wheel. He had on a brown cashmere overcoat and carried a thick leather briefcase. A much younger man emerged from the passenger side. Susan had an impression of handsome dark eyes, mustache, white teeth, cleft chin, and a skier's tan. The younger man wore a green baseball-style cap with SECURITY on the visor. Weston made the introductions.

"Jack Webster, the Chief of Security. Kurt Mallon, his deputy. Meet Dr. Susan Cullen. She runs the Biohazard Lab I was telling you about, Jack."

Webster, a former FBI man, had a pale, fleshy face with piercing blue eyes and short gray hair going rapidly white. He looked Susan over as if he suspected Dr. Weston of pulling his leg. "My God," he said. "I must be getting old. Ancient. I've got a granddaughter near your age, Dr. Cullen."

"Not by ten years at least," Susan said, her breath steaming in the cold air. "Thanks anyway."

"Pleased to meet you, Doctor," the young deputy said, extending a gloved hand. To Dr. Weston he offered only a deprecatory smile. Susan got the distinct impression the two men did not like each other.

Weston clapped his hands together. "Let's get this show on the road," he said, glancing at the rapidly lowering sun. "Jack, you got the call, why don't you give Dr. Cullen the facts?"

Webster chuckled. " 'Just the facts, ma'am,' is that the idea? Excuse the old joke, Doc," he said, turning to Susan. "Why don't we start at the scene of the crime."

The temporary mortuary was in a single-stall garage on the corner of the storage building. There was nothing on the outside to denote its function. No sign on the access door, which was located on the far side. The security chief produced a tagged key from his pocket, unlocked the door, and pulled the door open.

There were lights on inside, but no heat. The cold seemed to radiate up from the concrete floor. The first thing Susan noticed was a portable mortuary table, empty, and beside it a hospital gurney, occupied. The cadaver was draped in a sheet, but the arms and legs were sprawled out in such a way that the frost-covered, marble-white fingertips of one hand protruded from under the sheet.

Webster busied himself lighting up a cigar. It was obvious the presence of the body made him uncomfortable. He compensated for his uneasiness by assuming a light, bantering tone of voice.

With clenched teeth holding the cigar, the senior security cop used both hands to flip open a notebook he'd extracted from his briefcase. "Okay, like we used to say at the Bureau, these are the particulars: Sunday, about ten after one in the morning. We log a call from the mortician—a Mr. Quentin Jones from Skowhegan; he comes in whenever the necessity arises. He wants to report a stolen cadaver. First thing I assume is, it's a prank call. We don't get a lot of missing cadavers here in Sprauken, Dr. Cullen," he said, waggling his tufted white eyebrows. "This is the first since I came on as chief. Okay, like I say, I respond. I find Quentin in here, wringing his hands. I know he's upset because his toupee is on crooked."

Webster chuckled at the lame joke, then paused to shift the cigar to the other side of his mouth. "He tells me he transported the deceased from the clinic to this place, began pumping out the bodily fluids prior to injecting the embalming agent, and then went out to the commissary for supper. Apparently he stayed several hours, drinking beer with a few of the locals. He came back after midnight to discover the deceased was no longer on the premises. Mr. Jones concluded that somebody was playing a sick joke on him. Somebody crazy enough to open the overhead door, back a car in, and remove the deceased. Then he noticed the fire exit door was ajar and he checked it out and realized his first guess was dead wrong."

Deputy Mallon grinned at Susan as if to say, *Give the old guy a break; he's nervous.*

Webster looked up from his notes and indicated the fire exit, which had a push-bar release. "The deceased was removed via that door. There was fresh snow on the ground and a nice, easy-to-follow trail of footprints heading in a straight line into the wooded area behind the building. One set of prints by the way. They've since been obliterated, but we got some good plaster casts of bare feet."

"Tracks left by bare feet?" Susan asked.

"You heard me," Webster said with a nervous grin. "Bare feet. Okay, I give the mortician my spare flashlight and we follow the footprints. Exact distance, as we later determined, four hundred and forty-two feet. The footprints lead us directly to the deceased, who was facedown in the snow at the base of a tree."

Webster removed a file folder from the briefcase and handed it to Susan. "Pictures," he said.

The color photographs had been taken at night, illuminated by a bright strobe that made the ice-covered trees look unreal, as if formed from blown crystal. The cadaver was that of a thin, middle-aged woman. Her arms and legs were sprawled out.

A frozen snow angel, Susan thought, examining the pictures. The trail of footprints, which appeared as black shadows in the photos, made it look like the cadaver had walked in a straight line until it bumped into the tree and fell facedown in the snow.

"We looked all over for another set of footprints," Webster explained, gesturing with the cigar. "Found only virgin snow."

"What state was the cadaver in when you found it?" Susan asked.

"Frozen solid, near as I could tell," Webster replied. "I figured someone carried the thing out there, dropped it, and then backed off, keeping to the same footprints. My deputy disagrees. Right, Kurt?"

Deputy Mallon nodded. "The casts indicate the prints were

made by someone weighing no more than a hundred and twenty-five pounds.''

''Which just so happens to be what the deceased weighed,'' Webster added.

Susan handed the pictures back to the security chief and approached the gurney. She lifted the sheet and made an unhurried visual examination while Dr. Weston explained that the deceased, a clerical worker, had been in ill health for some time, suffering from extreme hypertension. The cause of death was attributed to sudden, massive cerebral hemorrhage.

Meanwhile Webster puffed nervously on his cigar and joked with Deputy Mallon. When Susan completed her preliminary examination and dropped the sheet he appeared greatly relieved.

''I agree with Dr. Weston this is no ordinary prank,'' he said. ''What I'd like to know is, who would do such a gruesome thing, and why? Also *how* they did it.''

He grinned around the cigar stub. ''I'm dying to know,'' he added.

5:05 P.M.

Bernie Simms found it helpful to think of his blessings before he had to actually look at his supper. Supper at the Veterans' Hospice in China, Maine, was not conducive to giving thanks. Bernie had been admitted to the facility to play the last great waiting game; under the circumstances an appetite was hard to come by. On the bright side, the hospice had two good, slate-bed, regulation-sized pool tables, one of which was cut low enough for the guys in wheelchairs. They had a good library of paperbacks, a big-screen projection TV, and a collection of old war flicks, including the ever-popular *Hellcats of the Navy*, featuring Ronald Reagan.

Bernie's buddy Sam Carnovitz, who was hanging in there with one bad lung between himself and eternity, old Sam always got a kick out of *Hellcats*.

''Beautiful, huh?'' Sam would say, squinting at the big

screen. "They showed clips of this in Reagan's film bio at the Republican convention, like as if he'd really been in combat as a navy pilot."

"Yeah? I thought he *was* in the navy," Bernie always said, just to bait him, bring the color to his buddy's cheeks.

"Ah, for chrissake," Sam would retort. "The man was sitting out the war in Hollywood, pretending to be a soldier in the movies. Clark Gable was ten years older than Reagan, and *he* joined up and flew bomber missions over Germany. Not Ronnie. At the time he had a phobia about flying, for chrissake. You ask me, he had a phobia about dying for his country."

That was as close as he and Sam ever got to the subject of dying. Bernie Simms had an inoperable heart aneurysm that could burst at any time. A growing tumor threatened Sam's remaining lung. Terminal, the both of them, like virtually all the other veterans at the hospice. Sam joked about his "bad airbag" and Bernie made cracks about his "bum ticker" but that was as far as they took it.

Come to think, Sam Carnovitz was another blessing to count before a supper of gray beans, green ham, and beets that looked like gallstones. Bernie didn't want to think about the food, or the weight loss he was suffering. It was becoming increasingly difficult to look on the bright side, but Bernie was only a couple years shy of his three-score-and-ten, and he'd lived a full life, and he wanted to make his exit with some semblance of dignity, if possible. So he kept counting; out of habit, out of need.

His one serious regret was the financial situation his wife would have to face. In all the years of their marriage Louise had never even balanced the checkbook, that was Bernie's department, and now she would have to handle a big mortgage, overdue taxes, unpaid hospital bills. The prospect of leaving that mess behind ruined Bernie's sleep, but there was nothing he could do about it. No hope of making it right, unless his weekly lottery ticket came in.

And how long were the odds on that? Longer than life itself.

Until the blond-haired punk arrived. Bernie had seen him

from the solarium window. The new BMW caught his attention. It came up the drive too fast for the season, skidded, braked to a lucky stop just shy of the banked snow at the curb. The youngster who emerged from the vehicle had a moddish haircut and an expensive leather jacket. He wore driving gloves and Vuarnet sunglasses suspended from a loop around his neck. He walked with a jauntiness that Bernie found irritating. Who did this boy think he was? Didn't he know men were sick in here? Was this some unfortunate veteran's son, grandson, nephew, what?

Bernie sauntered into the foyer, casual as can be, and checked out the punk kid entering Dr. Bertram's office. Dr. Bert was the director of the Veterans' Hospice. He was himself a veteran of the Korean conflict, a kindly man respected by most of the terminals. Even Sam Carnovitz liked him, and Sam hated doctors.

The punk was in Bertram's office for what seemed an inordinately long time. To Bernie, by now intensely curious, that meant the punk was at the hospice for an out-of-the-ordinary reason. He wasn't simply visiting a relative. When the punk emerged from the office with Dr. Bert at his side, Bernie made sure he was close enough to overhear.

To his surprise, Dr. Bert addressed him.

"Hey, Bernie," he said, gesturing. "Come along to the lounge; you may want to hear this."

"Hear what?" Bernie said, trying to make eye contact with the young man. The punk looked away, studying the ceiling.

"You'll find out," the doctor said firmly. "Bottom line, it concerns money."

Bernie followed, his interest piqued. Sam joined him in the lounge, and most of the others who were well enough to move came too. When the room was about two-thirds full— twenty-six terminal patients in all—Dr. Bert stood up and made the introduction.

"As you boys all know, the hospice program here is funded by the VA, and so we're in touch with most of the other government agencies. Recently I was contacted by a Pentagon outfit known as DARPA, which in plain English is the Defense Advanced Research Projects Agency. DARPA wanted to know if I'd let you gentlemen listen to a proposition from a certain defense contractor—they'd rather not say who—and I said okay, we'd give 'em a listen.''

The punk stood up. He'd put away the designer sunglasses and now he didn't look so bad, or so damned jaunty.

"My name is Tony," he said. "I won't give you my last name, for security purposes. You're all veterans and you all understand that.''

No last name. Security purpose. Very mysterious and intriguing. Bernie was aware of Sam Carnovitz breathing heavily beside him. Struggling to keep himself upright, at semiattention in his chair.

"I can't give you a lot of details, except to say that I'm one of a team of civilians working on a project we consider vital to the defense of this country. There are many elements of the project, and I've been cleared to mention only one. We are presently testing a certain . . . drug. The drug is experimental in nature. The intention of the drug is to help prolong life in a combat situation, but it may have side effects. We need to determine exactly how serious these side effects might be. In short, gentlemen, we're looking for volunteers.''

Somebody laughingly asked how much it paid. The punk, to everybody's surprise, said these magic words:

"Fifty thousand dollars.''

That got their attention. The lounge was instantly buzzing. Tony No Last Name had to raise his voice. "That's correct, gentlemen. We are budgeted to pay each volunteer fifty grand. Of course we're not paying that much money for nothing.'' He paused to read from a notebook. "For that sum, each volunteer must sign a release form, a sort of contract, that exculpates my company, and the U.S. government, from any further financial indemnity, should the volunteer suffer debilitating side effects as a result of the experiment.''

Sam Carnovitz had his hand up. "Hey, Mr. No Last Name, can you define the word *exculpate*?''

"Certainly," the young man said. "It means to prove blameless. In this case it means you and your heirs would be giving up the right to initiate a lawsuit. You understand what *exculpate* means now, sir?''

"I knew already," Sam said. "Just wanted to see if you did."

Everybody laughed, including the young man with no last name. Bernie noticed that he had a lot of white, white teeth. Capped, maybe. Then Dr. Bert got up again.

"You don't decide a thing like this on the spot," he cautioned. "Think it over. At two o'clock tomorrow I'll be in my office, and if any of you want to enter this special program, come in and see me and we'll discuss it further."

That was the last they saw of the punk named Tony, until the day the yellow bus came to take them away. By then Bernie had stopped counting his blessings.

6:25 P.M.

The spray from the shower nozzle was hot and soothing. Steam filled the tiled stall as Susan soaped herself. The experience in the temporary mortuary had chilled her to the bone. Partly it was psychosomatic, she knew: the sight of the frost-covered female cadaver made Susan imagine the sensation of eternal cold. Most of her previous investigations had involved living human beings, industrial workers who suffered from undiagnosed ailments, usually the result of a biohazard in the work environment. Exposure to toxic gases, trace elements of heavy metals and the like. The rare instances when she had had to examine a cadaver or conduct an autopsy had until now been within the familiar confines of her own lab, where it was easier to think of the deceased as simply a repository of information, a puzzle to be solved.

Unlike the frozen snow angel.

Never a morbid person, Susan nevertheless had trouble erasing that image from her mind. The soothing shower helped. The hot, stinging water made her feel very much alive. As she stepped from the shower stall her trim, high-busted figure was rosy pink from the heat. The hard spray had left her breasts feeling tender. Patting herself dry with a thick, soft towel she thought of Eliot, who would just be getting home from his last lecture at the University of Virginia Medical School. She had promised to phone him. It was disturbing to realize that she wasn't looking forward to making the call.

Susan slipped on a terry cloth robe and sat down at the vanity mirror to blow-dry her hair, aware that she had promised to be in the lobby of the White Fox restaurant in little more than half an hour. As she fluffed her hair, preparatory to switching on the dryer, she ruefully recalled her brief exchange with the limousine driver. In answer to the question about whether or not her avid skier friend was a boyfriend, she had replied, somewhat offhandedly, "Sort of."

Sort of? Eliot would be appalled. He considered himself her fiancé. No date had been set, but the idea of formal marriage had been settled, so far as he was concerned. The copper-haired girl in the mirror stuck out her tongue. Another immature habit of which Eliot disapproved.

Act your age, he would say, and smile in that slight, condescending way of his.

Susan shrugged off the robe and walked naked through the opulently appointed suite. Like most defense contractors, Sprauken International treated the notion of executive perquisites seriously. Although Susan was not technically part of the management team, as director of the Biohazard Lab she was accorded the same privileges as high-ranking executives. Even in the remote Maine facility these perks included maid service, a hot tub and sauna, an on-call masseuse, and a spectacular view of the stark white mountains enclosing the valley. She deliberately scuffed her feet on the thick carpet and enjoyed the tingling sensation of static electricity as it gathered on the cooling surface of her skin, making her hair fluff out. When Susan reached for the garment bag a spark jumped from her fingertip. She jumped involuntarily, then laughed at her own foolishness.

You're a renowned scientist, she chided herself. *Behave like one.*

The valet service had returned her best black dress. She

peeled away the plastic wrap and checked to make sure the dress was neatly pressed. From a pocket in the garment bag she removed a new bra-and-panty set, one of Eliot's many Christmas presents. As she stepped into the silky underpants Susan glanced at the telephone next to the bed, made a face, and decided she would put off the call until after dinner.

The vantage point was perfect for surveillance of the inn. He positioned his vehicle on the hilltop, calculating that the distance was about five hundred yards. Far enough away so an unlit vehicle was invisible, but the inn, with all its bright lights, came easily into focus.

The binoculars were 10×40 Minoltas, more than powerful enough to discern a human figure at that distance. He swept the binoculars over the inn, counting floors. She was on the third floor, on the east side, facing him. He counted windows, left to right.

Bingo.

He made a fine adjustment on the focus and braced his elbows on the armrest. The car motor idled quietly. The heater sighed; almost a feminine sound, he thought, irritated. Smothering. Vaguely threatening.

The bitch. She was half naked, slipping into sexy little panties. Was she teasing him? Did she know he was there in the dark, watching every move, every slink of her hips?

No, that was impossible. From her vantage the night must appear impenetrable. He watched, his pulse thudding, as she climbed into a slinky black dress. Who the hell was she trying to impress?

Doctor Bitch. Women had no place in medicine, didn't she know that? Not even as nurses. In the old days the nurses had been men, for that matter. He'd heard that somewhere. No doubt it was true. It was also true that in the old days women kept themselves covered unless they were whores, and if they were whores you could do anything you wanted to them, even kill them if you felt like it.

The good old days. It was time to get back to the good old

days. His hands tightened on the binoculars. He imagined his hands tightening on her throat.

In the dark he smiled.

Dr. Weston was waiting in the restaurant lobby. Susan almost walked right by him. At the clinic he'd been dressed in a flannel shirt, jeans, and work boots. Now, neatly groomed in a dark serge suit and a peacock-blue silk tie that accentuated his piercing eyes, he looked very much the Chief of Medicine. Serious and daunting. The spell was broken when he grinned, shook his head admiringly, and said, "Wow."

"Pardon?"

"I said you look stunning," he said. "Goddard is probably expecting you to show up wearing a lab coat with a bunch of leaky pens in your pocket. Wait till he gets a load of you in that getup."

"What's wrong?" Susan said, involuntarily checking to see if her seams were straight.

"Are you serious? Nothing's wrong. You look elegant, Dr. Cullen. The big boss is sure to be impressed, that's all I'm saying."

"Uh, thanks." Quite suddenly the idea of a business dinner with the famous Dr. Kenneth Goddard was slightly unnerving. Her confidence began to evaporate.

Goddard was now president of the combined MGS-Experimental divisions. Back in the days of the Apollo program he'd been a mission commander who once helped avert disaster by jury-rigging a complex piece of guidance equipment. After the Apollo missions had concluded, he left the astronaut program and entered the private sector. In addition to holding a doctorate in theoretical electronics, he was renowned for developing super-high-tech instruments that resulted in lucrative Department of Defense contracts for his divisions.

"He knows why I'm here?"

"Sure he knows," Dr. Weston said, leading her into the restaurant. "Goddard is a wizard. He knows all and he sees all."

"You're making me nervous," Susan hissed.

Weston chuckled. "Don't be. The great man hasn't eaten a pathologist in weeks."

"It's just that most of the company execs are paranoid about the Biohazard Lab. They assume I've been sent in to assign blame when something goes wrong."

"Relax," he said. "For your information it was the great man himself who requested the lab. And you."

That should have been reassuring, but by the time Susan entered the small, private dining room her stomach was as tight as a clenched fist. The black dress was all wrong, she decided; it signaled that she was an attractive female. She should have worn a conservatively cut suit, establishing that she was, like Goddard himself, a respected scientist.

Kenneth Goddard was already at the table.

"Dr. Cullen?" He stood up, extending his right hand. He was a thin, ascetic-looking man with a high, freckled forehead and hair so white it was almost translucent. Susan immediately noticed his remarkably pale eyes; his irises appeared to have been drained of color. He'd been reading a report and wore half-lensed glasses that had slipped to the end of his nose. Something about his slightly distracted, professorial manner put her immediately at ease.

"Unfortunately I have to be back at the plant in an hour," he said apologetically. "We're running tests on a new piece of equipment tonight, can't be helped. So if no one objects we'll dispense with the cocktails and proceed directly to the meal. I've taken the liberty of ordering for both of you."

Conversation ceased while a waiter circled the table, setting out an array of covered dishes and decanting a bottle of red wine.

"I'm relieved that your lab was able to respond so quickly," Goddard said when the waiter had retired. "This ugly business with the, ah, incidents must seem like a morbid but harmless hoax to an outsider, Dr. Cullen. Maybe even a waste of your time. I assure you it is not. In an enclosed community like this rumors spread faster than any virus. And like a virus they can infect the well-being of both the work force and the entity itself."

"The entity?" Susan had been expecting to hear the technobabble typically affected by project engineers. She was somewhat surprised by the former astronaut's courtly manner of speech.

"The company," Goddard responded. "I am convinced that whoever arranged this, um, disturbing hoax means to inflict real harm to the company, particularly to the MGS Division. As Dr. Weston will no doubt confirm, there are a number of activist groups in this state that oppose the defense industry. Last year they sponsored a referendum that would have banned all DOD contractors from the state. Fortunately it didn't pass, but you get the idea."

Susan almost choked on the wine. She was stunned by his analysis, which seemed to be curiously out of step with reality. "You think the two incidents are the work of *protesters*?"

Goddard smiled distantly. His remarkably pale eyes became the color of thin smoke. "Activists, protesters. Or it could be the work of a competitor. There are several other defense contractors who would stop at nothing to disrupt our work force, take over our contracts. The point is that when this story leaks—and it will, eventually—we have to be ready with a rational explanation. If we fail, the activists will have a field day, and so will our competitors. They'll find a way to blame it on toxic waste, or radiation leakage, or some other wild and frightening theory."

Susan noticed that Dr. Weston had turned his attention to the first course, a dish of vegetables, veal, and Italian sausage billed as *vitello alla molese*. She got the impression he'd heard all of this before and was waiting to see how she would react to Goddard's conspiracy theory.

"As far as I'm aware," she said carefully, attempting to keep her thoughts in order, "the Missle Guidance Systems Division develops computer systems and radar devices. So the toxic chemistry involved is minimal. Any radiation leakage would be nonisotopic, with no danger of harming the environment. I don't see where toxic waste or nuke issues enter into it."

Goddard nodded. "The radical element isn't overly concerned with the truth, Dr. Cullen. They will do whatever they can to inflame public opinion. When we're put on the defensive and have to deny toxic violations, then we're already losing. In the media, denial implies guilt. But I don't mean to burden you with a lot of political static. You needn't worry about who is responsible for this hoax—our security people will take care of that. You can concentrate on the how. Do your thing, give us the data, we'll go from there."

"Yes, of course," Susan said, not quite sure to what she was agreeing.

"When is the lab due to arrive, by the way?"

"Noon tomorrow, if it doesn't run into another snowstorm," Susan replied.

Goddard shrugged. "It's been one of those winters."

Having stated his views, the former astronaut turned his attention to the meal. Apparently conspiracy theories did not adversely affect his appetite, because he ate with great relish. Goddard was so thin that Susan couldn't help wondering how his body metabolized all the carbohydrates in the rich food. She picked at the elegantly prepared stuff on her plate, feeling compelled to smile whenever either of her male dinner companions commented on the quality or taste.

When the opportunity presented itself, she glared daggers at Weston. He smiled and winked, which was infuriating. Goddard appeared oblivious to any conflict between the two physicians. He spooned up the last of his sorbet, glanced at his watch, and announced that he had to leave.

"Dr. Cullen," he said, taking her hand as he stood up, "this has been a pleasure. I look forward to reading your report."

When she was certain that Goddard was out of hearing range, Susan turned to Tom Weston and said, "You bastard, why didn't you tell me?"

Weston licked his sorbet spoon and grinned. "Tell you what, that the great astronaut is a bit of a paranoid? That he tends to blame activists or other defense contractors for anything that happens to go wrong at Sprauken?"

"Something like that."

"I started to this afternoon and then thought better of it," Weston said. "I figured you could draw your own conclusions. Would you have reacted differently if I'd warned you?''

"I don't know,'' Susan said, her anger dissipating. ''I hate surprises, that's all.''

Weston chuckled. ''A medical detective who hates surprises? Come on, Susan. Give me a break. There was no way I could prepare you for Kenneth Goddard. He's a genius engineer, a super administrator, and a pretty nice guy with this one odd quirk: we get a flu bug sweeping through and he's convinced the boogeyman is responsible. The way we all handle him is to just smile and nod and go about our business. I'd advise you to do the same. Now, let's skip the postmortem, shall we? Can I buy you a drink?''

The explanation made perfect sense. Susan decided there was no reason to be angry, but she wasn't in any mood for socializing.

"Some other time,'' she said. ''I've got to, ah, make a phone call.''

If she was aware that his eyes followed every shift of her curves as she made her way to the elevators, she gave no indication. She was already concentrating on what she would say to Eliot.

11:58 P.M.

Sleep came hard at the Veterans' Hospice in China, Maine. Often it did not come at all. Tonight was one of those nights.

"You awake, Sam?''

"Yup.''

"You thinking what I'm thinking?''

"Expect so. What are you thinking, exactly?''

Bernie and Sam shared a room. With the lights out, Bernie was sometimes reminded of those nights long ago at summer camp, when he and his bunkmates had lain awake trading tall tales and lies. Mostly the lies had been about girls. That was the difference now. He and Sam never talked about girls. Mostly they talked about the old days. Prime-of-life days.

Good times. Tonight, for a change, they talked about the punk. Tony No Last Name.

"All my life I made a study of faces," Sam said. He was sitting propped up with pillows so his lung wouldn't fill. "Ever since I was a kid, I watched and studied. For instance the way my Aunt Sadie looked at my Uncle Phil. You could write a book with what she said in one look. And my wife Ruthie, God rest her, I knew she was in love with me before she did, just from the look on her face."

"I don't trust him," Bernie said firmly, trying to get back to the subject of the fifty-grand offer.

"Exactly my point," Sam said. "The smug look on that young face, you're right not to trust. It wasn't only family I studied. Strangers, too. On the subway you can always tell the sad ones, the crazy ones, the mean ones. Those sick or dangerous types try to fool the world, hiding behind this mask they assume, but they can't fool Sam Carnovitz. I looked, I studied, I learned. And this boy selling us the bill of goods, he didn't even try to hide his true feelings for us."

Bernie said, "He's lying about the money."

"No, wait. Not so fast," Sam said, becoming animated. "See, that's the mistake you make. You see something wrong, that he's lying—and in this I agree, of course he's lying—and you assume it is the money he's lying about. Because you are worried about the money, am I right?"

"I've got financial difficulties," Bernie said haltingly. "You know about that."

"I do. And this could be a way out, this fifty thousand he promises. Except he is lying."

"But you just said—" Bernie stopped. He was beginning to get agitated. And when he got agitated, his heart beat faster.

"I know what I said, my friend," Sam said in a soothing tone, attempting to calm him. "The smug boy was lying. But not about the money. No, no. He's lying about this 'experiment.' A lifetime tells me this. He comes into this place, he knows what it means for us to be here, and he has nothing but contempt for us. We are sick old men. We are not human to him. We are not even faces. And because he does not look past the sickness, he misjudges us. He assumes we are afraid of death and therefore he tries to sell us this little story about a drug that prolongs life. At most, he says, there may be a few side effects.''

Bernie turned on his side. That eased the pain in his chest, for a time. ''So he's lying about this miracle drug?''

Sam nodded. ''Of course he's lying. You think a big company would pay fifty thousand dollars to a dying man if there was danger only of a few side effects?''

''It *is* a lot of money,'' Bernie agreed.

''Never mind side effects. Whatever that young man wants to do to us, it must be fatal. This experiment of his, it figures to kill us. The fifty grand is to keep the relatives happy.''

They lay in their separate beds, staring into the darkness for a while. Letting the idea soak in. It was Bernie who broke the silence.

''You know what I'm thinking?''

Sam coughed. When he had his breath back he said, ''Sure. You're thinking: 'So what if it kills us?' ''

''Exactly,'' Bernie said, happy for the first time in weeks. ''As long as Louise gets the money, so what? What have we got to lose? A few weeks or months? Is that what you're thinking, Sam?''

''Yes,'' he said. ''Also I'm thinking I'd like to study a few more faces. New faces, no offense.''

Bernie laughed. ''No offense,'' he said.

Wednesday, January 7

In her dream she was buried under a mountain of warm snow. The idea of warm, suffocating snowflakes was so disturbing that Susan woke up with a start and discovered she had fallen asleep fully clothed. The telephone was on the pillow next to her head. A glance at the clock on the nightstand indicated that Eliot would surely be home by now.

Groggily she sat up and dialed the familiar number. Still no answer. She could imagine exactly what it sounded like inside the big house as Eliot's extensions rang simultaneously in the kitchen, the study, the bedroom, and the master bath. He had made her promise to call and now he wasn't there; he hadn't even bothered to switch on his answering machine. No doubt there was a reasonable explanation, but Susan found that her unintended nap had not improved her tolerance for reasonable explanations. She slammed the receiver down.

The nerve. Wide awake, it came back to her. Not the dream about suffocating snow, but what she had been worrying about moments before she nodded off: the sural nerve in the posterior calf of the late Robert J. Simpson. The correct procedure would have been to perform a biopsy of the peripheral nerve as soon as feasible; distracted by the interview with R.N. McNeil, Susan had neglected to do so. Important evidence of nerve or muscle activity might be contained in the sural tissue and every hour that went by decreased the chance of its being preserved.

Susan grabbed the down parka Dr. Weston had loaned her and hurried out of the suite. A few yards down the hall she remembered the insulated boots and decided it wasn't worth the effort of unlocking the door to get them. The clinic was only about a half mile away, how cold could it get?

Very cold indeed, as she discovered to her dismay.

The sky was clear, studded with pinpoint stars, and the packed layer of snow alongside the roadway crunched squeakily under her thin suede boots. A steady wind frosted the backs of her denim-covered legs. With the hood up the parka kept her head and upper body reasonably warm, but her lower legs and toes were quickly numbed. She stamped her feet as she strode rapidly along, hands jammed deep inside the down-filled pockets. Ahead she could see the lights of the clinic, the faint trace of red neon over the entrance to the ER.

She hurried toward the lights. Oddly enough they seemed to keep receding into the distance, mocking her. In Charlottesville, Virginia, home base for the Biohazard Lab, a half-mile walk was nothing. She and Eliot frequently wandered for miles on quiet, back-country roads. Here in Maine, at the height of winter, a half mile was a perilous journey. For the first time in her life Susan perceived cold as life-threatening. She understood how easy it might be to perish from exposure. Without the parka her core body temperature would have been dangerously lowered in a matter of minutes. As it was her feet felt as if they had been encased in blocks of ice.

By the time Susan reached the cheerfully illuminated ER entrance she was having trouble bending her knees. The jeans were more like cold, brittle sheet metal than fabric. The night-duty nurse looked up from the romance novel she was reading and said, "Yes, Miss? Can we help you?"

Susan attempted to explain who she was through chattering teeth. She took a deep breath and tried again. The nurse had never heard of her. Susan produced her credentials. The nurse studied her Sprauken identification card, handed it back, and said, "Fine, Dr. Cullen. Sorry about the hassle, but the security people came by earlier in the evening and asked us to be sure no unauthorized personnel entered the facility.''

"No problem," Susan said. She shifted from foot to foot, trying to get the circulation flowing in her toes.

"Anything wrong?" the nurse asked, looking down at Susan's thin, fashionable boots.

"No. Just damned cold out there," Susan said.

"Ten below, not counting the windchill.''

"What?''

"I said it was ten below zero. Even so, I'm surprised you got so chilled walking from the parking lot to the building.''

Susan explained. "I walked over from the executive inn. They haven't assigned me transportation yet.''

The nurse looked startled and said, "I see.''

Susan headed into the clinic, wincing as the blood began the painful, tingling process of warming her feet and lower legs. The nurse waited until she was out of range before picking up the telephone and punching in a number. She glanced at the lurid cover of the romance novel as the phone began to ring.

Room 144-B was icebox cold. The LED on the thermostat indicated an air temperature a few degrees above freezing. It felt much colder to Susan as she slipped on a white lab coat and a pair of thin surgical gloves. Intellectually she knew the low temperature was necessary to help delay the natural decaying process of the cadaver. Physically her body demanded a tropical environment. Hot sun and swaying palm trees.

All the more reason to work fast. After the biopsy she would find transportation back to the inn and plunge directly into the hot tub. With that pleasant thought in mind she went to the gurney and turned back the lower part of the sheet, exposing the left calf area. Exposure and excision of the sural nerve would have been easier if the cadaver were facedown. Without help Susan did not intend to try repositioning the remains of what had been a large, well-nourished male. True, she might have gotten assistance from the night shift orderly, but what she wanted to do was get in, strip the specimen nerve, get out, and return to the warmth of her suite.

Simple enough, in theory.

In practice she had to practically tear the room apart to find the most rudimentary of tools, a scalpel. Apparently the county medical examiner brought his own instruments, or left them locked up in some other part of the clinic. Finally she found a new foil-wrapped scalpel and returned to the gurney with the blade poised.

Susan stepped back involuntarily.

Something was wrong. The lower leg was not in the position she'd left it in. She distinctly remembered turning the ankle to the right to expose more of the calf area. Now it was twisted to the left.

Impossible.

Susan shivered, telling herself that she was mistaken. Obviously she had intended to reposition the calf and neglected to do so. Her imagination had supplied a picture of the completed action. That was what fooled her.

Stop acting like a silly medical student, she thought, taking a deep breath of the cold air. During her four-year pathology residency Susan had attended or supervised more than a hundred autopsies, and countless surgical biopsies. It would be ridiculous to get spooked at this stage of the game. The cadaver had been in place for four days; it could not possibly have moved.

When her heartbeat had returned to something like normal she proceeded with the excision of the sural nerve. From all appearances the unfortunate Mr. Simpson had had a perfectly normal physiology. The nerve was located precisely where it should have been in the cutaneous layer. Susan deftly stripped it and then took a small sample of the striated muscle tissue underneath. When the lab arrived she would have Chester Oswald, her medical technician, run an electrophysiologic series before fixing the nerve for histologic stains.

She separated the muscle tissue into three portions. Working quickly she put the first two into a Formalin solution: one intended for light microscopic examination, the other to be immersed in special fixatives prior to electron microscopy.

The third, which she placed in a separate petri dish, would be quick-frozen in nitrogen and later delicately sliced into transparently thin slide sections by Oswald, who was a genius with a microtome knife.

Susan had her back to the gurney, was facing the work counter where she'd placed the samples, when she heard a creaking sound. She finished peeling off the surgical gloves and waited for the sound to stop, unwilling to turn around. It did not. Her heart thudded so hard it made her head feel light.

"Is this what you do for fun at two in the morning?"

Dr. Weston was standing on the other side of the gurney, glancing with sleepy eyes at the exposed calf muscle. His boot soles squeaked on the rubber tile floor.

"The ER nurse gave me a buzz," he explained, yawning. "Said there was a pitifully underdressed M.D. on the premises who appeared to be suffering from a case of frostbitten toes."

Susan was still shivering as she allowed herself to be led away from the gurney.

"Are you serious? This is the best you can do for frostbite—a tub of warm water?"

Tom Weston had taken Susan to a small treatment room in the ER, removed her suede boots, and immersed her aching, icy-to-the-touch feet in a basin of water heated to normal body temperature. Now he was leaning in the door and shaking his head, his blue eyes bright with amusement. "We can always amputate," he said. "Or maybe you'd rather stick your toes in a nice new microwave."

"I mean," Susan said, splashing her feet in the basin, "is this really necessary? It's three in the morning. I'd rather be home in bed."

"Where's home, exactly?" Weston asked.

"Charlottesville, Virginia, for the last few years. The lab is an affiliate of the new biotech facility Sprauken endowed at the medical school. We run research programs there when we're not on assignment elsewhere."

"Which is most of the time?"

"Well, yes. A lot," Susan said, wincing. It felt as if shards of ice were melting in her toes.

Like most physicians, Susan hated to submit to treatment with another doctor. Her considerable diagnostic talents did not extend to her own body. Although she was willing to accept his view of the dangers of light frostbite—certainly he knew more than she did on the subject—she had to wonder if Tom Weston's insistence that she bathe her feet might be a sneaky way of initiating physical intimacy. As if to confirm that view, he knelt down, dipped his hands in the basin, and began to massage her ankles.

"That hurts," she announced.

"Be glad," he said. "That means you're getting blood flow. Not too much capillary damage."

As he worked down, stroking and squeezing the soles of her feet, the pain dissipated and was replaced by a vague, slightly disturbing sensation of pleasure. Susan had never had her feet massaged. It felt good. Afraid she might fall asleep right there in the ER, she drew away and announced, "Thank you, that's enough."

Weston stood up. "Anything you say, Doctor. I'll give you a ride back to the inn. Unless you'd rather walk."

He warmed up the Jeep and brought it around to the ER entrance. Susan discovered that her feet had swollen too much to fit into the suede boots. She was glad to find the inn lobby deserted when Weston dropped her off. It would have been embarrassing to be seen limping in in a pair of green surgical booties.

Susan threw away the Darvon tablets Tom Weston had given her for the pain. She slept deeply. The dream about the suffocating snow did not return that night. Instead she dreamed that the phone was ringing, and that she made no attempt to answer it.

5:01 A.M.

Things were going wrong at the clinic.

Dr. Tom Weston, who had rounds to make at seven, had

gone back to his office after returning Susan to the inn. Proximity to the lovely pathologist only served to remind him of the empty bed that awaited him at home. The emptiness was not something he cared to confront right at the moment. He decided to bring his files up to date in the quiet hours before dawn.

It had not gone well. First the coffee maker in his office had gone beserk. He'd filled the reservoir with water as usual, but when he flipped the switch a blue spark arced right through the hot plate. The plastic housing heated up and the smell of scalded coffee grounds combined nastily with that of melting plastic. To make matters worse, when he pulled the plug out of the socket he got a jolt that made his wrist sting.

What the hell was going on with the power?

Returning to his desk, Tom flipped on the computer screen and punched in the access code for his file on current patients. He hit the LOAD button and got gibberish on the screen. Machine language scrolled by at an alarming rate.

"Son of a bitch," he said quietly. Then he shut off the computer and began to methodically check all the cable connections. Power supply to computer, computer to monitor, computer to hard disk-drive, computer to keyboard. The normal drill.

He was inspecting the back of the keyboard to make sure the connector pins were secure when the monitor began to glow. Dr. Weston stared at the luminous screen in disbelief. He checked to see if the power switch was off. It was. For good measure he disconnected the power supply from the surge protector.

The screen continued to glow.

How very odd, he thought. Must be a fused relay on the switch. He decided to log an early call into the computer service's answering machine and thumbed through the Rolodex until he located the number. He picked up the phone and started to punch in the call.

"Damn," he said.

The phone was alive with humming static. The call would not go through. Tom put the receiver down and leaned back in his chair, gazing from the computer to the coffee machine.

Had to be a problem with the generating plant, he decided. Current out of phase or something like that. Making the electronics crazy.

He waited about ten minutes before trying the computer again. This time it seemed to be functioning properly except for one small problem. When he called up the file he discovered to his dismay that the floppy disk had been erased. Gone, blank. Either he'd mistakenly erased it himself, or else the strange power surge had somehow caused it.

Why a power surge at five in the morning?

"I give up," he said aloud, and then cringed. He wasn't in the habit of talking to himself. Clearly a cup of coffee was in order.

In the empty cafeteria Tom used a gas range to boil water for instant coffee. He was on his way back to his office when a bloodcurdling scream erupted from the ER.

It was a male scream, loud and tormented. Dr. Weston dropped the coffee cup and broke into a run. The rubber soles of his jogging shoes squeaked as he rounded corners.

The first thing he saw when he careened into the ER was the night shift R.N. getting up off the floor. Her face was pale, frightened.

The screaming man appeared to be dancing alone. He was clutching his right wrist as he spun around, agonized by the pain. Blood from his hand spattered to the floor.

Two other man circled him warily, obviously at a loss for what to do. Dr. Weston recognized Kurt Mallon, the security deputy, and Tony Faro, chief engineer from the Experimental Division. Faro was one of Goddard's so-called Whiz Kids. Blond-haired and barely in his mid-twenties, Tony usually affected the boyish, smug expression of an Eagle Scout who had gotten all the merit badges without much effort. Now he looked uneasy, uncertain of what to do.

Suddenly the wounded man caught sight of Weston. "Doc! Please! Give me something!" he began to plead, his voice choked with pain.

The shaky R.N. helped Tom restrain the wounded man, who calmed down a little when a painkiller was promised. The injection took effect quickly, and Tom was able to administer an antiseptic rinse to the wound, which was what the R.N. had been attempting when the injured man went wild with pain.

After getting a good look at the open wound, Tom confronted Tony Faro and Deputy Mallon. "This man has been bitten," he announced. "Any idea what happened?"

Tony and Deputy Mallon exchanged loaded glances. Tony hesitated before saying, "It was a guard dog. The damn fool made a sudden move, the thing went for him. Right, Kurt?"

"Yeah, right," Deputy Mallon said without much conviction.

Tom frowned with impatience. He hated to be lied to, especially when a patient's well-being was at stake.

"Any chance the, ah, *dog* was rabid?" he demanded, addressing himself to the young engineer, who was clearly in charge.

"None," Tony answered, flashing a white, wolfish grin of perfect teeth. His eyes, however, remained expressionless.

"You're certain?"

"Yeah. Absolutely," he said. "Look, just patch him up, okay? He put his hand where he shouldn't, that's all that happened."

Tom knew they were lying, but he got the distinct impression that pushing for the truth would not be effective. He "patched up" the wounded man as requested, obtained a dose of antibiotics from the clinic pharmacy, and asked that the patient return later in the day to have the hand X-rayed for possible bone damage. It was the best he could do, under the circumstances.

Dr. Weston knew damn well it wasn't a dog bite. He knew what dog bites looked like. He also knew what kind of damage human teeth could do.

11:46 A.M.

When the trailer truck towing the lab arrived a little before noon, Susan was waiting in the clinic parking lot. The sight of the big green-and-white trailer never failed to lift her spirits. It was a bright sunny day under a gunmetal-blue winter sky, and the anxiety she'd experienced in the bleak, early hours of the morning was largely forgotten.

The truck air horns tooted. Susan clapped her mittened hands together and waved. The door opened and a diminutive black man descended from the cab. He made a thumbs-up sign and grinned, ivory teeth splitting his darkly complected face.

"Ozzie!" Susan cried.

She rushed out to embrace Chester Oswald. In Susan's opinion he was one of the best histocytologists in the business. Nobody knew cell and tissue testing better. Oswald, whose sexual preference was unabashedly male, was under five feet tall, the result of a childhood spinal deformity, since corrected. The difference in height meant that when Susan hugged him his face ended up between her breasts. As usual Ozzie took full advantage, giggling wildly as he nuzzled her.

"One of these days I'm going to switch to girls," he announced. "Are you still available?"

Susan ignored the jibe. Ozzie didn't approve of Eliot, whom he considered a dreadful snob. A native Virginian descended from the "Hundred Families," Eliot sometimes refered to Ozzie as "that colored dwarf." It was a sore point with Susan, who didn't understand how the two men she cared the most about could so loathe each other.

"Any trouble on the run up from Boston?" Susan wanted to know.

"Just that freak storm that shut down the turnpike," Ozzie said.

"I wish you'd let me hire a regular driver," Susan said. "I worry about you on these long road trips."

"Uh-uh, momma, ain't no way am I gonna let a teamster get his hands on my baby," Ozzie said, affecting a jive accent.

The tone was light and taunting, but he wasn't kidding. The roving Biohazard Lab was his creation as much as it was Susan's. He had helped design the layout and had overseen construction. It was Ozzie who came up with the wish list for the test equipment. Ozzie who helped her design CYTO, the micrographic computer system that diagnosed tissue and blood samples. CYTO compared key elements of an in-lab slide with a vast library of slide images in the computer memory, arriving at a probable diagnosis in a fraction of the time it would have taken by the old system of manual comparison. They had exceeded budget, of course, but the result was inarguably the most well-equipped pathology lab on wheels.

"This a high-tech baby," Ozzie liked to brag. "Want to know what *state of the art* means, check it out."

Susan's full professional confidence returned as she and Ozzie positioned the big trailer near the clinic, running the power and telephone cables into the building. They had the lab at an acceptable work temperature and the CYTO program on-line with the mainframe in Charlottesville by two o'clock.

Susan turned the nerve and tissue samples over to Ozzie. She took charge of preparing the blood smears. Although her training as a clinical pathologist was of necessity wide-ranging, Dr. Cullen's particular interest was in the field of hematology, the study of the blood. This expertise was particularly useful in determining how mere traces of industrial toxins, often extremely difficult to identify, managef to adversely affect the health. Susan could read blood cells like a book. She knew how to coax secrets from the slide preparations by the use of dyes and disclosing agents, many of which she had developed for specific, rare industrial poisons.

As she adjusted the bright field of the microscope, Susan experienced a familiar sensation of physical and mental well-being. She was about to enter another world, one whose boundaries were defined not by the power of the microscope lenses, but only by the limits of her diagnostic imagination. The feeling of comfortable, confident intimacy with her work was something she had never shared with Eliot, or with any man. Such a thing was not, she supposed, possible. Maybe in books or movies, certainly not in the real world. She would just have to be content with the satisfaction of doing good work. That's what she was thinking as she slipped the first slide into the field and leaned forward, gazing down into the soft white light.

Susan was happy again.

Dr. Alvin Nash came out of the OB-GYN surgery, peeled off his gloves, and threw them against the wall. He was pissed off. Ordinarily he liked a chance to do a straightforward surgical procedure. It kept him in trim, mentally and physically, and left him better prepared to deal with any emergency that might occur while he was delivering a baby. But this was getting ridiculous: two D and C's in less than an hour, both necessitated by first-trimester miscarriages!

Not one but *two* of his girls miscarrying on the same day for a total of five miscarriages in less than a week! It boggled the mind!

Nash knew the statistics: on average, one of every five pregnancies might be terminated by spontaneous miscarriage, usually in the first trimester. His own clients had always been well below the curve. The result, he secretly concluded, of his own holistic style of treatment. Keep the mother healthy and the baby would be just fine.

Now the statistical curve was snapping back like a whip. Quite suddenly a third of the confirmed pregnancies in Sprauken had ended in miscarriage. And *that* was unacceptable. The more he thought about it, the more his anger turned to an uneasy feeling that somehow he was to blame. Maybe was overlooking a symptom the women had in common. There had to be a connection, but what? He decided to pull the files of all his pregnant patients, his "girls," and go over them entry by entry, looking for abnormal similarities.

The decision to take some kind of action helped Nash get control of his temper. He peeled off his greens, went directly to his office, and asked his receptionist to get the Portland Path Lab on the line. He took the call in his office, with the door shut.

"Yeah, right," he said. "Dr. Nash here, from the Sprauken clinic. You people ran a battery of blood tests on a patient of mine, Ruthann Glover. Test batch 23-651-4. I need to confer with the technician who ran the batch. I've got a few questions about the results."

2:25 P.M.

Dr. Bertram was seeing them one at a time. Bernie Simms, eager to get the meeting over with, fidgeted on the hard wooden bench outside Dr. Bert's office. When his buddy Sam Carnovitz emerged he flashed a thumbs-up and smiled enigmatically, but refused to discuss what had transpired.

"You'll find out," he said. "You're a patient here, correct? So be patient." Sam could be maddening sometimes.

At last it was Bernie's turn.

"Give me the papers," he said immediately. "I'm going to sign."

"Have a seat, Bernie," Dr. Bert said. "Take a load off your feet."

Bernie sat.

"I'm obliged to point out a few things," the doctor said. "Such as the fact that by agreeing to participate in this experiment, whatever it is, you may be putting your life at risk."

Bernie smirked. "Come on, Doc. Every day my life is at risk. What's the difference?"

"There could be a big difference. The young gentleman who was here yesterday, he didn't give us much information. For all we know this drug they're testing could be painful."

"I know from pain, Doc."

Dr. Bertram polished his glasses. "Bernie, I've got your service record here. You were in the Airborne, a paratrooper. You made, it says, fifteen combat jumps, is that right?"

"If it says. At the time I wasn't counting."

The doctor nodded. "Exactly my point. Guys like you, good paratroopers, you didn't think about tomorrow."

"Hey," Bernie said. "In those days we never knew if there would *be* a tomorrow. It was a big war and nobody knew, really, how it would turn out. Not at the time. They said jump, we jumped. Was it so different in Korea?"

"Let's stick to you, Bernie. What you want from this."

"That's easy," Bernie said. "I want the money. I never

thought I'd be in a position I couldn't work, provide for my wife. Things haven't been easy for her lately. I want to make it up, leave her fixed.''

"Of course," the doctor said. "And for that you're willing to make one last jump, am I right?"

"You want to put it that way, sure. Tell me straight, Doc, is there any reason they can't use me for this?"

Dr. Bertram shook his head. "No reason at all. But I've got to tell you, I don't altogether trust these folks. You may not be aware of this, but the military—and don't let's kid ourselves, a defense contractor is the military—they don't have a clean record in regard to experiments on civilians, or soldiers, for that matter.''

"What are you getting at, Doc?"

The doctor put on his glasses. His eyes were grim. "There have been certain unfortunate incidents. Right after nuclear weapons were first developed, hundreds of soldiers were intentionally exposed to fallout radiation to see what toxic effects it had. Many of them died years later, from very painful forms of cancer. Later, when germ warfare was the big thing, veterans like yourself were exposed to the germs. And then when the CIA wanted to test a new drug, LSD, they gave it to people who didn't even know they were being tested. One of them jumped out a hotel window.''

"This is different," Bernie said impatiently. "I'm going into this with my eyes open. I know it could kill me, whatever it is.''

"For the money."

"Of course for the money. Doc, the way it is with me and Louise, we've been through a lifetime. If some young punk comes in here and says, 'Bernie, we'll pay your wife fifty grand if you'll stand up against a wall and be shot,' I'd do it.''

"You're getting excited now, Bernie. Remember your blood pressure.''

"Of course I'm getting excited, and how could I forget my bum ticker? That's exactly why I'm going to do this thing, and not you or nobody is going to talk me out of it. Now give me the papers, please, so I can sign.''

"You won't reconsider?"

"I'm all decided. I'm going to make this jump, and the hell with the parachute."

Dr. Bertram sighed, then opened his drawer and removed a sheaf of papers.

3:22 P.M.

The device pleased him. He had designed it, built it with his own hands in a few spare hours at the assembly shop. He knew the young technicians got a kick out of seeing Kenneth Goddard tinkering with a soldering iron. It contributed to his legend.

This is the same dude walked on the moon, okay? he imagined them saying. *Runs the whole goddamn division, and what does he do to relax? He's right there in the shop, creating these sophisticated little electronic devices! Beautiful little things! Doesn't even refer to a schematic, just* does *it, you know? The man is a genius.*

Goddard smiled to himself, unaware that his lips were twitching. He had been awake and active for thirty-six hours. He couldn't remember the last time he'd allowed himself a full night's sleep. Sleep was a waste of time and energy.

He readjusted the earphones and swept the pretty little debugging device along the baseboards of his office. If the instrument detected an electronic bug it would chirp like a bird. He didn't really expect to find a bug in his office—Security swept every day with their own sophisticated detectors—he just liked to do things with his own hands.

You couldn't be too careful about bugs. The Defense Department was intrigued with PULSE, the new weapons system being developed and tested by the Experimental Division, but there were certain congressmen on the Appropriations Committee who were unabashedly squeamish: a leak at this crucial stage might result in shelving the project.

Goddard ran the detector over the air vents, along the lamp cords, around the phone jacks—anywhere it might be expected to pick up a signal. There was nothing. Satisfied, he unplugged the earphones and returned the detector to the safe. He then used the direct computer link to transmit a coded memo to the NSA desk in Langley, Virginia.

ATTENTION: RICHARD D. DUBOIS, CHIEF INTELLIGENCE OFFICER, DATA RETRIEVAL, he typed, watching the words flash on the screen. DEAR DICKIE, REQUEST IN-DEPTH SECURITY REPORT ON SPRAUKEN EMPLOYEE, SUSAN CULLEN, M.D., DIRECTOR BIOHAZARD LAB. ANY AND ALL DATA. REGARDS FROM APOLLO.

Goddard checked his spelling, pressed the SEND button, and watched the memo sweep from the screen. Thirty seconds later the ACKNOWLEDGE signal flashed and the code machine cycled off.

The intercom buzzed. Goddard picked up the receiver.

"Yes?"

"Just a reminder, sir. You're due back at the test facility in twenty minutes. Your car is waiting."

"Thanks."

PULSE. He smiled. Goddard experienced a deep sense of satisfaction whenever he thought about the new system. A radical improvement on the old Pandora Project, PULSE utilized pulses of extremely high energy microwaves to neutralize the nervous system. The phenomenon had been established in theory for years, but no working model had ever been successfully developed until Goddard stumbled on the idea of combining the HEM pulses with radio waves at the opposite end of the spectrum. ELF, extremely low frequency, had until then been in use only for long-distance communication, principally to submarines that could not be reached over normal airwaves. ELF penetrated through the earth and into the seabeds. In pulsed combination with HEM, it was capable of penetrating into the depths of the human mind, short-circuiting the central and peripheral nervous systems as effectively as any of the outlawed biochemical weapons.

The preliminary tests had been stunning, in every sense of the word. Much work remained to be done before PULSE functioned in a way that would, Goddard believed, change the nature of human warfare. Abandoning the project because a few squeamish congressmen objected was unthinkable, hence his obsession with security.

Goddard was pleased that Colonel Bentley, the liaison from the Defense Advanced Research Projects Agency, was impressed with the initial test runs. Impressed, hell. He was blown away by the possibilities, and had filed a five-star report to his DARPA superiors. The colonel had hinted that there would be no problem with the budget if the tests continued to be favorable.

If it's hot, throw money at it, that was basic DARPA policy: Don't worry about the bottom line, just get us a working model.

Before securing the office safe, Goddard removed a plastic pill bottle. He shook two of the small black capsules into the palm of his hand and swallowed them dry. He started to put the bottle back, then changed his mind. It was going to be another long night. He needed to be alert and he believed the amphetamines helped focus his concentration. They had side effects, of course. The most obvious being weight loss. He'd been eating like a trencherman lately, but the pounds were still slipping away.

No problem. When the live testing was finished he would lay off the pills and sleep for a week. Let Tony Faro, his chief project engineer, handle the cleanup phase. That was the best thing about young Tony. He was a son of a bitch, personality-wise, but you could trust him to handle the small, nagging details.

4:05 P.M.

Susan kept a small calculator pad at hand while reading the slides. She was adept at entering numbers by touch, allowing her to concentrate on the cell count. The fingertips of her right hand moved instinctively over the pad as she manipulated the slide with her left hand.

She didn't need to look at the total on the calculator to know that the numbers were seriously out of whack.

"Ozzie?"

"Yo."

"I need your eyes."

Chester Oswald finished his sequence at the cryostat, where he was preparing ultrathin tissue sections for examination, and slipped into her chair. They had been sharing the same tight working quarters for almost three years now and had developed a verbal shorthand. Ozzie knew Susan wanted his first impression, unsullied by her opinion. He gazed into the microscope. The only sound to disturb the quiet of the lab was the faint hum of the cryostat machine.

Several minutes passed. Susan waited patiently.

"Abnormally high lymphocytes," Ozzie said. "Way up there."

"Bingo," Susan said with a smile. "Also high monocytes and neutrophils."

"Virus?" Ozzie said. "That's the normal dig for a high white cell count."

"Dig" was his shorthand for *diagnosis*. A high incidence of lymphocytes in the blood usually meant that the immune system was fighting off an infection. As they both knew, blood chemistry could also be affected by a variety of rare toxins, prolonged exposure to nonisotopic radiation, or a bone marrow disease.

"We'll set up a full array of cultures," Susan said. "But if they were that sick, why didn't it show up elsewhere?"

"They?" Ozzie said, raising his eyebrows.

"Both samples have almost identically high white cell counts. Simpson, the engineer, was reportedly in excellent health. Fell from a ladder. Miss Farsi, the clerical worker, suffered from extreme hypertension. Cause of death: stroke and cerebral hemorrhage. No mention that she was ill with a virus. Nothing about it on their workups."

The little man shrugged, his eyes, as always, slightly protuberant. His expression was one Susan knew well. It meant he was intrigued.

"Anything unusual in the tissue samples?"

Oswald grinned. "Thought you'd never ask."

He escorted her to the computer terminal and insisted she

take his seat. The extending of small courtesies was another of the little games they played. It made it easier to coexist in the almost claustrophobic environment of the crowded lab. While she sat and looked at the screen, Ozzie reached over her shoulder and manipulated the keyboard.

"Striated muscle tissues first," he said, transferring the magnified image to the left of the screen. "We show a minimum of cytopath-type damage. That's to be expected, since the cadaver was kept relatively cool, and muscle tissues at the extremities are usually the last to undergo microorganic damage. Normal, so far. And boring. Who *cares* about dead leg muscle?"

Susan restrained the temptation to interrupt. That was another of their small courtesies. Ozzie, who tended to stammer in public, was prone to lecture when he had his special audience of one.

"The answer to that," he continued, "is that no one cares—unless there has been a rather fantastic report that the leg muscle continued to function after death. Then, of course, one becomes *most* interested. One takes a closer look."

He pressed a key, increasing magnification.

"Note the area around the dendrites. Cellular condition might, by the casual observer, be attributed to cytopathological damage—the normal process of cell decay. Let's have a look at typical cytopath damage in a normal striated calf muscle." He touched another key and a second image appeared on the right side of the screen, called up from the vast memory of standard tissue samples. "Note the damage is not at all similar. The dendrites—the tiny hairlike nerves—are basically intact, but in the standard sample the cell walls have been ruptured by typical cytopath action. The dendrites in the sample from the unfortunate Mr. Simpson reveal a curiously hardened cell structure."

"What caused that?" Susan asked.

Ozzie shrugged. "Beats the hell out of me. I never saw anything exactly like it. Neither has the CYTO program. I had it cycle through ten thousand samples, keyed on that characteristic. No matchups."

"An anomaly? Interesting."

"Sure is. Now keep your butt glued to the chair, cupcake; the show isn't over. Check out the chromatography." The technician's nimble fingers caressed the keyboard, wiping the slide sections from the screen. A full-color graph appeared. "Acetylcholine," he said. "Buckets of acetylcholine."

Acetylcholine, he reminded her, was a transmitter substance, released in trace amounts by the nervous system to trigger muscle action. The trace amounts were usually so slight that the substance was difficult to identify even with computer-driven chromatography. Ozzie's "buckets of acetylcholine" was actually something less than a microgram, but in the microscopic nerve dendrites, that amounted to saturation.

Ozzie tapped a few more keys, dredging up another graph. "As CYTO tells us, Mr. Simpson, age fifty-eight with a desk job, had significantly more acetylcholine in his system than an Olympic sprinter."

"Impossible."

Ozzie giggled. "Right. Just like it's impossible for a cadaver to get off a gurney and walk."

Susan shook her head, staring at the screen. "An injection of acetylcholine wouldn't stimulate muscle action."

"No," Ozzie agreed. "That's a by-product of nerve action. Introduction of electrical impulses might do it, however."

Susan made a face. "The frog's leg trick? Come on, Oz. It's one thing to make a muscle contract in a biology class. It's quite another to duplicate significant muscle coordination. Walking is complicated."

"I agree. I'm simply saying that if the nervous system is artificially stimulated with electrical impulses, the synapses will produce acetylcholine. It's one of the classic neurological experiments. Otto Loewi got a Nobel Prize for discovering it."

"Loewi didn't make dead things walk."

Ozzie's gentle hands moved to her shoulders, massaging her neck. She hadn't realized how tense she was. "Relax, Dr. Cullen," Ozzie said. "There has to be an explanation, right? That's the consolation of science. If we look hard enough in the right places, we can find a reason for any phenomenon. Or at least an interesting theory."

"So we just keep looking."

"That's what we do," he said softly. "So far we have high acetylcholine in the nerves and high lymphocytes in the blood. That's something to start with."

A buzzer sounded. The lab doorbell. Ozzie went to see who it was and returned with a sly look on his face. "Two gentlemen callers. Want to know if the lady pathologist is receiving visitors."

Susan went to the lab door. She realized, with a start, that the sun was already setting. Where had the day gone?

Tom Weston was standing awkwardly just inside the entrance. He looked intimidated by the crowded confines of the lab, as if afraid he might break something. He was accompanied by a plump, prematurely balding man with dimpled cheeks and a mischievous grin.

"This is Dr. Alvin Nash," Weston said. "Our resident OB-GYN. Also claims to be a pediatrician."

Susan shook hands. Behind her, Ozzie was trying to blend into the equipment. He didn't like visitors.

"Wow," Dr. Nash said, looking around. "This place looks like the inside of the space shuttle. I'm impressed."

The way his eyes flicked over her, Susan was convinced he was as impressed with her looks as he was with the lab. Clinical pathologists weren't supposed to be young and beautiful. They were supposed to wear tortoiseshell glasses repaired with electrical tape. Having endured the reaction many times, she was able to shrug it off. Another horny male.

"I assume you're here for the tour," she said to Dr. Weston.

"Yeah, well sure. Love to." Tom cleared his throat. "Fact is, Dr. Cullen, we'd like to ask a favor. That is, Al would. I mean Dr. Nash."

"For chrissake, Tom, quit stalling," Nash said, bumping past his friend. He came up close to Susan, closer than she found comfortable, although she didn't try to back away.

"We got a problem," Nash said to her, "and I'm hoping you can help us out."

"What's the problem?"

"Blood," Nash said. He dipped his hand into his jacket pocket and produced several sample vials. "I've had an unusual number of patients spontaneously miscarry in the last few days. So one of the things I did was express blood samples to the path lab at the Maine Medical Center. They usually do good work, only this time I think maybe they screwed up."

Susan said, "What makes you think that?"

"Because the results don't make sense. I've got five very healthy, very normal young women, normal temperature, no sign of viral infection, and they all show white cell counts that are off the chart."

"What?" Susan said, startled.

"Lymphocytes," Nash said. "Any reason five healthy kids should have ultrahigh lymphocytes?"

Thursday, January 8

12:02 A.M.

The night was sparking. Bits of granular white snow drifted by like static on a dark screen. Goddard sipped from a mug of heavily sugared black coffee. He stood alone on the catwalk, staring at the window without really seeing. In his mind the snow was static. The dark sky was a blank video screen. As if the world outside the test building was something that could be turned on or off, as he so desired. And if it lacked a control switch he could make one out of spare parts, he decided. Simple. Do it in his sleep.

An amplified voice spoke his name.

"Dr. Goddard? We're ready to resume testing now, sir."

He remembered, with a small, physical thrill, why he had wandered over to the deserted section of the catwalk. He didn't want Tony Faro to know about the pills. He slipped his hand into his pocket, took out the vial, and tapped an amphetamine capsule into the palm of his hand. He thought better of it, adding two more. Three would take him through the rest of the test. Three was more than he usually took at one time, but this was a special night. He deserved it.

Goddard swallowed, washing the capsules down with the sweet coffee. Immediately the sense of well-being returned. He realized he was abusing the amphetamines, that when the PULSE tests were complete he would have to confront the problem. It might even require a little medical assistance. Pills to counteract the pills. All very scientific.

"Dr. Goddard? Are you in the vicinity, sir? Please respond."

He moved along the catwalk, feeling almost weightless. Faro and the rest of the observation team were assembled on an area of suspended staging, forty feet above the target area. The lighting was such that Goddard could see them but they could not see him very clearly. The situation was pleasing: all those pale white faces peering into the darkness, looking for the boss. He recognized the liaison from DARPA. Colonel Benjamin Bentley, Jr., was the Pentagon money man—in his own way as important to the project as Goddard or Tony Faro.

They appeared relieved when he strolled into view, raising the coffee mug in a casual salute.

"The test is a go now, sir," Tony announced. "We're just waiting for the power to cycle on."

Goddard nodded. As he moved in to inspect the control console the young engineers on the observation team vied for his attention. He smiled and nodded to several of them. Names were a problem. He was too immersed in the technical aspects to concern himself with individual engineers on the team. He left that to Tony.

The arrayed video screens were really more of a convenience than a necessity. All relevant data were being tracked and recorded by computer with much more precision than was reflected on the monitors. Human observers, no matter how well trained, could only comprehend effects in a very limited spectrum. Even the computer system would take a significant amount of real time to digest all the data; keeping track of everything PULSE did was a lot more complicated than mere number crunching.

He called over to his chief project engineer. "You satisfied with the readouts, Tony?"

"Looking good, sir."

Goddard leaned against the safety rail and glanced down. Forty feet below, on a sawdust floor, the cages were in position, bathed in a circle of intense white light. Goddard wrinkled his nose. The stink from the cages was enough to make his skin crawl. The smell! And it would only get worse as the testing proceeded. Well, it couldn't be helped. In a few minutes, if things went according to plan, no one would care about the stench.

He turned to Tony Faro, who was standing quietly by, waiting for his signal.

"It's show time," he said.

12:58 A.M.

Susan lay awake in the darkened bedroom of the suite, staring at the window, where fat pellets of snow seemed to appear out of nowhere, drifting into the exterior lights. She was exhausted but wide awake, a familiar condition when things got hot at the lab. She and Ozzie had worked late, running a full battery of tests and smears on the new samples Dr. Nash had provided. Finding lots of interesting anomalies but no explanation for why five young women should share a startlingly similar blood chemistry. Was there a connection between blood levels in the resident population and the samples taken from the cadavers? It was too early to say. Tomorrow she would ask Dr. Weston to provide an array of samples from the clinic patients. Just as a precaution.

It wasn't the strange blood chemistry or the lab work that was bothering her, though. It was Eliot. After a long, shuddering soak in the hot tub she'd finally gotten through to him. Gotten through in the sense that they talked. Now, thinking about it, she wasn't at all sure that he'd listened to a word she said.

The conversation had started out fine.

"Sorry about last night," he began. "I went over to Mother's for dinner. It got rather late. I tried you about one-ish, but I guess you were dead to the world by then."

"How's Mother?" Susan asked dutifully.

"Great," Eliot said. "We had a long, really fascinating conversation about the wedding. Mother has some marvelous ideas."

Eliot's mother was a strong-willed, highly opinionated

woman who had devoted her entire adult life to her late husband, and then transferred all of her considerable attentions to her only son. Her soft, high-toned Virginia accent did not quite conceal the vague contempt she had for all young females. None of whom, she made it quite clear, were really good enough for Eliot. Susan thought of her as Dragon Lady.

"We haven't even decided on a date," she said uneasily. "How can you discuss it with your mother?"

Eliot ignored that. Apparently the matter had been settled. June was the only suitable month, and his mother had used her Hundred Family social connections to secure the country club facilities.

"The country club?" Susan said, incredulous. "Eliot, I thought we were going to get married in the college chapel and then sort of, well, elope."

He laughed. Eloping was for teenagers, he told her. As chair of the biology department he had certain obligations; he had to project a certain image. He had to think of his position, his family. His mother.

"We're making a statement, darling," he said. "We might as well do it in style."

Susan listened in disbelief as he outlined an entire week of dinners, parties, and receptions, to be presided over by Dragon Lady, of course. The seamstress, caterer, photographer, and florist had all been selected. Susan was too exhausted to put up an argument, and from Eliot's tone it wouldn't have done much good. Everything was decided.

"One other thing," he said, interrupting her as she tried to say good-night. "I cleared my calendar for the weekend and booked a flight. We have reservations at Ice Valley. Best suite at the lodge."

"Eliot, I'll be tied to the lab all weekend!"

"We'll discuss it when I get there," he said cheerfully.

And so she watched the snow drift by the window and waited for sleep to come. When the phone rang she assumed it was Eliot, calling to say he'd changed his mind about flying up for the weekend. Sighing, she hooked a finger around the receiver and dragged it to her ear.

It was Jack Webster, the security chief. His voice sounded strained.

"We've got another one," he said. "A deadwalker. I just saw it with my own eyes. I'm sending a car for you. It'll be waiting at the lobby entrance."

"Another what—"

But he had hung up. Susan dressed hurriedly. This time she remembered the insulated boots. She grabbed the down parka, a knit hat, and gloves. When the elevator failed to respond instantly, she ran down the three flights of stairs.

A white Saab skidded to a stop at the inn entrance a moment after she pushed through the door. Kurt Mallon, Webster's handsome young deputy, was at the wheel. He explained that he'd been on night patrol, checking the plant perimeter, when alerted via radio.

"The old man sounded pretty shook up," he said, accelerating through a turn, evidently undisturbed by the low visibility. Susan, always a nervous passenger, clipped on her seat belt.

"Where are we going?" she asked.

"East Meadow complex," he said. He seemed to relish the idea of fast driving on a snow-strewn road. "Number one twenty-two. Private residence."

A few minutes later he drifted through a turn and then downshifted. Susan, positive they were about to skid out of control, braced her hands against the dashboard, shut her eyes, and held her breath. When she opened her eyes again they were stopped a few feet from the rear of a parked ambulance. Mallon was grinning at her.

"Hey, I'm sorry, Doc," he said. "What the chief told me, I assumed you needed to get here pronto."

Shaken and too irritated to respond, Susan merely nodded and got out of the car. Jack Webster was waiting just inside the front door of a small two-story unit. In the light from the hall his fleshy face looked pale and drawn. A slow, steady thumping sound came from somewhere near the top of the stairs.

"Great, Doc." He sighed with relief. "Glad to see you. Damned glad."

Two hospital orderlies were standing in the shadows behind him. One of them had developed a facial tick that made it look as if his nervous smile were flashing on and off, battery powered. The other orderly fidgeted, chewing on an unlit cigarette.

"Lars Svenson," Webster said, referring to a notebook. "Accountant in the billing department. Divorced, sixty-two years of age. Left work at four o'clock. Showered and changed. Due to meet several of his buddies for a card game at six. Never showed. A friend called, got no answer, came 'round here about ten to make sure Svenson was okay. He wasn't. Found him upstairs, slumped over, cool to the touch. Dead of massive coronary, apparently while tying his shoes."

"When did the coronary occur?"

"Your guess is as good as mine," Webster said, shrugging. "Probably better. We assume sometime before six. Dr. Weston came over shortly after ten, pronounced Svenson dead. Ambulance team had another emergency—pregnant woman with severe hemorrhaging—so Dr. Weston instructed them to come back here and get the deceased when they had the time. No rush, he said. Right, boys?"

"Right," said the orderly with the nervous smile. "Told us he guessed Svenson was in no hurry."

The other orderly tittered. The laugh sounded like steam escaping from a kettle. "Dr. Tom guessed wrong," he said.

Webster sighed. He looked much older than Susan remembered. The joking confidence was not there. The hand clutching the notebook trembled slightly.

"Go on," Susan said.

"Dr. Weston left here at ten-thirty. Locked up. Left the keys with a nurse at the clinic and went into surgery to assist Dr. Nash with the hemorrhaging patient. Half an hour ago these fellows picked up the keys and came 'round here to load up the deceased. After observing the, uhm, thing, they called me. I called you."

The slow thumping sound from upstairs continued unabated. Susan noticed that it seemed to coincide with the flickering smile of the orderly. More of an involuntary wince. She was reminded of Trevor McNeil, the night shift R.N. who had reported the first incident. He'd suffered a similar nervous reaction.

"Where?" she asked, knowing the answer.

Webster pointed up the stairs.

"Ladies first," he said. "I'm getting too old for this crap."

He unholstered his revolver.

"Is that really necessary?" Susan said, starting up the stairs.

"You tell me."

He followed her, trailed by Deputy Mallon, who had also drawn his revolver. Susan felt silly. Nevertheless her heart began to thud against her rib cage as she mounted the stairs.

Thump. Thump. Thump.

No, not her heart, she realized—the other sound, coming from upstairs. Mustn't confuse the two. Behind her, Jack Webster was breathing heavily. The fact that both of the cops thought it necessary to draw their weapons bothered her almost as much as the thumping noise.

The late Mr. Svenson did not keep a tidy nest. There was a pong of stale cigars and dirty socks. A sad, lonesome, middle-aged kind of smell. The carpet hadn't been cleaned recently. Outside the bathroom a hamper overflowed with soiled linen. The door to the bathroom was open. Susan glanced inside and reflexively wrinkled her nose—the whole place needed a good scrubbing and airing out.

The lights were out in the bedroom. Susan reached inside, felt for a switch, and clicked it on. The ambulance gurney was collapsed on the floor just inside the door. Right where the orderlies left it. Nervous grin and the cigarette eater.

Thump. Thump. Thump.

The sound was as steady as a metronome. Louder in the bedroom, but still curiously muffled. She wanted to say something to Webster, anything, but her mouth was too dry.

Thump.

Thump.

Thump.

Susan took a deep breath and moved into the bedroom, sidling around the gurney.

Empty. The unmade bed was empty. There were clothes strewn everywhere. Mostly dress shirts. Svenson must have had a shirt for every day of the month. On the nightstand next to the bed was an overflowing ashtray and a stack of men's magazines. *Playboy*, *Penthouse*, *Hustler*. A pair of reading glasses perched on one of the well-thumbed magazines.

She found her way around the bed, unable to focus on the source of the thumping sound. It seemed to be all around her. She looked at Webster, who had not come through the door, and gestured helplessly.

He pointed his revolver at the closet. The bi-fold doors were closed. She waited for Webster to come inside and open the closet for her. Clearly he was not about to volunteer.

Thump.

Thump.

Enough. Susan tossed her head, marched to the closet, and flung back the doors.

Svenson was inside.

His upper body leaned awkwardly against the rear wall of the closet. His arms were loose at his sides. His legs were churning methodically, *thump thump thump*, as he attempted to go forward, chugging ineffectively against the wall.

"Oh come on," Susan said. Angry now, at what was obviously a hoax. The man was alive. Had to be.

Impulsively Susan reached out and put her hand to the side of Svenson's neck. She jerked back. His flesh was cool, room temperature. Quite impossible. Without considering the consequences Susan grabbed hold of his shirt and tried to pull him out of the closet.

Svenson fell. Susan spun to get out of the way. He brushed her as he went by, landing heavily on his back. The legs continued to churn steadily, as if attempting to pedal a bicycle. Behind her, Webster groaned as she knelt and stared at the glassy, lifeless eyes of the cadaver.

The man was dead. He had been dead for hours.

1:16 A.M.

The screaming was horrible. Goddard covered his ears and turned away. He felt short of breath. Something was wrong with the air. It was too thin. And his heart was racing into tachycardia, beating out of control.

He was beginning to feel weightless. The screaming made anything possible, even the failure of gravity. In another moment he would drift away.

"Dr. Goddard, are you okay? You look very pale, sir."

He grimaced and nodded, slowly dropping his hands from his ears. The screaming had faded into a low, guttural howl. He tried to focus on Tony Faro. The young man hovered nearby, obviously concerned.

"What went wrong?" Goddard asked him.

"Wrong, sir?"

Goddard cleared his throat. "The, uhm, screaming."

"Screaming? Oh, that. Nothing abnormal, if that's what you mean. We've got a howler in cage three. Doesn't take much to set him off."

"It sounded . . . tormented."

Tony shrugged. "If the noise bothers you that much we could rig up muzzles, I guess. Shut the bastards up."

Goddard was unable to look his young protégé in the eye. "Never mind," he muttered. "I thought for a minute something had . . . gone wrong."

Tony grinned and laughed. "Everything went perfect. Check out the meters, sir. We got an awesome pulse on that last sequence. Awesome!"

Awesome. There it was again, that word. Tony and the other kids on the staff used it frequently. Somehow, after the screaming, it seemed inappropriate. What did the screamer think? What did it feel?

It felt, Goddard was convinced, anything but awesome.

1:32 A.M.

Susan felt better when Ozzie arrived, laden with equipment. Jack Webster and the two orderlies were no help—they remained on the ground floor of the apartment, smoking and muttering amongst themselves. Leave it to the doctor was the attitude. Deputy Mallon had stayed in the bedroom, but he kept waving his gun around, and that made Susan almost as nervous as the sight of the dead feet slowly pedaling in the air.

"You can take a break now, Officer," Ozzie had told him right off. "We'll give a yell if we need anything shot, okay?"

"Okay," the deputy had said dully, apparently oblivious to irony. Holstering his weapon, he marched out of the room.

Ozzie slung the equipment cases on the bed and unsnapped the locks. He glanced at the prone body of Lars Svenson, noted the ambulating legs, and said, "Seeing is believing, huh? Come on, Doc, give me a hand with the BEAM machine. Susan? Hey, snap out of it," he gently chided. "We've got work to do."

It helped to maintain scientific discipline. Concentrate on the equipment, the details, on recording the data. Ignore the sweat on Ozzie's lip, the flutter in her own heart, and find out what was going on with the body that had once been a middle-aged accountant named Lars Svenson. And so they unpacked BEAM, the portable brain electrical activity mapping device, and plugged in the monitors.

"EKG is flat," Ozzie said, positioning the electrodes on the cool, fleshy chest. "Not even a trace of a heartbeat."

Susan had already determined that with a stethoscope, but this way they had a record of it on tape. Oddly enough, even without any heart activity there was evidence of slight blood pressure.

"Fluids being displaced by the flexing muscle," Ozzie theorized. He managed to reposition an EKG electrode on Svenson's thrashing leg, and recalibrated the BEAM unit to detect the slightest trace of electrical activity in the central nervous system.

Susan taped electrodes to the cadaver skull. Fortunately Svenson was bald, so it was not necessary to shave the head to achieve good contact. As she'd anticipated, the brain wave was completely flat. Whatever was happening to the dead in Sprauken, it didn't involve neurological activity above the brain stem.

Ozzie said, "This sucker is on-line. We're picking up faint impulses from the leg muscles. Not much, though. Old Lars is what you might call a low-watt zombie."

"Ozzie!"

"Sorry," he said. "Graveyard humor. How about we stand it up, see if all this leg activity can really make it walk?"

"Take it from me," Susan said. "It does."

Ozzie frowned. "I'm serious, Doc. Having it upright and walking may change the electrical field discharge. Right now there's almost no resistance to the muscle contractions."

He insisted. Susan, knowing he was right, relented and tried to help. Svenson had been no lightweight alive. Dead he seemed to have the density of lead. Fortunately Ozzie was stronger than he looked, and by bracing his bandy little legs he was able to heave the cadaver upright.

"I'll be damned," Ozzie said, amazed. "Look at it go."

And so they were able to collect data while the dead thing walked. It plodded forward until it came up against the wall and continued to thump in place, as if on a treadmill that had run out of room. Ozzie tried making it shift direction by nudging it away from the wall, but each time it would slowly inch around and come up against the same wall. Only the lower body seemed affected by the phenomenon. The head flopped on the shoulders, softly rattling the thin electrode wires taped to the skull; the arms were limp and totally unresponsive.

"Gruesome but harmless," Ozzie observed while monitoring the instrument gauges. "From what I can see here it seems to be nothing more than a muscular response to stimuli."

"I agree," Susan said. "But what stimuli?"

Ozzie shrugged. "A viral nerve disorder? Something that enhances the normal contractions of rigor mortis?"

"Impossible."

"Yup," Ozzie said. "Impossible. But there it is. The thing is as dead as the proverbial doornail and yet the leg muscles are functioning."

At 1:58 A.M. the contractions began to slow. The cadaver gradually stopped moving, like a toy whose spring had finally wound down. It remained in place, leaning against the wall, for sixty-eight more seconds, and then the knees suddenly buckled and the thing collapsed.

Ozzie looked down at the sprawled, motionless body and said, "I can't wait to slice this sucker up."

7:10 A.M.

The sun, pale and limpid, seemed to be struggling to rise above the mountains. Nowhere in its brief winter trajectory would it be overhead. Daylight was an interval of less than ten hours—it was the night that had substance in the valley.

The thought suited his mood exactly.

"Oh shut up," Tom Weston said into his shaving mirror, trying to shake off the morbid thoughts that had ruined his sleep. So what if the days were brief in January? By June he would be biking or playing tennis in the warm, extended twilight; the winter doldrums would be forgotten.

"Sorry, Jeannie," he said aloud. About the only time he gave in to the urge to speak to her was just after waking, in the familiar intimacy of the bathroom. Although it had been almost a year, he still felt it necessary to say her name aloud at least once each day.

Never forget.

Dr. Weston had no faith in an afterlife. For him all that remained of Jeannie was what had been locked into his memory. If he let that fade there would be nothing, not even a trace of her left in the world. So he kept the memories fresh, even though it caused him pain and sleepless nights.

Tom splashed cold water on his face and turned away from the mirror, searching for a dry towel. Jack Webster had telephoned in the middle of the night. The old cop had sounded giddy, as if he'd been drinking. Probably nipping at whatever booze Lars Svenson had left behind. And why not?

"Come on over," Webster had requested. "See the thing with your own eyes."

Half awake even before the ringing phone startled him,

Tom had declined. He was a curious, inquisitive man—that's what being an internist was all about—but he had no interest in frequenting a gruesome sideshow. Alive, Lars Svenson had been his patient; dead, he belonged to the pathologist. In this case Susan Cullen and her strange little lab assistant.

The scene Webster described wasn't exactly sleep-inducing. Tom had lain awake, trying to rid himself of the image of Svenson frittering away long after death, until the security chief called again an hour later to tell him the incident was over.

"That pretty gal brought in this fancy equipment and run all kinds of tests," Webster had said, his voice thick with drink. "She says they'll figure out what happened."

"I'm sure they will," Tom had replied. "Thanks for the call."

Then he had rolled over and tried to will himself to sleep. Not a chance. His mind was alive with a confused static of worrisome thoughts. Something was seriously out of whack in Sprauken, and it wasn't just that the cadavers kept kicking. In a way the hematologic profiles of Al's pregnant patients were more alarming than the deadwalking phenomena. All of the young moms had unusually high lymphocyte levels. White blood cell counts way beyond the normal range. Most had suffered spontaneous miscarriage or serious hemorrhaging. And yet none showed any sign of infection, viral or otherwise, nor did the symptoms indicate any of the common blood diseases.

What the hell was going on?

Tom decided to skip breakfast and head directly to the clinic. He was out the door, taking his first breath of the icy morning air, when the phone rang. It was still ringing when he unlocked the door.

"Dr. Weston? This is Tony Faro, over at the Experimental Division. Sorry to disturb you at this hour."

"You're not disturbing me, Tony. Go ahead." *Oh God,* Tom thought, *preserve me from the boy-genius types. Especially the one who acts as honcho for the big boss.*

"Well, Doctor, we've got a slight problem over here. Is there any chance you could meet me at Goddard's office?"

"This is a medical problem?"

"I'm afraid it is."

Tom hung up, called the clinic to inform them of his destination, and headed for the Sprauken Experimental Division. He drove at moderate speed, taking care on the patches of ice. He left the stereo off.

Tony was waiting in the lobby, chatting with a uniformed guard. Other than security personnel, the office suites were empty. He seemed anxious to get Dr. Weston out of sight before the first shift started to arrive.

The young engineer coughed into his fist. "This is a matter of, uh, some discretion," he said, coming across, as usual, like a diffident, slightly superior Boy Scout with peach-smooth cheeks and a perfect haircut. "You have any problem with that, Doctor?"

Weston shook his head, but he clearly resented the implication. He was a company physician, Chief of Medicine, fully aware of the importance of discretion.

"It's been a long night," Tony said, leading him down a corridor. "The trouble is Dr. Goddard. I'm afraid he's had a bit of a breakdown. Overwork and exhaustion."

"Breakdown? What kind of breakdown?"

"The mental kind," Tony said, tapping his forehead, making the sign for crazy. "The poor guy got a little unhinged last night. He's been working pretty extreme hours—we're in the test phase of a new project—and Dr. Goddard hasn't slept in several days. I guess the strain got to him."

Tom nodded. "What happened?"

"Well, he just went a little . . . nuts. Started raving. I got the impression he was . . . hallucinating? Can that happen when you're overtired?"

"Sure," Tom said.

He didn't bother asking why Goddard hadn't been brought in to the clinic. The answer was obvious. In the normal corporate world it was standard procedure to shield a senior executive; in the defense industry, with the mania for security, that went double. A man in Kenneth Goddard's position couldn't allow himself to be seen as weak or incapacitated.

So Tony was doing the boss an immense favor by covering up. Probably looking to earn another merit badge in brown-nosing, Tom decided, aware he was being unfair to the young man.

"I'll wait out here if you don't mind," Tony said, hanging back at the door to the office. "One thing, Doc. He's sort of rambling, okay? What he says won't make a lot of sense. What the old guy needs is sleep. Maybe you could trank him out?"

"We'll see." Tom didn't much like the "old guy" reference. In his early fifties, Kenneth Goddard wasn't exactly a senior citizen.

Dr. Weston hefted his black bag and entered. At first he thought Tony Faro had made a mistake—the office suite appeared to be empty. There was no desk as such, since the former astronaut preferred worktables, and only a few photographs on the walls. That was somewhat surprising, since in his day Apollo Commander Goddard had been photographed for innumerable publications.

"Hello?"

No response. Daylight washed tentatively through a row of high windows, elongating the stark shadows of the furniture.

One of the shadows was Kenneth Goddard.

He lay facedown on the rug beside a leather sofa, his tightly clenched fists covering his ears. Tom put his bag on a worktable—it was strewn with small bits of electronic equipment—and crouched, slipping his fingers around Goddard's right wrist.

"Easy now," he said. "It's Dr. Weston. Tom. We had dinner together the other night, remember?"

Goddard nodded rigidly, averting his face. His pulse was rapid and hard, better than a hundred and twenty beats per minute. The kind of pulse typical of extreme exertion, or acute panic.

"I'm okay now," Goddard muttered. "Nothing serious."

"Please take your hands away from your ears, Dr. Goddard. We have to talk."

Reluctantly he relaxed his fists.

"When was the last time you slept?"

Answering the question seemed to require considerable effort. "Sunday," he muttered. "I had a nap on Sunday."

"You're stressed out, Dr. Goddard. Exhausted. What can we do about that?"

"I'll be okay. I can sleep here on the couch. I often sleep in here—ask anybody."

Tom checked Goddard's blood pressure. High, but not dangerously so. "My advice, if you'll have it, is to go home, get under a hot shower, and go to bed. I'll give you a sedative that should help you sleep."

"Not necessary," Goddard said. He kept his eyes tightly closed, as if afraid of what he might see. "I just got a little nervous all of a sudden. It was nothing."

"Tony said you were hallucinating. That's not 'nothing.' "

Goddard muttered, "I've been drinking too much coffee."

Tom sighed. "Coffee won't make you hallucinate. Sleep deprivation will."

Goddard shuddered. He licked his lips, his breath coming in rapid gulps. "It's just, you know, the screaming smell. It got to me."

"The what?"

"The howler," Goddard muttered. He began to flail around, as if fighting something invisible. "The howler in cage three! Oh God what a noise. Tony says it's normal, but damn it I can't . . . can't *stand* to inflict pain. Make it stop! Please!"

Something creaked behind him. Tony Faro was standing there, a tight, knowing smile on his lips. Tom got the impression that he'd been there all along and had just decided to make himself known. The young project engineer couldn't quite hide his faint contempt for the older man shuddering on the rug.

"He's raving again, Doc. You better give him something."

Tom reached for his little black bag.

8:05 A.M.

Nurse Alters thought they looked like a row of zombies. She had taken over the ER shift at six, assuming that as usual she'd have the first few hours to catch up on paperwork. No such luck. Two or three patients were waiting when she got there, and more had been arriving ever since. All of them complaining of weakness and a "tired-out feeling," symptoms of a typical winter flu bug.

"I'm weak as a kitten," one woman complained. "I could hardly get out of bed."

Nurse Alters refrained from stating the obvious, that maybe the woman should have stayed in bed rather than clog up the clinic ER. An even dozen people with similar nonspecific complaints were now waiting to see Dr. Weston, who had been called away on an emergency. Nurse Alters tried to appease them by cuffing them for blood pressure and checking temperatures. It was an old ploy, but it worked. They waited for Dr. Tom without making too much of a fuss.

Now, at a time when she would usually be having her second cup of coffee, three more people stumbled into the ER. Nurse Alters knew what each one would say: "I'm feeling weak. I have no energy. I must be coming down with something."

The blood pressure readings were a little low, on average, but not dangerously so. Oddly enough there were no elevated temperatures. No swollen glands. No fever. With flu you'd expect at least a low-grade fever. To save Dr. Weston time when he did arrive, Nurse Alters took it upon herself to secure throat swabbings from each and every one of the complainants. Later she would draw blood samples, if Doctor thought it appropriate.

"I'm feeling, I don't know, a little funny," said the latest to enter the ER.

"Run-down?" Nurse Alters asked. "Weak as a kitten?"

"Yes," the man said. "That's it exactly."

"Take a seat please. Doctor will see you as soon as he gets back."

Nurse Alters was a cult movie buff. She glanced at her row of patients and thought, if that was the night of the living dead, *this* is the morning after.

9:25 A.M.

The Lars Svenson postmortem was performed in OR-2, the rarely used backup operating room at the clinic. Dr. Cullen was assisted by medical technician Chester Oswald. They had both scrubbed for the autopsy, so as not to introduce any microorganisms to the cultures Ozzie would be preparing from tissue samples. The normal precautions of antisepsis were taken, in the unlikely event that the cadaver was contaminated with dangerous pathogenic organisms.

They were gloved and masked. Wherever possible Dr. Cullen used plastic surgical blades, so as not to contaminate samples with metallic traces.

The autopsy was recorded by two video cameras, in addition to the usual audio cassette recording of the pathologist's step-by-step findings. Susan opened the proceedings with a visual examination of the deceased, and followed by probing the body with her gloved fingers.

Dr. Cullen: The decedent, Lars Svenson, is a well-developed Caucasian male of about sixty years. Height five feet eleven inches, weight approximately one hundred and eighty-five pounds. Readily discernible scars include a four-inch, stitched incision mark on the lower right abdomen indicating an appendix removed in childhood, and a two-inch crescent on the left knee, the result of a skiing accident, according to Mr. Svenson's file.

[pause]

Thorough examination of the epidermis reveals no obvious puncture marks or wounds.

[pause]

There is pronounced rigor in the upper limbs. Lower limbs and hip area remain supple, with no indication of rigor. Possible explanation: extremely high level of acetylcholine in the peripheral nervous system.

[pause]

I am proceeding with the cranial autopsy.

[a plastic scalpel incision on the thin flesh covering the scalp, followed by retractors to peel the skin flaps back]

Saw, please.

[high-pitched whine of electric bone saw, fitted with a special blade]

I have completed the V-cut. Skull thickness is within normal limits, approximately one-quarter inch at thinnest point. Elevators, please. I will now pry loose the segmented bone section. Segment removed. Dura appears normal. I will remove the dura. Ozzie?

[Chester Oswald visually examines the exposed brain]

Dr. Cullen: Do you see any sign of malformation?

Oswald: No. Appears typical.

Dr. Cullen: Thank you. That is my judgment also. I am severing the nerves and blood vessels at the base of the skull.

[Oswald assists, cutting nerve bundles as Dr. Cullen maneuvers the brain free of the skull cavity]

Dr. Cullen: Brain of subject weighs three pounds, one ounce. Within normal limits. Ozzie, it's all yours.

[Oswald slices the brain in sections, arranging a variety of tissue samples, while Dr. Cullen continues with the gross autopsy]

Dr. Cullen: I am proceeding with the Y-incision.

[pause]

The great vessels to the neck, head, and arms have been ligated, and I will proceed with the evisceration of the organs, beginning with the heart.

Thus Lars Svenson was subtracted.

Susan, working methodically, removed organs and tissue samples. Death was a puzzle: with patience and dexterity and the miracle of high-tech pathology it was a puzzle that could be solved. Examine and weigh the various parts, probe for flaws, slice and dice and render in minuscule portions for chromatography analysis and X-ray fluorescence and microscopic examination—it was all part of the process, nothing to fear.

So she reminded herself.

The last part of Lars Svenson to be subtracted was his spinal cord. The usual procedure would have been to take samples of the organs, return each to the body cavity, and neatly close the Y-incision. But with the deadwalker it was different. Susan elected to leave the body separated into its various parts, separately preserved in Formalin, or quick-frozen.

Somehow it seemed safer that way.

Tom Weston pushed through the swinging doors into the scrub room at a few minutes before 11:00 A.M. He'd been trying to tear himself away from the crowded clinic for more than two hours, and regretted missing the autopsy.

"Find anything interesting?"

Susan shrugged. "A sixty-year-old male with severely occluded arteries and lung tissue that looks like something you'd find in an ashtray." She placed her greens into a plastic bag, sealing the top. "Prostate enlarged, but that's normal for his age."

"Anything . . . *unusual* about the cause of death?" Tom asked.

"Nope. Massive coronary, just as you diagnosed." She peeled off her gloves and went to the sink. "I'd say Mr. Svenson's clock had run out. He had the classic three killers. High blood pressure, high cholesterol, high nicotine."

"That was Lars," Tom said, nodding sadly. "The guy loved fried foods, butter-drenched lobster, and Pall Malls. Three packs a day. I prescribed medication for the blood pressure but he was convinced the pills made him impotent. So he stopped taking the stuff." He paused, looking rueful. "We're making Lars sound like a damn fool, like he *deserved* to have a coronary. The real truth is he was one hell of a good man. A friend. Used to trout fish with me now and then. I'll miss him."

"Ever catch any?"

"Huh?"

"Trout," Susan reminded him. "Why you went fishing."

Tom chuckled. "You don't go fishing to catch fish. At least I don't. Fishing is an excuse to get out there under the big sky and smell the fresh air and hear the water singing. Of course if you *do* happen to hook up with a few speckled trout, so much the better.''

"That can't be a typical attitude."

"You'd be surprised," he said. "Stick around until spring and I'll show you."

"Very tempting," she said. And surprised herself, because it *was* tempting. "Come on, I'll buy you a cup of coffee, Tom."

He grinned. "There," he said, "that wasn't so hard, was it?"

Nurse Alters couldn't believe it. No sooner had Dr. Weston finished examining all the patients and hurried off to the OR than a new batch arrived. All with the by now familiar complaints: "I'm tired. I'm weak. I must be coming down with something. Can Dr. Tom see me?"

"Take a seat please," Nurse Alters said. "Dr. Weston has left for the morning. Dr. Nash is covering."

The doctor had requested that she draw blood from all those with the "tired feeling" complaint, just as a precaution. It was obvious, he'd said, that a low-grade flu was making the rounds. They'd know for sure which strain as soon as the throat swabs and blood tests came back. Until then all they could do was advise bed rest.

"It's probably nothing, but I feel really run-down. No energy.''

"Weak as a kitten?" Nurse Alters said. "Take a seat please, and roll up your sleeve."

"So," Tom said, feigning a casualness he did not feel. "The, um, incidents are not pranks or practical jokes?"

"No way," Susan said. "The deadwalking phenomenon has occurred at least once. I saw it with my own eyes. Which leads me to conclude the other two incidents also went off pretty much as reported."

"What happened? How was it done?"

Susan shrugged. They had gone into his office, so as not to be overheard. The coffee was out of the ceramic mugs he kept there, made from a brand-new coffee machine, which he'd bought to replace the one that had mysteriously burned out during the early-morning power surge. "Obviously some kind of intramuscular or neurological stimulus is taking place," she said. "The new BEAM unit is a lot more sensitive than a regular EEG, and it detected electrical impulses at a level you'd expect to find with normal nerve and muscle activity. It's possible that the impulses could be set off by a foreign substance. That's one theory."

"By 'foreign substance' you mean a chemical?"

She nodded. "Like I say, just a theory. Here goes: Assume, for the sake of argument, that Svenson and the others were exposed to a nerve agent of some kind. Not a toxic level, because all three died of natural causes, but an agent that incorporates itself into the chemistry of the nerve structure. Then when the host body dies, the chemical undergoes a change. The result stimulates the surrounding tissue."

"You can do that with dead muscle?"

"Sure. The old trick of making a frog leg jerk around by running an electrical charge through it. Galvanism, remember?"

Tom looked skeptical. "Yeah, right. But this isn't just a contraction in a severed frog leg. This is a series of complex movements."

"I said it was a theory," Susan said. "So far we haven't isolated any unusual toxins. We might be able to nail it down with the liquid chromatography. If nothing shows there, Ozzie has a hunch there's a microbe connection. Possibly a synthetic virus that attacks the peripheral nervous system. He's setting up a full array of cultures. We should know in a few days."

"Nerve toxins, synthetic virus? Am I hearing this right? Those sound like chemical warfare items."

Susan smiled, sipped the coffee, and looked directly into his eyes. "Yes," she said, "they do don't they?"

"Damn it, Susan, they don't manufacture things like that here. Sprauken is an electronic hardware facility. Nuts and bolts and radar screens."

"You're sure about that?"

He started to say he damn well was—then he remembered Goddard. The man had been raving about a "screaming smell,'' whatever the hell *that* was, about not wanting to inflict pain. And before that, the incident in the ER when smug young Tony Faro brought in the worker who had been badly bitten by human-sized teeth. Faro had lied about the injury for some reason. What had *that* been all about? And just this morning, the sudden epidemic of flu symptoms; was there any connection there?

"Pretty sure," he said uneasily. "And if there were chemical weapons at the plant, it still doesn't make sense. Lars Svenson was an accountant. I doubt he ever went near the plant buildings. His office is on the other side of the village."

Susan was nodding, agreeing with him. "Right. If all three of these people had been in the same workplace environment, we'd have somewhere to start. But it's been a pretty wide grouping, so far. A file clerk, a bookkeeper, an electrical engineer. Difficult to see how they'd all be accidentally exposed to an experimental toxin. Which leaves us with a couple of interesting possibilities."

"Such as?" Tom said, almost afraid to ask.

"Maybe the stimulating agent was administered after death."

"On purpose, you mean. An experiment. But why?"

Susan raised her eyebrows, staring at him over the cup. "Too dangerous to try out on live subjects?"

Tom shuddered. "I'd hate to think . . . What's the other possibility you mentioned?"

Susan's smile hardened. Her eyes glistened as she put down the cup and folded her hands. "That's what I wanted to talk to you about. I'd like you to supply us with as many blood samples of clinic patients as possible. I want to conduct a blood chemistry survey of the village. Because the other possibility is that everyone in Sprauken has been exposed. And it doesn't show up until you're dead."

11:20 A.M.

Tony Faro paced in the driveway outside the executive complex where Goddard had been sedated and put to bed. He was waiting for the marines. Specifically for Colonel Benjamin Bentley, Jr. The stiff-necked DARPA bastard. Just once Tony would like to see him crack a joke, or respond with a smile. It was like a grin cost money.

Never mind. He needed Bentley. When he made his move—and the time for that was soon, very soon—he needed to have DARPA backing him with the Pentagon. So what if the colonel was a flinty, ice-veined leatherneck? This wasn't about friendship, this was about power. He would stroke Bentley, find a way to win him over, whatever it took. Use him and then, if necessary, lose him. That was the success drill.

The marine arrived at the wheel of an all-terrain Land Rover. Tony slipped into the passenger seat. Something from Wagner was playing on the stereo. Another thing wrong with Colonel Bentley. He liked opera.

"What's the prognosis?"

"He's asleep, finally," Tony said. "I got one of the local quacks to dose him with tranks. You mind? Let's take it on the road, just in case the old boy wakes up and peeks out his window. He's paranoid enough as it is, without seeing us meeting behind his back."

Colonel Bentley put the Rover in gear. He drove at moderate speed through the slushy streets. Very few vehicles were out and about. The village of Sprauken never had a traffic problem, not with the staggered shifts and the four-lane access road to the plant. Traffic always flowed according to plan. Every aspect of company life had been anticipated and accounted for, down to the last detail. It was a policy of which Colonel Bentley vigorously approved.

"Nervous breakdown, huh?" he asked without any trace of compassion. "How long will he be out of action?"

Tony shrugged. "Unbelievable, wasn't it? The old boy gibbering like an idiot. All because of some sentimental attachment to primates." He shook his head. It was unbelievable how Goddard was falling apart under pressure.

"Can he function?" Bentley wanted to know. "Will this throw the test schedule off?"

"No way," Tony said vehemently. "Later today I'm arranging to isolate our human volunteers. We have thirteen terminal cases all signed off, nice and legal. PULSE remains a go. We can run without Goddard, if necessary.''

''Without Dr. Goddard's authorization?''

Tony tapped his fingers. It was tough getting the rhythm of Wagner. All that bellowing and cymbal smashing. Weird, unpleasant stuff. War music for psycho sopranos.

''There's a way around that,'' Tony said finally. ''DARPA could formally request reassignment of the project director.''

''Meaning turn control over to the chief engineer. You.''

''Give it some thought,'' Tony said. ''Poor Goddard. You saw what happened to him last night. Let's face facts. The old boy is losing it. Stressed out. He's got this idea that PULSE will end warfare. You've heard his routine. War without death, the dawning of a new age for humankind, et cetera.'' Tony chuckled. ''War without death? I mean, is that over the edge or what?''

Colonel Bentley parked the Rover on a deserted overlook at the outskirts of the village. Whirlwinds of snow danced over the valley floor. An icy white shroud encased the distant mountains.

''We've been worried about Goddard,'' Bentley said. ''This project is Grade One priority. He's under a lot of stress, as you mentioned. And there's the addiction.''

''You know about the pills, huh?''

''Sure we do. We've been monitoring his urine levels.''

Tony stared, not sure whether to be aghast or amused. ''You've been testing his *piss*?''

Bentley gave him a cool, squinty kind of look. Bemused and slightly contemptuous. He said, ''This is, potentially, a multibillion-dollar project. We have to be absolutely certain that the man in charge is functioning efficiently. If Goddard isn't functioning at the next test sequence, I'm going to recommend that he be sent to a substance-abuse clinic. They can get him off the amphetamines in a couple of weeks. Hell, it's speed, not heroin.''

''Yeah?'' Tony responded. ''In case you didn't notice, he was hallucinating. Seeing things. Confusing chimps with human test subjects. And that's going to be a real problem in the final test phase, when we bring in the quote, volunteers, unquote. I'm not sure he can handle it.''

Bentley gazed impassively at the windswept landscape. Even behind the wheel he gave the impression of remaining at attention. ''You seem to lack leader loyalty, Tony. Is *that* going to be a problem?''

Tony made a face. Didn't the guy get it? He said, ''My loyalty lies with the project, not with Kenneth Goddard. I want to see PULSE go forward. I want to see it in production. I want to see it *function*, damn it. And I thought you did, too.''

The colonel had a way of measuring out his words. As if his every verbal utterance was being filed somewhere. Maybe it was, Tony thought. DARPA bugging devices were more numerous than black flies on a wet day in May.

''We're expecting great things of PULSE,'' Bentley said. He turned to Tony. A ghost of a smile animated his thin lips. ''We think it has the potential to be a real killer. With or without Dr. Kenneth Goddard.''

''Just sit right there,'' Dr. Nash said to the young woman on the examination table. ''Don't move a goddamn inch.''

He hurried away, ambulating down the hall in what might unkindly be described as a mincing waddle—he was in a hurry but couldn't quite bring himself to run—and found Dr. Weston leaning over the ER nurses' station, scanning a medical form.

Nash came up, tugged at his sleeve. ''Hey, Tom, want to see something really weird?''

Weston looked up from the form. ''No, Al, I'd rather not see anything really weird, if you don't mind.''

Nash tugged him harder. ''Come on, I have a double patellar. You gotta see it, tell me I'm not crazy.''

''You're not crazy, Al. Okay?'' His brow furrowed. ''A double what?''

''See, I got you curious. Step into my lair, only take a minute of your precious Chief of Medicine time. Humor me, Tom.''

He followed Nash into the examination room. The young

woman was exactly where Dr. Nash had left her, seated on the edge of the table, wearing a blouse and panties.

"Peggy LaRue, meet Dr. Weston. Dr. Weston, Peggy LaRue. Okay, we're all acquainted now. Peggy's here for a checkup and her annual Pap smear. Like a lot of other people in the village she's feeling a bit run-down, maybe a touch of the flu, but other than that, no specific complaints. Right, Peggy?"

The young woman nodded. She was blushing. Dr. Nash was her gynecologist—he'd already seen the most intimate parts of her—but the ruggedly handsome Dr. Weston was a stranger. She wasn't accustomed to meeting strangers in her underwear.

"Okay. So I take her blood pressure, heartbeat, check that her lungs are clear, eyes, ears—the routine, right?" Nash said, speaking in a clipped, excited voice. "Everything absolutely normal. Peggy's the picture of health. Matter of fact she's so healthy, watch what happens."

Nash pulled a rubber hammer from his pocket and tapped at a spot just under her right knee. Both legs kicked out. Miss LaRue giggled. "That almost tickles."

Tom frowned. "Let me try that," he said, taking the hammer from Nash. He slipped his hand behind the young woman's left knee, tapped her right patella. Both legs kicked. Classic involuntary reflex—except that according to what he'd learned in medical school, the patellar reflex was supposed to be confined to the leg being stimulated.

It was as if the reflex was being echoed by the nerves in the other limb. Crazy.

"You wouldn't be putting us on, would you, Miss LaRue?"

Peggy blushed even more, shaking her head. "Is something wrong with me?" she asked Nash.

"Not a thing. You're twice the fun," he said lightly. Then, giving Tom a warning look, he added, "Right, Dr. Weston?"

Tom made himself smile. No point in frightening the patient. "Right, Miss LaRue. Just goes to show that no two people are made exactly the same."

Nash walked him out of the examination room, into the hallway. He stood close enough to get his glasses steamed.

"Okay, smart guy. Can you explain that?"

Tom frowned, shook his head. "Like you said, a weird reflex. Or maybe she really was faking it. A subconscious bid for attention?"

Nash grimaced. "Spare me the psychobabble, Tom. If it was just this one patient I might buy it."

"What are you saying, Al?"

"I'm saying I've been getting a double patellar reflex from every patient. It started yesterday afternoon. So when the Chief of Medicine thinks up a good explanation, be sure to let me know, huh? I'd be grateful."

He walked away, rubbing his glasses on his lab coat.

Tom went into the ER, found an empty cubicle, and pulled the curtain closed behind him. He dropped his pants and sat down on the edge of an examination table. The plastic padding was cool under his butt. He took a deep breath, then used the hammer to tap his right patella.

Both his legs kicked.

2:30 P.M.

They came for them in a yellow school bus. Bernie had been expecting a military vehicle, something official. Maybe even air transportation; who knew how far they were going, where the test site was located?

"Does it matter where?" Sam Carnovitz had asked.

"I guess not," Bernie had responded. They were sitting around the lounge, waiting. Dr. Bert had said it could be any time now. "For myself, I wouldn't mind a little hot weather. Arizona. Florida maybe."

That got a laugh out of Sam. "Listen to him. Florida. You think they come all the way to Maine from Florida? You think they got no Veterans' Hospice in Florida?"

"I'm ready for a change of scenery, is all."

Sam was still laughing. "Buddy boy, we gonna get a change in scenery. And where you're going, it could be hot. Hotter than Florida."

The bus arrived right after lunch. Bernie hadn't eaten. He was too nerved up with speculation. Where were they going? What would happen to them? It was no use with all the questions, but he couldn't help wondering.

The bus driver was no help. A big know-nothing, a mere driver, hired by the hour.

"How should I know where we're going?" he said.

"You're driving the bus, you must know."

"I'm following instructions is what I'm doing, mister. And my instructions are, I follow the BMW."

"The what?"

"Right there, ahead of us. Where he goes, we go."

There it was, the BMW again. And the young punk was at the wheel, Tony No Last Name. Hadn't even had the courtesy to greet them as they boarded the bus. Or were carried aboard; several of the volunteers were confined to wheelchairs. There he was with his fancy sunglasses and his driving gloves. Tony the phony, leading the short parade.

The ride was two hours in duration. First on a major highway, then off into the network of county roads. Very rural. Going roughly north and therefore inland, from what Bernie could discern. So much for Florida.

"As a kid I rode a bus like this," Sam said. He was looking chipper, sitting up and taking an interest. "Same color. I remember it had no heat. This bus has heat."

"I walked," Bernie said. "The school was nearby. When I got older we rode bikes."

"You had a bike? What a lucky kid you were. My father, a tailor, he could give us only what he made with his hands. I wore a nice suit to school, always a nice suit. Blue serge; it lasted."

The memory brought a smile to Sam's face and he slept for a while. Bernie didn't disturb him. Sleep was so precious.

At last they came to a small mill town, hidden away in the snowy hills. There were tall pines along the frozen river. Bernie looked for signs, wanting to know the name of the place. No luck. It was like a dozen small towns in central Maine. It didn't matter, he supposed.

The bus pulled up near a low brick building that might,

from the look of it, have once been an elementary school. The postwar boom in kids was over now, and in any event the old mill towns were dying. Tony No Last Name got out of his spiffy new BMW and boarded the bus.

"This is a kind of way station," he said. "A nursing home. You'll be kept here, and cared for, until we're ready to transport you to the test facility."

"When will that be?" someone asked.

"I can't say," the young man said. "No more than a week if all goes well."

"Goes well? What could go wrong?"

The boy smiled, showing his perfect teeth. "Figure of speech, gentlemen. Nothing is going to go wrong. You have my personal guarantee."

Sam woke up. "Are we there yet?" he asked.

"Almost," Bernie said.

4:05 P.M.

Goddard woke up listening for the scream. Under the tranquilizers his dreams had been muffled and indistinct. The images faded quickly. Only the echo of that chilling sound stayed with him.

Pull yourself together, Ken-boy.

He turned on his side, forced himself to sit up. Held his head in his hands until the dizziness passed. His mouth was furry and dry, as if he'd been chewing on a blanket. His head felt as if he'd been pummeled by huge, soft boxing gloves. Smashing, smashing, making his ears ring with the ghost of a scream.

It was the pills, he knew. Uppers and then downers.

Got to break the cycle. He'd been kidding himself, letting the black beauties do the thinking for him. How he loved that bright, sparkly feeling! The *newness* of it all. Goddard had developed a taste for amphetamines in the early days of his career as a test pilot, when the pills were prescribed for long-distance flights. He stopped using them when he was selected for the Apollo program. Years went by. Then, during the early, hectic stages of developing PULSE, he started on the pills again, relying on the stimulant to get him through the grueling all-nighters in the lab. Strung out like a grad student trying to finish a thesis. The drug helped Goddard focus his concentration on the complexities of developing the PULSE technology and made him feel young again, vibrant with energy.

That was over now. The development phase was complete. He had to kick the stuff again before Tony or the others began to suspect he had a problem. As to last night's incident, he'd slough that off as sleep deprivation—plain ordinary exhaustion. Nothing to be ashamed of there. He'd been keeping a brutal schedule. An inhuman schedule.

Goddard crawled from the bed and stumbled. He caught hold of a chair, tipping it over, and went to one knee. Amazing how his body seemed to be betraying him! He got up shivering and staggered into the bathroom, where he stood over the commode dry heaving, his belly doing flip-flops. That giddy nausea, almost like being weightless again. Nothing came up. Goddard caught sight of his pale, ghastly face in the mirror and winced. His complexion was green. The color of dead, putrefying flesh.

The panic came at him again. Rushing into his body, making every muscle tremble, every nerve resonate with panic.

Get hold of it, mister! Bear down! Breathe slow and easy.

He was snorting through his nose, gulping air. Hyperventilating. He reached for the shower nozzle, jerked it on full blast. Steaming water scalded his forearm. He jerked away, then managed to yank the handle over, turning the jet of water cold.

Better.

When the water temperature was bearable, Goddard braced himself carefully and stepped into the shower stall. His heart was trip-hammering as he ducked his head under the lukewarm stream. Gradually his pulse returned almost to normal.

That was when he heard it again, faintly. It seemed to come from the drain. A small echo of that terrible, humanlike shriek of fear.

A trick Ken-boy! Your mind is playing a trick! What it wants is a little black capsule. And another, and another . . .

Goddard crouched under the water until he could no longer hear the terrified screaming. Until he found a way to lock it away inside his head.

Ozzie stared at the chromatography screen, his dark face bathed in the pale yellow light. He tapped the computer keyboard, nudging the CYTO program to look at the results from a different angle. The graph remained essentially unchanged.

Lars Svenson's blood and tissue were saturated with the natural nerve stimulant acetylcholine, as Susan had suspected. The levels were even higher than those found in the samples taken from the first two deadwalkers. It was as if, in death, Svenson's deteriorating body chemistry had gone berserk. A blood sample drawn two weeks previous, at a routine hypertension checkup, had indicated a normal, barely detectible trace amount of the nerve stimulant.

So whatever had gone wrong with Svenson's neurochemistry had happened within the last two weeks.

"Damn and son of a bitch," Ozzie said.

"Swearing at CYTO is like cursing the darkness," Susan reminded him.

"Old CYTO knows better," Ozzie said, fondly patting the screen. "She knows I was cussing the situation, not the program."

"CYTO is a she?" Susan asked, amused.

"Mother of knowledge," Ozzie replied with a lopsided grin. "How's the population survey going? You still getting high lymphocytes?"

"Off the charts," she said, looking up from the microscope with a tired squint. "Just about every sample drawn from clinic patients in the last couple of weeks has a similar blood chemistry. A sizable part of the village population is complaining of flulike symptoms. The lymphocyte count isn't quite at a dangerous level, but it's not that far off, either."

"So how are *you* doing, lymph-wise?"

"Lymph-wise? Is that a word?"

"Is now," he said. "Come on, Susan, I saw you prick your finger and smear that slide. What did you find?"

She shrugged. "Higher than normal, but nowhere near the local average. White cell count about what I'd expect to find if I had a cold."

"Uh-huh. You have the flu? A cold?"

She shook her head.

"Neither do I." Ozzie pulled a couple of slides from the breast pocket of his lab coat. "My personal stash. The first is yesterday morning. The second is roughly twenty-four hours later."

"Your blood?"

"My very own. Check them out yourself."

Susan shook her head. "I'll take your word. What does it show?"

"A trend. My blood is still lower than this 'local average' you mentioned, but the white cell count is up thirty percent overnight."

Susan stared at him. His grin had faded. "So whatever it is, we're getting infected," she said.

He shrugged. "If it's a microbial pathogen. So far we've got nothing to indicate any widespread infection. So maybe what is happening, we're adjusting to the environment."

"Huh?"

Ozzie looked grim. His eyes, naturally protuberant, looked more swollen than usual. The result of hours in dim light, studying the various screens and graphs, or bent over a microscope. "I don't know whether the pathogen, if it exists, is a toxin or a disease," he said. "The blood counts could be responding to a substance entirely unknown to us. Maybe something is leaking into the environment here in Sprauken, Susan. And if it is, you can bet your beautiful white ass it's defense related."

Tom Weston went into his office and locked the door. He unplugged the telephone, turned off the intercom. Shut the blinds against the last faint pinkish streaks of the winter sunset, and flicked off the overhead lights.

He sat at his desk for a while with his eyes closed, but that didn't help. Finally he did something he hadn't done in months. He got down on the carpet and lay on his back with his hands laced behind his head and stared at the ceiling. The sensation of dread and terrible, terrible aloneness lay there with him. There was no escape.

It had started at the nurses' station. He was checking his appointment calendar—the Smoke-Free-Living Seminar he was supposed to conduct on Monday, what a joke—and suddenly it was staring him right in the face.

Jean's birthday. It was exactly one week away. Instantly he remembered her last birthday. Every blessed moment, every detail. They'd gone down to Boston for the weekend, taken a suite at the Ritz-Carlton. Just after sunset it started snowing like a bastard and they hadn't left the hotel for their long-planned night on the town. Instead they'd ordered up a bottle of champagne—outrageously expensive stuff—and then made love on the bed. Then on the floor. And later in the tub. Screwing around like a couple of lovesick kids, a honeymoon couple!

Son of a bitch! It was such a great time, such a great memory; why did it hurt so?

"You know how lucky we are?" Jean had whispered, grazing his earlobe with her teeth, like she wanted to maybe take a bite, savor his flesh. "Think about it, babe. Think about everybody we know, all the little miseries they have, the bad marriages, the cheating, the heartache. And we still get hot for each other. We can still fuck like it's brand-new!"

And how. And maybe it *was* luck, a fleeting, tricky kind of luck that brought them together, granted them a few happy years before snatching Jean away. That was luck, too. The meanest kind of bad luck that made an undetected aneurysm burst like a bullet in Jeannie's brain exactly ten days after her last birthday. The blood vessel ruptured about fifteen minutes before her shift at the clinic ended. What happened was, Jeannie passed out with a sigh, her fingers softly clutching at her stethoscope, and never regained consciousness. Ten minutes later her heart fluttered, then stopped beating.

There was nothing he could do. Not a thing! But that hadn't stopped him from trying. The frantic images were etched in his memory. Slamming the paddles against Jeannie's chest and hitting the juice, watching her body arch upward. Then listening, listening, straining to hear the faintest murmur. Some sign that life still dwelled within her. And hearing nothing. That awful silence!

Jesus! What had Goddard been squawking about, a screaming? Something he'd hallucinated, or dredged up from a nightmare. Tom lay on the floor of his office, in much the same position he'd found Kenneth Goddard, and decided that, given a choice, he'd take the screaming.

Anything was better than the awful, empty silence that had entered the world when Jeannie died.

6:10 P.M.

Ozzie was playing with the eggs. Rolling them through his gloved fingers, searching for imperfections. He held each egg up to a white glowing light, the old farmer's technique of candling that remained part of the laboratory process. The eggs were a special, fertilized variety, alive in the most vital sense, and Ozzie wanted to be sure each thin shell was perfectly intact. The vent hood made a soft, droning sound as it sucked up and sterilized the air in the lab.

As Ozzie worked he hummed an aria from *The Magic Flute*. Mozart, he knew, had probably died of a bacterial infection.

Having satisfied himself that all the embryos were alive and forming normally, he returned to the first egg, disinfecting the exterior of the shell with an ethanol solution. As he waited for the ethanol to evaporate, he sterilized the special egg punch by dipping it in a 70 percent solution of alcohol and passing the instrument through a flame.

He used the punch to make a tiny hole in the top of the egg, taking care not to puncture the embryo membrane just yet. He had already prepared a suspension of nerve tissue taken from the Lars Svenson cadaver, and drew the nerve solution up into a 6-millimeter syringe that had been fitted with a large-gauge needle. Holding the egg with great care, Ozzie inserted the syringe into the embryo membrane, depressed the plunger, and then sealed the small hole in the shell with ordinary Duco cement.

Satisfied that the procedure had not been contaminated, he marked the egg with a coded number and placed it in an incubating tray.

The live-egg method of microbe detection required an incubation period of approximately two days. Most of the known microphages would rapidly multiply inside the egg's fluid. When harvested, the virus and the antibodies it produced would be visible under a microscope. In most cases the host embryo would die in the process. Ozzie repeated the procedure with samples from the first two deadwalkers. Then, on Susan's instructions, he introduced tissue samples taken by Dr. Nash from the miscarried pregnancies, and throat swabbings from a variety of the clinic "flu" patients who had high lymphocyte blood samples. Dr. Weston had informed his patients that he was trying to isolate a "low-grade virus." As yet the Biohazard Lab detected no evidence of anything more than a coincidental connection between the deadwalking phenomena and the similarly altered blood chemistry of the resident population, but a thorough test sampling seemed prudent.

The last egg received a swabbing from Ozzie's own throat. That was his idea. The last egg was not coded. He simply signed his name to it with a soft lead pencil.

He finished humming the Mozart aria, removed his gloves, and sterilized his hands yet again. After donning a new pair of gloves, he removed a rack of glass tubes from the refrigerator. Each tube contained live, specially treated human cells, prepared by a commercial laboratory. Like the eggs they provided a basic growing medium for tissue cultures. Certain viral strains that did not respond to the egg fluid would flourish in the sealed tubes. Ozzie repeated the process, introducing samples from the cadavers and the live clinic patients, and last—and, he hoped, least—again tested his own throat swabbing.

He signed the tube "C. Oswald."

When the rack of glass tubes was safely installed in the incubator, he decided to take a break before continuing with the more routine serum tests. He approached the computer alcove where Susan was working.

"Dose of caffeine and organic acid?"

Susan looked up, bleary-eyed, from the gas chromatography display on the monitor. "I wish you wouldn't put it that way. But yeah, I need a cup of coffee."

He poured from a beaker. The lab had a perfectly adequate coffee maker, but Ozzie preferred the tried-and-true beaker brew that he'd developed a taste for in med-tech school. He handed the steaming mug to Susan and said, "Are we having fun yet?"

Susan glanced at the screen and shook her head. "There *has* to be a toxin present. An organic nerve agent, a trigger chemical, *something* that elevates lymphocytes and alters the peripheral nervous system chemistry. I'm just missing it somehow."

"Drink."

Susan sipped from the mug as instructed and tried not to make a face. Ozzie's beaker brew was strong enough to scorch tooth enamel.

"Maybe it dissipates," Ozzie suggested.

"Huh?"

"Maybe your unknown toxin dissipates. That would rule out the heavy metals. The old invisible ink trick. Now you see it, now you don't."

Susan shuddered. "Ozzie, you're giving me the creeps."

"Sorry. You get my point, though. Maybe what we're looking for is a nerve agent that is *designed* to be undetectable. The ultimate CBW weapon. Even the smallest leak of that deadly stuff might have spectacular effects."

"Chem-bio warfare? But Sprauken isn't involved in any CBW projects. I checked with Dr. Weston, just to be sure. They're strictly hardware."

Ozzie nodded thoughtfully. "So far as we know."

"Missile guidance systems," she insisted, remembering that Tom had made exactly the same excuses. "Radar. Communications systems. Things like that."

"Or that's what they want us to believe," he said. "This is a remote facility in an underpopulated state. Perfect for cooking up chem-bio weapons. And if the resident workers get accidentally exposed, blame it on the flu."

Susan shook her head vehemently. She just plain didn't want to believe it. Chemical biological weapons went against everything the Biohazard Lab stood for. "Come on, Ozzie. Remember, this is Kenneth Goddard's division. He's an electrical engineer. A former astronaut. Not a chemist."

"So?"

"So it doesn't make sense, that's all. Not a CBW leak. Not here. Has to be something else. An industrial by-product, maybe, that has toxic effects."

Ozzie's face was a mask. "Just noodling. Thinking out loud."

"We don't detect *something* tangible in the next twenty-four hours, I'll go to Goddard and ask him point-blank."

They left it at that, for the moment. Susan turned back to the screen, analyzing reactive agents, trying to pinpoint the presence of an unknown substance that altered the blood and produced strange effects in the nervous system. Her goal was to settle the most vital question: Was there a connection between what had happened to the cadavers and what was happening to the blood chemistry of the resident population?

"Come on CYTO," she whispered softly to the screen, "speak to me."

Ozzie, hard at work in his corner of the lab, was preparing serum tests. This was the so-called quick-and-dirty method for detecting a specific virus. The specificity itself had limitations: it could only reveal the presence of a known pathogen. Swine flu, Legionnaires', the A/Victoria flu strain, common Epstein-Barr, the meningitis group, and a host of others in the microbe hierarchy that were well known to medical science. While Susan searched for rare poisons, he looked for something alive: a virus or microphage.

As he diluted red blood cells in saline solution he thought, *Are you in there, invisible ink?*

On one of the serum tubes he signed his name: "C. Oswald."

Just in case.

The uniform came in handy. You wore the uniform, carried the badge, the gun, it was amazing: you could go anywhere, do anything. Like he was going to check out where the bitch lived and nobody questioned his being inside the executive suites, or denied him the use of a pass card. All you had to do was say "Security matter," and the dumb bastards would nod like they knew what it was all about. Like they were clued in.

He slipped the coded card into the slot over the door handle and pushed. A solenoid hummed, the lock snapped open; it was that easy. He went into the darkened room and closed the door behind him. No reason to be furtive. The bitch and her little colored sidekick were playing doctor at the lab. He had the suite to himself.

A little self-indulgence was in order. Deputy Mallon removed his holster and his jacket and fell backward on the bed. He lay there motionless, eyes closed, aware of her scent. A faint citrus smell. Reminded him of orange blossoms, that year they spent in Florida with his stepfather. What was he, ten years old? And he could still recall the smell of the blossoms! That was about the only good thing he remembered, the orange tree in the hardscrabble lot behind that fetid trailer. Hiding out there when the drinking got bad, when his mother came after him with the poultry shears.

Forget that shit.

Mallon sat up. He had work to do. A mission from the boss.

But first the creepy-crawl. He went to the closet. Dresses inside plastic sheaths, fresh from the dry cleaner. Expensive, fashionable things for going out, making the right impression. He stroked the fabric under the plastic covers, but it did not touch him. There was nothing of her in the clothes.

He knew where to go for *her*, but he was saving that for last. In the meantime, delaying the inevitable moment of pleasure, he checked out the bathroom. Fancy stuff. A tiled shower stall, a small sauna unit, a Jacuzzi hot tub.

A full-length mirror.

Mallon dropped his trousers, took off his shirt, and confronted his naked reflection in the glass. Tried to look himself in the eye, but he hated that shit, it made him dizzy. What it did, looking himself in the eye, it gave him that empty feeling. Like he was standing at the edge of a cliff, ready to leap into a cavern of emptiness. Better to check out his body. Inspect the flesh. That was pleasant, soothing. He worked out, the whole Nautilus routine, and it showed. Flat belly, tight buttocks, nice muscle definition.

What would the bitch think if she walked in, found him buck naked in her bathroom? Probably do that funny little scream women do when they're frightened. Like a picture he'd once seen in a magazine of a woman reacting to a bombing raid. Just this open mouth with no sound, but you could still hear it somehow, like when dogs can hear those high whistles.

Mallon grinned. His teeth were large and white, a nice contrast to his ski tan. A twenty-dollar whore in Lewiston had once told him he had a "show biz smile," whatever that was supposed to mean. Trying to worm a few extra bucks out of him. Fat chance. He'd used his "show biz" teeth to give her a little nibble. A bite, actually, not that it drew much blood. And she'd screamed like a child. *Eek eek!*

Mallon laughed.

The laughter sounded strange and exciting as it echoed in the tiled bath. Spooky. Like he was leaving a vibration of himself in the place. He went to the commode and stood there, gazing down into the blue-tinted water. Grinning, he directed a stream of urine into the bowl. Not bothering to be neat about it. That was the point. He wanted Dr. Bitch to suspect her privacy had been violated. Weird her out. Soften her up.

He dressed, taking his time. He tucked in his shirt, neatened his hair with her comb, cleaned his teeth with her toothbrush. His pulse was racing by the time he got to her bureau and began to open the drawers. Hitting the jackpot on the third try.

Sighing, he knelt by the open drawer and ran both hands through her lingerie. He crushed the silky things in his fingers just as, long ago, he had crushed the orange blossoms. And the butterflies. And whatever small animals that happened to stray near him. All crushed, soiled, punished for being weak.

Mallon closed his eyes and let the hatred wash through him. The hate made him strong; it purified his essence. Nothing could hurt him. Not beautiful, taunting bitches, not poultry shears, not the emptiness. Nothing.

Before leaving he placed the tiny microwave listening device on the telephone, as the boss had requested.

Every whisper, he thought. *I own every little whisper.*

"Say that again?" Ozzie asked.

Susan came around to the nook by the cryostat machine, where Ozzie was preparing slides of frozen tissue samples.

"This impression I have. That we're missing something crucial. A vital clue."

"Like what?"

Susan laughed. "If I knew we wouldn't be missing it, right?"

"You have a logic working at some level or other," he said, making a translucently thin slice with his microtome knife, then deftly transferring it to a slide. "I'm assuming that."

Susan rested her hip on the workbench, effectively blocking his access to the slides. Ozzie put down the microtome knife and waited for her pitch.

"Okay," she said, ticking off the points. "What do we know? One: we're picking up uniformly high lymphocytes in the blood chemistry of the resident population. Two: the blood serum of the same group shows a rise in triglycerides and acetylcholine, which may adversely affect the peripheral nervous system. Three: blood chemistry in the cadavers and blood chemistry in the living population are remarkably similar. Four: the nervous system is being subtly affected in the living, drastically stimulated in the dead. Five: we keep seeing a lot of other odd little quirks that don't conform to any known infirmity, but which might be the result of a previously undetected pathogen."

Ozzie nodded. "Unless something shows in the cultures."

Susan shook her head. "Maybe, but don't hold your breath.

Aside from the blood chemistry, there are no other indications of epidemic infection. The only common complaint of the clinic patients is a 'lack of energy,' which is explained by the lymphocyte level. There are no unusual fevers, no unexplained tissue inflammations. Tom—I mean Dr. Weston—says that until today the flu rate was actually *below* normal for the season. We'll have to wait on the egg and cell cultures before we can rule out a disease, of course, but I'm still inclined to concentrate our efforts on isolating a toxic substance.''

Ozzie chuckled and gestured toward the chromatography display. ''Isn't that what you've been doing all day? Searching for a rare organic poison?''

Susan picked up the microtome knife and balanced the lethally sharp blade in the palm of her hand. ''Yup. And not just organic, but heavy metal toxins as well. I've tried matchups for two thousand of the most common poisons, from arsenic to xylene. And come up with nothing. So what do we conclude?''

''We conclude we're up a creek and we've got to find a paddle. Fast.''

Susan nodded miserably. ''But CYTO keeps telling us there *isn't* any toxin present in the samples. That's a kind of clue, I guess.''

''Some clue, Sherlock,'' Ozzie said, alluding to the fact that he was more comfortable with medical evidence that could be observed, rather than an intuited diagnosis. He hated the guessing game.

Susan put down the knife. ''Think about it, Ozzie. Something brand-new is happening here, an undetected biohazard. Something outside of every documented case. Something that has a wide range of effects on blood, nerve, and tissue, alive *or* dead.''

Ozzie chuckled. ''And that makes you happy?''

Susan shrugged. ''It's a challenge. Test pilots have this term, they call it 'pushing the envelope'—the outer limits of the atmosphere. That's what we're doing here in Sprauken.''

''Pushing the envelope?''

''In a way.''

"Maybe," Ozzie said. "Too bad I suffer from aviaphobia."
"What's that?"
"Fear of flying."

7:32 P.M.

Goddard read the message again. He seemed to be having trouble focusing. Had it come through as machine gibberish? Was his decoding device out of date? He shut his eyes, took a deep breath, then looked again. This time the typescript was clear.

ATTENTION: APOLLO.

REQUESTED SECURITY PROBE SPRAUKEN EMPLOYEE SUSAN CUL-LEN, M.D., COMPLETE. EXTENSIVE BACKGROUND CHECK NEGA-TIVE. SECURITY CLEARANCE WARRANTED, UP TO AND INCLUD-ING THIRD LEVEL. PROCEED AT YOUR DISCRETION AND NOTIFY THIS OFFICE IF SUBJECT BRIEFED ON PULSE PROJECT.

REGARDS, DUBOIS.

His hands were trembling. What the hell was he looking at? Then he remembered transmitting a coded memo to Dickie DuBois at Data Retrieval in Langley. This was evidently the reply.

Susan Cullen, M.D.?

Right. The Biohazard Lab. Sharp young woman. He'd wanted to be sure about her security clearance before involving her in the PULSE project. Not that she would have to know all the details, or even the basic concept. Just enough to get an informed reaction, a new perspective on the project. Her medical background would be useful, especially during the final, human phase of the testing. Had he mentioned the possibility to Tony? Tony would handle the details. The boy was a great one for details.

Goddard discovered that if he put his hands in his pockets the trembling wasn't so noticeable. No need for him to hide. He'd been right in deciding to get back to work. His problem was a slight physical dependency on the black capsules. No big deal. He could handle it. His mind wasn't affected. He paced his office—instructions had been given that he not be disturbed by anyone except Tony—intending to walk off the jitters.

He was aware of the irony. It was steady hands that had saved his Apollo mission all those years ago. Steady hands and a perfectly concentrated mind. The incident with the busted servo motor had made him famous for a while. His fifteen minutes and a little more.

Goddard wandered over to the corner cabinet, where the model of the old moon-landing module was displayed. Hard to believe, but it was practically an antique now! He picked up the model and *just like that* the trembling diminished. So the event still had that kind of power over him. Amazing! Goddard shook his head, marveling at his suddenly steady hands.

It had been such a silly thing, really, that famous repair. All he'd done was figure a way to wire around a failed relay. Any aircraft electrician could have done the same. What made it glamorous was the fact that there were lives at stake. The situation had been exaggerated by the media. The module might have functioned even *without* the repair. No one had focused on that possibility, of course. The potential-disaster angle was the hot news, and it had worked to his benefit. Without the publicity there would have been no job offer from Sprauken after the missions concluded, no budget for research and development. Ultimately, if he hadn't fixed that dumb little servo motor, PULSE might not exist.

You never knew. Just as he'd never suspected that a doctorate in theoretical electronics would ultimately land him a slot on the Apollo team. It was all chance.

Except for PULSE. There the chance factor had been eliminated. If PULSE worked, if it was able to render a population helpless without inflicting death or permanent injury, the brutal art of warfare would be changed forever. When living human beings no longer died in the absurd confrontations of conventional fighting, the social evolution of the race would be improved, perfected. Goddard fervently believed that as the inventor of PULSE he would have a special place in history. *That* was true immortality.

And compared with the mighty currents of history, his little problem with the pills was truly insignificant. Who had cared that Edison was deaf? He was the father of electricity, that's all that mattered. Who really cared if Kenneth Goddard took a few more pills, just to get him through the night? How could it possibly harm the reputation of the father of PULSE?

It was settled. All you had to do was think it through.

Pleased with his line of reasoning, Goddard went into the executive washroom and retrieved the hidden vial of amphetamines and made himself well again.

8:05 P.M.

Tom Weston groaned and forced himself to get up. It required an extreme effort of will. The flood of memories had a sweet, narcotic pain that tended to paralyze.

You had to fight it.

He stood up, weaving dizzily. It was no good, opening the floodgates. The grief was self-indulgent. He was allowing himself to wallow in the aloneness, letting it take over his life. Jeannie would have kicked his butt. He could imagine her reaction:

You beautiful schmuck, life goes on!

And so it did. But something was wrong in the village. A strange life-in-death situation had developed. The inexplicable blood chemistry results at the clinic, the unreasonable frequency of miscarriages, the strange double patellar reflex in the nervous system, these were symptoms for which he had no reasonable explanation. As an internist, diagnosis was supposed to be his main strength! Even more disturbing than the blood chemistry of the living was what had happened to Lars Svenson and the others after death. Deadwalking. What did it mean? Would it keep happening? Would the phenomenon begin to affect the living as well as the dead?

Tom hadn't worked it out in his head—something in him

resisted examining the idea—but the incidents with the cadavers had retriggered his grief for Jeannie. He did know one thing. There was only one sure way of regaining his emotional balance. He had to get back to work.

He retrieved his parka and mittens and left the clinic by the side entrance, where he wouldn't be observed. The bone-chilling cold was back, an inescapable symptom of the long winter nights. He used to think of the cold as a challenge, something to be battled, overcome. Now it simply fatigued him. Cold, like death, was the enemy.

Physician, warm thyself.

He grinned, teeth stinging with the frozen air. Funny how he kept mixing up the old adage, confusing warmth with healing. What would a psychiatrist make of that? Not that he really wanted to know. Like many physicians—like most people, for that matter—Dr. Thomas Weston had a profound distrust of psychiatry. It was the new black magic, witchcraft got up in modern disguise. The mystery of human nature would never completely reveal itself to science. Or so he hoped.

The lights were on in the Biohazard Lab. Against the bleak winter night the place looked almost homey. On impulse he mounted the fold-down steps and knocked on the door. The gnomish technician with the coal black skin and the strangely protuberant eyes answered.

"Oh, it's you."

"Hi. Stopped by to check on my frostbite patient."

Chester Oswald looked skeptical. Then Susan came into view. She held up the pair of insulated boots.

"Never leave home without 'em," she said, "plus they dropped off my rental car, so we've got transportation."

Tom attempted a smile and said, "Then you won't need a ride?"

"No, I guess not," she replied, then appeared to change her mind. "Hey, Ozzie? Are you about finished here?"

The little man glowered, shaking his head. "I've got a rack of tissue samples in the cryostat," he said. "Have to wait for it to cycle off."

"Okay," Susan said. "Tell you what. I'll leave you the

keys to the rental and Dr. Weston will give me a ride back to the inn. That okay with you, Dr. Weston?"

"Absolutely," he said, feeling the smile become real.

"Ozzie?"

"Sure," Oswald said. "Of course." He started to turn back to his equipment, then added, rather sourly, "Better get to bed early, Dr. Cullen. You look beat."

Susan slipped on the insulated boots and zipped up the heavy parka. In the parking lot the rubber soles made bat-squeak noises on the brittle layer of snow. Her breath was a plume of white vapor. Tom walked at her side, slapping his mittens together, feeling somewhat uneasy. What did he hope to accomplish by making friends with Susan Cullen?

"I don't think your assistant likes me much," he commented.

"Ozzie?" Susan shook her head. "Don't be silly. He's just a little overprotective. Has the idea that all other males are sexual predators."

Tom chuckled. He tried to imagine himself as a sexual predator. What would he need, a fur loincloth, a disco suit, war paint, what?

"So I should be flattered, maybe?" he said.

"Just takes time with Ozzie. He's really a great guy when you get to know him. A brilliant technician. The lab couldn't function without him."

Tom unlocked the Jeep. "I got the impression he was jealous, for some reason."

"Ozzie?" Susan chuckled at the thought. "Well, maybe. But not the way you think."

He started the motor, let it warm up, and jacked on the heater. They made small talk during the short drive back to the inn—how darned cold it was, what a contrast to Virginia, and so on. Tom felt that he was failing miserably. He didn't know what he wanted from Susan Cullen, but it was certainly not a weather report.

"Can you come up for a few minutes?" Susan asked.

"Huh?" he responded, and mentally kicked himself. Now the question was not what did he want, but what did *she* want.

"I really ought to keep you up to date on the test results," she explained. "We're picking up some interesting anomalies in the resident blood chemistry."

"Oh," he said. "Sure. I guess I can spare a couple of minutes."

Susan frowned. "You have someone waiting? I should have asked, Tom. Are you married?"

He shrugged. "My, uh, wife is no longer with me."

"Oh."

You idiot, he thought. *Just tell her the truth. Tell her that Jeannie died and you still haven't gotten over it and until you do get over it you can't even think about being with another woman, not really.*

He smiled grimly and said nothing of the kind.

"This won't take long," Susan said lightly. "We could sit in the lounge if you don't want to be seen going into my suite."

"No," he said, clearing his throat. "That would be silly. Besides, I'd just as soon it not get around that we're concerned about local blood chemistry. You know how rumors take on a life of their own in a remote area like this."

"Sure," she said, leading the way into the lobby. "Dr. Goddard mentioned the same thing."

"Oh yeah," Tom said without enthusiasm. "Goddard. Well, I guess he has a point."

"And he's the boss."

The elevator door slid open. They stepped inside, keeping well apart.

"Yes," Tom said, smiling weakly. "There's that."

After switching on the lights inside the suite Susan went directly to the phone. "I'm starved," she said. "Have you eaten?"

He hesitated. What the hell was wrong with him? He was acting like an adolescent boy. "As a matter of fact I'm famished," he said.

"I'll order a plate of sandwiches. Okay by you?"

"Okay by me."

After placing the order with room service, Susan went to hang up her coat. Sliding open the closet door, she hesitated. Her outfits seemed to be arranged in a different order than she remembered. Well, maybe the room attendant had been tidying up. But why would a maid wrinkle the plastic covers from the dry cleaner? Never mind. Not important.

"Something wrong?" Tom asked.

"No. I'll just be a minute."

Susan went into the bathroom and splashed cool water on her face. What she really wanted was a long hot soak in the whirlpool. That would have to wait until after she'd packed Tom Weston off, back to whoever it was that made him so self-conscious about being seen in her company. An attractive man—not quite so handsome as Eliot, perhaps—but so strangely secretive and moody. Maybe it was the remote location. Too much communing with nature in the famous Maine woods.

On the way out of the bathroom she happened to glance at the commode. Odd. The seat was up.

Susan went to put it down and noticed that the toilet had been used and not flushed. She frowned. Was the room attendant a male, then? It was not a pleasant idea, that an unknown male had been using her bathroom, and making a sloppy job of it, too. Almost as if he wanted his visit to be obvious. She went to the sink and washed her hands again. Silly compulsion.

When she returned to the main room Tom was pushing a service cart over to the small dining nook.

"Here okay?" he asked.

"Fine."

Susan brought her briefcase to the table, removed a thick, ragged-edged computer printout. As they shared the plate of sandwiches, Susan pointed out the anomalies CYTO had picked up in the blood chemistry and tissue samples.

"You already know about the high lymphocytes," she said. "Now we've identified unusually high triglycerides, and a corresponding decline in healthy red cells. We have identical readings from virtually every blood sample tested. Simpson, Farsi, Lars Svenson, and the half-dozen women who suffered miscarriages in the last week or so. And we're seeing the same results in blood drawn from the 'flu' patients. It would appear that the entire population of the village is affected. And the curve is going upward. Something is changing the blood chemistry here in Sprauken."

Tom nibbled on a sandwich and glanced at the printout. "I don't get it," he said. "If it was a flu bug we'd be seeing fevers, swollen glands, nausea, not just this 'tired feeling' syndrome."

Susan said, "Remember the blood problems could be the result of a toxin, not a virus. And don't discount the miscarriages. Very often that's the first sign that a pathogen is present in the environment. Fetuses are supersensitive to the presence of toxic substances."

His eyebrows went up. "Toxin? Did I hear that right? You mean a leak from the plant?"

"It's possible."

Tom gave her a long, hard look. "Are you telling me there's a connection between deadwalking cadavers and what is happening to otherwise normal pregnancies? Because if there is, I don't get it."

Aware that he was upset, Susan tried to be soothing. "I'm saying there *may* be a toxin present, so far undetected, that has a variety of effects on the human body. Certain effects when alive—the high blood counts—and certain effects after death. The postmortem reactive muscle activity, for instance."

Tom shuddered. That was a hell of a way of describing a deadwalker: postmortem reactive muscle activity.

"The company has a damn good toxic-containment policy," he said. "We have a fully staffed safety inspection team. I just can't believe there's a leak big enough to affect the whole village."

"I don't know the source," Susan said. "We can't get a line on that until we've identified the toxin. And if there *is* a leak, the toxin is a new substance, something CYTO has never sampled before. It's possible that the leak might be measured in parts per billion, that it is *so* toxic that the merest trace in the environment is producing significant changes in blood and nerve chemistry."

Tom stopped chewing on his sandwich. Suddenly he'd lost his appetite. "You're serious, aren't you? You think it'll get worse."

"I'm serious, yes. Or maybe cautious is a better word. Remember, detecting biohazards is my specialty. I've seen some pretty gruesome cases. Solvents that ravage the bone marrow. Exotic gases that can destroy the lymphatic system thirty seconds after inhalation. Heavy metal poisons that accumulate over the years and cause inoperable brain tumors. Contaminated dust that causes irreversible nerve damage, and so on.''

Tom put the remains of the sandwich back on the tray.

''Sorry,'' Susan said. ''It's just, this may be a chance to isolate a rare toxin before it does any lasting harm. Usually by the time the Biohazard Lab is called in there are some very sick or dying people. This time I think we're getting an early warning.''

''Warning?''

''The deadwalkers,'' she said, gripping his wrist. ''The deadwalkers are trying to tell us something. And we've got to listen. That's a crude way of putting it, maybe, but we can't deny the evidence.''

Tom stared at the slim hand, then at her. Her pale green eyes were blazing. He suddenly knew what had attracted him to the young pathologist. It was not her lovely eyes, not her beauty, not even her intelligence. It was her passion. She cared passionately about her work, her life.

''What do you want to do?'' he asked softly.

''I want to confer with Kenneth Goddard,'' she said. ''I want to ask him who is allowing poison to escape, and why. And I want to stop whatever is leaking before it's too late.''

''Well,'' he said. ''That's simple enough.''

Later, after Tom had mumbled a good-night and kissed her briefly (and awkwardly) on the cheek, Susan lay in bed and shivered. It was not the wind howling outside, or the room temperature, or even her misgivings about Eliot and the wedding. It was what she'd found in her bureau drawer.

Chaos.

Someone had gone through her lingerie. Twisting the sheer material, tearing it, ripping it to shreds. Her silky private things, many of them gifts from Eliot, had been violently rended. It had been done with a hatred, of that she was convinced.

Someone hated her. Someone wanted to tear at her, destroy her. Someone wanted to rip her to shreds, as her intimate clothing had been ripped and destroyed. That was the message in the bureau.

The phone was right there beside her, inches from her hand. Susan played with the idea of calling the security force. Talk to Jack Webster or that young deputy of his. But what would she say? Someone used my toilet? Someone ripped my panties? It sounded so lame when you put it that way. So juvenile. Why did she feel so threatened by such a minor intrusion on her privacy? It was not like she'd been raped or physically touched in any way.

So why was she terrified?

Maybe the thing to do was call Eliot. She lifted the handset, touched the buttons on the phone. No. Eliot would see it as an opportunity to remind her that she was a woman, and therefore prone to hysteria. He would be condescending.

Calm down, my dear, there has to be a rational explanation. Call the authorities, if you really must. But really, Susan, don't you think you're overreacting?

Forget Eliot. And if you couldn't call the man you were engaged to marry, who *could* you call?

Tom Weston? A possibility. No doubt he would hurry back to her room. But the kind of comfort he had to offer—he had actually trembled when he kissed her, on the cheek yet!—was more than Susan was prepared to deal with at the moment. Things were confused enough with Eliot. No need to bring an attractive, recently divorced male into the equation. She had to work out a few things with Dr. Thomas Weston before she could feel right about calling him in the middle of the night.

Finally she punched in a number. It was picked up on the first ring.

"Ozzie?" she said. "Did I wake you?"

11:59 P.M.

There was a glitch in the program. Tony had narrowed it down to the fail-safe cycle, but no matter which way he tried to reroute the data, bypassing fail-safe, the program still failed to run. And without computer backup, PULSE would not function. Eight hundred million dollars worth of super-sophisticated hardware remained as unresponsive as a car with a dead battery. It was infuriating.

"Get the programmers up here," Tony said disgustedly. "Fucking number crunchers. Damn software was supposed to be foolproof."

"You sure it's the software?"

Tony jumped. He hadn't been expecting that voice.

"Uh, hello, sir," he said. "I thought you were going to give it a pass tonight, let me handle the test."

"I'm fine," Goddard said. "What seems to be the problem?"

"Glitch in the program. PULSE is off-cycle, and we can't bring it back up until the fail-safe system gets the correct signal."

Goddard nodded, directing his attention to the computer screen that had baffled his chief engineer. "Tell me the sequence of events, okay, Tony? Exactly where in the program does it refuse to trigger PULSE?"

Tony frowned. His area of expertise was hardware. He relied on the programming department to design software according to the project specifications. When the computer failed to run he was at a loss—and there was nothing quite so unnerving as being asked a direct technical question by Kenneth goddamn Goddard.

"Just somewhere in the fail-safe sequence, sir. There's nothing wrong with the equipment, but the computer thinks there is, and so it's shutting us down. Maybe if we could program it to override the fail-safe?" He knew it was a mistake even as the words left his mouth. Goddard, the dotty bastard, was a bug on backups, on fail-safe systems.

"Give me a few minutes here before you roust the programmers," Goddard said, moving to the nearest terminal.

"Anything I can do, sir?" Tony asked.

Goddard shook his head, began punching keys. In less than a minute he isolated the point in the program sequence where the fail-safe command shut everything down. Goddard glanced at the screen and chuckled. "Hell," he said. "You can do something for me, Tony. Get me a screwdriver."

"What, sir?"

"A screwdriver. I think I've found your 'glitch.' "

It was maddening. Goddard was supposed to be in bed, sedated. Now here he was, bright-eyed and bushy-tailed. Maybe a little *too* bright-eyed. But he seemed steady enough, and if the big boss wanted a screwdriver, he damn well *got* a screwdriver.

"Come on, Tony. This might be fun."

"Where are we going?" the younger man asked, trailing Goddard along the catwalk.

"Out on the rim," Goddard replied. "We're going out on the rim."

Tony followed up a ladder to the next catwalk level encircling the PULSE prototype, which loomed over the target area. He had no choice but to play along with the boss. The old spacewalking bastard was full of surprises. The way it was supposed to happen, Tony was running tonight's test series—a kind of dress rehearsal for how he would handle the job if the big boss went into a mental meltdown, as had seemed inevitable until moments before. Colonel Bentley was giving Tony a chance to prove he could fill the slot as Special Project Director, if and when Goddard was terminated. After which he could write his own ticket.

What Tony figured, he'd split off the Experimental Division, make it his personal fiefdom. The kingdom of PULSE. Bring in more of the young turks from bio weapons, develop PULSE into the kind of weapons system that fatcat Pentagon generals would fight over.

"The thing about a fail-safe system," Goddard was saying, sprinting up another ladder, "any fail-safe system, is they tend to be supersensitive. Kick out at the slightest excuse. And that's the whole point, right? The safety factor. Sometimes all it takes is a little surge. Too much power through a minor circuit and the master program gets nervous, pulls the plug."

Christ on crutches, the old guy was babbling! Power surges? The trouble was in the software, some goddamn glitch in the program.

"If I remember correctly, the breaker is right about . . . *here*."

Goddard paused, looping one arm around the ladder rung to steady himself. Tony had to come up short, the boss man's feet almost in his face. Then he made the mistake of looking down. They were clear of the catwalk, out on the rim. Holy shit. It was a direct drop of forty feet to the floor. Except, Tony realized, a falling body wouldn't even hit the floor clean. A falling body would be impaled on the cages in the target area.

Tony hated heights. Always had, ever since he was a kid. He could feel the sweat oozing like cheap machine oil from his palms as he clung to the ladder and listened to Goddard droning on about power surges and . . . what the hell was he saying, something about Christmas tree lights?

"You know," Goddard chuckled, prodding a maze of shielded cables with the screwdriver, "those old-fashioned light strings? One bulb blows and the whole tree goes dead? Then you have to check out every single light bulb? Of course this particular circuit isn't wired in series, but the effect is the same. The computer senses a break and shuts down the whole system, using the fail-safe sequence."

Tony closed his eyes, hugged the ladder. "I knew that," he said.

Goddard, the bastard, laughed. "The computer will also identify exactly where the break in the circuit occurred. *If* you happen to know the command," he added, rubbing it in. He released a retaining screw, flipped back a shield on a small electrical box, and used the screwdriver to reset a cutout switch. "There," he said. "It's just a matter of logical troubleshooting."

"Can we get down now?" Tony said. "Sir?"

In the cages forty feet below, the test subjects began to rattle the bars and scream.

Friday, January 9

It was the smell that woke her. An acrid, burning kind of smell. Ruthann sat up in bed, suddenly wide awake. She'd been dreaming that she was pregnant again, a pleasant dream for a change. The bed was empty beside her. Peter was on the third shift for the next two weeks, and she was still on regular daylight hours, so the pleasant work of making another baby, as Dr. Nash had suggested, would have to wait.

The smell. Was the apartment burning? Was the complex on fire? No hint of flames disturbed the dark. The night sky gave no glowing hints of fire. Was she imagining the smell, was it some strange part of her dream?

Ruthann got out of bed and put on a robe. She looked for her slippers, couldn't find them, and went downstairs in her bare feet. The odor grew stronger, more acrid. Not fire exactly, she decided, but something very, very hot.

The kitchen area was glowing. A faint pink light radiated from the walls. The stove! Had she left the stove on? It didn't seem possible. She was very careful about the stove, about all the appliances.

Ruthann rushed into the alcove. It was the stove, all right, and all four top burners were glowing cherry red.

"You little fool," she said, admonishing herself. "How could you go and do a dumb thing like that?"

Relieved, in a way, not to find an actual fire, Ruthann

began the business of turning the dials counterclockwise, to the OFF position. She was stunned to discover the dials would not move. They were already *in* the OFF position. And yet the burners were glowing away as if she had a Thanksgiving dinner planned.

So the stove was malfunctioning. She'd never heard of a stove that malfunctioned by turning itself on. There was only one thing to do—unplug the damn thing and call Maintenance first thing in the morning.

At first Ruthann started to reach for the heavy, three-prong plug with her bare hands. Then she thought better of it. Pete, a quality control inspector at the MGS Division, was always warning her about the dangers of electrical shock in the home. Ruthann got a thick towel from the downstairs bathroom. She went back into the kitchen resolutely, wrapped the towel over the plug, and yanked it loose.

There. Done.

Ruthann leaned against the sink and waited for the burners to stop glowing. *Must be a trick of my eyes*, she thought. *I've been staring at those burners so long I think they're still on. Of course they* can't *be, not with the stove unplugged.*

But the burners remained on, plug or no plug. The cheerful rosy glow did not diminish. After fifteen minutes by the clock, Ruthann filled a pot with water and began to pour it on the burners. Steam rose from the coils.

"You turned yourself on," she admonished the appliance. "Now you can damn well turn yourself *off*, you stupid stove. I wanna go back to sleep. You understand?"

Thirty minutes later the burners finally stopped glowing. By then Ruthann was soaking wet and in no mood for sleep.

PULSE cycled off. Colonel Bentley, who'd been conferring with Tony Faro during the test sequence, hurried over to the control console.

"Congratulations, Dr. Goddard," the colonel said, pumping his hand. "It's everything you promised. I'm impressed. I'm sure my superiors will be equally impressed with my report."

Goddard walked over to the rail, glanced down at the silent cages.

"Come on," he said. "Let's get down to ground level, check it out firsthand."

"Anything you say," Bentley responded.

As Goddard turned, heading for the elevator, he missed seeing the glance that passed between Tony and the colonel. It was not a friendly glance. Tony was pissed off at Goddard's adroit handling of the test, and the marine was savoring the moment.

The elevator was an open cage with a limited capacity. Goddard and Bentley rode it down alone. "As you know," Goddard said, "we ran that particular phase at less than one tenth of available power."

The colonel nodded and said, "I must admit I had my doubts. We all did. This isn't the first time we've financed this kind of project. Were you around for the old Pandora?"

Goddard shook his head. "I read the literature, of course. PULSE is the same basic principle, but the method of execution is quite different."

Colonel Bentley's ironic laughter sounded just a bit like a dry cough. "You're damn straight the execution is different. Pandora didn't work worth a damn. We dumped millions into it, all under the hidden budget, of course. Enormous waste of time and money."

Goddard fingered the bottle of pills in his pocket. He didn't need them, not now. He was on a natural adrenaline high.

The little elevator chugged to a stop. The target area technical team was waiting, all of them grinning, giving him the thumbs-up. Just beyond, brightly illuminated by the overhead lights, were the test cages. The technicians were shoveling antiseptically treated sawdust through the bars, trying to cover the stench. What did it matter? PULSE had functioned superbly.

"What's the survival rate?" Goddard demanded.

"Hundred percent, sir. All the chimps survived. Take a look at the monitors, sir. Heartbeat and blood pressure are virtually normal, but the brain waves are in deep alpha pattern."

Colonel Bentley strolled to the nearest cage. He borrowed

a cattle prod and shoved it through the bars. Goddard winced but didn't stop him—it was best not to argue with DARPA's main man.

Zap! The colonel jolted one of the larger males. Normally it was quite vicious. Now, although clearly conscious on some level, it did not respond to the painful electric charge. The chimp's nervous system was short-circuited, unable to transmit messages to the brain. The colonel dropped the prod in the sawdust and came back, brushing his hands.

"So," the colonel said softly. "When do we try it on humans?"

5:45 A.M.

Bernie Simms tended to be an early riser. Had been all his life. At the hospice he'd continued to get up and about before most of the others. Early morning was a good time for him. Also it was best to avoid the rounds of bedpans and medication that served to remind him of his infirmity.

It was no different at the Cage. Sam Carnovitz had come up with the descriptive term only minutes after they checked into the nursing home. Tony No Last Name, the young punk in the BMW, had sped off before the nursing staff took charge, and it was immediately obvious that the personnel at the short-term care facility had no idea what was in store for the veterans.

"This place is just a holding area," Sam said. "A not-so-fancy cage. They keep us here, isolated, until they want us. Nobody knows nothing. Isn't this the way I said it would be?"

Bernie agreed. Sam had it figured. Between the two of them they were able to determine that the nursing home was privately owned, that it relied on Medicaid referrals for most of its business. The business, it seemed, was bedding gravely ill patients who were awaiting placement in a long-term facility or hospice. The place had no recreational facilities whatsoever. No library, no game room, no big-screen television, no pool tables. Just beds, rarely empty.

"They got 'em coming and going," Sam said. "Big turnover. It's a dumping-off area, this place; a cage without bars. They'll come for us in the middle of the night, this company with the big secrets, that's my prediction. And when we're gone, no one on the staff here will even notice. It'll be like we never existed."

What mattered to Bernie was that the money was in an escrow account, and would be transferred directly to Louise at the conclusion of the experiment. It would come as a great surprise to her, that sum of money. A provision of the contract had forbidden the volunteers from contacting anyone on the outside. This was to maintain, it was implied, the national security.

"Making the victims feel important is what it is," Sam decided. "Like we're contributing to science. To the defense of the nation."

"Maybe we are," Bernie said. "Maybe what they're going to do to us will save lives."

"It's possible," Sam conceded. "Like when they were testing for yellow fever, you mean? Those men who volunteered to let the infected mosquitoes bite them?"

"Something like that," Bernie said.

"We'll see. I got an idea, though, whatever they got in mind for us, it's worse than getting bit by a few mosquitoes."

Just staying in the Cage was bad enough. Could it possibly get worse? Bernie shuffled from one end of the corridor to the other, walking and waiting.

7:05 A.M.

Dawn was less than impressive. A pinkish glow behind the mountains, almost totally obscured by low cloud cover. They were talking snow again, Ozzie remembered; they were always talking snow in this godforsaken spot. They had nothing better to talk about. "They" being, of course, the local yokels.

Ozzie sipped a glass of orange juice, nibbled his toast, and waited for Susan. He was the only customer in the dining room. Sunrise, such as it was, played itself out behind a wall of triple-insulated glass that overlooked the valley and the faintly darker ring of mountains.

Why couldn't the Biohazard Lab have been dispatched to the Sprauken facility in central Florida? Why Maine, in January?

Lighten up, Oswald, he thought. *Drink your cup of caffeine derivative and get with the program.*

Susan had been freaked-out when she called his room the night before. Convinced that someone had been prowling her suite, going through her things. He'd done his best to calm her down, but the normally imperturbable Susan Cullen had been truly frightened.

At first Ozzie thought she'd been having a nightmare. Babbling about some beast who'd ripped her lingerie. Sounded like that creep Eliot on a bad night, maybe. Those southern males were all the same, no matter how refined they tried to act, or how many advanced degrees they compiled. *The Hundred Families of Virginia my ass,* Ozzie thought. And then, gradually, he'd started to make sense of what she was saying, and he realized it wasn't a nightmare, someone *had* been trashing her things, and it couldn't possibly be Eliot, no matter how much he'd have liked to blame the son of a bitch.

"Call Security," Ozzie had advised. "Report it. Also we can tell the inn manager, have him check out the staff."

"I feel like a fool," Susan had responded. "It was just some underwear, right? I mean, so what? Lots of people have access to suites at the inn. Repairmen, maintenance workers. This place is not exactly a private domicile."

Ozzie was adamant. "I think you should at least mention it to what's-his-name, Jack Webster. The security chief."

"You really think it would do any good?"

"Who knows? And have 'em change the lock. Or even change suites, if it will give you peace of mind."

Susan was much calmer. "I think I'm overreacting," she'd said. "Must be all those lymphocytes in my blood."

Ozzie had laughed. "Yeah, that's it. Listen, how come

you're alone up there? I thought you were entertaining Dr. Weston.''

"Give me a break, Oz. He just stayed for a sandwich and a glass of milk. There's nothing going on there, believe me.''

"Really? Too bad.''

"I thought you didn't like Tom. I mean Dr. Weston.''

"Yeah, well I've been thinking it over,'' Ozzie had said. "I think you should have a fling with him, get Eliot out of your system.''

"Come on, Oz. I'm engaged to Eliot.'' There was a pause. He heard her take a deep breath. "Sort of engaged,'' she'd corrected.

He chuckled. "Is that like being sort of pregnant? Never mind, don't answer. Listen, you want me to come up, keep you company?''

"I'll be fine. Sorry to wake you up.''

"Don't apologize. I don't get that many late-night calls from beautiful women. Or beautiful men, damn it.''

In truth he was flattered that she'd turned to him. Susan Cullen was probably the most important person in his life at the moment. Selecting him to help put the new roving lab together was a great opportunity. As it stood now he could have his pick of positions at any biohazard facility in the country. In the world, probably. Or he could move into pure research if he so desired. Not that he did. The medical detective work the lab handled was more exciting, more varied, more damned *interesting* than any other long-term research projects. The world of white mice would just have to get along without Chester Oswald, thank you very much.

"Ozzie?''

He looked up from his plate of toast as Susan plopped herself down at the table and said, "About last night . . .''

"Forget it,'' he said. "You manage to get some sleep?''

"Some,'' she admitted. A bleary-eyed waiter appeared and silently poured her coffee. Susan indicated that she didn't want breakfast.

"See that vague pink thing out there?'' Ozzie said, gesturing. "That's the sun. Impressive, huh? Jesus, no wonder the blood chemistry is weird up here. Sunlight deprivation.''

Susan looked startled.

"I was just kidding," he said.

"Check it out," Susan said.

"Are you serious? You want me to check out effects of sun deprivation on blood chemistry?"

She nodded. "CYTO can link up to the literature. There have been several studies on light deprivation recently and I'm not familiar with the results."

He sighed and rolled his eyes. "Yes, Bwana Doc. As you wish."

Susan leaned forward and spoke earnestly. "We can't leave any stone unturned here, Ozzie. This is important."

He made a face, but he knew she was right.

Goddard had taken to sleeping in his office. Well, not sleeping exactly. More like a quiet interlude. What he did was lock the inner door, take off his tie and his shoes, and lie down on the Naugahyde couch. Sometimes he would put on the headphones, listen to some music. He preferred Yamanakabushi, the Japanese contemplative songs, or maybe Rampal with that light, soaring flute. The kind of stuff he liked was sometimes called New Age, he had no idea why. What was new about Buddhist mood music? The staff knew what he preferred, and kept the stereo rack supplied with fresh CDs.

He closed his eyes and let the quiet tones drift through him. Who needed sleep? Sleep was a waste of time. The "little death," they called it. Edison had slept only a few hours a day. Of course if the grand old man had had amphetamines he might *never* have slept. Think of the marvelous things he might have invented!

Goddard smiled. It had been a very successful evening. First he'd surprised Tony by troubleshooting the supposed glitch in the program, and it was always difficult and satisfying to surprise the young man. Proved he still had a thing or two to learn from the master. Young Tony had been getting just a little big for his Cal Tech britches lately. Even better than besting Tony, the test sequence went off exceptionally well, better than could be hoped. Colonel Bentley, by nature very reserved, had been openly enthusiastic. Goddard had the impression that Bentley and Tony were bickering over minor details. A personality conflict, not unusual when you mixed an ambitious young engineer with a seasoned Pentagon bureaucrat.

The best thing about last night was that he'd been in control. This time there were no foolish overreactions about the chimps' screaming. *Naturally* they screamed. They were frightened. It was normal for a primate to screech when frightened or aroused.

The point was, they had survived direct exposure to PULSE. And there were indications that the damage to the nervous system was reversible, as Goddard himself had predicted. After a few hours the chimps, although still unable to respond to stimuli (Goddard found the term *paralyzed* distasteful), began to show an awareness of their surroundings. Eye movement increased. The primates would be constantly monitored in the following days and weeks to determine if the capacity for normal brain and nerve functions returned.

The final, human test phase now looked like a go. Goddard was aware that Tony had made all the arrangements, that a volunteer group was on standby, but final approval was still up to Goddard. He was determined that human testing be delayed while the long-term effects of PULSE were evaluated. The Pentagon was pushing for the human phase, of course. That was to be expected. Kid Tony would just have to learn how to handle Colonel Bentley.

His thoughts were interrupted by the intercom buzzer. Hadn't he directed that no calls be put through? Goddard sighed, slipped off the headphones, and padded in his stocking feet to the intercom.

"Very sorry to disturb you, sir, but Dr. Weston is on the line and he says it's a medical emergency."

"What? Wait a sec, put him on," Goddard said. "Dr. Weston? What's this about a medical emergency?"

The physician was apologetic. "I guess I didn't make myself clear, sir. I told your secretary that Dr. Cullen and I needed to discuss a possible medical emergency with you. I didn't mean to imply we were currently in a state of emergency."

"You better explain."

"I'd rather not do it over the phone, if you don't mind."

Goddard's eyes flicked around his office. Hadn't he just swept the place for bugs? Was the line secure? "I understand," Goddard said carefully. "What do you suggest?"

"Your office or the clinic. Whatever is convenient for you, sir."

Goddard grinned. "I know just the place," he said.

9:00 A.M.

Tony loved his BMW. It was his beautiful baby, his dream machine. He backed the automobile carefully out of the garage and let the engine idle. He monitored the gauges until the thermostat in the cooling system clicked open, indicating that the cylinders were properly warmed. Ready for takeoff. Before putting the transmission in gear he slipped a cassette into the deck and adjusted the volume. Tony liked heavy metal. His current favorite was a raunchy band called Pretty Poison. As he drove he adjusted the space expander until it sounded like Pretty Poison was jamming in the rear seat.

Fuck that opera shit. And fuck that uptight bastard Colonel Bentley. Last night had been a major downer. Bentley had been dazzled by Goddard's I'm-the-genius-who-made-this-project-fly routine, just lapping it up. Well, maybe Goddard *was* a technical genius, but so what? The question was, could he continue to function as head of the Experimental Division, given his addiction and his weakness? Could he provide leadership? Could he make the hard choices?

The Really Big Question: Was Kenneth Goddard ready, willing, and able to deliver PULSE as a functioning weapon system? Would he kick out the jams and prove what they all knew in theory was possible, that PULSE could scramble the human brain in a microsecond? Would he deliver what the Pentagon really wanted: a brand-new, rewrite-the-strategy-books killing machine?

The Really Big Answer: The old boy simply didn't have the guts. He still believed in his silly, unworkable idea about taking death out of the war-fighting equation. When the human test phase commenced, old Mr. Apollo would shatter like brittle glass.

Tony knew how to guarantee a Goddard mental meltdown. He had it wired. The human testing would go seriously awry and when Goddard freaked, Colonel Bentley would realize there was only one man truly on top of the situation, one man who knew all the angles, anticipated all the problems, one man with the chill-out attitude required to keep PULSE on track.

Tony slowed the BMW, keenly aware that the roads had been salted and that the corrosive mixture of salt and snow was detrimental to the well-being of his automobile. It would require a thorough cleansing, with special attention to the undercarriage. Up ahead he spotted the cop car exactly where it was supposed to be. A Saab, dull but useful, like the man driving it.

He pulled in to the adjacent space, tapped his horn. The cop got out, came to the window like a good little boy. Tony waited a beat, then thumbed the switch and let his window hum down.

"Morning, Kurt. Beautiful morning, huh?"

Mallon glanced at the gray sky and shrugged. He never knew what to say to Tony Faro. The guy had a mouth on him, you had to watch out. "Yeah, I guess it is," he said.

"Equipment functioning?"

"Working perfect, Tony."

Tony curled his upper lip. "We better keep it formal on your end, Kurt. A man in my position, I'm not supposed to get friendly with a guy in your position, capiche?"

Mallon nodded warily, shoved his hands in his pockets. It was cold and windy, but Tony always did things in his own way. So if he wanted to make dumb conversation, fine. Mallon had the goods, and they'd get down to that eventually.

Tony was saying, "If it got around, you on a first-name basis with me, it would be pretty obvious we're working together. And this is supposed to be our little secret, right?"

Mallon nodded. "Right, Mr. Faro."

"You're catching on, Kurt. So tell me, you manage to make that little installation I suggested?"

"Sure. Piece of cake."

Tony grinned. "Sure you don't mean piece of ass?"

"Huh?"

Huh? That was beautiful, Tony thought. That was the dumb bastard summed up in a word. He said, "Nothing, Kurt. I just mean the lady is attractive. But of course you've met her."

"Yeah, I met her."

Tony was still grinning. It made Mallon uncomfortable. He averted his eyes, cleared his throat, and said, "You want the tape or what?"

"Sure. She have anything interesting to say?"

Christ, it was truly pitiful, the stupid dork was starting to stamp his feet, like a goddamn counting horse. Were all security cops this dumb?

"I didn't listen," Mallon said uncertainly, handing over the cassette.

"Come on, Kurt, do you expect me to believe that? Of course you listened. You had to see if the device was functioning correctly, right? So what did she have to say? Anything interesting, or was she too busy humping that sawbones who runs the clinic?"

Mallon hesitated. "They were talking like doctors."

"Oh, really?" Tony laughed. "How did you expect them to talk?"

Mallon hastened to explain. "You know what I mean. Medical stuff. They're worried about a toxic leak or something."

That perked Tony up. "What? A toxic leak?"

"Some kind of poison that's messing up people's blood. I'm no doctor, Mr. Faro. I just got the impression they're worried about chemical warfare. That's the word they used. Chem-bio warfare."

"I'll check it out," Tony said.

Mallon bent lower, until his breath started fogging the

chrome on the BMW. "Is that what you guys are up to?" he asked. "A chemical warfare kind of thing?"

Tony stared at him until Mallon shifted his eyes away. The whipped curr reflex. "Never mind what us guys are up to, Kurt. You were in the military. You know how the system works. Classified information is released only on a need-to-know basis, and you don't need to know. What I want you to do, just hang loose. I'll get back to you about this lady doctor."

"Sure thing, Mr. Faro."

As the BMW pulled out Tony gunned it, spraying slush all over Mallon's polished boots.

Susan searched for metallic elements. Her earlier tissue analysis had focused on organic poisons, since the organics were more prone to affect the peripheral nervous system. Even with the considerable assistance of CYTO, capable of searching through thousands of base comparisons for organic toxins, she had come up with a big fat zero. The computer had struck out.

Now began the dull, repetitive work of preparing bone and tissue samples for a series of metallic tests: neutron activation, spectophotometry, X-ray fluorescence.

Susan remained convinced she was missing something. A vital clue still eluded her. Maybe the answer was a metallic poison. Or a combination of toxic chemicals that produced bizarre results. A toxin that linked blood lymphocytes with the nervous system. A toxin that sometimes behaved like a virus or microphage.

"What we're looking for," Ozzie had said, "is a master of disguise."

Ozzie. What a crazy idea of his, that she should get Eliot out of her system. Like he was a virus. Well, Ozzie had microphages on the mind. He was back there right now, hunkered down in his little alcove, running a whole new series of serum tests. Susan could hear him humming above the noise of the air vent. That familiar tune of his, something from an opera. Funny man. He liked to say that in another life he'd been born not colored, but a coloratura, a soprano specializing in high notes.

A smile played over her lips as she recalled her anxious, late-night phone call to him. He had instinctively known how to treat her fears seriously and at the same time dispel them. Ultimately she had decided not to contact Jack Webster at Security. An investigation—and she had no doubt it would be inconclusive, given that there was no actual evidence except the torn lingerie—would only distract her from more important work. She would simply have to be on her guard—and of course she intended to keep the door bolted.

Susan was preparing a bone sample in a sterile mortar when Tom Weston arrived unexpectedly. This time Ozzie was cordial. More than cordial.

"Your gentleman caller," he said with a wink. "I can't decide, is he ruggedly handsome or handsomely rugged? What's your opinion?"

Tom entered the lab hesitantly, as awkward as ever around the delicate lab equipment. "Goddard has agreed to meet with us," he said. "He wants to see us right now. Can you break away?"

Susan looked to Ozzie, who gave her the high sign. "You kids just leave the lab to me. Go on, have a blast," he urged, practically shoving them out the door.

As they approached the Jeep, Tom said, "I can't figure that guy out. Was he making fun of me?"

"Do you care?"

"Yeah," he responded. "I think I do. He's a friend of yours. I want him to think well of me."

Susan found herself grinning as she slipped into the passenger seat. It was exactly the right thing to say. Her estimation of Tom Weston went up several notches. If only he wouldn't act so deferential around her. She wasn't fine china; she wouldn't break.

Weston explained that Goddard had agreed to meet them at the Experimental Division, in the fabrication shop where he sometimes took up the soldering iron and joined his staff of skilled technicians. Security, always a concern at Sprauken, was exceptionally tight at Experimental. The two physicians were delayed for more than twenty minutes, until the guard got a direct verbal release from Goddard himself.

"Sorry, Doc," said the guard when he finally waved them through. "I guess you know what it's like now, huh? Just kidding."

Tom smiled weakly and put the Jeep in gear.

"What'd he mean by that?" Susan wanted to know.

Tom gave her a sidelong glance. "You really don't get it? No, I guess you haven't had to deal with that particular headache. He meant waiting for a doctor. We have chronic delays even at the clinic, which is more than adequately staffed. I keep trying to get the scheduling on real time, but somehow we're always backed up. Al and I did this study once, found the average delay was forty minutes, and then had the receptionist push all appointments up an extra forty minutes to compensate. Smart, right?"

"I guess."

"Then you guess wrong. Within half a day we were backed up again with the same average delay. I *still* don't know what went wrong," he added, laughing. "The faster I go, the behinder I get."

"I do know *that* feeling."

Tom parked near the shop entrance, where Goddard's green Mercedes took up two spaces. He started to get out of the Jeep, then hesitated. "What are you going to say to the big boss?"

Susan shrugged. "Express my concern. Ask him to undertake a thorough search for a toxic leak. State my belief that if the white cell count gets any higher we should notify the CDC."

"The Centers for Disease Control?"

Susan nodded. "You have any problem with that?"

"No," he said, opening the door. "But don't be surprised if *he* does."

A slender, gray-haired man wearing company overalls and dark safety glasses came out of the shop and waved. When he lifted the glasses Susan recognized Kenneth Goddard.

"Dr. Cullen, we meet again," he said, taking her hand.

"Welcome to my la-*bor*-atory," he added, giving the word a humorous, Vincent Price twist.

Today his gray eyes were bright, his glance penetrating. Setting a rapid pace, he led them through the fabrication shop, warning Susan not to look directly at the heliarc welding machines that were stitching together sheets of aluminum. As each part was assembled a technician removed it from the jig and touched up the welds with a grinder. The sound was deafening. Goddard, grinning happily, had to shout to make himself heard.

"Side-scanning radar! We're putting together a new prototype! That's classified, of course!"

He ushered them into a smaller room and shut the heavy door behind them. The noise was diminished by a few decibels. "This is where I mess around with my little toys," he explained, indicating the workbenches strewn with electronic gear. "The place is shielded and I personally sweep it every day."

Susan's expression indicated her confusion. Did the division president actually do his own custodial work? Goddard, sensing her uncertainty, chuckled and said, "Sweep it for bugs, Dr. Cullen. Listening devices. Our competitors would love to know what we're up to here."

Susan glanced at Tom. He made it obvious he wanted her to go first. She hesitated, then began. "Dr. Goddard, we're concerned about—"

"Never mind the honorary title," he said. "I'm not a physician. But before you explain this potential medical emergency Dr. Weston mentioned, tell me what you've learned about these sick jokes with the cadavers. How was it done? Any line on the perpetrator? Any idea *why* they want it to look like the dead are coming to life?"

Susan was taken aback. The statement she had rehearsed vanished from her mind. "I have no idea," she stammered.

"Are you serious?" Goddard looked incredulous. "No idea at all? What have you been doing these last few days?"

Susan took a deep breath. "How about some coffee?" she blurted.

Goddard backed down and agreed they would have coffee

and discuss the situation. If anything, the shop coffee was even more acidic than the stuff Ozzie concocted in the lab. But with a cup in hand Susan felt more in control. It was amazing how easily Kenneth Goddard unnerved her.

"I know that's not what you intended when you requested the Biohazard Lab," she began, "but we're conducting a parallel investigation. The deadwalking phenomena, naturally we're all curious about *that*, but we've also discovered a disturbing trend in the resident blood chemistry, and we feel that has to take precedence."

"Oh?" The remark was neutral.

She described the situation with the blood samples taken from the clinic, and how they seemed to echo the test results from the three cadavers.

"Are you telling me we have an epidemic in the village?" Goddard wanted to know. "This is the first I've heard of it."

"Not an infectious epidemic," Susan corrected. "At least we don't think it's a virus, although many of those affected interpret their symptoms as a 'flu bug.' Maybe that's just as well, for the moment. We don't want to start a panic, but there are indications that the residents of Sprauken have been exposed to an unknown toxin. Whatever the toxic substance is, it seems to affect the blood as well as the peripheral nervous system of the living. In the dead—well, you know about that."

Goddard looked skeptical. "This sounds pretty fantastic, Dr. Cullen. What toxin are you talking about?"

"That's what we don't know. Not yet. I'm hoping you could help us."

Goddard put his coffee mug down on a workbench and folded his arms. "You're the pathologist," he said. "How could I possibly help? My expertise is in theoretical electronics."

Tom, who'd been letting Susan run with it, cleared his throat and interrupted. "What, uh, Dr. Cullen needs is a list of all chemicals in use at the plant."

"But surely that's available," Goddard said impatiently. "Why come to me?"

"There are lists and there are lists," Susan said firmly. "If

Sprauken is involved in the manufacture of chem-bio weapons we need to know about it. I'm thinking specifically of nerve agents.''

Goddard was clearly at a loss. "Chem-bio weapons?" he asked softly. "Are you serious?"

"Dead serious," Susan said.

"No way," Goddard said, straightening up. "No way would I allow chem-bio weapons in this facility. If you knew anything about me, Dr. Cullen, you'd know I am absolutely opposed to that kind of thing. I've spoken out against biological warfare time and again. We all have to share this little planet. We can't risk polluting it with deadly diseases and horrible nerve agents. Science has to find a way to *stop* the killing.''

He was obviously deeply offended. Susan didn't know what to say, except the obvious. "I'm sorry," she said. "I didn't mean to imply that you were—"

"Hold on!" Goddard interrupted, his eyes glittering. "Wait just a damn minute. Maybe you're on to something here, Dr. Cullen! It's possible that a deadly substance has been introduced into the village by outside forces.''

Tom signaled her to end the interview, but Goddard was already off and running.

"Agitators, saboteurs," he said, his eyes hooding. "We have our share of clever enemies, Dr. Cullen. Just ask Dr. Weston. I've shared my thoughts with him on that subject. He'll tell you. I wouldn't put anything past them, not even a thing as horrible as you suggest.''

Goddard veered off on this new tangent: the enemies who were out to destroy his reputation. He went on at length about his respect for the environment, his strong opposition to careless use of toxic substances.

"We selected this site because of the natural beauty, Dr. Cullen," he said. "And believe me, we work to keep it that way.''

"I'm sure you do," Susan said. "I'm not trying to point the finger. A toxic leak can be an accident. Maybe *no one* is at fault.''

Goddard stared so hard Susan felt as if she was being

X-rayed by his oddly colorless eyes. Finally he spoke. "What do you want from me?"

"I want you to authorize a total search of the plant," Susan said, ready with the request. "Concentrating on airborne toxins."

Goddard licked his lips, scratched idly at his face. His eyes dulled and suddenly he seemed to have lost interest in what she was saying. "Is that all? A search for leaking toxins?"

"For now, yes."

He waved his hand. "Then go ahead. And when you've finished with that, Dr. Cullen, can you do me a favor?"

"Of course."

"Do the job you were hired for. Find out why the dead are walking. It's very important to me. I have to know why."

1:35 P.M.

Ozzie was scanning an article on sunlight deprivation in the *New England Journal of Medicine* when the trailer seemed to shift slightly. He dimmed the computer screen and waited to see who was about to enter the lab. The slight shift usually meant someone was on the outer step. Was it Susan? But she had gone out to the plant to organize an inspection and wasn't expected back until much later, and anyhow he knew her distinctive tread. This was a stranger.

He waited. When no one knocked or rang the buzzer Ozzie got up and looked through the small window. He immediately noticed the white Saab sedan with the Sprauken Security emblem on the door. Had it been parked there earlier? He didn't think so.

The trailer shifted again. Damn it, what was going on? Ozzie opened the door and leaned out into the cold air.

"Hello?" he shouted. "Who's there?"

He heard the sound of boots hitting the icy pavement of the parking lot and then the handsome young deputy with the ski-bum tan and the white teeth came around the front of the trailer.

"Hi there," Deputy Mallon said. "No cause for alarm. We got a report there was a stray cat on the roof of the trailer. Just dropped by to check it out."

Ozzie squinted. Cat on the roof? What was he talking about?

"False alarm," the cop said. "Or else maybe it got down by itself. You know how cats are," he added.

"Ah, sure," Ozzie said uncertainly.

The cop waved, strolled to his cruiser, and drove off. Ozzie waited until he was out of sight, then went around to the front end of the trailer to have a look. He couldn't see anything but the weather head where the power and phone cables entered the lab. Was it possible that a stray cat had climbed up there via the phone line?

"Oh, who the hell cares," Ozzie muttered, and then hurried back inside. It was cold, too cold for pondering little mysteries about cats and cops.

He returned to the computer screen and finished scanning the article. Now he could report to Susan what he'd suspected all along. There was no evidence that sunlight deprivation affected the blood chemistry. All it did, these dark winter climes, was make people go a little soft in the head.

For example, a cop who had nothing better to do than scramble around on a trailer roof looking for a phantom feline.

"Don't jump to conclusions," Tom said. "The man is under a lot of stress."

Susan was skeptical. The meeting with Kenneth Goddard had been disturbing. "He's a paranoid delusional," she said. "I find that pretty scary, considering."

"The point is, he agreed to your requests. He authorized a search for toxic leaks. Come on, Susan, you knew he had his quirks before you went in there."

"Quirks?" Susan rolled her eyes. "Paranoid delusions are not 'quirks.' Did you see the way his mood changed? And the way his eyes were dilated?"

The Jeep bounced over a frost heave. Tom slowed to a crawl. "Maybe I shouldn't tell you this, since he's my patient, but Goddard has a chemical dependency problem. He's hooked on amphetamines.''

''Speed?''

Tom nodded. ''Amphetamines tend to increase normal paranoia. Mood changes get exaggerated. Considering his addiction, Goddard's behavior is normal.''

Susan shook her head. ''Nothing is normal around here. I'm no expert on drug abusers, but I do know one thing.''

The road was clear ahead. Tom shifted gears, began to pick up speed.

''We can't trust him,'' Susan said. ''We can't trust anybody but ourselves.''

Tony walked the perimeter of the test area, snapping his fingers and bobbing his head. He was listening to the Cullen tape on his Walkman and he wanted the animal handlers to think he was rockin' and rollin', as usual. No one else was allowed to wear a Walkman on the job. As Chief Engineer, Tony made the rules. The Walkman was an indication of status, and he never missed a chance to flaunt it.

Bee-bop-a-shoo-bop. This broad from the Biohazard Lab was trouble. He could tell that, just the way she jived the clinic sawbones, Dr. Weston. Lymphocytes, changes in blood chemistry, mysterious toxins—what did she know? All that medical training, millions of dollars in equipment, and the lady didn't know shit.

It was laughable. Or would be, except for the trouble she could stir up, dead wrong as she was about the toxins. Broad like that had connections, medical experts she could get on her side, go to the media, maybe get a subcommittee to hold hearings. That right there would screw up his career plans, even if PULSE survived congressional scrutiny.

Bee-bop-a-bam-bam. Best thing, head her off at the pass. Stop her before she got a line on the real action, that would blow her socks off.

The tape ended. Tony switched off the Walkman. He decided to give Deputy Mallon a new assignment.

*　　*　　*

The Atmospheric Sampling Collector was a very simple device, about the size and shape of a jar of cold cream. Inside was a specially treated filter. Susan unscrewed the lid and held up the jar.

"Please be sure to mark down the exact location for each collector," she said, speaking to a group of twelve safety inspectors. "Make sure the lid vent is turned all the way counterclockwise. That will insure that we get air circulating over the filter."

She had been briefing the inspection team for almost thirty minutes. It was a delicate undertaking. Their first reaction had been quiet resentment: an outsider was telling them they hadn't been doing an adequate job. Susan, who had often run into the problem, patiently explained that no insult was intended. The plant had an exemplary safety record, thanks to the staff of professional safety inspectors.

"But no matter how good you are, or how dedicated, you can't be expected to detect an 'invisible' safety hazard. The filters in these ASCs are sensitive to a wide range of toxins, so if there are trace amounts in the plant atmosphere, we'll know within forty-eight hours."

Susan didn't mention the changes in blood chemistry or the widespread "flu" complaints. She had presented the air sampling as a "special experimental test" and there had been surprisingly few questions from the inspection team. Although it was technically owned by the parent company, Sprauken employees considered the Biohazard Lab on par with a government agency. As the lab director she was respected and feared. A bad performance rating from Dr. Cullen could ruin a career.

"Use your own judgment," Susan said, trying to break through to the team. "Ventilating systems need to be sampled, of course. And areas like cafeterias, rest rooms. Also the commissary, library, recreation rooms. The idea is, we want to sample any area frequented by a wide range of employees. Understood?"

She waited for questions. There were no questions.

7:28 P.M.

The weekend got off to a bad start when Susan received a call from the security officer at the village gate.

"Got a fella here says he knows Dr. Cullen. Claims he's expected. Seems a bit . . . guess you'd say hot under the collar."

Damn! She'd forgotten Eliot was coming in on the afternoon flight.

"Fairly tall? Light brown hair cut short? Brown eyes?"

"Can't see much of his hair, ma'am. Got a hat on, don't you know, one of them knit ski jobs. You want we should let 'im through?"

Ten minutes later Susan was in the lobby of the inn, her nose pressed against the plate glass door. Headlights appeared. Her heart began to pound. It had been a very long day, mentally exhausting, and she wasn't ready to deal with Eliot's slow-burn southern temper.

Then the first thing he did, when he got out of the rental car, was blow her a kiss from his gloved hand.

"My fault," he said. "I should have called from the airport. Forgot about security clearance."

He had on a new ski parka and the nylon made a slippery sound as they embraced. Susan was so surprised and relieved by his cheerful mood that she felt her eyes begin to moisten.

"I'm famished," he said, giving her another playful squeeze. "What's for supper?"

"The restaurant has a full menu."

"They got hush puppies?" he said, exaggerating his soft Virginia drawl. "Ain't got hush puppies, ain't got a full menu. But this bein' Maine, ah guess ah'll try me one a them lobster-type critters."

Susan laughed. He had the good-old-boy inflection down perfectly. At times she preferred it to the condescending Hundred Families attitude he adopted whenever they discussed his position at the university, or their pending marriage, or the Dragon Lady. Especially the Dragon Lady.

"How's your mom?" Susan asked sweetly.

"Never mind Mother," he said with a sly grin. "You're the only woman in my life."

It was exactly the lie she wanted to hear.

They met in a crowded meadow, in the merry month of May.

Sprauken International had opened a new headquarters for the Bio-Tech Lab in Charlottesville, Virginia. It was a sleepy college town not far from the Blue Hills area, and Susan found it invigorating to be in an undergraduate atmosphere again. This time she didn't have to attend classes, of course, nor was she expected to teach, although she had agreed to give an occasional lecture on toxic hazards at the medical school. That was to be the extent of her affiliation with the university—or so she thought.

On her first Saturday in Virginia the weather was so lovely she just had to get out of the lab building. With the top down on her aging but cherished VW Super Beetle, Susan headed out into the country without any particular destination in mind. She was surprised and a little dismayed to encounter a minor traffic jam in an otherwise quiet valley of rolling hills and horse farms. Then she learned that one of the estates was hosting a bluegrass music festival for charity. From a distance the big striped festival tents looked almost medieval.

Well, why not? As Susan parked the Beetle she couldn't help noticing the tall, good-looking country boy who was directing traffic into a beautiful meadow. Dressed in faded jeans, the boots the locals called "kickers," and a summer-weight Stetson, he favored her with a big grin and a pair of deep brown eyes that glistened under the brim of the hat. Susan smiled back—what the hell, it was one of those times and places where you traded sparks with handsome strangers.

Later, sitting on the grass and listening to a couple of fiddle players dueling a familiar tune almost to death, she was astonished when the handsome cowboy plopped down and handed her a sweating-cold bottle of beer.

"You must be one of them college gals," he said. "Now don't get spooked, I ain't gonna bite."

Susan soon realized that the cowboy was playing a role, the macho man, and obviously expected her to respond as a coquettish coed. She decided the safest bet was to be polite but keep her distance.

"You work around here?" she asked, meaning the horse farm.

"I been known to shovel out a stall or two," he admitted.

"The labors of Hercules."

"Huh?"

But Susan didn't quite believe that "huh?" The cowboy was putting her on. It was tiresome—she'd never been good at role-playing and as a pre-med student hadn't had time for the usual games between the sexes. Susan sipped the beer and made polite, if somewhat forced, conversation for about fifteen minutes, then excused herself for the ladies' room (in this case a row of portable johns) and never returned. The easy way out of an uncomfortable, if somewhat stimulating, situation.

Three days later they were both embarrassed to find themselves playing radically different roles. Susan arrived at the biology department lecture hall with a tray of slides and some notes, having agreed to give an informal talk on new methods of detecting heavy metal toxins in the blood. Dr. Eliot James, the department head, met her at the podium.

They both did double takes.

"You lose the hat?" Susan asked. "Or did a horse eat it?"

"I'm devastated," Dr. James whispered. "I had no idea. Sprauken employees don't drive beat-up Volkswagens."

"This one does," Susan said, and glided by him to the lectern.

After the lecture they laughed about it, and Eliot—he had a doctorate in biology, of course, but didn't use the title except at formal academic functions—admitted that the bluegrass festival had been staged on his property and that he had volunteered to help with the parking.

"Somehow a tweed jacket just didn't make it," he said. "And I *have* mucked out a few stables, though not so many as Hercules. Thank God."

"Come on, admit it. You thought I was a coed and you were trying out pick-up lines."

They were in the faculty lounge, having coffee. Eliot shifted nervously and said, "No way. Just your typical southern hospitality gambit. Making a pretty stranger welcome. And then you promised to come back, but what you really meant was adios. Didn't you feel just the tiniest bit sorry for that good old boy you left sprawled on the grass?"

"I thought he was a cowboy."

"Cowboys are in Texas." Eliot grinned. "Around here they're good old boys. It's a way of life."

Susan was introduced to Eliot's way of life over the next few weeks. On campus he was very much the proper head of a department. He seemed to relish the political infighting that was endemic to any university, and he was good at it, obviously. It didn't hurt that he came from a wealthy family that had, in the past, made generous endowments to the college. On weekends he lived the life of southern privilege, overseeing the maintenance of his country estate, hosting relaxed but lavish functions that had made him well known among the social elite of the county.

Eliot was charming, handsome, sexually adept, and seemed to take it for granted that Susan wanted to marry him. Most of the time she did. But from the beginning she'd been interested in Eliot James the man, not Eliot James of Blue Hill Estate and the Hundred Families and the glossy articles in *Southern Living*. Susan wanted to love an individual, not a tradition or way of life, and that was a distinction that Eliot didn't really understand.

"Sorry, sir. No lobster available tonight."

It was no big deal—Eliot preferred beef to seafood—but Susan was curious. The glass tank in the main dining room had been teeming with lobsters only yesterday.

"No one is sure what happened, but something went wrong in the tank," the waiter explained. "If the water temperature isn't just right, or the salinity is too far off, the lobsters die pretty easy. And this morning there were three dozen dead lobsters in there. The head chef just about had a fit."

Susan asked if the lobsters had been disposed of, and appeared disappointed when the waiter assured her they had been thrown away.

"Sweetheart, relax," Eliot admonished her. "I'll have the filet mignon. We'll try the lobster some other time."

When the waiter left with the order Susan explained that in light of the unexplained symptoms that were affecting the community, the Biohazard Lab was collecting data on all unexplained phenomena. Even a phenomenon as far afield as the sudden expiration of a tankful of crustaceans.

"So you think the elevated blood counts may be a result of food poisoning?" Eliot asked, bemused. "Or water contamination?"

Susan shrugged. "We're feeding data into the CYTO program. Looking for similarities to any other blood and/or nerve disorders."

"And what does the computer say?"

"So far, nothing," Susan said. "It appears to be a totally unique situation. We haven't been able to isolate a toxin. There are simply no points of comparison, at least not any that make sense."

Eliot smiled and touched her hand. "I've got a suggestion," he said. "We have our dinner here and dessert in your room. And tomorrow we fall headlong down a lovely white slope."

"What?"

"Skiing, sweetheart," Eliot said. "We're going skiing, remember?"

"But I *can't*, Eliot!"

"I'll teach, you follow. We'll start off with a simple snowplow."

"No, I mean I can't leave the lab. It's just impossible."

The food arrived before Susan could convince him that it was her duty to remain at the lab. He'd come more than a thousand miles to see her and it didn't seem right to spoil his supper with argument. And then later, in bed, pure physical attraction took over. Whatever their problems as a couple, none of it seemed to matter when they made love.

Maybe *that* was the problem.

*   *   *

He crouched in the darkness of the custodian's closet, pressed the headphones to his ears, and listened. The bugging device was functioning beautifully, just as Tony Faro had promised. It was like he was in the room with them. In bed with them. The panting, the urgent whispers, it all washed over him like a hot red wind that settled into his head, coloring his thoughts.

The bitch. Playing hard to get, stuck up, like she'd never heard of sex. The big-deal scientist. And all the time she was hot, begging for it. Listen to her now!

The whore!

It was going to be a pleasure, toying with her. She'd never know what hit her. That was the best part.

Saturday, January 10

Jon Tanborg decided to kill himself after hearing the weather report. The sons of bitches were predicting more snow. Tanborg had about had it with snow, and cold, and living. He'd been sitting in his busted Barcalounger all night, nursing a pint of rye whiskey that made him feel mean and dirty and small. Sitting in the Barcalounger was punishment. It was the last thing Diana gave him before walking out the door.

"I'm taking the car," she'd said. "I'm taking the silver place setting my mother gave us, and the Wexford crystal. You can keep the goddamn chair. You can rot in the goddamn chair, you miserable bastard."

Diana was right. He *was* a miserable bastard. Tanborg had been suffering from clinically diagnosed depression for at least three years, a depression enhanced by creeping alcoholism. He had grown to loathe himself as a more mentally secure person might loathe a painful carbuncle or a tumor. His self-hatred was also directed at anyone who expressed concern for his condition. Diana had been the first victim. After months of anguish she had finally left him, unable to cope with his bleakness and his anger. Dr. Weston, that smarmy know-it-all, had advised him to take medication and see a therapist. A therapist!

But Tanborg didn't want to relieve his depression. Not anymore. All he wanted to do now was cease to exist. It was

148

the simplest solution. All he had to do was summon the energy to get up out of the Barcalounger and go out to the garage.

He finished the pint. The whiskey burned into his brain, reinforcing the decision he'd been in the process of making for the last three years. He heaved himself up from the chair and staggered to the kitchen. He broke the whiskey bottle in the sink. Let somebody else clean up the mess—he wouldn't have to worry about *that* anymore.

The rear door of the kitchen opened into the single-stall garage. There were five other stalls in the complex, all separated by cinder block fire walls. Thanks to the building code, Jon Tanborg could cease to exist in the privacy of his own motor vehicle. A used Ford Escort he'd picked up after Diana split.

Now that he was on his feet and moving, it seemed easier. What was the big deal? All you had to do was get in the car, fire up the crappy four-cylinder engine, and roll down the windows. Fall asleep and never again have to endure the pain of waking up. Couldn't be simpler.

After starting the engine Tanborg noticed the gas tank was only a quarter full. He debated driving to the gas station, going through the process of filling the damn thing, and returning home. No way. A quarter tank would do it. If he went out for fuel the mood might leave him and then he'd be back in the Barcalounger in the dead of winter, and where was *that?*

The garage began to fill with fumes. The exhaust had a nasty sweet aroma, like burning cookies. That was what Tanborg took with him into the darkness. Burning cookies.

8:01 A.M.

It was harvest time in egg city. Ozzie finished his first cup of lab coffee and went to check the incubator. The white eggshells stared at him like rows of blank eyes. Ciphers that he was about to solve, or so he hoped. He had injected the live, fertilized eggs with a variety of blood and tissue samples. Any microphage present in the samples would have rapidly multiplied inside the cells of the egg tissue by now. The most easily detectable proof of a virus would be the death of the chicken embryo, and that was easily determined.

He switched on the sterile air filter, put on a pair of sterilized gloves, and opened the incubator glass. A puff of warm air escaped, making his eyes water.

"Come to papa," he whispered, reaching for the first egg.

The candling process that allowed him to inspect the embryo was not much different from the old method employed by farmers. His "candle" was a powerful white light source inside a darkened box. It rendered the eggshell translucent.

When Ozzie first inoculated the eggs he'd done so in the belief that the strange blood and neurological disorders in the village were almost certainly the result of a microphage. A living infection. Over the past thirty-six hours his thinking had changed on that subject. He now agreed with Susan that the most likely candidate was a toxin. An exotic poison rather than an infection.

He held the first egg up to the light. The embryo was alive. No evidence of viral infection. One down.

Two down.

Three down.

It became routine. All of the embryos were alive. The last to be checked were the eggs inoculated with blood and tissue samples from his own body. The eggs signed "Ozzie."

He found that his hands were trembling. *Got to cut down on the caffeine,* he chided himself. Taking a deep breath, he reached for the egg with his name on it and placed it over the light source.

The embryo was alive.

All alone in the lab, Chester Oswald began to giggle. Nerves. Too much coffee.

10:30 A.M.

It was like being back in school. Not medical school, elementary school. First grade. She felt small and nervous and slightly dizzy. The dizziness was partly on account of the strangely tilted horizon. With so much cloud cover obscuring the view, the slanted edge of the ski slope became the edge of the world, and it was an edge she was in danger of falling over.

"Keep both poles planted firmly in the snow," the instructor said. "Like this, just ahead of your body weight. What we're going to do, boys and girls—and, uh, ladies and gentlemen—is we're going to start out with a simple, old-fashioned technique called the snowplow."

The correction after "boys and girls" was for Susan's benefit. The others in the novice class were all children, several of them hardly more than toddlers. Four-year-olds and they were more at ease on skis than she was. Maybe because they were closer to the ground. Susan was both amused by the situation and mildly humiliated.

"Just relax," Eliot had advised. "It's all in fun. Everybody has to start somewhere. Believe me, you're not the only novice skier in Ice Valley."

Right. Easy for him to say. The lesson was being given on a gentle slope within full view of the lodge. Breakfasting powder freaks had a perfect view of Dr. Susan Cullen falling flat on her derriere. An even better view of that same derriere waggling in brand-new sky-blue ski pants as she struggled to right herself with just the poles, as the instructor advised.

"Don't worry about falling," the instructor said. "The snow is nice and soft today. We had—what was it?—five inches of fluffy stuff last night. It's a perfect day for a first-timer. Conditions are excellent. You tried this yesterday, for instance, there was this layer of crusty ice made it tough even on the experts."

After half an hour or so Susan began to feel more comfortable. Partly she was getting used to the skis, learning to control them, partly it was because Eliot had stopped watching the show and had departed to the upper slopes, promising to return shortly after her lesson concluded.

"You're beautiful even when your ass is soaking wet,"

he'd said, kissing her. "On second thought, maybe you should try falling forward, just for a change."

The bastard. No, that wasn't fair. It *was* funny, the way she kept losing her balance. You couldn't blame Eliot for laughing. She was laughing herself. But there was something about the tilt of his smile that made her resentful. She hadn't wanted to come to this damn mountain. She had work to do at the lab, important work, and it wasn't fair to dump all of it on Ozzie and take off for a day of kidding around.

Eliot had promised to get her back to Sprauken by six at the latest. They would leave sooner if it began to snow heavily. Surprisingly, he hadn't made that big a fuss about canceling their reservations at the lodge. He seemed to be trying to placate her on a daily basis, in hopes that she wouldn't take umbrage at Dragon Lady's dominance of their wedding plans.

"It's traditional to feel nervous about a wedding," he'd said the night before, when she expressed her anxiety. "I'll be shaking like a leaf when the big moment comes."

That was for her benefit. Eliot wasn't the shaking leaf type. When the moment arrived he would be in total control. Or rather he would share control with his mother, who would be orchestrating the entire event. And as much of their life together as she could manage.

"Okay," the instructor was saying. "Let's spread out along the ridge and we'll try going down this little slope. Ready? Okay, get yourself started. Keep your toes pointed slightly inwards, but don't let the points of your skis cross or you'll go boom. That's right. Excellent!"

It wasn't really that difficult, once you got the hang of it. Susan practiced gliding down the gentle slope for the rest of the lesson, very pleased with herself.

The binoculars had a way of throwing things out of scale. People who were really a hundred yards apart appeared about to collide. It was dreamy. It was like watching a movie in his head. He was an eye secretly floating over the winter landscape, disconnected from his body. He could follow behind Dr. Bitch in her hot little ski pants and she had no idea. Not a clue.

The fact that she was a novice presented an intriguing

number of possibilities. The thing to do was keep her under surveillance and wait for an opportunity. Then when it happened, it happened. Blame it on Mother Nature.

He liked that. Now there was a *real* bitch, Mother Nature. Old Mother had a lot of tricks up her sleeve, but that didn't mean you couldn't help her out.

"I knew you'd like it, if you gave it a chance," Eliot said.

He'd just finished a run on the charmingly named Suicide Slide and his eyes were glistening and the color was high in his cheeks. He looked sexy and confident and Susan couldn't remember exactly why it was she'd been irritated with him.

"It feels so *fast*," Susan said. "I can't be going more than five or ten miles an hour but it feels like a hundred."

"And you enjoy it."

"Amazing, huh? And you're talking to a woman who has never intentionally exceeded the speed limit. When I was a teenager I simply could not understand why the boys were so fascinated with going fast. Now I know."

Eliot smiled. They were standing at the bottom of the teaching slope, in what proved to be a brief patch of sunlight. For one giddy moment Susan imagined that they looked like the perfect ski couple. Handsome and windblown, exquisitely matched. A postcard. Then the opening in the clouds snapped shut and the sun stopped glinting off the snow and she struggled to retain the feeling.

"Good thing you didn't develop early on as a speed freak," Eliot said. "You might have married some greaseball with a hot car."

His smile revealed a slight trace of contempt at the thought of Susan paired with anyone other than Eliot James of Blue Hill Estate and the Hundred Families. The feeling of being newly in love evaporated like her steaming breath in the cold air. Why did he always have to spoil the moment with a reminder of who he was, and who she would be when they married?

"I want to try a real slope," Susan said. "I want to go fast."

"Better not overdo it the first time out," Eliot said, chuckling. "If you're not afraid to risk a little tumble, you could try Eezee Duzit."

"Easy does it?"

"The novice trail. Very gentle incline; you can't get in real trouble. We'll take the chair lift."

The trick of following a target was to keep one step ahead. Anticipate the target's next move, and be there waiting. He'd learned that in Special Forces, when he first made the elite recon unit. Those were the days. It was fine before the lieutenant got in his way. Never mind that now. Concentrate on Dr. Bitch and her visiting boyfriend.

Mallon cut in at the lift line, managed to score the chair directly in front of the lovey-dovey couple. Then all he had to do, hold his mirrored sunglasses in his hand and he could watch them in the reflection on the lenses.

They were kissing, right there for all the world to see. Mallon felt the gorge rise in his throat. The thought of someone else's tongue in his mouth was so repulsive it made him shudder. That's what *she* had done, after she cut him with the poultry shears. Trying to make him hush up, pretending she loved him. Stupid drunken cow, she didn't even know how to kiss a little boy; she had to do it like he was a man, like he wasn't her natural born—

Stop. Mallon squeezed the memory shut and bolted the door in his head. You wanted to keep a target in view, you had to concentrate. You had to anticipate the target's next move.

Then you made *your* move, and next became last.

"I'll be right behind you," Eliot promised.

The chair lift had been more exhilarating than she'd expected. It started off low to the ground and then in places swooped rapidly upward, thirty feet in the air. Eliot's lips were hot, questing. Susan experienced a pang of guilt. She should be responding to him, seizing the moment, and instead something made her turn away, breaking the kiss before it really got going.

"Playing hard to get, huh?" he'd said, kiddingly. "We'll

see about that. You'd be surprised what goes on in these trails, when folks get out of sight.''

Susan pretended not to know what he was hinting at and he let it drop. Then she decided she didn't want to be followed, not the very first time down the novice slope.

''Tell you what,'' she said. ''You go on up to the expert trail and we'll meet at the bottom. At the lodge.''

''You're sure that's what you want?''

''Eliot, honey, you'll just make me nervous and then I'll fall for sure. Besides, you'll be bored to death on the novice slope. You said as much.''

''Yeah, I guess I did. And come to think of it, I wouldn't mind another blast down the Slide.''

They parted under the chair lift. Susan followed the trail to the south face, as instructed. Taking her time, perfecting her technique. Other skiers swooped by, looking smooth and graceful, tucked into racing form. A good-sized young male in a lime-green parka and ski mask almost knocked her over. He did not turn to apologize or even to acknowledge the near miss. He'd been ahead of them on the chair lift, riding alone—she recognized the parka. There was something about the way he moved that looked familiar. Someone she'd seen in Sprauken, perhaps. Susan let it go. No sense letting some rude jerk spoil her fun.

There was a red flag stuck in the snow at the entrance to the first trail.

DANGER: LIGHTNING RUN CLOSED DUE TO ICY CONDITIONS

Susan reflected that she would not be inclined to risk an expert trail called Lightning Run even had it been open. She pushed on another thirty yards to the next opening. A sign was propped up against a nearby tree.

EEZEE DUZIT

That sounded exactly her speed.

The trail curved to the left, hemmed in by tall, snow-frosted spruce trees. The first incline was steeper than she'd expected, then rapidly leveled off before the next curve. Just a little tease, but it was all she could do to keep her skis from crossing.

She paused at the bottom of the first incline to catch her breath and found herself facing a large opening in the trees. At that moment a window in the clouds opened again, bringing on a patch of clear blue sky, and for a couple of minutes she had a spectacular view all the way across the valley floor.

That was Sprauken, far off to the east. It looked like a toy village, with the frozen lake reflecting blue, the scattered apartment clusters, and the darker smudge of the manufacturing facility at the far end. The streets radiated out like points of a star from the plant buildings, she noticed. A pattern. And something about it rang a bell, though for the life of her she couldn't quite think why. It was like having a word on the tip of her tongue. Maddening.

What was there about the placement of the plant and the streets and the rest of the village that seemed so familiar?

Then the clouds closed in again, shrouding the mountain, and she was faced with the prospect of getting down a slope that appeared to be steeper than she'd been led to believe. If this was a novice trail she'd hate to see an expert version. Even the spruce trees, with their sharp, jutting lower branches, looked menacing.

Susan pushed off cautiously, determined to proceed at her own pace, despite the fact that Eliot was, in all probability, already racing for the bottom. They would have a nice lunch at the lodge and then have a serious talk about Susan's premarital jitters. Before Eliot left for home she wanted to be reassured that their love was strong enough to survive the Dragon Lady's meddling.

She was thinking about Eliot as she slipped over the rise. Acceleration was sudden and rapid. What the hell? She glanced down. There was *ice* under her skis! Before Susan could react she shot forward, out of control. This wasn't a slope, it was a sheer cliff, so steep the soft snow had been blown away, exposing a slick layer of ice.

Somehow she'd been diverted to Lightning Run!

There was no time for questions or coherent thoughts. Only

a struggle to stay alive. Susan lost her poles on the first turn, in a vain attempt to stop. She skidded sideways, accelerating so fast that the blood rushed to her head. A blur of bristling tree branches loomed. She raised an arm to shield her eyes. The sharp branches missed, and she was falling headlong down a sheet of ice.

The notorious Lightning Run was so named because it cut like a jagged white lightning bolt through the thick trees. It had been engineered to test the skills of experts. Each abrupt jag in the trail had been artificially steepened to provide maximum acceleration into the turn. Injuries were common. Head or spinal injuries could be, and had been, fatal.

Susan never knew how she lost the first ski. It was just gone, airborne, rocketing away like an Exocet missile. The loss scarcely made any difference as she flopped and bounced from her feet to her knees, then twisted backward. She clawed desperately at the ice with her mittens, trying to slow down. It had no effect. A turn loomed and she was thrown in another direction, skittering over a series of moguls like a pebble skipping over the waves.

It was a bad dream, a nightmare of vertigo. More trees rushed upward, seeking to impale her on stubby, spearlike branches. She shot through, cutting off part of the turn, and emerged on the chute, a banked run that dropped at forty-five degrees. The other ski vanished.

Free-fall.

He pictured Dr. Bitch broken at the base of a tree, ski pants turning crimson. A rag doll. The picture in his head made him smile.

Mallon couldn't resist checking out the damage. He switched the signs back at the top of the run and tucked into racing form. Old Lightning was nasty under ideal conditions; iced up it would require all of his considerable skill.

As he swooped through the first turn he grinned, his white teeth bared against the wind. His speed and skill made him invulnerable. He was a tiger, a wolf, a destroyer of flesh and silk.

Die for me, Dr. Bitch, he urged. *Die for me.*

*   *   *

It was the flying part that saved her. Without the skis as ballast Susan lifted into the air. She shot over the icy lip of the chute. Up she went. For a heartbeat she seemed to hang in space. She had a glimpse of the mountainside falling away under her. Then she dropped straight down into a world of spruce boughs. She fell through the boughs, the needles scratching her face and hands. Breaking her fall.

She landed flat on her back with a thump that knocked the wind out of her.

I'm dead, she thought.

Passing out would have been a blessing; instead she remained vividly conscious, aware that her lungs were empty, that her heart was beating like frenzied bird wings against her bruised rib cage. Looking up, all she could see were torn spruce boughs and dancing pinpoints of light. Stars. It was true; when you hit your head you saw stars.

Slowly she was able to get her lungs working. Susan took inventory. Her toes and fingers worked and she sure as hell could feel all the bruises and scratches. Conclusion: no spinal trauma. She was disoriented and dizzy but she'd never lost consciousness, so there was probably no danger of concussion.

Thank God for flying. If she'd hit the trees from the side the massive trunks would have done brutal damage. Instead she'd fallen straight down through the boughs. Lucky to be alive.

When she was able to breathe almost normally, Susan got to her knees. She began trembling uncontrollably. Delayed reaction.

Come on girl, get it together. You still have to find a way down the mountain.

Hot chocolate. That's what she was thinking about as she crawled from tree to tree, clinging to the lower branches. My kingdom for a cup of hot chocolate. And the warmth of a fireplace, and Eliot's strong arms around her.

She was thinking about Eliot again, wanting him, when she became aware of a high-pitched noise. Distant at first and then rapidly getting closer. Like a bat or a bird or claws scratching on ice.

Scree-scree-scree.

Skis. Skis cutting over the ice. Not out of control but handled with precision. Susan crawled to the edge of the run, ready to wave her arms, make herself seen. Maybe it was the ski patrol, alerted by Eliot. She was still a few yards from the opening, partially shielded by the trees, when the skier flashed by.

The lime-green jacket. The ski mask and a glimpse of white, ferociously grinning teeth. Susan saw him as a blurred streak, and then the *scree-scree* of the skis faded and she was alone on the mountain.

"You're angry and cold and frightened," Eliot said. "You made a mistake, okay? Once you recover you'll realize you're being melodramatic."

"Oh, for God's sake," Susan said through chattering teeth. It had taken her more than an hour to work her way down the slope, going from tree to tree, digging her boots into whatever footholds she could find. The cold had been bone chilling, exhausting. Her ribs ached.

Now she was finally inside the lodge, wrapped in a thick blanket, not a yard from a roaring fire, and she was *still* cold inside. The cold she could handle though. What she wasn't ready for was Eliot's skepticism.

"I'm telling you, *somebody tried to kill me.*"

Eliot shook his head, exasperated. "Come on, honey. Talk sense. Who would want to kill you?"

Susan glared at him. He was supposed to be comforting her, not treating her like a hysterical fool. "I don't know. My guess is the man in the lime-green parka."

"The lime-green who?"

"I thought about it while I was crawling down the mountain and I'm pretty sure the same man was hanging around near the beginner's slope, using a pair of binoculars. I couldn't see his face but something about the way he moved convinced me I'd seen him in the village."

"That's possible," Eliot said. "Ice Valley is the closest ski resort to Sprauken. There's nowhere else to go."

"He *must* have been following me. He was ahead of us on

the chair lift. He must have switched the signs, knowing I was a novice skier."

Eliot was smiling that superior smile of his. "Wait a second, honey. Did you hear what you just said? He was following you and then he was *ahead* of us on the chair lift. If he'd been following then he'd have been *behind* us, right? I mean think about it."

Susan squeezed the mug of hot chocolate until her hands ached. She was so frustrated she wanted to scream. "Ahead, behind, it doesn't matter. Maybe it *wasn't* the guy in the green parka who did it, but *somebody* switched the signs and I damn near got killed."

Eliot stroked her arm. She'd seen him use the same gesture on his hunting dogs. Tender but firmly in control. "I don't doubt the signs were changed, Susan. But that doesn't mean somebody was out to get you. Could have been a prank. Kids fooling around."

He made it sound so reasonable. A prank. Kids fooling around. That was how the cops would see it, too. Susan was just another hysterical, frightened woman, if you looked at it that way.

"What I don't understand," Eliot said earnestly, "is who would be out to harm you?"

Eliot didn't know about the prowler who'd been through her room, and Susan was in no mood to tell him about it now. He'd find a way to dismiss the incident, just as he'd found an explanation for the switched signs on the icy ski run. She was tired. Tired of explaining. Tired of being condescended to by Eliot.

"Take me home," she said. "I want to go home."

His eyes lit up. "Back to Charlottesville with me?"

She shook her head. "Back to the lab. That's my home."

5:45 P.M.

"What happened is, the car ran out of gas," Tom Weston said. "The poor bastard was in there long enough so the carbon monoxide caused brain death. He's on the respirator now. Clinical death will ensure a few minutes after we shut off the life support.''

Susan stared at him, uncomprehending. She had just endured a two-hour drive back from Ice Valley with Eliot. Neither of them speaking much. During the course of the long, slow drive over slippery mountain roads her anger had been replaced by a sense of loss and confusion. She felt that her life was in danger and Eliot's first reaction was to mock her fear. When she needed him most he wasn't there for her. The last thing he'd said, after dropping her off at the lab, was, ''When you come to your senses, call me.''

Then he'd left immediately to get the last flight out of Portland. Ten minutes later—she'd barely had time to get her coat off and say hello to Ozzie—Tom Weston was at the door with news about an attempted suicide.

''Tanborg's only relative is his ex-wife,'' Tom explained, ''and she's threatening to sue if we *don't* pull the plug, so there's no problem with getting permission.''

''Pull the plug?'' Susan said. ''Excuse me, I'm having trouble following this.''

Tom looked at her with concern. ''Are you okay, Susan? You look pale. What happened is, this patient of mine tried to kill himself. Car running in his garage. He was found before his heart stopped beating, so technically he's still alive.''

''And you're going to shut off the life-support system?''

Tom nodded glumly. ''Tanborg is brain dead. A vegetable. His heart is failing.''

Ozzie left his workstation, where he'd been communing with CYTO, and joined them, his bugged-out eyes glistening with interest. ''Don't you get it?'' he said to Susan. ''We can monitor the exact moment of death. If the body exhibits the deadwalking phenomenon, we'll be right there to collect data exactly as it happens. We might be able to isolate the stimulus. That's what you had in mind, right, Dr. Weston?''

Susan made an effort. The same facility for concentration that had enabled her to endure the rigors of medical school came into play. By focusing on the matter at hand she was able to shunt Eliot into another part of her mind. She would deal with it later.

"Might be worth a try," she said. "But what makes you so sure it will happen this time?"

Tom checked his shirt pocket for the pack of cigarettes that wasn't there. The old smoking instinct was still at work. "Percentages," he said. "It happened to the last three people who died here. Why not the fourth?"

Tony was acting pissed.

"You dumb oaf," he said. "I said give her a scare. Not arrange a fatal accident."

Deputy Mallon wouldn't look him in the eye. He just kept stirring his coffee with his finger, a filthy habit that made Tony feel like gagging. Instead of answering, Mallon just kept nodding. Looked like one of those damn bobbing-head dolls.

"What the hell were you thinking?" Tony demanded.

"The action was within the assigned parameters," the deputy muttered. "I saw my chance and reacted accordingly."

Now he was talking like a cop, mouthing those mangled legalisms that cops used to make themselves sound smart. Tony wanted to keep Mallon off balance, that way he was more easily manipulated. So he acted pissed about the attempt on Dr. Cullen's life. In truth he was just a little disappointed that it hadn't worked.

"You implied that the target was to be taken out," Mallon was saying.

"Kurt? Can I have your attention? Watch my lips: You will do exactly as I say, nothing more, nothing less. We're in a very delicate situation here. Is that understood?"

Deputy Mallon nodded sullenly.

"Your little trick failed and now the target—what a charming description of a gorgeous piece of ass—the target knows somebody is out to get her. Has she reported it?"

Mallon shrugged. "There's nothing she can prove."

"I asked you a question, Kurt. Please respond. Has she reported the attempt on her life?"

"Not to us."

"Tell you what, Kurt. Take your dirty finger out of that coffee cup and get over there and activate that bug you installed at the lab. You did install it, right?"

"Affirmative."

Affirmative. What a rock head. Still, Mallon had proved he was willing to kill, and you never knew, that might be useful one of these days. Or nights.

"Move it," Tony said. "Kick out the jams."

Drs. Weston and Cullen had sandwiches in the clinic cafeteria while Ozzie set up the monitoring equipment. Susan, who thought she wasn't hungry, found herself eating every bite of a ham-and-cheese, even the crust. Nervous energy.

"Something is bothering you," Tom said. "Is it the prospect of observing another deadwalker?"

"I'm fine. Really."

"You are like hell," Tom said. "You look like you've been scared half to death."

Susan couldn't hide her surprise at his on-the-money guess.

"Damn," he said, taken aback by her reaction, "that *is* what happened. Something frightened you. Tell me about it."

She found herself describing the incident of the intruder in her suite and the close call she'd had on the mountain. He listened attentively, his brow furrowed with worry.

"Let's think this through," he said. "You report a possible toxic leak and the next day some company goon is on your tail. It can't be a coincidence."

"You think it was Kenneth Goddard?" Susan said, incredulous.

"Not personally, of course. But your work at the lab must be making Goddard, or someone close to him, very nervous."

"It doesn't make sense. The company owns the lab. They could just call off the investigation. Make us leave."

Tom reached out, placing his hand over hers. "Just give it a little thought. Sure, they could throw the lab out. They own the lab and for that matter the village. But they don't own you."

"No," she said, not quite sure what he meant.

"You really do care about this, Susan," he said. "You're convinced lives are endangered. So throwing the Biohazard Lab out of town wouldn't stop you, would it?"

She shook her head, amazed at how well he knew her. "I'd contact the CDC. I'd alert all the medical publications, the media, whatever it takes."

Tom Weston was grinning. "I *knew* it! And they know it, too, just from your record. You can't be trusted to follow the company line if lives are endangered. You'll follow your conscience."

Susan was uneasy. "Anybody would," she responded.

"I'm not so sure," he said. "I think you're pretty special."

10:45 P.M.

The body was wired for sound and pictures. BEAM, the brain electrical activity mapping device, was in place, monitoring the flat brain wave and the numerous tiny electrical fields still present in the central and peripheral nervous systems. Blood pressure, heartbeat, EKG, temperature, respiration, all monitorable life signs were wired. An intravenous device was in place, capable of drawing blood samples at predetermined intervals, or on command. Video cameras had been positioned in each corner of the room, with a master control tied into sensors activated by any movement in the limbs.

Jon Tanborg was about to be granted his last wish.

"What a waste," Susan said.

Having had to deal with the sick and the dying and the dead, Susan had limited sympathy for suicides. They threw away what others struggled for; they not only sought to end life, they mocked it, and by extension all those who strove to improve the human condition.

The respirator that forced air into Tanborg's lungs made a dull, clunking sound. As if impatient to stop functioning.

"Any time you're ready," Tom said, his voice strained. He never looked at an unconscious, respirated patient without being reminded of his late wife. "I've closed off the east wing of the clinic, so we won't be disturbed. The R.N. assigned to the deathwatch has been transferred over to Maternity. She was glad to go."

"I don't blame her," Susan said.

Ozzie stood up behind the video monitors, where he'd been checking coaxial connections. "Don't get all weepy now," he said. "This chump took the pipe. He wanted to die. And now he's maybe going to help us out, like it or not."

Susan nodded. Ozzie had a point, as usual. "Well," she said. "The other three died before midnight and became active sometime after. So I guess we should stick to the pattern." She glanced at the brain-dead patient and hesitated. "Who's going to do it?"

"Tanborg was my client," Tom said. "I'll do it."

He stepped forward and shut off the respirating machine. Almost immediately the heartbeat became erratic and feeble. Blood pressure plummeted. The body began to die.

Tony had the tape in his pocket when he went in to meet with Goddard. Proof positive that Dr. Susan Cullen was abusing her position as head of the Biohazard Lab. Proof of her disloyalty to the company. Tony hadn't decided for sure if he would share the tape with Goddard, but it gave him confidence to know he had the hole card if the big boss ever called his bluff.

Five minutes later his hole card was a joker. Worthless.

"I appreciate your concern about Dr. Cullen," Goddard said. He was pacing his office in his stocking feet, having complained of a painful skin infection. As he talked he kept wandering back to the worktables, where the project blueprints were unfurled and weighted down with his shoes. "The fact is, I'm already aware of her concern. We had a meeting yesterday, at her request. She and Dr. Weston are very worried about the deteriorating health situation here in the village."

Tony smirked. In his estimation Tom Weston was a loser, a man without ambition. Why else would he waste his career at an employee health clinic in a podunk place like Sprauken? He had to be a quack. Real doctors were into high-risk surgery. That's where the money was.

"Yeah," Tony said. "The poor twits are worried about a toxic leak. I heard about it," he added, patting the tape in his pocket.

A wasted touch. Goddard wasn't even looking at him. The old buzzard was still on the pills, that was for sure, the way he was dancing around on his itchy feet, pouring over the project designs he already knew by heart.

"I know, I know what you're thinking," Goddard responded. "There *is* no toxic leak. No chem-bio weapons are being tested. That was my first reaction; that Dr. Cullen is just plain wrong. And then I gave it some thought."

Here it comes, Tony thought, readying himself for another of the boss's famous diatribes. He expected to hear about mysterious saboteurs, hidden enemies, the usual drivel of a mind frayed by chemical stimulants. Goddard surprised him.

"Throw out everything else and you're left with this: Dr. Cullen has irrefutable evidence that the health of the civilian population has deteriorated in the last two weeks," Goddard said, staring up at the fluorescent lights as if composing a lecture. "As you know, we began preliminary PULSE testing two weeks ago. Could there be a connection, I asked myself?"

Tony sighed. "It's just the goddamn flu bug is going around. She's making a big deal out of a few runny noses."

Goddard ignored the interruption. "The answer requires a complete recalculation, factoring in high-energy microwave leakage. I checked over the existing data and concluded that PULSE has side effects we hadn't anticipated."

Toy stared. Was the old dude finally going truly bonkers? Was this the beginning of mental meltdown?

So *what* if PULSE had a few side effects? It *worked*, that's all that mattered to the Pentagon. They wanted a weapons system, and a weapons system was expected to inflict death or debilitating injury. That was the whole goddamn point that Goddard kept missing! There was no such thing as a weapon to end war. That old chestnut had been tossed into the fire long ago, about the time they invented battleships.

"My original calculations clearly underestimated the residual effects of the PULSE phenomena," Goddard was saying, babbling away in an oddly pitched voice. As if trying to drown out some other, smaller voice in his thoughts. "Testing should never have been initiated in proximity to a civilian population."

"Oh come on," Tony interjected, losing patience. "This isn't a civilian population. These are Sprauken employees. We own them. The village itself is a hundred miles from the nearest population center. Besides, the testing phase will be over in another week, and then everything will go back to normal."

Goddard looked up from the blueprint and focused on Tony for the first time. "I'm recommending that we delay the human test phase until we can devise a method of shielding PULSE. A delay will also give us a chance to reevaluate the data, fine-tune the equipment."

Tony was speechless. Postpone the human test phase? This was beautiful. This was exactly what he needed. Now Colonel Bentley would have to remove Goddard from the project.

"You better write it down, sir," he solemnly advised. "They'll want to have it in writing."

"Queen of diamonds," Tom said. "Bad luck lady."

"What?"

He was playing solitaire, flipping the cards out on the spare bed. Jon Tanborg's heart had ceased beating about ten minutes before. Ozzie was monitoring the fall in body temperatures, checking the BEAM unit for any electrical impulses registering in the nervous system. No one spoke of the death, now that it was a fact. The waiting game had begun.

"*The Manchurian Candidate*," he said, still dealing out the cards. "Frank Sinatra, Laurence Harvey. Harvey plays this soldier got brainwashed in Korea. The way they control him is, they call him up on the phone and say, 'Why not pass the time playing a little solitaire?' and when the queen of diamonds comes up, he goes into a trance, ready to be programmed. Great movie."

Susan said, "I read the book."

Tom grinned. "You know what? I believe you. Most people, they tell you they read the book, what they really mean is they saw the movie and they've always *intended* to read the book but haven't quite got around to it. Ace of spades."

"Another bad luck card?"

"Not for me," he said, slapping the card down. "Means I win."

"What do you win?"

"A three-day trip to Saint Thomas, when this is over. Hell, maybe I'll take a week. Find a palm tree close to the water and sit under it and read a movie, maybe."

Susan laughed. She understood that he wanted her to laugh, and she was willing to oblige. She also understood that the casual reference to a Caribbean holiday was not by accident. It was a subtle come-on, an opening gambit. She let it go, for the moment.

"We could double up, if you want," Tom suggested.

"What?"

"Double solitaire," he said. "I've got an extra deck."

Susan declined. She wasn't in the mood for cards. In her mind she was trying to see another pattern. The pattern that tantalized her from the mountain, when the village had been in view, briefly. She kept seeing a grid or a map, something about Sprauken that was so obvious it had become invisible, like a stairway hidden in the patterns of an Escher lithograph.

"A map," she said aloud.

"Sure, go on," Tom said. "Take a nap. Ozzie and I can handle this."

"No, a *map*. Of Sprauken. Is there one available?"

Tom looked up from the cards, his expression puzzled. "Are you going to tell me why you want a map?"

"Is there one?"

"Sure. In my office. Well?"

"Tell you after I've looked," Susan said. "It may be nothing. Just a kind of hunch."

He put the cards down and left. Five minutes later he returned with a survey chart of the village area. The surrounding hills and peaks were marked for elevation. Several red pen lines had been drawn through the outlying wilderness.

"Jeannie and I used to do a little hiking," he explained.

"Jeannie?"

"My, uh, late wife."

"Late?" Susan looked up from the unfurled chart. It took a beat, and then she understood. She understood a whole lot about Tom Weston. His diffidence, his ambivalence, his shifting moods. "I'm sorry. When did it happen?"

"A year ago," he said, obviously eager to change the subject. "So does it help, the map?"

Susan studied the map of Sprauken, but her concentration had been broken. The pattern didn't seem to be there. It was maddening, trying to dredge something up out of her subconscious.

"I'm probably imagining things," she said. "Only I have this very strong feeling that something important is staring me right in the face."

Ozzie sighed and sat down. "Great way to spend a Saturday night, huh? Waiting for a stiff to lead the last dance. Give me those cards. What we'll do, boys and girl, we'll play a little poker. Stud, nothing wild."

"We need four for poker," Tom said.

"We got four," Ozzie said jerking his thumb at the body. "That's the dummy hand."

11:30 P.M.

The target area tech crew assembled for a pep talk from the old man. This was to be the final test in the animal phase, and according to scuttlebutt the results had already exceeded expectations. Goddard was not known to be generous with praise, but the crew expected a commendation, or at the very least a "job well done."

What they got was a lecture on personal safety.

"Each and every member of this crew is hereby instructed to observe the existing safety rules. No exceptions. You will wear the field helmets and the antistatic suits. You will keep behind the shielded barricades until the all-clear is given. You will submit to the routine neurological examination at the completion of testing. Violation of any of these rules of conduct will result in reassignment and a drop in pay grade. Any questions?"

There were no questions. In the Experimental Division the

phrase ''any questions?'' was strictly rhetorical. Questioning company policy was considered to be as potentially corrosive as a toxic leak. It was simply not done.

''Fine,'' Goddard said. ''As soon as we have PULSE on-line we will proceed with the final test in this sequence. After conclusion of the test, all members of the tech team will be debriefed by Chief Engineer Faro or one of his subordinates. Your clear, concise impressions and observations of changes in the primate behavior will be entered in the data bank. That is all.''

Dismissed, the crew members returned to their stations. Those directly involved in animal handling went to the cages. The chimps, believing they were about to be fed, began chattering and shrieking. A mother chimp huddled as she nursed her infant, protecting it from the larger males, who at times appeared jealous of her attention.

''Is that really necessary?'' Goddard asked Tony, pointing out the mother-infant combination in the crowded cage.

''Of course, sir. Statistically we need data on how PULSE affects mammals with a smaller body mass. A chimp infant is similar to a human infant in that respect. Also the psych team wants to know if the mothering instinct is totally eradicated, or if the effect wears off after time.''

''Good point,'' Goddard said. ''Keep me informed.''

After the consultation with his chief engineer, Kenneth Goddard headed directly for the closest rest room, where he locked himself in a stall, removed his shoes and socks, and began to furiously scratch his itching feet and ankles. The itching spasms were a side effect of long-term amphetamine abuse and sleep deprivation. Goddard was aware of that, but it didn't make any difference.

He scratched until the blood ran from his fingernails.

Mallon listened. The silence was louder than his beating heart. He crouched in the darkness of the custodian's closet, and remembered another dark closet, another kind of silence. Years ago.

It was not a closet, not exactly. More of a shed attached to the back of the trailer, where his stepfather kept his tools.

Hammers, saws, drills. Kurt, age eight, wanted to borrow a hammer to pound nails into an old wooden crate he'd found. Not to build anything, just for the pure joy of swinging a hammer.

It was absolutely forbidden to enter the shed, of course. That was part of the fun, too. Rooting around for the tools, he soon discovered why his stepfather wanted him kept out of the shed. In an old, beat-up trunk he found bottles of liquor and, deeper in the trunk, bundles of photographs. The photos were of women engaged in various types of sexual activity. They were horrible and fascinating and frightening, those photos. Kurt was just starting to look at the pictures, really look at them, when his mother began calling his name.

Git yer butt inside, you miserable little brat! Git here, where is you? Kurt? Kurt!

She was drunk. He could always tell instantly, the funny way her voice changed. Panicked, he closed the shed door. There was no lock inside, so he shoved the trunk up against the door. By then his mother was yelling for his stepfather, and then the two of them were outside the shed, screaming drunk.

Kurt hid inside the trunk. He pulled the lid down and lay curled among the photographs. He covered his ears, trying to block out his mother's taunting voice. It worked. All he could hear was the muffled beating of his heart, and the terrible, waiting silence that finally ended when the trunk lid flew open.

You like them pitchers, boy? That what you after, them pitchers of dirty women? Well go on, look at 'em! Open yer eyes and look or I'll get them poultry shears 'n jab yer eyes out!

Momma, please.

"Shut up!" he shouted.

The sound of his own voice brought Mallon back to the present. He was supposed to be monitoring Dr. Cullen's suite. Only Dr. Cullen wasn't in there. And she wasn't in the lab. Tony Faro wanted to know her whereabouts and what she was doing. Mallon was supposed to find out.

The panic came over him for a few heartbeats. He was

losing control. Tony would never understand. Tony would find out about his service record, have him fired, make sure he never got another job in security.

Mallon burst from the closet, momentarily dazzled by the lights. There was no one around. He could prowl the halls to his heart's content.

What he needed, he realized, what he absolutely required, to clear his head, was a creepy-crawl. He got out the pass card, and slipped it into the lock, and went into Dr. Bitch's room.

"Hello? Dr. Cullen?"

A silly precaution. She was not there. She was off somewhere with Dr. Weston, doing God knows what. Not at Weston's place, though; Mallon had checked that out. He had to find them, Tony had made that clear, but first he needed to renew himself.

He opened the blinds. Reflections from the exterior floodlights touched parts of the room like a faint fog. The shadows were pleasing. He felt at home. Mallon stripped and walked naked into the bathroom. The tiles were cool under his feet. He found her soap and her shampoo and went into the shower stall. He showered, taking his time. Using her soap to cleanse his body. Scrubbing his maleness. He shampooed his hair and let the soap rinse away until every extraneous thought and memory swirled down the drain, leaving his mind as squeaky clean as his hair.

What if she came back?

Then he would deal with it. He would make a decision and act on it. Another decision, and so on. The decisions, he knew, would invoke a very long period of silence in Dr. Bitch. Forever and ever and ever. No more lucky escapes.

She did not return.

Mallon dried himself with her towels, shaped his hair with her blow drier. He walked back into her sleeping quarters feeling powerful and confident. He was in control again. Tony would be proud.

Tony would . . . appreciate him. And that was better than love.

Mallon could see himself in the full-length mirror. Sculpted by the shadows. The image in the mirror was large, menacing. The image was afraid of nothing.

The creepy-crawl would not be complete until he made his mark. How? He let the loathing wash though him like a powerful transfusion until at last he had decided. Then he went to her mirror and made himself known.

Colonel Bentley requested an informal meeting with the project director while they were waiting for PULSE to cycle on-line. He had seen Goddard's confidential memo detailing apparent side effects on the civilian population, and wanted to discuss the situation.

"We appreciate your concern," he began. "But Sprauken International is not at risk in this particular situation. You have no legal obligation. As I understand it, all employees sign an ironclad release as part of the contract. Which guarantees that Sprauken cannot be held responsible for any injury beyond a specified monetary settlement based on the employee's salary. Nor is the federal government culpable. Is that not correct?"

Goddard stared at him, surprised. "Excuse me for asking, Colonel, but who showed you that memo?"

Bentley smiled. "I have my sources. That's not important. What's important is that you understand the situation. There is no danger of Sprauken being at financial risk in this matter."

"I'm not concerned with the financial risk," Goddard said. "I'm talking about the unanticipated side effects. We need more and better shielding. Or, as I mentioned in my memo, we should consider evacuating the village before we start the next phase."

"Evacuate the village?" Colonel Bentley scoffed. "Might as well put a big sign on the front gate. SECRET TESTING IN PROGRESS."

"Then move PULSE to a more isolated location."

"That would take, what, a year? Longer? Bear in mind the company is contractually obliged to continue without delay. PULSE must go forward on schedule. The importance of the project outweighs any possible risk to the work force."

Goddard fingered the bottle of pills in his pocket. "What happens if I refuse to go forward?"

Colonel Bentley's manner was polite and thoughtful. They might have been discussing the weather, or the latest sports news. "If you refuse to authorize the next test phase, we'll have no choice but to replace you."

"You could do that?"

"Not me. General Vance would contact the Sprauken board of directors."

"Ah, yes, the board," Goddard said with a small, twitching smile. He well knew what the board would do if it had to choose between pleasing the Pentagon and pleasing Kenneth Goddard. "Will you forward my memo detailing concerns about possible side effects? Just for the record?"

"Of course."

"Very well." He glanced at his watch. "It's show time."

Tony took his sweet time tying his Reeboks. He was crouching outside the door to the room where Goddard and Colonel Bentley had retired for a private meeting, and all he could hear were tones and inflections. It didn't really matter if he heard it word for word.

That snide bastard Bentley had been contemptuous when Tony slipped him a copy of the memo. Now, with Goddard's weakness documented, the colonel's personal opinion no longer mattered. There was only one man capable of taking over the project on short notice.

They would have to come to him. That was a nice thought. Tony finished tying his Reeboks and moved away from the door. He didn't need to overhear the conversation. It didn't matter what Goddard said to the colonel. Events would determine the outcome. He had it wired.

BOOK II

Pulse

"The boundaries which divide Life from Death are at best shadowy and vague. Who shall say where the one ends, and where the other begins?"

Edgar Allan Poe

Sunday, January 11

1:05 A.M.

"Aces and eights," Ozzie said. "You know what that means."

"Remind me," Tom responded.

"Dead man's hand. Wild Bill Hickcock got it in the back holding aces and eights. Bad luck. You really ought to fold."

"I'm staying," Tom insisted. "I don't believe you have the third jack."

Ozzie made a face and folded his hand. "That wipes me out. Susan, you want to sit in? I'll take over the monitors."

Susan begged off, convinced that the elaborate deathwatch was a waste of time and effort. Nothing was going to happen to the new cadaver. The expiration had been perfectly normal. No muscle or neurological activity had occurred. Not even a twitch.

She unrolled the map of Sprauken for maybe the tenth time. Looking for the pattern that had to be there. Street patterns. Patterns of apartment clusters. Hiding a clue, a secret. The key.

"Anything I can do to help?" Tom wanted to know.

"Not unless you're a mind reader. Of the subconscious."

"How about word association? I say 'blood' and you say . . ."

177

"Red." Susan sighed. "Thanks, but that won't help. I'm looking for a pattern, not a word. Has something to do with the way the village and the plant are situated. Or maybe it doesn't. Damn it! What's wrong with my brain?"

Ozzie gently massaged her shoulders. "We're all overtired, kid. Stressed out. Put the map away and try to relax."

Susan rolled up the chart. He was right. You couldn't make the pattern emerge by trying to force it. If in fact there *was* a pattern. Maybe her mind was just playing tricks, malfunctioning under stress.

"What about this man you thought you recognized at the ski resort?" Tom wanted to know.

Susan shook her head. "His face was covered. It was just the way he moved. Reminded me of someone I'd seen here in the village, I don't know who. Sorry."

"Hey, quit apologizing." Tom grinned and fanned out the deck. "Go on. Pick a card, any card."

Susan was reaching for a card when the room brightened. It was one in the morning and no one had touched the lights, and yet the room was suddenly brighter.

"Check out the monitors," Ozzie said urgently. "They're burning out."

All of the video monitor screens were glowing incandescent white.

Tom said, "I don't get it. How could four tubes blow all at the same time? Something like this happened to my computer screen a few days ago. I figured it was a power surge."

Susan touched one of the monitors. Her fingertips seemed to pick up the strange glow. She had expected the screen to be hot, but there was no more heat emanating than usual. "All of this equipment is tied into the mainframe," she said quietly. "There are adequate surge protectors. If amperage exceeds the recommended limit, the breakers cut out. Therefore it can't be a power surge. Right, Ozzie?"

Chester Oswald nodded. He was staring not at the glowing monitors, but at the bed where the body lay, wired and taped and tethered to the lab equipment. His voice was a husky whisper.

"Don't blink, kids," he said. "I think I saw it move."

* * *

Mallon prowled in the shadows around the Biohazard Lab, away from the streetlights. The trailer was dark, locked up. He could break in, check it out, but what good would that do? He knew little of science or labs. He imagined bubbling beakers, dangerous chemicals. Best to leave the place alone. Dr. Bitch wasn't in there, that was all that mattered.

She was not at the inn or the lab or Dr. Weston's place. Where the hell could she be?

He was heading back to the cruiser when he glanced up at the clinic building. At the far end of the east wing, figures were visible against the drawn shades. Somebody moving around in there. What was going on at this hour of the morning?

Mallon decided to investigate. What the hell, he was the deputy, he was *supposed* to investigate.

In the cages the shrieking had subsided to a few frightened whimpers. The mother chimp cradled her infant silently, no longer rocking on her haunches. Soon all of the primates were motionless. Terrified eyes relaxed, became dull and glistening and empty.

"What level is this?" the colonel inquired. He, Goddard, and Tony Faro were high above the target area, observing the chimps on shielded monitors.

"We're running at twenty-two percent of max power," Tony replied. "PULSE will continue at this level for another, let me see, eight minutes. The next sequence increases to thirty percent of max. That sustains for twenty minutes, with pulse sequences that should thoroughly scramble the primate nervous system. Or the nervous system of any living thing in the target area."

The colonel glanced at Goddard, who seemed to be holding up very well indeed. The former astronaut barely shuddered, for instance, when the infant chimp slipped from its mother's arms and rolled to the dung-spattered floor of the cage.

"And your team remains convinced the effect can be dupli-cated at long range?" Bentley asked.

"More than ever," Tony said, radiating confidence. "Extreme high-energy waves on the PULSE frequency can be delivered from a range of a hundred miles or more. Which means an existing satellite system can be utilized. Hell, we could use the space shuttle.''

"An intriguing idea," the colonel said. "Do you agree, Dr. Goddard?"

Goddard stirred. "As a matter of fact, I do."

The colonel was well aware that the former astronaut had expressed strong interest in accompanying a PULSE weapon into low-level orbit, should the system ever be tested in space. Of course the decision for deployment would not be made until the ground-based prototype had been thoroughly proven.

"So all we have to do," Tony continued, "is find the optimum sequence of pulses. When we have that, we can erase the human nervous system like you'd erase a bad audio tape."

Above them the prototype pivoted on counter-weighted gimbals, ready to release another sequence of high-energy pulses at the target area. Controlled by the computer program the weapon positioned itself perfectly. For the caged primates there was no escape.

"Is the data being recorded?" Susan asked.

"Beats me," Ozzie replied. "The monitors are flaming out. I can't tell if the signals are recording or not."

Movement in the left calf and foot of the cadaver had been observed. *Was* being observed. The toes were flexing in spasms. The calf muscle contracted and twitched. Tom was using a stethoscope to check for any signs of heartbeat or ventricular activity, in case the EKG recorder was not functioning.

"Absolutely nothing," he said, pulling the stethoscope away from his ears. "I'm prepared to certify that Tanborg is just as dead now as he was ten minutes ago. Brain dead, body dead. Anybody got any idea what's making the muscles contract?"

"The way those monitor screens are glowing, my guess is we're being bombarded with a strong electronic signal,"

Susan said, her voice shaky with excitement. "I think maybe that's what's stimulating the muscle nerves."

Susan had taken out a notebook and was writing down her impressions. She had just finished *magnetic field? check cathode response* when the room darkened perceptibly. Her first reaction was to assume that the power had failed. Then she realized it was merely the monitor screens. All of them had burned out in the same instant, leaving the room in relative darkness.

"You feel that?" Ozzie whispered.

"What?"

"Like static electricity in the air," he said. "Making the hair on my neck tingle."

Did she really feel it or was the tingling due to the power of suggestion? The consideration of such subtleties ceased abruptly when the cadaver legs began to make walking motions. Pedaling slowly in the air, exactly as Lars Svenson's legs had done. Susan's own knees felt weak, as if her nerves were resonating with tension. It took all her strength not to turn away from the bedside.

Something grabbed her hand. Tom tightened his grip and she responded by squeezing back. She got the distinct impression that his nerves were just as frayed as hers. Was it fear of the unknown, the human dread of dead things, or were they being affected by the same outside stimulus that was making the corpse muscles contract? As they watched, the motion of the slowly pedaling legs gradually shifted the body to the edge of the bed.

"It's going to fall off," Tom said. "Should we stop it?"

"Hell, no," Ozzie said. "See what happens. Hey, is that my imagination or are those wires almost glowing?"

He indicated the hair-thin wires that connected the body to the various monitoring devices. Susan squinted. There was either a faint bluish glow emanating from the wires or her eyes were being tricked by the dim light. If the glow was real, it had to be the result of a very powerful electrical field. Something strong enough to knock out normal electrical systems. Something strong enough to produce startling side effects in dying nerves and tissue.

"Look out!"

Quite suddenly the thing was upright and walking. It was coming directly at Susan. Tom yanked her out of the way as the body slowly staggered by, trailing the torn, glowing wires.

The squat, naked body of the late Jon Tanborg clumped forward, heading for the door. The head flopped uselessly from side to side. Arms and torso were limp. Susan, acting on impulse, rushed ahead and pushed open the double doors. The body clumped awkwardly through the doorway, more machinelike than human, the loose wires skittering on the floor tiles.

Then Tom was beside her saying, "Is it trying to escape?"

"No," Susan said uncertainly. "There's no brain activity involved. Muscle action is drawing it in that direction. Watch what happens when it comes to the end of the hallway."

At the end of the hallway the body bumped up against the wall. The legs continued to thrash up and down.

"That's how Svenson's body responded," Susan said, remembering. "It went as far as it could in one direction and just kept walking in place. Like a compass needle following a magnetic line."

Tom followed the thing to where it had come up against the wall. He watched the legs thrash in slow, steady rhythm, his complexion drained and pale.

"Know what this reminds me of?" he said huskily. "Some sort of big, gruesome toy. A nightmare windup doll. What I want to know is, how do we shut the damn thing off?"

Midway through the last sequence of pulses, Tony switched off the lights in the target area. He hadn't bothered to clear the procedure with Goddard. He wanted the element of surprise to put the old boy off balance.

"What the hell's going on?" Goddard said, startled by the sudden change.

"Take a look, sir. Over the edge. Colonel, can you see the effect? It'll maybe take a few seconds for your eyes to adjust."

The two men stared down at the dimly lit target area.

"They're glowing," the colonel said, surprised. "The bars on the cages are glowing."

Goddard shut his eyes, relieved. For a few horrible heartbeats he thought he'd been hallucinating again. Now that he knew the others could see the same phenomenon, the explanation came to him. Clever boy, that Tony. Trying to impress the colonel.

"The static field effect," Goddard said. "PULSE is generating so many megawatts of power at high frequency that it radiates an electrical field. Any unshielded metallic substance is likely to respond. That's what you wanted to show the colonel, right, Tony?"

"Right, sir. I thought it might be nice to document the effect. Kind of awesome-looking, hey, Colonel Bentley?"

The colonel did not reply. He stared down at the glowing cages, the comatose chimps bathed in the faint blue light produced by the field effect.

"What happens at a hundred percent power?" he wanted to know.

Beautiful, Tony thought. *What a beautiful question.*

"Dr. Goddard?"

Answer him, you wimp, Tony silently urged. *Tell him what he wants to hear.*

"This level is more than sufficient," Goddard said uneasily. "At thirty percent the targets are rendered helpless."

"Yeah, I can see that," the colonel said, exasperated. "What I want to know is, how high do you have to crank it up before PULSE kills the little bastards?"

1:35 A.M.

The faint murmuring echoed through the unlit corridors. Creepy stuff. Indistinct voices. Skittering sounds that made no sense. Deputy Mallon upholstered his weapon, made sure the safety catch was disengaged. The fire doors to the east wing of the clinic had been locked—a very unusual happenstance—and he'd had to use his master key to gain entrance.

What was going on? What was Dr. Bitch hiding? He had to know. Gun in hand, he padded silently down the corridor.

Mallon was aware that Tony Faro was involved in a power struggle for control of the Experimental Division. The rumor had been circulating for months. So when Tony first approached him, Mallon had been honored. The hip young engineer had implied that for his cooperation he would be rewarded with Webster's job. Chief of Security. With access to all intelligence and personnel files. As Chief, Mallon would have the power to expunge certain facts from his service record. Facts that, if they ever came to light, would mean instant dismissal, maybe even prosecution for perjuring himself on his job application.

Facts like that ridiculous psychiatric discharge from the army. Fucking doctors had been out to get him. He hated doctors. In particular he hated women doctors. It was hate that gave him purpose. Hate that kept certain excruciating memories buried. Hate that made him strong.

He turned to the left and the murmuring voices became louder, more distinct.

"It's so damn obvious," Susan said, rattling the map. "I can't believe I couldn't see it. It was right there from the beginning, staring us all in the face."

She spread the map out on the floor. Tom and Ozzie waited for her to continue.

"Okay, over here is the temporary morgue. Scene of the first incident. The body walks precisely in this direction. It keeps on walking until the muscle tissue freezes solid. Or until the stimulus ceased."

"But what stimulus, exactly?" Tom wanted to know.

Susan shrugged. "I only know the source. Not what's causing it."

"The source? But how?"

"The pattern. Can't you see the pattern? Okay, we've plotted the line the first deadwalker followed. The second was right here in the clinic, witnessed by Nurse McNeil. The body was attempting to go in this direction," she said, tapping her finger against the map, "only it bumped up against a wall almost immediately. As did Lars Svenson, from this point over here.''

"I still don't get it," Tom said. "Those are all different directions. Random, I'd say. What does it prove?"

Susan laid a straightedge on the map. "You're correct, it does look random. Unless we take the trouble to extend the lines. Where exactly would the deadwalkers have crossed paths if there had been no impediments to their progress?''

Carefully she extended the first line. Then the second, the third, and finally the precise direction of the last deadwalker. The lines all intersected at the same point.

"The plant," Tom said. "The lines cross over the Experimental Division."

Susan nodded. "The changes in blood chemistry convinced me the leak had to be a toxin. I was wrong. You saw what happened to the electronic gear tonight. Everything went haywire. Now what, exactly, do they manufacture at the Experimental Division?''

Tom scratched his head. "Guidance systems. And high-power radar."

"Equipment that generates microwave pulses?"

"Yeah, I guess. That's what radar is, right? Microwave pulses? Can microwaves alter human blood chemistry? Or damage the nerves?''

"That's what we need to find out," Susan said.

Ozzie got to his feet. "I'm going back to the lab. I'll get CYTO on-line and print out all the available literature."

Susan said, "Fine. While you're doing that, Dr. Weston and I are going to take his Jeep out for a spin."

"We are?"

Susan answered by linking her arm in Tom's and steering him to the nearest exit.

The infant chimp was dead. Crushed when a large male toppled over. A technician freed the small, lifeless clump of fur and bones and placed it in the mother's arms. She did not respond. The dead infant slipped from her breast.

"Excellent," Colonel Bentley said. "If PULSE erases the

mother instinct, it can erase *all* instincts. Even self-preservation.''

Goddard appeared agitated. He paced near the cages, scuffing the sawdust. ''I feel confident the damage is reversible, if the pulse burst does not exceed certain limits. Clearly tonight's sequence exceeded that limit. Much work remains to be done. We need to develop tolerance guidelines, safety levels, and so on.''

''Yes, yes,'' the colonel said, pretending polite interest. ''Very commendable, I'm sure.'' He borrowed a cattle prod and satisfied himself that the big males remained inert. There was a *zap!* and the sharp odor of seared flesh. When he was done administering powerful electric charges, with no response, he looked up to see Goddard hurrying away.

''Dr. Goddard! Where are you going? I want you to show me the data on power levels.''

Goddard waved him off and hurried away.

''What's his hurry?'' Colonel Bentley asked.

Tony grinned. ''Off to the bathroom to give himself a fix. Pop a few more pills. You better follow him, Colonel.''

Bentley removed his uniform hat, wiped his brow. Prodding chimps was hot work. ''Yeah? Why is that?''

''You're taking samples of his urine, right?''

''Fuck off, Tony.''

Tony smiled.

''What's it going to take, huh? When are you and the Pentagon brass going to smarten up and realize you need a new project director?'' he said. ''You and me, Colonel, we could work together. With me in charge, this weapons system is going to rock and roll.''

Bentley was cool, calculating. ''The matter is under consideration,'' he said.

''He's going to snap,'' Tony promised. ''He's going to break like an old rubber band.''

The colonel shrugged. ''We'll see about that.''

They never made it past the first checkpoint. The road to the Experimental Division had been blocked off.

"I'm Dr. Weston," Tom said, leaning out the window. "There's an emergency. I have to get through."

"Sorry, Dr. Weston," the guard responded uneasily. "I'm not authorized to let you through. Or anyone else, for that matter."

"Since when did you set up roadblocks here?"

"Just the last two weeks. Kind of a security exercise, they told us."

Tom checked out the roadblock. There were several sand-weighted barrels and a heavy truck parked perpendicular to the street. No way to force the Jeep through.

"You want me to call the office, put in the request?" the guard asked.

"Never mind," Tom said. "I'll do it myself."

He rolled up the window, put the Jeep in reverse. "Strike one," he said as they drove away.

"Is there another way in?" Susan asked.

"Not directly," he said. "Not by road, anyhow. Better fasten your seat belt, this could get bumpy."

"What are you going to do?"

"Try out the four-wheel drive. What the hell, I paid for the option." Tom circled around to the north, cutting through a cluster of residential housing. Susan, disoriented, had no idea where he was heading. Tom downshifted, skidding the rear wheels, and they emerged on a bluff overlooking the rear of the plant.

"Believe it or not, this is a beautiful meadow come spring. Right now the hillside is covered with about six feet of densely packed snow. The wind tends to blow away the light stuff, leaving the ice behind."

Susan squinted, but the headlights extended only so far. After that the night was impenetrable. "There must be a fence," she said.

Tom nodded. "Good guess. But if I remember it correctly, the fence is about eight feet high. With the snow buildup and a little momentum we can drive right over it."

He engaged the four-wheel drive and put the transmission into the lowest gear. The tricky part was getting up over the frozen embankment. He cruised along the edge until he spotted a dip in the snowbank, and then gunned the engine. Susan braced her hands against the dashboard. They hit, churned up over the edge, and slid for a few yards on the compacted snow.

"Beautiful," Tom said.

There was a *chunk!* and the wheels cracked through the crust.

"My fault," he said. "Never should have stopped moving."

He began to rock the vehicle, shifting quickly from forward to reverse, coaxing the wheels out of the rut.

"You want me to get out and push?" Susan offered.

"Hang tight," he said. "I've almost got it."

The Jeep teetered. The wheels caught, dragging them out of the rut, and Tom quickly shifted gears. "Got to keep an even speed," he explained. "I've seen the boys do this on the lake, racing on the ice."

They weren't moving particularly fast, but Susan found it frightening. No road, no painted lines, just whiteness spinning away, disappearing as the headlights seemed to carry them forward. They might have been heading for the edge of the world, into the unknown dark.

"How far?" she asked.

"Hard to say. We'll know when we get there."

She never really saw the fence. Just a glimpse of wire glinting in the headlights. The Jeep hit the submerged fence posts and ripped through. They were inside the plant perimeter. Tom had cut his lower lip on the steering wheel.

"Teach me to keep my big mouth shut," he said, wiping the blood away with his sleeve. "Okay, we're in like Flynn. Now let's see if we can pay a surprise visit to the Experimental Division."

They almost made it. Tom had pulled up next to Goddard's Mercedes when another vehicle, running without headlights, slid to a stop, tapping the Jeep's rear bumper.

A powerful flashlight blinded Tom as he stumbled from the Jeep.

"Hands over your head. You, too, lady."

Deputy Mallon confronted them with gun drawn.

"You should know better, Dr. Weston. Violating security is a serious offense."

"We have to see Goddard," Susan said, moving toward the deputy. "It's a medical emergency."

"Dr. Goddard requested assistance?"

"Well, no. Not exactly. But we have to see him right now."

Mallon waved the revolver. "Get back in the vehicle, Dr. Cullen. You do the same, Dr. Weston. I'm going to escort you back to the main gate. If you try another stunt like this, I'll have no choice but to place you both under arrest."

"You wouldn't dare," Tom said, blustering.

"Try me," Mallon snapped, waving his revolver.

They returned to the Jeep.

"Strike three and we're out," he said to Susan.

Mallon followed them to the main gate, escorting them through security, and then pulled alongside. "No hard feelings," he said to Tom. "Just doing my job."

Tom waved. As the cruiser pulled away he hit the dashboard with his fist and said, "Shit! How the hell did he catch us like that?"

"He must have been following us," Susan said. She huddled in the front seat, shivering.

"Why would he do that?"

"I don't know," Susan said. "But it's him, Tom. He's the one."

"What?"

"The man in the ski mask and green parka. The man who tried to kill me on the ski slope. I knew it the moment he came swaggering out of the cop car. The way he moves."

Tom turned to her, his jaw dropping open. "Why didn't you say so?"

"I was afraid," she said. "Afraid he might shoot you."

3:31 A.M.

Hour of the wolf, Bernie Simms thought, lying awake on the hard, rubberized hospital mattress. *Hour of the damned wolf.*

In the darkness he could hear Sam Carnovitz struggling to fill his single, diseased lung with bad air. Poor Sam. The nursing home stunk of carbolic acid and unemptied bedpans. It smelled of incontinent death and the inferior cologne the nurses daubed on themselves to cover the ghastly funk of despair.

The Cage, that was what Sam called the nursing home. A cage without bars. It was enough to make a man long for the relative comforts of the Veterans' Hospice. At least the Vets had the pool tables and the big-screen television and the Saturday wheelchair races. In this godforsaken hole there were only the rows of beds and the hourly ministrations of a nursing staff that made a ceremony out of not meeting your eyes.

Die if thou must, for I see thee not.

Bernie couldn't find it in his heart to blame the nurses. Why should they put themselves out for a collection of terminally ill old men who thought so little of themselves that they had willingly signed away whatever rights to life remained?

Fifty grand, Bernie thought. *I'm lying here in the stinking dark for a lousy fifty grand*. Enough, he reminded himself, to pay off the mortgage for Louise, and the overdue property taxes, and the unpaid hospital bills. Maybe enough left over to buy a plane ticket to Virginia Beach so she could visit Brenda and the kids.

Bernie shut his eyes and tried to remember what his grandchildren looked like. Small, blurred faces. That was all he could conjure up. Good kids, Louise had said. She'd been to see them twice in five years. Or was it three times? No matter. He'd been too ill to accompany her, and in any event didn't want his grandchildren to recall him as an ailing old man, an invalid with a bum ticker. Better they remember the grinning, black-haired young paratrooper in the old photograph.

It was the dead hours of the night that were the worst part. The hours when he could feel the pain thudding in his damaged arteries, and the fear of ceasing to exist became a tangible thing as real as the aneurysm in his heart. When the time came he would, he fervently hoped, find the courage to face it with his head up, his eyes open.

Soon, the young punk Tony had told them before speeding

off in his fancy BMW, soon. The bus will come and take you to the location and shortly after that the experiment will begin.

Bernie imagined death arriving on an old yellow school bus. He rather liked the idea.

"As soon as I get you back to the inn I'm calling Jack Webster," Tom Weston vowed.

"Kurt Mallon works for Webster," Susan reminded him.

He nodded. "True. But I can't believe Jack would be involved in an attempted murder."

Susan, recalling the bluff old cop with his cigar and his bad jokes, tended to agree. Then again, she wouldn't have thought Kurt Mallon capable of malice. "I just don't want to get sidetracked," she said. "The important thing is to find out what they're doing at Experimental. If we can't get Goddard to stop it, we may have to make arrangements to evacuate the village. Alert the proper agencies, with or without company approval."

At that hour of the morning the inn was silent and dim, seemingly deserted. A sign at the reception desk indicated that the concierge could be contacted by telephone in case of an emergency. The building was asleep.

"This place gives me the creeps," Tom said. "Come on, I'll walk you to your room."

Susan almost told him an escort was unnecessary, then thought better of it. As they waited for the elevator to rise, Tom reached for her hand absently, as if out of long habit. When he realized what had happened he blushed. "Sorry," he said. "I wasn't thinking."

He had been, though. Thinking about Jeannie. Weary and slightly confused he had done the automatic thing, seeking comfort from the woman at his side. But it was the wrong time, he decided, and possibly the wrong woman.

Susan smiled. "Keep not thinking," she said, returning his touch.

The dim silence that hovered over the inn extended to the third floor. She found the plastic pass card in her purse and clicked the door open. "I better give Ozzie a buzz," she said, reaching for the lights. ''He'll stay at the lab until he's ordered to get some sleep.''

The lights came on. She didn't scream exactly. More a choking sound. Turning to run, she bumped into Tom.

''Holy shit,'' he said, looking over her shoulder.

At first it looked like snow. Fluffy white stuff spewed from the mattress, stirred into flurries by the motion of the door. Then he saw the long, jagged knife cuts that had torn the bed apart. The mattress had been eviscerated. Susan's clothing was similarly ripped and slashed to shreds, scattered everywhere. It was a scene of frenzied destruction, so violent the room seemed to throb with anger.

A threat had been scrawled on the mirror in red lipstick:

DIE

DR. BITCH

DIE

''Come on,'' Tom said. ''Let's get out of here.''

Susan nodded wordlessly. She never wanted to see the room again. Deciding not to wait for the elevator, they hurried down the stairs and out into the predawn cold. Tom insisted they lock both doors of the Jeep.

''You can stay at my place for now. I'll deal with Jack Webster first thing in the morning. If he doesn't come through I'll contact the State Police, or the FBI, whatever it takes.''

Susan, always fiercely independent, felt the need of a protector for the first time in her life. The hatred emanating from the room had made her feel weak, helpless. Whoever had slashed the bed and scrawled the threat on the mirror had been acting out an even greater rage. A rage directed at her.

''Kurt Mallon,'' Tom said, steering carefully through the empty, icy streets. ''He followed you to Ice Valley, tried to kill you there. He followed us tonight. It had to be him.''

''It doesn't make sense,'' Susan said. ''I hardly know the man. Why would he want to kill me?''

''There's something wrong with him. Something missing,'' Tom said. ''Jeannie never trusted him. Not from the first time he came into the clinic.''

Susan took a deep breath, hugging herself. *Calm down. You're safe now.* She glanced at Tom. "Jeannie was your wife?"

He nodded. "Jean had good instincts about people. And Kurt Mallon gave her the creeps. She told me once . . . she said, 'That boy has eyes like the snowman.' "

"What did she mean?"

"Dead eyes," Tom said. "Like he was frozen inside."

"I never noticed his eyes. All I saw was that big smile."

Tom snapped his fingers. "Damn! I just remembered. Mallon was there with Tony Faro when they brought in the injured worker. Maybe *that's* the connection."

He told her about the worker whose hand had been severely bitten, and his feeling that Tony and Deputy Mallon had been lying about the incident.

"Who is Tony Faro?" Susan wanted to know.

"Chief Engineer at the Experimental Division," Tom explained. "Goddard's personal Whiz Kid. He's ambitious and ruthless. Everybody in Sprauken knows that he wants Goddard's job as Director of Special Projects. Everybody but Goddard, who tends to be oblivious to things like company politics."

"And you think this Tony person is involved with Kurt Mallon?"

"I don't know," Tom said. "I intend to find out."

Susan telephoned the lab from Tom's apartment.

"Any progress?" she asked.

"I'm gonna give this computer a great big kiss," Ozzie said, his voice feverish with excitement. "There's not a lot in print about electromagnetic pulses—most of the research has been classified—but what there is, CYTO has found. I'm going through the data now. One thing jumped right out: a common symptom of exposure to high-impulse microwaves is a marked increase in the level of lymphocytes in the blood."

"That fits. Any known neurological side effects?"

"CYTO is running that right now. The problem is, most of the research has been done by defense labs. A lot of the data seems to have been suppressed or arbitrarily classified, so it's hard to nail down the evidence.''

"I'll be there in a couple of hours.''

"Get some sleep," he advised. "Preferably not alone.''

"You're incorrigible.''

"My middle name," he said.

Just before hanging up she asked, "Hey, Ozzie, have you got the door locked?''

"Locked and deadbolted," he reassured her. "You want to get in, use the key, because I'm not unlocking. Not for nobody.''

When she hung up, Tom was there, handing her a bourbon-laced hot toddy. "You forgot to mention what happened to your room," he said.

"I didn't forget," she said, taking the drink. "Just didn't want him to worry about me.''

Tom smiled wearily. "You know what my mother would have called you?''

"I can't imagine.''

"A peach. You're a peach, Susan Cullen." He clinked his glass against hers, made it a toast. "You know what we're up against here, don't you?''

"Sure. The company.''

"And not your average company, either," he said. "Sprauken International, a very large and powerful defense contractor. Also the Pentagon. Specifically, DARPA.''

"What, exactly, is DARPA?''

"Defense Advanced Research Projects Administration. They handle the very hush-hush stuff. It just so happens there's a DARPA officer in the village. Colonel Benjamin Bentley, Jr. Dollars to gold-plated donuts he's mixed up in this.''

Susan sat down and sipped at the drink. It was hot and heady, exactly what she needed. Tom had gotten a fire going in the fireplace, and reflected flames danced over the pine-paneled walls. The place felt cozy and safe. Already the violence displayed at the inn seemed a distant thing, almost unreal.

"I'm not used to this cloak-and-dagger stuff," she said. "I feel silly and inadequate.''

"That's the last thing you are," Tom said, sitting cross-legged by the fire.

Susan closed her eyes and leaned back in the chair. "This drink is going right to my head. I need to sleep for a few hours."

"What the doctor ordered." He chuckled. "Sometimes the old remedies are the best. I'll take the couch out here. You can have my bedroom."

He excused himself and went to get extra blankets and bedding. Susan put down her drink and followed him into the bedroom. Acting on impulse she slipped her arms around his waist from behind and rested her head against his broad shoulders.

"Tell you what," she murmured. "We'll share the bed. I need someone to just hold me tonight. Think you could do that?"

He turned in her arms, lifted her chin, and looked into her eyes. "I think I could manage," he whispered.

He parked the cruiser around the corner, behind a snowbank, out of sight. Adrenaline had cured his fatigue. The look of fear on her face had been thrilling. A heartbeat later she'd hidden it, drawn the mask, but for just that moment they'd both known exactly who he was.

Mallon got out of the cruiser and looked up at the apartment complex. The last light had gone out in Dr. Weston's apartment and now the building was no more than a rectangular silhouette, blocking the pin point stars. Did Dr. Tom know? Had she told him?

Mallon's lips drew back. His teeth ached pleasantly with the cold. He felt like a wolf, a predator. He wondered if they whispered his name in fear. It was a good thought, a powerful thought, and he held it.

Dr. Bitch and her new lover.

Get it while you can, he thought.

6:05 A.M.

It started five minutes into the morning shift. Nurse Alters barely had time to sling her purse on the back of the chair and take a few sips from her go-cup of hot chocolate when they started pouring into the ER. Well, not pouring, exactly. Stumbling, limping, dragging listless feet. The barely walking wounded.

"What's wrong?" she asked the first individual who presented himself at the admittance desk.

"Me and the wife, we're both of us sick."

Nurse Alters responded with her best clinical smile. "Indeed. Can you be more specific?"

"Ethel woke up in the middle of the night with the shivers, or the jitters, or some damn thing. Couldn't stop shaking. Like her nerves was all riled up. Shook so much it woke me, and then I got 'em, too."

"Got what, Mr. Bradford?"

"Shakes. Jerky kind of feeling in the muscles, like if you'd rubbed up against a live wire."

Mr. Bradford was certainly a live wire, Nurse Alters thought, examining his lined and haggard face, the gray stubble on his chin. If Bradford had rubbed up against poor Ethel, it was no wonder she had the shakes.

"Kinda tingly type of sensation," Mrs. Bradford said, joining her husband at the desk. "Extremely distressing. And when that stopped—and it ended for both of us at exactly the same moment—well, then, we both come down with nausea and headaches. Migraine kind of headaches."

"Do you often suffer from migraines, Mrs. Bradford?"

"Nope. Never have. All we can figure, we had some kind of food poisoning. Or maybe something in the water, since we didn't all eat the same food last night."

"All?" Nurse Alters said, lifting her pretty, plucked eyebrows.

"Yep. All them others followed us in; they're from our building."

Nurse Alters sighed, gazing at the rows of haggard, worried faces. There were more every minute, all of them crowding into the ER. Thirty or more sick and frightened people.

"The same building." Nurse Alter sighed. She opened her notebook. Doctor would want to know. "And what building is that?"

"The East Meadow complex," Mr. Bradford said. "Right up near the plant entrance. Very convenient," he added.

Closing his eyes hadn't helped. Neither had the soft Yamanakabushi music in the headphones. Sleep was simply not available for Kenneth Goddard. The thing to do, he decided, was just relax, let things unwind inside his head. He would worry about sleeping after he'd settled the issue of live testing.

The human volunteers Tony had recruited were to be bused in and subjected to a low-level PULSE sequence in less than forty-eight hours. So he had a day or so to make his case, establish his authority over the project. DARPA would strongly resist any delay, as Colonel Bentley had made clear. Tony was apparently siding with the Pentagon, despite his personal conflicts with Bentley. Unfortunate, but it couldn't be helped. That left Goddard alone in his conviction that the human test phase should be delayed. True, the volunteers were terminal patients whose lives were already in jeopardy, but it wasn't only the volunteers, it was the resident population that troubled him. The villagers.

There was no way to adequately shield the village from high-energy microwaves. Goddard had been over the problem again and again. The wave pulses were simply too strong and pervasive. Levels intended to stun the neurological system in the target area were obviously still strong enough, at the rippling edge of the wave, to produce serious side effects. Nerve damage. Blood damage. Other symptoms that might not show up for years.

His fingers moved to the pill bottle. It was not time for a dose yet, but touching the bottle gave him comfort. When he needed it, it was there. The security freed him to think.

Goddard remained convinced that PULSE, which from a range of more than a hundred miles could render an army helpless in seconds, was the weapon to end warfare. But he was equally convinced that peacetime civilian populations should not be needlessly exposed. He was prepared to fight for his convictions, if only he could find the right angle, a convincing means of dissuading his powerful Pentagon bosses.

What to do?

Goddard opened the pill bottle. First things first.

Susan woke up wearing a soft flannel nightgown. She was aware of Tom in the bathroom, the sound of a toothbrush being vigorously applied. Her hand stroked the soft material. The gown was not hers. That left one alternative. It must have belonged to Tom's late wife.

She rolled over, uncertain of how she felt. They had slept in each other's arms, too numbed by exhaustion to make love. The feeling had been so natural, so right, that she had accepted it. She wasn't falling in love with Tom Weston. She already loved him. That was the thought she had taken into sleep.

Now, lying awake in a bed where, not so long ago, another woman had loved and slept with the same man, she was not so sure of her feelings. Was it fear and anxiety that drew her to Tom? Physical attraction? Or was it an emotional rebound from Eliot?

Eliot. He had not crossed her mind until that very moment. Surely that meant that she no longer loved Eliot James, that she had never really loved him. If she and Tom had been thrown together by circumstance, if their mutual attraction was not lasting love, but simply a human longing for comfort, then so be it.

Let it happen, Susan decided. See where it goes.

Tom returned from the bathroom fully dressed. He sat on the edge of the bed and gazed at her with tired blue eyes. "This is pretty scary, huh?"

She knew exactly what he meant. It was as if he shared her thoughts.

"The next day or two is going to be crazy," he said. "We won't have a lot of time alone. But I don't want to lose this wonderful, scary feeling, Susan. You think we can hang on to it?''

"Are you really frightened?''

"Sure,'' he said. "I don't fall in love every day.''

"Hold me,'' she said, and threw her arms around his neck. She was just starting to taste the toothpaste on his lips when the telephone rang.

It was Ozzie, calling from the lab.

Chester Oswald had consumed so much of his beaker-brewed coffee that his hands were trembling. His eyes had the same slight quiver as he eagerly outlined the medical detective work that had taken him through the night, into the morning.

"Where's lover boy?'' he asked Susan as she entered the lab.

"Paying a visit to Jack Webster, the Chief of Security.''

"Your eyes are sparkling,'' Ozzie said with a mischievous grin.

"Sleep deprivation,'' she retorted. "Come on, spill it. What did you find?''

He indicated the fresh pile of computer printouts. "This was like pulling teeth,'' he said. "If I was a paranoid type, I might conclude that the defense industry and the Feds have a common interest in discouraging research into the physiological effects of electromagnetic pulses. By the way, EM pulses include everything from high-tension wires to microwaves. Radio and television broadcasts. The fact is, just about everybody on the planet is under a constant barrage of man-made electromagnetic pulses. We can't escape.''

"Any *need* to escape?'' Susan said, reaching for the stack of computer paper. "Come on, Ozzie, what did you find?''

"Patience, my child. I was up all night with this. Least you can do is let me explain in my own way.''

"Shall I set up the lectern, Professor?''

Ozzie grimaced. "Trouble with friends is, they know you too well. Okay, we'll start with defining microwaves, or is that too simple for you?''

"Go ahead. Like I said, it's been a while since I took a

physics course. And theoretical electronics was never my thing."

Ozzie nodded, lacing his long, slender fingers together. "Microwaves are a category of electromagnetic waves ranging in size from one centimeter to thirty centimeters. Anything shorter is light; anything longer is a radio wave. The major difference between microwaves and, say, infrared radiation, as far as we're concerned, is that, unlike sunlight, microwaves can penetrate the entire body."

Susan settled back, risking part of a cup of the dreadful beaker-brewed coffee. Ozzie would take his time, spell it out clearly. Much of what he covered she already knew, in vague terms, but his nightlong research had uncovered medical specifics that, ultimately, helped make sense of the strange effects experienced in the village of Sprauken.

"How much of the microwave radiation is absorbed into the human body varies with the frequency of the wave," he continued. "Maximum effect seems to be at those frequencies below one gigahertz. That includes television signals and most radar pulses. The studies I've been able to find indicate that there is no particular danger from television signals unless you happen to be within a few hundred feet of a broadcast antenna."

"What about radar pulses?"

"That's where it gets controversial. The government studies conclude there are no ill effects unless you're virtually on top of the radar unit, in which case you can get your brain poached like an egg. Or develop instant cataracts, or possibly pancreatic cancer. Nongovernment studies—of which there are only a few—indicate that certain side effects—in particular, changes in blood chemistry and subtle neurological damage—can occur from a considerable distance."

"How far?" Susan wanted to know.

Ozzie shrugged. "That's where the research falls apart. How far away is safe? Microwaves can be narrowly focused—that's why we use them for broadcasting to satellites—and therefore most radar and communication devices are carefully aimed where they won't make contact with humans. Up in the air, between communication towers, and so on. Sideways leakage is usually minimal. Of course, if the generating device is especially powerful—in radar systems that detect incoming missiles, for instance—the area of dangerous exposure levels can be quite large. Several square miles.''

That fit. So far the most seriously affected group in Sprauken seemed to be those who lived in the apartment complex nearest to the Experimental Division. They had experienced not only blood chemistry changes but significant neurological distress as well, according to the reports from the clinic.

''Naturally I instructed CYTO to concentrate on the radar data because we know that this plant builds high-powered radar systems. Most of the stuff, naturally, is about detecting moving objects with microwave pulses. That's how radar works. You send out a pulse, listen for the echo, send out a pulse, and so on. Of course the whole thing happens very quickly. Many pulses per second. CYTO found a lot of literature on pulse studies and the pulse study material eventually led me to the albino rats.''

Susan sat up straight. ''What? Albino rats? Are you serious?''

''You got something against albino rats?''

''Matter of fact, yes. Albino rats and white rats and brown rats. The whole rat race gives me the creeps.''

Lack of sleep made Ozzie prey to fits of the giggles. The ''whole rat race'' comment reduced him to tears. When he'd regained control of himself he took a deep breath and said, ''You'll be happy to know that whoever ran this particular series of experiments wasn't too crazy about the poor little critters, either.''

''Rats are not 'poor little critters,' Ozzie. They're rats.''

''Be that as it may, albino rats are useful for certain kinds of lab experiments. Detecting genetic changes and so on. Also, as rats go, they're fairly smart. Your average albino rat can learn to run mazes, ring bells, and so on.''

''Remind me to stay out of mazes,'' Susan said.

''In this particular experiment,'' Ozzie said, indicating the printout, ''the rats were subjected to varying microwave pulses. The study concludes that certain pulses caused the rats to suddenly get stupid. Forgot how to run the mazes. Forgot they were rats.''

"Neurological damage?"

He nodded. "And brain damage, of a sort. In the concluding remarks one of the lab technicians has this to say: 'It was almost as if their brains had been erased of all instincts. They did not respond to further stimuli, not even the presence of food.' "

"Brain erasure. That's like science fiction, Ozzie."

"This wasn't a pulp novel, Susan. It was an accredited scientific study. It never got much publicity in the medical community because, as you pointed out, no one gives a damn about rats. Albino or otherwise."

"You didn't call me up at the crack of dawn to tell me about rats."

"No," he said. "But once CYTO picked up that study, I was able to backtrack and retrieve data that applies to human physiology. You ever hear of the Pandora project?"

She shook her head.

"Cute name, huh? Pandora opens the box and evil is loosed upon the world. It was a Pentagon project, funded by the Defense Advanced Research Projects Agency. Otherwise known as DARPA."

A tingle went down the back of Susan's neck. "I've heard of them," she said. "Tom says there's a DARPA officer in the village."

Ozzie raised his eyebrows. "A coincidence?"

"I no longer believe in coincidences. Tell me about Pandora."

"I can only tell you some of it. A lot remains classified. The project was initiated when the Russians started beaming microwaves at the U.S. Embassy in Moscow. Remember that?"

"Vaguely."

"Well, apparently they were using microwaves to activate bugging devices. Monitoring phone lines, electric typewriters, cable machines, and so on. We were doing the same thing, of course, so the Feds tried to keep a lid on the incident. It got leaked because embassy employees, including the ambassador and his staff, complained of bizarre symptoms. Blood problems similar to leukemia. High incidence of miscarriage. Neurological distress. Sound familiar?''

Susan nodded miserably.

"They called it the Moscow Signal. Once I had that information, CYTO found me a study that was done at the Walter Reed Army Institute of Research. What they did was irradiate monkeys with the Moscow Signal to see if they could induce biological or behavioral changes in the animals.''

"And did they?''

"Most of that remains classified in the Pandora files. An interesting item made it past the censors, however: the chromosomes in the peripheral blood showed aberrations in forty percent of the lymphocytes.''

The jokes about rats and mazes were no longer quite so amusing. Susan's spirits began to plummet. "That's pretty close to what we found in the resident population here.''

"Damn straight it is,'' Ozzie said. "But that's not what scares me. What scares me is that DARPA was so interested in the classified results they urged the Walter Reed facility to, quote, 'develop a human program.' The suggestion was made—and I found this in the official minutes of a congressional committee, by the way—that, quote, 'human subjects be required for six to eight months and that they could be obtained from Fort Dietrich,' unquote.''

"They used human test subjects?''

Ozzie nodded grimly. "The project director for Pandora testified before Congress that low-level microwaves could penetrate the central nervous system of monkeys. In his opinion human study was required. The implication was that a pulsed microwave device might be developed as a weapon.''

"And was it?''

"Classified,'' Ozzie said, bringing his fist down on the printouts.

"So what happened to Project Pandora?''

"No data available, except that it ceased to be funded under that name about ten years ago.''

"So it was a failure?''

"No way of knowing,'' he said. "The research could have continued under secret funding.''

"You say CYTO picked up some of this information from congressional publications?" Susan said.

"Yes. Public testimony before any of the committees is entered into the Congressional Record."

Susan hunched forward. "I've got an idea. Can CYTO find out exactly who was called to testify about the Pandora project?"

Ozzie gave her a doubtful look. "Yeah, sure. Might take a while to run it through. It would save time if I had a name to match up. You have a particular name in mind?"

"I do," she said, and told him.

Ozzie entered the name in the computer and had CYTO cycle it into the retrieval file for the Congressional Record. They sat back and waited, sipping gingerly at more of the beaker coffee.

7:58 A.M.

Webster wasn't supposed to put sugar in his coffee. He got around it with the dunk method. Dunk four or five heavily powdered donuts in the coffee and it tasted just fine. On an ordinary day he would expect to get a mild lecture from the affable Dr. Tom, who knew all about his blood sugar problems. This was shaping up as no ordinary day.

"What I figured," the worried-looking physician was saying, "I figured I had no choice but to trust you on this, Jack. If I went to the State Police or the FBI it would get back to you anyhow."

Webster dunked, tasted the coffee, dunked some more. It was a delicate operation, balancing the sweetness level. "You're telling me Kurt has been harassing Dr. Cullen?"

Tom Weston sighed, shook his head. "I wish it was that simple."

"Tell you what, just start at the beginning. Put it in order and let me see if I can follow, okay?"

Weston took a deep breath and began by outlining what

they knew of the deadwalkers and the unexplained medical symptoms that had been plaguing the rest of the community.

"You're telling me that creepy stuff with the bodies was no trick?" Webster interrupted. "It really happened?"

"You saw Lars Svenson's body with your own eyes, Jack."

Webster made a face. "Sure I did. Still didn't believe it. Figured somebody was toying with that thing somehow."

"Dr. Cullen thinks the deadwalkers and the unexplained symptoms are all tied in with the strong EMPs leaking from the Experimental Division."

Dunk. Webster looked up over his coffee cup, his eyes suspicious. "Strong what?"

"Electromagnetic pulses. That's what radio waves are. And microwaves. The pulses coming out of Experimental are powerful enough to affect the human nervous system. We assume they're testing some sort of weapons system in there, or a radar device. That's where Deputy Mallon comes into the picture."

He described what had happened to Susan at Ice Valley.

"She says Mallon was following her. He was there near the base of the mountain, he was there on the chair lift, and he came down the slope looking for her right after the signs were switched. And he was right behind us when we tried to sneak through the plant perimeter."

Webster nibbled the donut, slurped at the coffee. "Not the kind of evidence that will stand up in court," he commented.

Tom rubbed his jaw, exasperated. "I'm not asking you to arrest Mallon. I just want him to stay away from Susan."

"I'm still not clear on the motive."

Tom's eyes darted nervously about. He drummed his fingers on the chief's desk top. "Okay, I might as well just say it. The reason I hesitated before reporting these incidents, it occurred to me that if certain individuals in the company wanted to discourage Dr. Cullen's investigation, they might approach the Chief of Security. And that the Chief might order his deputy to put Dr. Cullen under surveillance, maybe scare her a little. If that's what happened, you have to know that Mallon is getting out of hand. He's dangerous."

Webster slammed the coffee down. "Whoa! Now hold on

just a damn minute. Is that what you think? That I'm behind these incidents?''

Tom smiled weakly. "I don't know what I think, Jack. I figure you for a straight shooter, but you're a company cop now, just like I'm a company doctor.''

Webster used a napkin to sop up the spilled coffee. His voice had softened considerably. "Hell, the job does mean a lot. Saved me from a park bench in Saint Pete. Plus it pays well. But let me make something perfectly clear, son. No job pays enough to condone an attempted murder. Or the kind of harassment you're describing. You say Kurt has been prowling in her room, slashing up her things?''

Tom nodded. "Whatever he's doing, he's getting more violent. The first incident was just clothing in a bureau drawer. Last night everything in the room was cut up, plus the mattress was slashed, and he left a threat on the mirror.''

"You're positive that Mallon is responsible?''

Tom shook his head. "I'm not positive of anything. I'm just hoping there isn't more than one crazy out there. It was Deputy Mallon on the mountain, Susan will swear to that. And whoever got into her room has access to a pass card. I assume a security officer could swing that?''

"He could,'' Webster agreed. "Question is, did he? Shouldn't be too hard for me to determine, one way or the other.''

"So you'll check it out?''

Webster sighed. "Don't see as I have any choice. I may be a company flatfoot now, but that doesn't mean I'll tolerate a rogue cop on my beat. Leave it to me, Doc.''

"That's what I was hoping you'd say,'' Tom said. He got up, zipped up his parka. "You're not kidding me, you know.''

"What?'' Webster said, puzzled. "Kidding you about what?''

"How you get sugar in your coffee,'' Tom said, grinning. "The old powdered donut trick.''

"Have a heart, Doc. What do you want from me?''

"I want you to live forever,'' Tom said. "Is that so much to ask?''

* * *

The CYTO screen was blinking.

"Bingo," Ozzie said, staring at the name on the monitor.

"Well what do you know," Susan said. "Lieutenant Colonel Bentley was the Pentagon liaison for Project Pandora, representing DARPA. And now, seven years later, and a full colonel, he's in the village as a guest of Sprauken International."

Ozzie said, "Coincidence?"

"Like bubonic plague was a coincidence," Susan said. "The colonel is here because he's an expert in pulse weapons. That clinches it, Ozzie. I don't give a damn what kind of war toys they're building at Experimental, they've got no right to endanger a civilian population. I'm going to confront Kenneth Goddard on this."

"He might decide to fire you. What do we do then?"

Susan thought long and hard. "Are you with me on this, Ozzie?" she asked.

"Sink or swim," he replied immediately.

"Okay. If Sprauken gives us the heave-ho, we'll go independent. Set up a new biohazard lab. Probably be on a slightly smaller scale."

"Small is beautiful," Ozzie said. "Look at me."

"There's a risk involved," Susan warned. "These boys play hardball, especially if it involves a juicy Pentagon contract."

"Throw 'em your best pitch," Ozzie said. "Fastball on the inside, chin high."

They were interrupted by a fist pounding against the lab door. Before unlocking, Ozzie checked out the scene through a small vent window.

"Big Mercedes limo out there," he said.

"I'll be damned."

Susan hurried to the door, slipped back the bolt, catching the limo driver by surprise. He relaxed, dropping his gloved fist.

"Excuse me, are you Dr. Susan Cullen? Dr. Goddard would like a word with you."

"Well, that's just fine," Susan said. "Because I'd like a word with him. Let me grab my coat."

She closed the door, leaving the driver on the steps.

"This is perfect. When Tom gets back, tell him I've gone to see Goddard."

Ozzie nodded and said, "You're not back in an hour, or if you don't call, we'll get out the cavalry."

"It'll be fine," she said, slipping into her down parka. "Keep an eye on Dr. Weston for me. He tends to get excited. I mean he'll be worried. Oh, you know what I mean."

"Sure I do," Ozzie grinned. "Question is, do *you* know what you mean?"

Susan hurried out to the limo, expecting to be driven to the executive office building, or the plant itself. The driver, racing ahead of her, managed to get to the rear door before she did. To her surprise, Kenneth Goddard was waiting inside the vehicle.

" 'Morning, Dr. Cullen," he said. "Please make yourself comfortable. I've got a proposition for you."

"Great," Susan said, slipping into the seat opposite him. "I've got one for you, too."

The light was wrong. Mallon squinted through the binoculars, trying to get past the glare, but the rising sun was behind the Mercedes and he couldn't make out who was inside. It was Goddard's vehicle, of course, but Tony Faro sometimes used it, and Mallon wanted to know who Dr. Bitch was meeting, and why. Was he the subject under discussion? Was she going directly to the top with her suspicions? Did she have any evidence linking him to the Ice Valley incident or the trashing of her suite? He didn't see how that was possible, but still, the very idea was disturbing.

Mallon dropped the binoculars and tuned in the security frequency. There was no activity on the radio, no indication that anything unusual was under way.

The Mercedes was pulling away, heading for the main road. He put the cruiser in gear and followed at a discreet distance. It wouldn't do to be seen tailing the boss's limousine. Nor did he have a good reason to pull it over, check out who was inside the tinted windows.

He fretted, gripping the wheel harder than was necessary.

Last night, in the early hours before dawn, he'd felt triumphant. Indomitable. Now he wasn't so sure. He could handle Dr. Bitch, no problem there, but Goddard was another story. Goddard made it complicated.

There was too much he, Mallon, didn't know. Tony, a stickler for security, was purposely keeping him in the dark. The idea that things were progressing beyond his control made him uneasy. And for Kurt Mallon it was only a brief transition from uneasiness to rage.

9:05 A.M.

Susan read the cable for a second time. "I'm not sure I understand," she said. "Who is Apollo? And what is the Pulse project?"

The limousine was idling on a hill overlooking the Experimental Division. The driver, instructed to leave the vehicle, stood nearby, kicking at bits of frozen snow, while he puffed on a cigarette.

"Apollo is me," Kenneth Goddard explained. "Just a silly code name. What you have in your hands is a security clearance. I assumed that eventually you'd have to be briefed on the project."

"This isn't what I expected," she said uncertainly.

A slant of wan sunlight played over the whitened landscape, making the ice-shrouded mountains look flat and unreal, like jagged cutouts along the horizon. Susan felt as if she were being asked to play a scene from a movie: confrontation with a powerful man, a certified American hero. The limousine, the banished driver, the majestic landscape; it all contributed to a sensation of dreamlike unease.

Goddard very deliberately rolled down the sock on his left ankle and scratched, his brow furrowed in concentration. That was another thing Susan hadn't been expecting, the strange dichotomy between the former astronaut's jittery, nervous mannerisms and his steady, sober manner of speech. He delivered his lines as if they had been written down and memorized long ago.

"I'm hoping we can work together on this, Dr. Cullen," he said, rolling up the sock. There was a faint tinge of blood under his fingernails.

"Work together?" Susan had intended to give him hell about endangering the health of the village. His attitude was so unnerving that now she wasn't sure how to proceed.

"On PULSE," he said. "We've been testing a remarkable new device. A defense system like no other in existence."

Take your chance, Susan thought. Go for broke. She said, "Does this new device generate microwaves?"

Goddard looked startled. His complexion was pasty and his hair was as thin and translucent as strands of monofilament fishing line. Susan had the impression that he was disintegrating inside, holding himself together by force of will.

"Microwaves are part of the process," he acknowledged. "How did you know?"

Susan told him about the electrical field they'd detected while monitoring the last deadwalker, the material CYTO had retrieved from various unclassified sources, indicating that many of the symptoms in the village, including involuntary muscle response, could be explained by the presence of powerful microwaves.

"Basically we had eliminated all the other possibilities," she said. "If I hadn't been sidetracked into hunting for toxins, we'd have come up with it sooner."

He nodded happily, as if delighted at her discovery.

"Remarkable detective work," he said. "You only have part of the picture, but the basic information is correct."

Anxiety formed a lump in her throat, but Susan forced herself to keep pressing, to ask the crucial, nagging question. "Why did you lie to us?" she said. "You must have known your 'remarkable new device' was causing the problems. You deliberately misled us."

Goddard pressed his thumbs to his nose. A line of sweat began to advance downward from his hairline. "Please believe me, Dr. Cullen, I didn't intentionally lie. I really had no idea the deadwalking phenomenon was being caused by leakage from PULSE, and I was simply too involved in the testing program to pay much attention to medical complaints in the village."

Oddly enough, Susan almost believed him. Kenneth Goddard appeared to be a man in torment, and she was convinced the problem was much deeper than drug dependency. Some fundamental conflict was wrenching at him, causing deep psychological distress.

"What happened to change your mind?" she asked.

The sweat dripped into his eyes. He blinked rapidly, then mopped his forehead with a handkerchief. "Is it stuffy in here?" he asked. He tried to tuck the handkerchief back in his pocket and missed.

"A little," Susan said.

Goddard cracked a window and gulped at the cold air. "What happened to change my mind. Good question. Excellent question. What happened is, after you notified me that a 'toxin' might be leaking, I went back and recalibrated our detection devices." He paused to gulp more of the cold air, then lay back against the headrest and closed his eyes. "Unfortunately, I must agree with your conclusion. There is no toxin, of course, but each time we've tested the prototype a dangerous level of microwaves has leaked into the area surrounding the plant."

"You told me outside agitators were responsible. Or a competitor."

"My first reaction, yes. Naturally I didn't want to think that PULSE was at fault. We took great precautions to shield the device. Obviously it was not enough."

Susan made her decision. "No thanks," she said, trying to hand him the cable. "I don't want any part of this. All I want is an assurance that no more leaks will occur."

When Goddard wouldn't take the cable, she placed it on his knee. After a moment the thin sheet of paper fluttered to the floor of the vehicle.

"I understand your reluctance," he said. "You think I've violated your trust."

Susan hesitated. "Didn't you?"

"It doesn't matter now whether I did or not, or what my intentions were. What matters now is that I need your help. Unless the situation is rectified, the PULSE leakage will certainly continue, and at considerably higher levels."

"But you're in charge," Susan said. "Just turn off this device, whatever it is."

Goddard retrieved the cable from the floor of the vehicle and forced it into her hands.

"Let me explain something to you, Dr. Cullen. I am, nominally, the Special Projects Director, but there are many other individuals involved at a high level. Representing various interests. The Pentagon, for instance, is insisting that the tests resume almost immediately. They have nearly a billion dollars invested in the project and they want to see the results. The reality is that *they* own the project. *They* call the shots."

Susan put the security clearance in her purse for the time being. She wanted it out of her sight. She had no desire to be made privy to defense secrets, or enter the arcane world of power struggles at the executive level. But it appeared she no longer had a choice in the matter. With Goddard clearly losing control, someone had to take responsibility.

"What kind of weapon are we talking about?" Susan asked. "What does it do?"

Goddard was smiling again. Suddenly he seemed to be trembling with excitement. "I think . . ." he began. "Handled correctly, I think it could change the world."

First things first. Before Webster initiated an investigation of his own deputy, he wanted proof of malfeasance. A little hard evidence. Could be the lady had an overactive imagination, panicked easy. As he drove to the inn to check out the allegations, Webster had it in the back of his mind that he just might sit down to one of the restaurant's sumptuous breakfasts. Hell with the donuts and coffee. Have a real meal for once; start the day off with a bang.

He was thinking steak and scrambled when he strolled up to the desk and asked for the manager.

"Mornin'," Webster said affably.

"Morning, Chief. What brings you in here on this fine day? Burglary? Arson? Murder?"

Webster chuckled. It was a running joke. Sprauken, with its carefully controlled population, had no crime rate to speak

213

of. In the five years the village had existed, there were, to date, no recorded incidents of burglary, arson, or murder. There had been one case of rape, a belligerent welder who assaulted his ex-wife, and the guilty party was now welding lobster traps at the state prison in Thomaston. Rape was a serious crime in Maine. Webster felt lucky to have had only a single serious incident in five years. Most of the lesser crimes involved domestic disputes: assaults, drunkenness, and so on.

"Just a routine check," Webster assured him. "The thing is we're running an inventory, bringing the security files up to date."

"Good idea, Chief. Hey, you want in for the Wednesday night poker game?"

"You mean since Svenson died?" Webster asked, narrowing his eyes.

"Yeah. All due respect to the dead, we got a tradition to uphold. There's a seat open if you're interested. Great bunch of guys."

Webster said, "Gambling is illegal."

"Come on, Chief. We'd love to have you. You know all the guys."

"I'll pass," Webster said. "Never been much for card games."

"You think it over, Chief. It's more a social occasion."

"About the security inventory. Passkeys. About how many are floating around?"

"Can't say offhand," the manager said. "I can check the slots, you want. Ten or a dozen, I guess, for the chambermaids and maintenance."

Webster made a mark in his notebook. "Ten or a dozen. Fine. Try to nail it down exactly, whenever you have the chance. I think Kurt was here couple nights ago, checking out the same thing."

"Kurt?"

"Deputy Mallon," Webster said offhandedly. "He picked up a passkey, right?"

"Now you mention it, sure. Said it was a security problem. Only don't get me wrong, it's not a passkey exactly. We use what they call the coded-card method. Cheaper in the long run; you don't have to make up new keys every time a guest accidentally flushes 'em down the loo, or whatever the hell it is they do with keys.''

The manager reached into a slot behind the desk and handed Webster a slim plastic card. ''This is a pass card, open any door in the facility. You can put it right in your wallet, like a credit card. Same size. Of course we change the codes every month or so.''

''Very convenient. Tell you what, I'm just going to stroll around, have a look see.''

''Anything wrong, Chief?''

''Not a thing. Just routine.''

Webster took the stairway rather than the elevator, so as not to alert the manager to what floor interested him. The stairs were a mistake. He'd been smoking too many cigars lately. Now his heart was thumping like he'd run the quarter mile.

''Now that would surely kill me,'' Webster muttered to himself. ''A quarter-mile run.''

He took a few moments to catch his breath and orient himself to the third floor. At the far end of the corridor a chambermaid was working her way along, room by room. Good. He preferred to check out Dr. Cullen's suite before the staff started messing around. See if Dr. Tom and the lady were maybe making a big thing out of nothing.

Webster slipped the plastic card into the slot above the door handle. The lock unit buzzed. The door clicked open.

He stepped inside. One glance was enough to convince him there had been no exaggeration. This was a crime scene. He put the Do Not Disturb sign on the handle and slipped the bolt.

''Holy mother of god.'' Webster sighed, perched carefully on the edge of a chair for a good long look at the place before he began wading through the mess.

The room was in chaos. The mattress, as Dr. Tom had said, was sliced open. Eight or ten long, jagged cuts. Stuffing torn out in handfuls. The pillows had been ripped apart, spewing fluffy down all over the floor. Some of the tiny feathers clung to the walls. There were bits of torn and shredded clothing everywhere. On the floor, the bed, hanging over the lamp shades. The bureau drawers had been gutted and smashed. A strong, flowery scent hung in the air. Webster was puzzled until he noticed the smashed perfume bottle.

A tube of red lipstick had been used to scrawl a message in foot-high letters, covering the full-length mirror:

DIE

DR. BITCH

DIE

Short, Webster thought, and right to the point.

"He what?" Tom asked. He realized he was almost shouting and tried to calm himself.

"Came and fetched her," Ozzie said. "Susan was going to see him. He showed up in that big green limo and saved her the trouble."

"And you let her go?"

Ozzie was amused by his anxiety. "Have a seat, Doc. Take a load off your feet. Coffee?"

"No thanks." Tom sat down, tried to force himself to relax. There was no reason to suspect that Susan would be in any physical danger from Kenneth Goddard. He was letting his protective instincts get the best of him. Just the same, he intended to check up on her within the hour.

Ozzie said, "You know the woman for a couple more days, you'll discover she comes and goes as she pleases."

"You're right, of course. Sorry I spoke out of turn."

"No need to apologize. We can both worry about her."

The strange little man seemed kind and sympathetic. Tom responded, feeling just a bit like a crazed adolescent. "So, uh, tell me about this boyfriend of hers," he asked. "The fiancé. How serious is it? Does Susan really want to marry him? What's he like?"

Ozzie giggled. His froglike eyes were glistening with tears of amusement. "Man, you really got it bad."

"I'm out of line?"

"Didn't say that. I was speaking of that four-letter word

gets everybody in so much trouble. L-O-V-E. Now, what do you want to know about Eliot James, aside from the fact he's a terrible snob, cute as a button, and rich as Donald Trump?''

Professor James was, in Ozzie's opinion, totally wrong for Susan. He was convinced she had been manipulated into setting a wedding date before she was really sure she wanted to get married.

"The man just wants another ornament in his life," Ozzie said. "He's got the prestige job, the big estate, social position; now he wants a pretty, intelligent wife to cap it off. Park her right next to his Mercedes coupe, take her out for a spin on weekends."

Tom laughed. "You really have it in for the guy."

"It's like this: Mr. Eliot James looks at me and sees a little colored man who should be holding up a lamp at the gate to his driveway."

"You think there's any hope for me?"

"Hope for what? Holding up a lamp? Forget it, you're too tall and too white. 'Scuze my sense of humor. Yeah, I do think you've got a pretty good chance. You really want to know, though, you'll have to ask the lady."

The telephone rang. Ozzie cradled the receiver between ear and shoulder. His eyes never left Tom. "Yeah, the doctor's in. Sure, I'll tell him." He put the receiver down. "Emergency at the clinic. That was a Dr. Nash. He wants you over there stat."

10:10 A.M.

The strobe stunned her eyes. Susan got up from the camera chair, blinking at little white dots. A minute later Goddard was pinning a laminated security pass to her blouse. He seemed very pleased, like a proud father. It was strange and not a little frightening.

"First we'll tour the target area, view the prototype. Then you'll have a basis for comparison."

Susan had agreed to visit the Experimental Division, lured

by his request for help. Something about filing a report that would, in his opinion, set everything right.

"As director of the Biohazard Lab, you'll lend a lot of credibility when I make my case," he said, leading her to an atrium where a half dozen motorized golf carts were plugged into battery chargers.

"The facility is larger than it looks," he explained. "These save time and energy."

Susan sat down in the adjoining seat as Goddard steered the cart through a maze of corridors. They emerged into a huge, aircraft hanger–sized building. The air was cool. She was glad she hadn't shed her down jacket. Goddard seemed unaffected by the temperature. The sweat was still trickling down his brow. Susan remembered that he had an amphetamine problem. Evidently he was kicking, and his body was sweating out the poison. She wondered how much the drug withdrawal was affecting his mind. Was he suffering from delusions and paranoia, common to amphetamine addiction? If so, the best thing to do was play along until she could get free of him.

An area in the center of the hangar was illuminated by powerful lights. Scaffolding had been erected around the illuminated area, and catwalks loomed high overhead, where, amidst the lights, an ominous, cannon-shaped object was visible, suspended from the roof beams. Goddard steered the cart to a place under the scaffolding. An open-caged elevator was waiting.

Goddard slid the gate back, followed her into the cage.

"It feels rickety," he said. "But the lift is rated for a thousand pounds, so we're safe."

Safe was a relative term, Susan reflected, hanging on to the safety bars with both hands. The cage jerked to a stop at the highest level of the catwalks.

"Mezzanine," Goddard joked, pulling back the gate.

White-coated technicians swarmed around a bank of monitors and a large computer console. No one paid any particular attention to her presence in the restricted area, or asked to see her pass. Being with Goddard was good enough.

The large object she had spotted from the distance was not

cannon-shaped, she decided when she saw it close up. More like a fat telescope, except that it was pointed the wrong way. The main body of the prototype was about twenty feet in length, not counting a hornlike extrusion at the business end. The whole device was suspended on a large gimbal, and counterweighted, so that it could be easily and accurately aimed by relatively small motors.

Goddard led her to the catwalk rail. The barrel of the prototype was almost close enough to reach out and touch.

"This is it," he announced. "PULSE. The section at the top is the vacuum pump. The pump feeds directly into the next chamber, which houses a beam-forming diode. Do you know anything about microwave propagation, Dr. Cullen?"

"Very little," she readily admitted.

"Not particularly complicated," Goddard said. "Much simpler than, say, a charged particle beam. Requires considerably less energy, too. What PULSE does, basically, is generate several signals of very pure frequency. What makes this prototype unique is the fact that it renders the signals into rapidly sequenced electromagnetic pulses. The pulses are extremely powerful, and of very short duration. A burst of pulses, if you will. The burst disrupts any other electrical field, including the natural electrical field generated by the primate nervous system and brain stem."

Susan didn't respond. She was gazing down into the illuminated target area, where workmen were busily erecting portable partitions that divided the area into a series of small cubicles. Like a giant rat maze, she thought, and the addition of chairs and tables meant the maze would be occupied not by albino rats but by human beings.

"I assumed our focusing device was adequate, but it now appears there has been significant sideways signal leakage from the horn," he said, gesturing at the business end of the tube. "It is a much less powerful pulse, although your research indicates the effect is not, unfortunately, insignificant."

"No," Susan said. "The pulses are strong enough to alter human blood and stimulate muscle responses in cadavers. I consider that pretty damn significant."

Goddard licked his lips, as if parched for water. "Yes,

yes,'' he said. "I share your concern, but I remain convinced PULSE can change the way we wage war. Fatalities will be a thing of the past. Why bother killing an army when a two-second burst from PULSE will render them helpless?''

"What's your definition of *helpless*?'' Susan asked.

"Unable to move, function, or think. Unable to fight or threaten.''

"So the victims might as well be dead, if your PULSE beam has made them into vegetables.''

Goddard became agitated. "No, no, it's not like that. Not like that at all. The damage to the nervous system is not permanent, we've shown that with the chimps. In time the effect wears off, the brain stem recovers. Surely that's better than wiping out an entire population? Or poisoning the environment with radiation that remains toxic for thousands of years? Can't you see the difference PULSE will make? PULSE will do away with the need for nuclear weapons, Dr. Cullen! It will change the world!''

There was no arguing with the man. He was a devout evangelist, ready to preach the gospel according to PULSE. He believed he had invented the weapon to end war. PULSE was his gift to humankind.

"This prototype is primitive. Overbuilt,'' he continued. "Capable of generating far more power than we've found to be necessary. With what we've learned here we can build a PULSE generator a tenth this size. Small enough to transport in an average aircraft. Jet fighters could fire PULSE bursts, rather than missiles or bullets. It could be retrofitted to existing tanks and gunships. In a decade, maybe less, we could have a PULSE weapon that fires like a rifle or handgun. Imagine, Dr. Cullen, a world where armies can fight but no one dies! War would become a chess match, a civilized method of settling rivalries.''

Was it the drug, Susan wondered, or the effects of withdrawal? Or was Goddard simply mad enough to believe his weapon would never be developed into a killing machine? Did he really believe that humankind was searching for a safe way to wage war? If that was the case, Susan thought, soldiers would be firing tranquilizing darts, not exploding bullets. The grim history of the twentieth century had revealed, time and again, that any new technology, from microbes to fusion, would be used to rain death and destruction, if at all possible. That was the lesson of chemical warfare, biological warfare, atomic warfare, and all the sophisticated hardwares that enabled humans to exterminate each other over vast distances.

PULSE would be no exception. If anything, it would be seen as a convenient means of violating the ban against chemical and biological weapons.

"Come on," Goddard said, clapping his hands together. "I'll show you the chimps. They're alive, Dr. Cullen. Living proof!"

As they rode the elevator down to the ground floor, Goddard's nose began to bleed. He was unaware of it until Susan produced a tissue from her purse.

"How odd," he said, tipping back his head. "Five years in the Apollo program, my nose never bled."

No, Susan thought, but five months of amphetamine abuse might do it. Crossing the target area, they had to dodge a dolly loaded with a pool table.

"All the comforts of home," Goddard commented. "That's Tony's idea. Great with all the little details, that boy."

"You're really going to test PULSE on humans?" Susan asked.

He nodded, leading her through a fire door into an adjacent area. "In forty-eight hours," he said. "Unless we can change their minds."

"Whose minds, exactly?"

"DARPA," he said. "I've been spending their money, now they want results."

"And they can countermand your orders, just like that?"

"No," Goddard said, blotting his nose with the tissue. "What they'll do is fire me. And if that happens, the project will be completely out of my control."

He pushed through another door. The smell hit Susan all at once. It was overpowering. She coughed, her eyes brimmed with tears. The air was hot and putrid.

"They really ought to do something about the ventilation

in here," Goddard said. "This is so bad I'm surprised the chimps can stand it."

A dozen cages were crammed into the room, set up in two rows of six. Antiseptically treated sawdust had been shoveled through the bars, but it did nothing to reduce the odor. At first Susan thought the chimps in the cages were dead. Then, overcoming her urge to retch, she was able to discern the faint glimmer of life in the dark, empty eyes. The second thing she noticed was that the eyes did not blink. Were the animals blind, or had their most basic instincts been erased?

The animal handler appeared from behind the cages. He wore a dirty pair of dungaree overalls and his right hand was in a flexible cast. He did not look pleased to see Goddard, and the displeasure was transferred to Susan.

"I was just cleaning up," he said defensively. "Hard to keep up with these friggin' monkeys, believe me. I almost liked it better when they were active, except we had to use a straitjacket on that big male. Vicious bastard. Not anymore, though. Gentle as a kitten."

"You're doing a splendid job," Goddard said, ignoring the filth and the mess. "Any progress to report?"

"Sort of," the man said, avoiding eye contact. "Another one died this morning. One of the females. We put the body in cold storage, like you said."

Goddard was aghast. He seemed to have forgotten Susan. "What happened?"

The handler shrugged. "Damned if I know. Choked to death, I guess, like the other two. They seem to get this spasm in the throat, and if you don't get to 'em quick, they stop breathin'. Weren't my fault, not this time."

Goddard recovered his composure. "Thank you. That will be all."

The handler was only too glad to hurry away.

"We've had some losses from this group," Goddard said. "Another reason I want to go over the data. These chimps were exposed to PULSE at thirty percent of capacity. Obviously the level was too high. They survived, most of them, but the recovery rate has been very slow."

"Recovery rate?" Susan said, incredulous. Most of the

animals were motionless, barely breathing. They had been rigged up for intravenous feeding, a glucose solution, apparently. "My God, what were they like before?"

"Totally incapacitated," Goddard said. "I admit, the improvement is subtle, but watch this."

He picked up the broom the handler had dropped and gently prodded a large male chimp through the bars. After a while the animal flinched and shifted slightly.

"Yesterday it didn't move at all," Goddard said triumphantly. "What's happening is that slowly they're relearning how to interpret signals from the brain stem. By this time next week I expect they may have relearned the instinct of hunger, and we'll be able to put them on solid food."

Susan felt sick. It was obvious to her that the chimps had sustained massive neurological damage. Hunger and the avoidance of pain were so deeply rooted in all mammals that the absence of such instincts indicated severe mental impairment.

"I've seen enough," Susan said.

Goddard seemed puzzled by her reaction. In his mind the chimps were well on the road to recovery. Outside the cage room Susan paused to catch her breath.

"We've got to do something," Susan said. "You can't expose human beings to PULSE."

"Not yet," Goddard agreed. "We need to study the data."

Not ever, Susan thought. *Not ever.*

11:15 A.M.

Dr. Tom Weston's heart was pounding with such force that it seemed to boom in his ears. His hands were shaking and his knees were weak, and to make matters worse the ether was making him dizzy.

Ether. This was back to the dark ages of surgery!

"We've got three choices," his buddy Al Nash had said. "We can cut into this girl without anesthetic, in which case the shock may kill her. Or you can calculate her body weight and put her on a respirator and administer the gases, in which case *you* might kill her. Or we can do it the old-fashioned way, with ether."

"Ether? Are you serious? I doubt we even *have* any ether in the clinic."

"Then you better find some, buddy boy, because I'll be damned if I'm going to take the fourth option, and that's to do nothing and watch her die of acute peritonital poisoning."

Tom hurried to the clinic pharmacy, but his first guess was correct. The clinic did not keep the volatile ether in stock. Then an inspiration struck and he ran out into the parking lot, skidded up to the Biohazard Lab, and begged Ozzie to tell him that, yes, the lab had ether.

"Easy," Ozzie had said. "Sure we're got ether. What are you, an addict?"

"What?"

"Sniffing ether fumes. Used to be a popular addiction amongst physicians."

"Acute peritonitis," Tom explained. "The Medivac is grounded because of the weather, so we can't fly her to Portland. Dr. Nash is cutting."

"I didn't know Nash was a surgeon," Ozzie said, handing over a pint can of ethyl ether.

Tom was already running. "No choice," he said.

There was always a choice, of course. The prudent thing to do, from a legal standpoint, would be to send the girl to Maine Medical Center by ambulance. It was possible she might survive a two-hour trip over snowy roads, and in any event the responsibility would no longer be theirs. Al Nash never even considered such an option. Jenny Pearson was five years old, one of the first babies he had delivered in Sprauken, and he was damned if he was going to let a child he had brought into the world expire because the attending physicians didn't want to risk a lawsuit.

Al was already scrubbed when Tom got back to the clinic.

"I've sedated her slightly," he said. "She was already delirious with pain and fever. I don't think she has any idea what we're about to do."

"Al, where does Jenny live?"

"East Meadow complex," Al said. He scowled. "What does that have to do with her peritonitis?"

"I'm not sure," Tom said. "Except that her home is only a few hundred yards from the Experimental Division. It may fit into the pattern Dr. Cullen is investigating."

"Save it, Tom. I need to concentrate on the immediate needs here."

"Sorry," Tom said. "Thinking out loud. What about the mother?"

"In there with her. She stays."

"If she can handle it," Tom said.

Al gave him a funny look. "The mom can handle it. She was eighteen hours in labor with this kid. Try excreting a watermelon for eighteen hours, Tom. Do that and you can handle most anything."

"Take it easy," Tom said, taking his place at the scrub sink. "I've got the ether."

"Sorry," his old friend said. "Who I'm worried about is not the mother, Tom. It's you. You look almost as sick as that kid. Are you ready for this? Hell, we haven't even got a qualified OR nurse on duty. The family could sue us from here to Hades if we goof this up, you know."

Tom nodded. He knew the risk. As an internist in generalized medicine, he had great confidence in his diagnostic abilities. As a seat-of-the-pants anesthesiologist he was afraid of aggravating an already grave situation. His distrust of "old-fashioned" medicine was profound. He believed that in the good old days surgeons killed almost as many as they saved. Ether, which first came into use in 1846, was about as "old-fashioned" as medicine could get.

"What scares me is not a lawsuit, Al," he said. "What scares me is, I'm afraid we're going to lose her. Her white cell count is extremely high. The peritonitis must be well advanced."

It was Tom Weston's experience that appendicitis in children usually occurred over a period of hours or even days. The symptoms were almost always severe abdominal pain accompanied by nausea and a low fever. Even in cases where the appendix had perforated, leading to peritonitis, the physician and the family usually had at least a few hours in which to arrange surgery. Often Dr. Weston was aware of a potential case days in advance, and planned accordingly.

This case was like nothing he had ever encountered. Little Jenny Pearson, hale and hearty moments before, had suddenly collapsed at the breakfast table. There had been no complaints of pain or nausea, no loss of appetite. According to her mother, the child had turned gray before her eyes, then suddenly collapsed into a fetal position. The ambulance crew assumed that the little girl had ingested a household poison. They ransacked the kitchen, finding nothing that could have caused such an instantaneous reaction. After being rushed to the clinic ER—already overcrowded with clients complaining of various nerve-related ailments—blood had been drawn and hurriedly tested. Jenny Pearson's appendix had ruptured without warning, spewing deadly bacterial poisons into her bloodstream.

The nearest practicing surgeon was two hours away. Al Nash elected himself cutter, as he had actually performed an appendectomy or two during his residency, nearly eight years before.

"We've never done abdominal surgery here," Tom reminded him. "We always send them to Portland."

"Crack that can of ether, big guy. And try not to let Jenny or her mother know you're scared shitless."

He tried. And once the cutting actually began, once he realized that Al Nash did indeed remember each step of the classic operation, then he began to relax. He administered the anesthetic the dreaded "old-fashioned" way, by dripping ether onto a gauze mask covering Jenny's nose and mouth. Mustn't overdo it, he kept reminding himself, recalling the old horror stories about children who never came out of ether anesthesia.

The mother, despite Al's prediction of steadfastness, fled the moment the scalpel sliced open her daughter's belly. Tom didn't blame her.

"I've exposed the cecum area of the large intestine," Nash said. "There's the perforation. No trace of a fecalith. Possible necrosis of the appendicidal tissue. Drain, please."

Nash inserted a drain into the ruptured appendix, spent twenty minutes carefully cleaning the area of all visible pus and secretions, and prepared to close the incision. The actual removal of the appendix would be undertaken at a later date, after Jenny's blood count had returned to normal.

As soon as the stitches were in, Tom removed the gauze mask from Jenny's face. Pulse and heartbeat had remained fairly strong throughout. Her eyes flickered, and there was every indication that she would come out of anesthesia quickly. Al Nash ordered intravenous antibiotics to begin immediately and then strode out to find the girl's mother before Tom had a chance to congratulate him on a job well done.

He had peeled off his greens and was washing up, feeling just a bit shaky, when he remembered Al's observations of the affected area. *No fecalith,* he had said. A fecalith was an obstruction to the appendix, the cause of swelling and eventual perforation. If there hadn't been a fecalith, why had the appendix suddenly perforated? And why had Jenny been struck down without the usual warning signals of peritonitis? Was it due to proximity to the Experimental Division? Could microwave leakage affect the inner organs, producing such unusally quick symptoms? Or was he just being paranoid, willing to blame the mysterious leaks for every recent illness in the village?

Tom didn't have much time to ponder the possibilities. He headed straight back to the Biohazard Lab to see if Susan had checked in.

After sealing Dr. Cullen's suite, Jack Webster drove around to Kurt Mallon's apartment. Mallon's cruiser was parked outside. The shades to his bedroom window were drawn. The boy was getting some shut-eye after a late shift. Perfectly normal activity.

The temptation was to go in there and ask him point-blank: *Hey kid, some perp with a sick mind trashed Dr. Cullen's room, left a threat on the mirror. Is that sick someone you by any chance?*

The evidence so far was hardly compelling. It had been established that (a) the doctor had seen Mallon in the vicinity shortly before she survived a potentially fatal skiing mishap; (b) Mallon apparently had Dr. Cullen, and possibly Dr. Weston, under surveillance, and was able to intercept them at the Experimental Division; (c) Mallon had obtained a card that gave him access to all the rooms at the inn.

Circumstantial at best. Any half-assed defense attorney could get the case laughed out of court if a prosecutor was imprudent enough to file charges. Before he could go any further, Webster had to find either hard evidence or compelling motive.

He decided to start with motive. Back at the Security office he reached for the Rolodex and looked up the number of an old crony who was still active in the Bureau.

"Steve? Jack Webster. Hey-hey, Steve-a-reeno, I knew you when. What do I mean when? When I was an SA and you were a rookie still tripping on your dick, *that's* when. Those were the days, huh? You bet I remember J. Edgar, that faggy Fascist bastard. Don't worry, I'm positive he can't hear me. They don't have phone taps in hell—at least I *hope* they don't."

Webster thought about putting his feet up on the desk, settled for the chair instead. While he chatted about old times with Steve he reached into the bottom drawer, got out a cigar, and peeled the cellophane.

"Yeah, listen, it's great. The hell with retirement. I got a nice little town to look after here. A great benefit package, even better than the Feds. And the area, Steve. Fishing, hiking, skiing, whatever you want. Mostly what I do is, I've got this bass boat, right? Yeah, just like one of those dumbass tubs you see on TV. And come spring I put on the funny hat and throw some beers in the cooler, and trailer the thing around the lake country. Steve, I swear to you there are largemouth bass so big they could swallow me and the boat and the trailer. Absolutely. Of course you're invited. You ever get up this way and you *don't* stop in I'll be all over your case. Yeah. Well, check it out if you're curious. Sprauken International is security conscious as a bastard, and they prefer to hire ex-Feds, I guess because that impresses the Pentagon. So you'd have that advantage, you want to apply for a job."

Webster took a long, luxurious puff on the cigar. How could anything that felt so good be bad for his health?

"Why I called, aside from checking to see if you're screwing up like you always did, is I've got a favor to ask. Now don't get all edgy, Steve, you know damn well I wouldn't ask you anything might jeopardize your pension. What I need, if you could punch in this name. Mallon, M-A-L-L-O-N. Kurt, K-U-R-T." Webster followed with Kurt's Social Security number and date of birth. "Whatever you can find. Start with Juvy. I think he grew up in Florida, and he did time in the military. I've got a partial service record here, he turned in a dupe with the job application. I want the complete service file on this boy, if you can get it. Anything juicy. And Steve? I'm serious about the bass fishing. Absolutely."

Webster put down the receiver, concentrated on blowing smoke rings. All he could do now was wait.

Goddard had insisted that she type her report directly into the code machine. *Report* was a misnomer. It was really more of a memo, an informed professional opinion. Susan was dubious about whether her word would convince a powerful Pentagon agency to suspend testing on a billion-dollar weapons project, but Goddard seemed to think it might help, so it was worth a shot.

FROM: DR. SUSAN CULLEN, DIRECTOR BIOHAZARD LAB, SPRAU-KEN INTERNATIONAL

ATTENTION: BUREAU OF SPECIAL PROJECTS OVERSIGHT [BOSPO] DEFENSE ADVANCED RESEARCH PROJECTS AGENCY [DARPA] DEFENSE CONTRACTOR LIAISON [DECAL]

SUBJECT: LEAKAGE OF HIGH-ENERGY MICROWAVE PULSE, ENVIRONS OF SPRAUKEN, MAINE.

AFTER INTENSIVE INVESTIGATION OF NEUROLOGICAL AND HEMATOLOGICAL ABERRATIONS IN RESIDENT POPULATION, THE BIOHAZARD LAB RECOMMENDS ALL HIGH-ENERGY MICROWAVE PULSE TESTING BE SUSPENDED UNTIL FURTHER EVALUATION OF DATA IS CONCLUDED. IRREFUTABLE EVIDENCE THAT PULSE LEAKAGE ADVERSELY AFFECTS HEALTH OF RESIDENTS. NERVE AND BLOOD CHEMISTRY DAMAGE DOCUMENTED. HEALTH RISK INTOLERABLE.

REPLY REQUESTED.

Susan used two fingers to punch at the keys. When she was satisfied with the results she pushed the SEND key, as Goddard had instructed, and the words were wiped from the screen.

I never mentioned the deadwalkers, she thought. Then again, if DARPA doesn't respond to health threats to the living, they certainly wouldn't care what happened to the dead. Better this way. Keep it simple. "Health risk intolerable," that got the message across in no uncertain terms. Now at least she was on record.

"Dr. Goddard? Are you there?"

They'd come back to the executive office building to use the encoding machine. As soon as they got inside the door Goddard had taken off his shoes and socks. In bare feet he showed her how to use the encoding machine, which was no more complicated than a personal computer. Then he had vanished into an adjoining room.

"Dr. Goddard? I sent the report. You want to check it out, make sure they got it on the other end?"

Susan got up from the desk. Strange, she thought she heard the faint chirping of a bird. Impossible.

"Dr. Goddard?"

It was not a bird sound, she decided; then again, it wasn't quite human, either. Determined to investigate, uncertain of what she might find, Susan entered the adjoining room. It was not, as she assumed, another office or workroom, but a large executive bathroom. Done up in the best Sprauken style. Lots of black marble tiles and deep mirrors. It was the mirrors that confused her at first. The sight of herself receding into infinity.

Then she heard the sound again, and knew he was weeping. She found him slumped in a corner. His naked ankles were raw and inflamed from the scratches. His nose had started bleeding again. Two thin red threads had already stained the black marble.

When Goddard spotted her, the first thing he tried to do was hide the empty pill bottle. When he saw that it was useless he covered his eyes with his trembling hands and said, "Gone, all gone. I don't remember taking that many. Somebody is *stealing* from me."

Susan soaked a washcloth under the cold water. She tipped his head back and began to blot up the blood under his nostrils. His eyes stopped flitting and locked onto her.

"Help me," he said. "Please help me."

12:01 P.M.

He woke up in a cold sweat, reaching out to stop her. He was a child hiding in the shed and she was coming at him with the poultry shears.

You filthy boy.

Mallon sat up, tried to shake free of the dream. He was not a ten-year-old boy. He was not hiding in a shed behind a trailer in Florida, and his mother was not chasing him with poultry shears. His mother was dead. She could never threaten, never touch him again.

He had to do something to stop the nightmares. They were beginning to intrude on reality. There were times when he thought he saw his mother out of the corner of his eyes. Just a glint of sharp steel, darting around a corner, a furtive shadow he could never quite bring into focus. And her voice was never far. That peculiar voice, thick with alcohol. *Come here, boy. See what momma's got for you.* Sometimes it was a treat: candy or a new toy. Other times it was the back of her hand, or an unexpected, intensely disturbing kiss on the lips.

You never knew what was coming from her. You had to be ready to run and hide. Or stand and fight. He'd never quite had the courage for that, not with *her.*

Mallon dragged himself from the sweat-soaked bed and jerked open the curtains. Snow was falling. More goddamn snow. The whole world was dead, frozen. The good thing about snow, it covered your tracks.

You filthy brat, the voice said.

"Shut up," he said. *"Shut up!"*

"We've got two days," Susan said. "We can make a whole lot of noise in two days, if need be."

Ozzie had borrowed a phone book from the clinic. He was checking off numbers for the daily newspapers, television stations, the governor's office, the Public Health Department, the local branch of the AMA (fat chance *they* would be much help, he thought, but you never know), any person or agency who might conceivably have an interest in a public health hazard in a remote village in Maine.

"If we don't have a positive answer by tomorrow morning, we'll arrange to hold a press conference."

"Here?" Ozzie said, looking around the lab.

"Not in the village. The media would never get past the front gates. We'll hold it in Augusta, the state capital. On the steps of the State House," Susan said, warming to the idea. "That will get some attention."

Ozzie began transferring the list of phone numbers to the computer. "What about them?" he asked, clicking away on the keyboard.

"Who?"

"The volunteers Goddard mentioned. The human test subjects. Any idea who they are, when they're scheduled to arrive?"

Susan shook her head. "I'm not sure Goddard knew. He was leaving it all to one of his subordinates. I got the impression the subjects were somehow connected to the military."

"That would make sense," Ozzie said. "According to CYTO, soldiers from Fort Dietrich were used in Project Pandora. I think the volunteer situation should be our first priority, agreed?"

Susan nodded. "Absolutely. If what happened to the chimps is any indication, humans exposed to PULSE will be rendered brain dead. Goddard has convinced himself the neurological damage is reversible, but I saw no evidence of that."

She had managed to get Kenneth Goddard home and into his own bed, where she administered an intravenous injection of Thorazine to help ease his anxiety. Sedated and drowsy, he seemed grateful for her kindness. Calling the clinic hotline, she arranged for around-the-clock nursing. Tom Weston, alerted shortly after he concluded emergency surgery, had agreed to check on the patient and try to persuade him to voluntarily check into a detox facility. Presumably Tom was over there now.

"It's not just the amphetamines," Susan reflected. "I think this whole business has driven the man half crazy with stress."

Her hours with Goddard had been nerve-racking, but she came away with a sense of what compelled him. The PULSE project was a temptation he could not resist. Perfecting the device, building a functional prototype, it was the challenge of a lifetime, akin to taking part in the astronaut program. At the same time he needed to convince himself that PULSE was really a good thing. He couldn't bear to be the inventor of a grotesque killing machine. Hence the delusions. A different sort of man would have just gone ahead and made the deadliest weapon possible, never mind the conseqences. In some ways Susan admired Goddard for at least struggling with his conscience, screwed up as he was.

Ozzie remained skeptical. Results counted with him, not motivations. "They find out he's the one who got you to file that memo and stir up trouble, you know what they'll do to him?"

"What?"

"Take away his big green limousine. And his title, and whatever else the executive wolf pack can strip off him."

"He'll be fine," Susan said. "Don't forget, he's Kenneth Goddard, the Apollo hero. Sprauken won't fire him—too much danger of a backlash from Congress."

"Not us, though," Ozzie said. "We're expendable."

"We'll land on our feet," Susan promised. "Something good will come of this. I can feel it."

"What's that?" Ozzie said, smiling. "Woman's intuition?"

"Call it a hunch."

Tony whistled as he set about altering the computer program for the human test sequence. Changing the program was simple. He used Goddard's access code, called up the file called SEQUENCING: POWER LEVELS & DURATION. It was simply a matter of adding one little zero. Kenneth Goddard had decided the first phase of human testing would use a maximum of ten percent of available power.

Tony made it one hundred percent.

That was it, his big plan to discredit the boss and take over as Special Project Director. So simple a ten-year-old hacker could have done it, provided he had the access code. That was the beauty, Tony thought, it was perfect. Add one little extra zero and a baker's dozen of elderly duffers would go to their reward a few weeks ahead of schedule. Zapped into eternity.

Goddard would freak out, guaranteed. He would blame himself for the error. Lapse of concentration due to drug abuse. The final mental meltdown.

Colonel Bentley might suspect who had really altered the program, but there was no way he could prove a thing. Besides, the colonel *wanted* to see what PULSE could do at full power. He'd as much as said so.

"Faro!"

Think of the devil. Tony flinched, then cooled himself out. He casually locked in the altered program and turned off the computer screen.

"Yes, Colonel?"

As usual Bentley looked as if he had a spine made from machined titanium. The ultimate uptight, upright marine. "At ease" meant he let his eyebrows relax. Now here he was holding a sheet of computer printout by the edge, between thumb and forefinger, as if it were a piece of soiled toilet paper.

"You have a problem?" Tony asked, forcing a smile.

"No, *we* have a problem. Check it out."

Tony read the memo. He looked up, puzzled. "How the hell did that crazy broad find out about the project?"

Colonel Bentley snatched the memo back. "I was going to ask you that very question and then I came to my senses and decided to look into it myself. Item: Goddard arranged to get a security clearance for Dr. Cullen. Item: Goddard gave her the grand tour this morning. Item: this memo was entered into the code machine in his office."

"And was it sent?"

"Of course. And Goddard's code machine routed copies not only to DARPA, but also to the Congressional Defense Oversight Committee."

Tony closed his eyes and gritted his perfect teeth.

"Fortunately the committee won't be back in closed session until Tuesday," Colonel Bentley said. "I'll see that DARPA sends an officer over to brief them to our point of view, but there's no guarantee the members will see it our way. They may decide to go along with Dr. Cullen's recommendation to hold off on testing. I never met a congressman who didn't love a delay."

"How is DARPA going to respond to the memo?" Tony wanted to know. He had an idea, another perfectly simple idea, and there was no reason it wouldn't work.

"In the negative, of course. You think we're going to let one softheaded M.D. throw a monkey wrench in a billion-dollar project?"

"Of course not," Tony said. "Has the response been cabled yet?"

Colonel Bentley shook his head. "They're waiting on me."

"Keep 'em waiting," Tony suggested. "Better yet, keep *her* waiting."

"What are you suggesting?" Colonel Bently said.

"I'm suggesting we move the test up. Run it tonight. That way we have the human data base we need, no matter what happens with Congress."

Colonel Bentley stared at him. Giving nothing away. "You can do that?" he asked softly. "You can pull off a midnight run?"

"Watch me," Tony said.

1:00 P.M.

When Tom Weston entered the lab, stamping snow from his boots, there were thin blue electrical wires protruding from under a flap on his parka. He was so happy to see Susan that he momentarily forgot the piece of equipment in his pocket as he sought to embrace her.

"Easy," Susan said, laughing. "I'm breakable, if you squeeze hard enough."

"Sorry. After an hour with Kenneth Goddard I'm a bit raw around the edges."

"How is he?"

"Nothing wrong with him a month in detox and a decade in therapy won't cure," Tom said, peeling off his parka. "Part of the time he thought he was back in outer space. Kept saying he felt weightless. I'd say he was long overdue for a leave of absence. Now what's the word on this big test he kept mumbling about? Is that for real? He seemed to think stopping it was up to you."

Susan briefed him on the memo she'd sent to DARPA, and the course of action she and Ozzie had agreed on if the memo failed to halt testing on the prototype.

"Basically we need to mobilize the media," she said. "We'll give DARPA twenty-four hours to make good. If they don't we'll go public."

"Do they know you intend to do that? Go public I mean?"

"No," Susan said. "At least I didn't mention that in the memo. Although Goddard seems to think his office was bugged. I'm not sure. Could have been speed freak paranoia."

"Maybe not," Tom said. "And that reminds me," he said, removing a small electronic unit from the parka. "I ripped this out of the Jeep. One of the many options I've never used. Maybe Ozzie can give me a hand rigging it up in here."

"A radar detector?"

"Sure," he said. "I figure if a cop's radar gun will set it off from half a mile away, whatever they're doing in Experimental ought to make it scream like a banshee."

Ozzie quickly wired up a voltage converter, plugging the radar detector into a twelve-volt line. "Sort of tickles me to think a made-in-Korea gadget might blow the whistle on a billion-dollar project," he said, patting the little unit.

The telephone rang. They all jumped. Susan answered. Covering the mouthpiece, she said, "For you, Tom. Dr. Nash at the clinic."

"Not again," Tom said. He grabbed the phone. "Al, what's wrong?"

"Easy, pal," Nash said. "I've got everything under control. I just had a talk with the Chief of Medicine at Maine Medical Center, and he's agreed to send two of his best internists over to the clinic to assist with the overload of clients in the ER."

"Beautiful," Tom said. "How'd you manage that?"

"Abject begging," Nash said. "I cried, I pleaded. Has Dr. Cullen isolated this mysterious toxin she was worried about? There's a rumor about a nerve gas circulating. I'd like to quell that if I could."

Tom looked at Susan, who was listening in on an extension. She shook her head.

"No truth to the nerve gas rumor, Al," Tom said. He added, cautiously, "Dr. Cullen will be issuing a report in another day or so. There's no reason to panic. We expect the symptoms to cease, and things will get back to normal."

"Can't tell your old buddy what the big secret is yet, huh?"

"Soon, Al, soon. But not over the phone."

"Okay. Grab some shut-eye, Weston. You left here dead on your feet."

Tom rang off. Susan hung up the extension and said, "He's got a point. We could all use a few hours' sleep. We'll need clear heads if we have to orchestrate a media blitz."

Ozzie elected to stay at the lab.

"Three's a crowd," he said with a wink. "You kids want to be alone. I'll catch a few z's right here on the cot. It won't be the first time."

"Call us if DARPA responds to the cable," Susan fretted. "Or if the radar detector goes off."

"Relax," Ozzie assured her, urging them out the door. "I've got it under control."

The driveway was empty. For a moment Mallon thought he was early. He checked his watch. Right on time. Then he realized that Tony Faro's BMW would be stored in the garage, out of harm's way. Tony was a prudent man, a thinker, a planner. Tony had a vision, and now it seemed he was willing to share it, for he'd been surprisingly friendly over the phone.

"Come on by," he'd said. "It's Sunday afternoon; we could watch a little gridiron action."

"I'm off duty," Mallon had stammered.

"Hey great. See you in half an hour, exactly."

Mallon parked his cruiser in the empty driveway, locked it, and walked up a neatly shoveled sidewalk. There was a Christmas wreath on Tony's door. Probably still had the tree up. Somehow Kurt couldn't visualize Tony Faro decorating a Christmas tree. He was the type who would hire someone to do it.

The door opened before his fist could descend.

"Hey, Kurt!" A gleaming smile split Tony's face. "Come on in, buddy."

"Afternoon, Mr. Faro."

Tony put a friendly arm on his guest's shoulder, swept him inside the door. The smile vanished. His eyes went hard.

"Something wrong, Mr. Faro?" Mallon asked.

"Not a thing, buddy boy."

He raised a finger to his lips. Mallon understood that he was not to talk. Tony led him into a living room, spacious by village standards, and indicated that Mallon sit on a suede leather couch. Mallon sat. The leather was as soft as a woman's purse. It made him feel tingly and ill at ease.

"Beer?" Tony was behind the bar. Mallon, not knowing if he should speak, merely nodded. A bottle of imported beer came sailing through the air. Mallon caught it.

"What do we have here, a great little play-off game or what?"

The question was rhetorical as Tony used a remote control to activate a television screen. The smash-'n-crash noises of pro football filled the room.

"Leapin' lizards!" Tony shouted above the noise. "Look at them linebackers pull to the left. Go get 'em. Stomp his ass into the Astroturf!"

Mallon fidgeted. What the hell was Tony trying to prove? That he was one of the boys? He put the beer bottle down. The cap didn't twist off and Tony hadn't bothered to open it.

"What'd you say, Kurt? You want to hear some rock 'n roll? No problem!"

Tony touched the remote control. The stereo came on, nearly drowning out the football game. Heavy metal. Mallon hated heavy metal. He hated music of any kind.

"This is my favorite thing!" Tony shouted, gesturing at the television. "Watch how they move. It sort of goes with the music, don't you think?"

Mallon did not reply. On the monitor, huge robotlike figures clashed in slow motion, a blur of bright uniforms.

Tony placed a gym bag between Mallon's feet and sat down on the couch. He was very close. Mallon wanted to move away—he didn't like being touched—but Tony snaked an arm around his shoulders and pulled him close. Close enough so Mallon could feel the moist breath in his ear.

"We might have an insect problem," Tony said. "An infestation. Bugs, Kurt, electronic bugging devices. They're everywhere. You just sit still and listen, okay?"

Mallon nodded. His hands clenched until his knuckles went white. Tony Faro's voice was practically inside his head.

"Now inside that gym bag is a twelve-pound magnet. You put the bag on a stack of computer tapes or disks, it will erase them, got it? Just nod."

Mallon nodded. He knew about magnets and computer tapes. He'd seen it on a television cop show.

"Dr. Cullen is becoming a problem," Tony said. "She has been collecting data that may be damaging to national security. I can arrange to zero-out the mainframe memory in Virginia, but I can't do anything about the terminal in the lab, or any disks she may have stored there. That's where you come in, Kurt old buddy. All you have to do, pass the magnet over any disks you find. Think you can do that?"

Mallon nodded. More than anything he wanted Tony Faro to stop breathing moist air in his ear.

"Just remember (a) magnet, (b) computer disks. It's very simple. The hard part is sneaking into the lab without getting caught. No witnesses, Kurt. Go in at night. Be discreet. You think you can be discreet about this?"

Mallon nodded again.

"Add that to the list, Kurt. (A) magnet, (b) computer disks, (c) discretion. We're in a sensitive area, here. National security. Your country is depending on you. The company is depending on you. And I, fool that I am, *I'm* depending on you. Tell me you won't fuck up this time, Kurt.''

Mallon nodded.

"No, tell me. Whisper it, Kurt. Whisper it like you really mean it.''

Tony tugged at his earlobe, waiting.

Kurt whispered, "I won't fuck up, Mr. Faro.''

In a voice loud enough to carry over the football and the rock 'n roll, Tony said, "You're beautiful, you know that, Kurt? You're a beautiful person. Have another beer?''

Mallon's first beer was still unopened. Also, he noticed, there was no Christmas tree.

It happened very naturally. Nothing awkward about it.

Tom showered first. He let the hot water thrum against the back of his neck. As a relaxant it was better than a stiff drink. He shaved, found that he liked what he saw of himself in the steamed-up glass, and entered the bedroom wearing a bathrobe.

"Your turn,'' he said to Susan, who was wrapped in a large bath towel.

Tom got into bed while Susan showered. It sounded like distant rain on a summer day. He lay flat on his back, fingers laced behind his head, and tried to examine his feelings. That was supposed to be very important, examining your feelings. It was not something that came naturally to him. Still, he wanted to know why he felt so right about Susan Cullen. Why it seemed there was a place for her in his heart, a place that did not intrude on his memories of Jeannie.

Because you're falling in love, you big goofus.

I'll always love you, Jean of my dreams.

Fine. Now try not to think so hard. Let it happen. Enjoy your life.

The weight of sorrow and grieving lifted away, replaced by a quiet sensation of total contentment. Susan came back into the bedroom and dropped her towel.

"Know what I think?'' she whispered, climbing under the blanket. "I think this is going to be great.''

It was.

Sunday Evening,
January 11

5:32 P.M.

"Creamed corn," Bernie said. "From the can."

"Where else?" Sam retorted. "They got maybe fresh corn on the cob this time of year? Sure it's from the can."

For the occasion of Sunday dinner they had decided to get out of bed and eat at the card table. This was discouraged by the nursing staff, but Sam put up such a fuss they conceded. The card table was near the window, with a steam radiator under the sill. The glass was fogged with moisture. It didn't matter: night had fallen and there was nothing to see.

"I never liked cream corn," Bernie said.

"So don't eat it."

Bernie Simms had no intention of eating the creamed corn, or the grayish beets, or the so-called chicken breast, or the slime-green gelatin square. Waiting had soured what little remained of his appetite. Formerly a robust man of 190 pounds, who had no trouble swinging Louise around when the mood struck him, he was down to a scrawny 140 or so. Partly that was his bum ticker: shedding the weight made each heartbeat that much easier. The rest of it was in his head. You quit eating when you were getting ready to quit living, is what the cardiologist had told him. The man was right.

"Maybe they decided not to use us," Bernie said.

"They already paid us the money," Sam said. "They'll

240

use us. You should relax. We've been waiting here only five days so far. It could be weeks more. You know how the government likes to make us wait.''

"This isn't the government. This is private enterprise.''

"Big business," Sam said. "Big government. What's the difference? Your wife Louise is now provided for, which is a load off your mind, am I correct?''

"Yeah," Bernie said. "Sure.''

"So what's your hurry?''

To change the subject, and elevate his mood if possible, Bernie agreed to play cribbage. Sam was the better player, and delighted in winning, which made it something of an ordeal. It was either cribbage or the television, and in the remote, central Maine mill town where the rest home was located, reception was limited to two channels. The mountains blocked the signals; they had no cable—it was that kind of place.

Sam shuffled the cards and dealt rapidly. There was nothing wrong with his hands. His hands, Bernie noticed, were like those of a much younger man.

"Did I tell you about the jar?" Sam asked.

Bernie shook his head. Did he mean bedpan?

"Something I saw in an old movie. A brain in a jar. They kept it alive in there, these scientists.''

"You're thinking of *Frankenstein*," Bernie suggested.

"Maybe. I don't remember the monster. All I remember is this jar with a brain inside. And the brain was alive. They had it hooked up to wires and you could hear what it was thinking.''

"Not *Frankenstein*," Bernie said, turning over a card. "Another movie, I can't remember the title.''

"Doesn't matter. Only it gave me this idea. There's nothing wrong with my brain. Inside I'm sharp as a tack. I can still add a column of figures, I can still review all the facts of a situation and come to an intelligent conclusion, I can still remember exactly what Lotte Lenya smelled like when I passed close by her in the Carnegie Delicatessen in 1949. She smelled like white grapes, in case you're interested.''

Bernie said, "She had a voice like smoke.''

Sam nodded. "Exactly like smoke. On the records it sounds higher, but in person, no.''

Bernie tried to steer the conversation to jazz singers and the musicals of Bertolt Brecht. The idea of jars and brains gave him the creeps. But Sam wasn't buying. He had something to say on the subject.

"I'm thinking, maybe this jar idea is a possibility. It's only my lungs are dying. Inside his brain Sam Carnovitz is very much alive. So put me in a jar—I mean the modern equivalent, something very high-tech—and I'll be content."

Bernie shuddered.

"For me the intellect is the most important," Sam said. "Also the smell of white grapes, and all the other things I remember. A lifetime."

"It was just a silly movie, Sam."

"You think I don't know? Of course I know. I'm speaking of comfort. This morning was very bad for me, if you recall, and so I invented this idea about the jar. I am suggesting you do the same. You have a good mind, Bernie. Invent something to hope for. You require something different, a mechanical heart, perhaps. A new drug that repairs the flesh."

Bernie shook his head. "What crazy ideas you have."

"Not so crazy. The mind is a wonderful thing. In the desert a man sees water, and it comforts him."

"Play the cards, Bernie."

As he watched Sam's nimble fingers move the pegs around the cribbage board, Bernie thought, *A drug that repairs the heart, is it possible?*

Sam was adding up the points, in his head, of course, when the punk with the blond haircut, Tony No Last Name, sauntered into the ward.

A fist clenched in Bernie's heart. This was it.

"Can I have your attention," the young man said, reading from a clipboard. "You're being transferred to the test facility. Transportation is waiting. The nursing staff will assist in the transfer. I expect your complete cooperation in this matter. Thank you."

Several of the men had questions. The young man raised his hand like a traffic cop, cutting them off. "Save your questions for later. Right now the important thing is to get this show on the road."

Sam Carnovitz deliberately shuffled the cards. "What's the hurry!" he called out, and then fell into a fit of coughing.

"National security," the young man responded. "You'll have to trust me on this."

The transportation that had come for them was not, as Bernie had imagined, a yellow school bus. The transportation was two white vans, rented from Avis. Sam got a kick out of that.

"They try harder," he said.

Jack Webster was settled deep in his recliner, drinking a diet cola because it reminded him of beer and watching the New England Patriots blow a huge play-off lead, when the call came through. Jack knew on the first ring who it was. He had a good instinct for phone calls.

"Yo, Steve-a-reeno," he crooned into the receiver. "How come you're working on Sunday? Favor for a friend? He better be a good friend, huh? Tell you what this good friend of yours is going to do. He's going to send you a round-trip ticket from Dulles to the Portland International Jetport, which you'll think is a pretty funny name when you see the place. Get yourself up here just before the fishing season opens, we'll try for the first salmon. You know about that? First salmon caught is supposed to go to the White House, the president has it for dinner. Old Maine tradition. Few years ago the guy who hooked the first salmon reneged. Said the hell with the White House, it was his fish. Some nerve, huh?"

Webster had clicked off the sound on the television. As he chatted with Steve he stared at the luminous screen. Helmets collided. The ball was torn away from a red jersey. In Super Slo-Mo it looked like a bomb leaving an aircraft. The Pats were disintegrating.

"No, I'm not pulling your leg, Steve. I'm serious. Absolutely. I've never actually fished salmon, so what we'll do, we'll hire a guide. That's right, he'll even bait the hook if you want him to. Of course we'll probably be using lures, not bait. Damn right it sounds like a great time. . . . Okay, sure, I'm ready for a load of dirt. Go ahead and hit me."

The FBI file on Kurt Mallon was not extensive, as the Bureau had never had cause to initiate an investigation involving him. The Bureau did, of course, have access to records kept by the Division of Juvenile Crimes, State of Florida. Steve had also obtained a duplicate of the complete file on Mallon's U.S. Army service record.

"What did he do as a kid?" Webster asked. "Steal a car? Drug problem? What?"

Kurt Mallon had never stolen a car, nor, so far as the Florida DJC had determined, did he indulge in drugs. Mallon had come under the authority of the Juvenile Enforcement system only once, for a destruction-of-property offense. He made restitution and was put on probation.

"He what?" Webster said. A chill went down his spine as Steve described the crime. "Tell it to me slow."

At fifteen Mallon had been arrested at an apartment complex in Hallandale, where he had allegedly destroyed numerous items of women's clothing. The clothing had been hung out to dry. According to the responding officer's deposition, Mallon had been cutting up lingerie with a pair of poultry shears when apprehended. The boy testified that he was disturbed by the recent death of his mother, who had fallen down a flight of steps while inebriated, and the caseworker recommended he be released to the custody of his stepfather, who had moved to Conway, New Hampshire.

"And that's it?" Webster said. "Nothing else in the Juvy file?"

The Bureau had no further record of Kurt Mallon until he entered the military three years later, on his eighteenth birthday. After fourteen months of active duty the onetime candidate for an elite Special Forces unit had received a psychiatric discharge. The discharge resulted from an incident involving an assault against an officer. The officer happened to be a female.

"What kind of assault, exactly?" Webster asked. "He use the scissors again?"

Kurt Mallon had attacked the female officer with a six-inch Bowie-type knife, of the kind issued to Special Forces personnel. The female was herself a Special Forces graduate, as well as a martial arts expert, and she had disarmed Mallon in full view of his company.

"I'm surprised he wasn't court-martialed," Webster said.

Kurt Mallon had been hospitalized for pyschiatric observation prior to an arraignment. While hospitalized he had assaulted a U.S. Army psychiatrist. The psychiatrist was female. Prior to the assault she had concluded that Mallon had been abused as a child, and that he had a deep fear of, and hostility toward, all things female.

Webster sighed. "What I don't understand, how come the army didn't press charges?"

The service file was sketchy in that regard. Apparently Mallon had agreed to a psychiatric discharge, preexisting condition, in lieu of a trial—in effect he pled nolo to the assault charges and let himself be cut off from any service-related benefits.

"They were saving money," Webster said. "Get this disturbed individual out of the military, let society deal with him. And I was sap enough to hire him. Beautiful."

Webster made polite conversation, reiterating his invitation to come fishing when the season opened, but his heart wasn't in it. He felt physically ill. He had genuinely liked the boy, liked his enthusiasm for the job, his willingness to learn. A bad call. By hiring Kurt Mallon, he had exposed the community to a potentially psychopathic individual who was all the more dangerous because he had the trust and access accorded to an officer of the law.

It was an ugly situation that had to be fixed. Jack Webster heaved himself out of his easy chair.

"You bastards piss me off, you know that?" he said to ball players on the television screen.

They made love, fell deeply asleep, and then woke to find themselves making love again. It was as if they had been sharing the same erotic dream and responded in exactly the same way at the same moment.

"You know what I want?" Tom said, after catching his breath. "I'd give my left nut for a cigarette."

Susan kissed the tip of his nose. "You're welcome to the

cigarette, but I now have a proprietary interest in keeping your, um, *equipment* in place.''

Tom grinned and gave up the idea of a smoke. There were no cigarettes in the apartment, and in any case he was not about to abandon the luxury of Susan's arms to search for a dose of nicotine.

''I have a question,'' he said, staring at a certain spot on the ceiling. ''You don't have to answer if you'd rather not.''

''Ask away,'' Susan said.

''Are you going to marry Eliot James?''

Susan giggled. She was not the giggling type; it just escaped her lips as an effervescence of joy. ''I was never really going to marry him,'' she said. ''I just hadn't found the right way to say no. Satisfied?''

''Totally.''

They drifted off, arms and legs entwined. Tom dreamed that the bed was a raft, that it was summer on the river, that he and Susan were together. When he woke up he was greatly relieved to find that the most crucial part of the dream was true. Susan was real and he loved her. In the dim light her hair was like finely spun, copper-tinted gold. The discovery pleased him. He looked forward to many more discoveries along that line.

''What happens next?'' he asked, nudging her awake.

''You mean with us?'' Susan said. ''Or you mean the situation?''

''Both, I guess. I'm assuming Sprauken will fire us.''

Susan sat up, hugging her knees to her chest. She'd been dreaming that it was summer—the heat had come on and the bedroom was relatively warm—and her mind wasn't quite ready to engage in contemplation of the future. After a few moments' consideration she said, ''If they *don't* fire me I'll resign. I can't play their game.''

''You'll give up the Biohazard Lab?''

She nodded quickly. ''Not the work, though. I want to start over again, do it right this time.''

Tom smiled. He had the same thing in mind, or did he? Did Susan want to make a life with him, or was he projecting his own fantasy?

"Of course we'll need a similar base of operations," Susan said dreamily, her fingertips lightly brushing the naked flesh of his shoulders. "A roving lab, but independently financed. Not a company store. Ozzie and I have been talking it over. We'd need to get legal advice, but we're hoping we can set up as a nonprofit. Raise funds that have no strings attached. Go wherever we're needed."

"I see," he said.

Susan stopped stroking. His muscles had tensed. "You sound disappointed," she said.

"I was hoping we could work something out. Make a life together."

She slipped down, resting her chin in the crook of his neck. It was amazing how well they fit together. "I thought that's what I was describing," she said. "A life together."

"You were describing a new biohazard lab," he said. "I'm not a pathologist, or a medical technician. I have no expertise in toxins, or neurological disorders, or blood diseases for that matter. I'm not a specialist."

Susan said, "The last thing we need is another specialist."

"Right," Tom said. "So you'll be off roving the world, taking on the toxic bad guys and the criminal polluters, and I'll be at some little clinic somewhere, making sure I have enough tongue depressors and throat swabs."

"You did good work here," Susan said, chiding him. "The people rely on you."

"All I'm saying, we can't be together if we're *not* together."

"Agreed," she said. "If the lab idea doesn't work out, we'll try something else. I started to say the last thing an independent biohazard lab needs is another specialist. Specialists tend to screen out any symptoms that don't fit into their area of expertise. I did it with toxins—I preferred to ignore any evidence that didn't point to a toxic leak. I *wanted* it to be a toxic leak. Ozzie focused on microphages to the exclusions of everything else. We missed the big picture until it was almost too late. If it wasn't for the deadwalkers, we might *never* have solved it."

"Keep talking," Tom said. "You're starting to make sense."

Susan sat up again, her pale green eyes glistening with

excitement. "What we've needed all along is a generalist to help keep the specialists on their toes. A physician with an informed, holistic approach to medicine, an open mind, and a willingness to listen."

"You're describing a good internist," Tom said.

Susan kissed his lips and said, "I'm describing you."

7:10 P.M.

"In my opinion," Sam Carnovitz said, "this is not so bad. Could be worse."

The rental vans had been waved through the security check-points and driven directly into the main building of the Experimental Division. By then Bernie had seen the name of the company displayed in several signs and logos. Sprauken International. He knew nothing about the corporation except that it was a huge conglomerate. So at least the check would be good.

The vans had delivered them into what appeared to be a large hangar, although there were no aircraft in evidence. The van windows were tinted, obscuring his view, but Bernie glimpsed a large scaffolding construction put into stark relief by powerful lights high up in the hangar rafters.

The next thing he saw, when the van came to a stop, was the lounge area of a nursing home.

"They're making us wait again," he said, nudging Sam.

Sam squinted, studying the lounge area. "Something's wrong," he said. "It's a fake. I can tell a fake when I see one."

As he helped Sam down from the van—he insisted on moving under his own steam, no wheelchair for tough old Sam—Bernie saw that his friend was correct. The "lounge," set up in the center of a much larger open area, was contrived of partitioned cubicles and items of furniture appropriate to a Vets' hospital. A pool table—not even regulation size, Bernie noted—a few card tables and chairs, a couple of colorless couches, a television. That was it.

"They want us to feel comfortable," Sam whispered.

Sprauken technicians, wearing dull gray overalls with "Sprauken Experimental Division" stitched on their lapels, helped the volunteer group from the van. Those who were incapacitated were transferred directly to the cubicles. Bernie and Sam, being of the more or less ambulatory group, were encouraged to make themselves at home in the lounge area.

"You fellas just relax now," the boss technician suggested. "Play cards, watch some tube, whatever. There are extra beds in the cubicle when you feel tired. We want you to get acclimated to the surroundings this evening. The supervisor will brief you on the actual test procedure tomorrow morning."

Bernie helped Sam into a chair, then approached the boss technician.

"Excuse me," he said. "What about this big test? What's going to happen to us?"

"Like I said, you'll be briefed first thing in the morning."

He started to turn away. Bernie grabbed his sleeve. "Are they going to give us a drug?" he asked. "What are they testing here?"

The technician patted his hand reassuringly. "Relax, Pops. This is just a psychological study. You know, what makes you tick. They'll explain it all later."

A psychological study? Bernie was vaguely disappointed by the whole tawdry setup. He had envisioned a sci-fi scenario, with figures in germproof suits, and bubbling test tubes. What they were getting was yet another version of a runaround.

He found Sam staring up toward the distant ceiling of the hangar.

"Can you see?" he asked.

Bernie looked. A net of fine black mesh had been suspended fifteen feet or so overhead, obscuring the view. He could discern a few lights twinkling through the net, almost like stars in a night sky. All else was shadows.

"I can't see much of anything," Bernie said.

"There's something up there," Sam said. He leaned forward, lowering his voice. "Equipment and stuff. Like a big camera, maybe. I think we're under observation."

"That makes sense," Bernie said. He told Sam about the psychological aspect of the test, according to the technician. "They're seeing how we react to a new environment, I assume."

"Psychological, schmychological," Sam scoffed. "It only means they intend to play tricks on us. Wait and see."

"What kind of tricks?" Bernie asked.

Sam grimaced. "The kind of tricks they pay you fifty thousand dollars for, that's what kind of tricks." He paused, glanced around at the hospice environment, and seemed satisfied. Color had returned to his cheeks. "I notice they got cribbage. You wanna play me? I'll go slow."

"Sure, Sam, why not?"

Sam shuffled and dealt. The other ambulatory vets gravitated to the pool table and began wagering on the outcome of a game of eight-ball. In a strange and disturbing way it was as if they'd never left the hospice. Sam was well on his way to his usual cribbage triumph when Bernie happened to look down at the floor.

"That's odd," he said. "There's sawdust on the floor, like a saloon. What do you make of that?"

Sam tapped his cane on the floor, sending up little puffs of the antiseptically treated sawdust.

"More like a circus," he said. "And we're in the center ring."

Colonel Benjamin E. Bentley, Jr., stood at the observation rail with his hands clasped behind his back. He was resplendent in full uniform. No wrinkle marred the material. No speck of dust adhered to his neat array of campaign ribbons. His shoes were spit polished and boned to the exact degree of gleam he'd learned first at his father's knee and later at Annapolis. Bentley had taken an unusual measure of care in dressing; these were, after all, American military veterans. Given the opportunity, he had intended to pass among them, acknowledging their courage in stepping forward when the call for volunteers went out.

But when he observed the sorry group disembarking from the vans, his resolve weakened. A phantom platoon. Sick old men in mismatched pants and shirts, in bathrobes, in wheel-chairs, lying motionless on gurneys. Pathetic. If this was courage, it was a variety he had never before encountered. It was obvious these derelict old men no longer had the will to live. They had given up. To greet them would be demeaning. Tony Faro's way was better: keep your distance, observe from on high or via the monitors.

Colonel Bentley swiveled his shoulders and faced the young engineer who had, by his own initiative, seized effective control of the PULSE project. "Time?" he asked.

"Soon," Tony replied. He was chewing gum, snapping it sharply as he gazed down at the target area. In a few minutes he would activate the circuits and begin the complicated process of warming up the prototype. "They've just been informed that the test will not be administered until tomorrow morning. That should cool them out."

"I see," Bentley said with a note of disapproval.

Tony Faro gave him a look. Would the guy ever lighten up? "Hey, Colonel, what do you want, huh? You want me to tell 'em we're planning to zap 'em with a pulse that will short-circuit every nerve in their bodies? I tell 'em that, some of those old duffers will keel over and die before we even get the unit warmed up."

Colonel Bentley nodded. Tony had a point. "They do know the severity of the test procedure? That they may be permanently incapacitated?"

Tony did his best to hide his smirk. *Permanent* was the right word. Bentley was playing it very cagey, the neutral observer routine, but he wasn't kidding Tony. DARPA wanted proof that PULSE was a killing machine, and they were going to get it. In spades.

"Yeah, sure they know," Tony said. "They signed all the paperwork. We're covered."

The marine cleared his throat. It had the effect of making his chin even more prominent. Tony could tell that he was uneasy about something. Excellent. The idea was to keep the colonel slightly off balance, if possible.

"When the sequence starts," Bentley said. "How long until the effect takes place? Is there a possibility that the, uh, volunteers may panic? Bear in mind that everything is being recorded in great detail."

So that was it. The colonel didn't want any gruesome scenes documented on the videotapes. Screaming and yelling, that kind of stuff. Might look bad if the subcommittee ever got the chance to review the data.

"Don't worry, Colonel. They'll never know what hit 'em."

The Biohazard Lab was dark. Mallon circled the clinic parking lot in his cruiser, as he would during any routine patrol, and observed no signs of life in the lab. Regrettably he did not have a passkey, so gaining access would necessitate a break-in. What kind of alarm or security system protected the lab's extensive inventory of equipment? He didn't have a clue, and Tony Faro had been no help at all.

"How the hell should I know?" the engineer had bristled. "You're the security cop, you figure it out. Just make damn sure you don't get caught."

Easily said. If the break-in was to remain undetected—and that was the whole point, according to Tony—it would require considerable cunning and finesse. You couldn't just hack the door down or bust in a window, Mallon reasoned. This was an undercover search and destroy. This was political action.

He parked the cruiser behind the lab, well out of the area illuminated by the clinic floodlights. He took several deep breaths. It was important to have the mind clear and focused before starting a mission, a lesson that had been drilled into him at the Special Forces training camp. He got out of the cruiser and quietly closed the door. The air was crisp, much colder than at first impression. As always, snow threatened, with an overcast cutting visibility even further. He would have liked to extinguish the parking lot floodlights, but that would attract attention, rather than deflect it. Traffic up to the clinic ER entrance was more or less constant; fortunately the narrow arc of the headlights failed to connect with the lab. All in all it wasn't a bad target.

Mallon opened the trunk and tried to remove the gym bag Tony Faro had given him. He tore one of the handles. Damn!

The magnet was adhering to the trunk with great force. He discovered how to free it by prying carefully at the corner of the gym bag and easing it away from the metal. All a matter of finesse.

Recon began at the rear of the lab trailer. There was only one window, much too small to permit entry. The door was securely fastened with a deadbolt. There would be no convenient tripping of the lock with a credit card, the cop show trick that so rarely worked in real situations.

As he'd suspected, the only plausible point of surreptitious entry was by way of the roof. He'd taken a quick look when installing the electronic bug on the phone line. He remembered a vent hood, possibly a skylight. The roof also had an added advantage—he was less likely to be seen up there.

Mallon checked to be sure he had his tool kit, then slung the gym bag over his shoulder and approached the forward end of the trailer. Getting up onto the roof was more difficult than he'd anticipated. There was an ice buildup along the edges; footholds were minimal.

What you had to do, you had to swarm up by main strength, just like the obstacle course in boot camp. You had to simply go for it.

He heaved himself up, managed to get his leg hooked over the edge, and dragged the rest of his body into place. His heart began pounding as the first sparks of adrenaline rushed into his bloodstream. In the darkness Mallon grinned to himself. He was alive, in control. Too bad Tony Faro couldn't see him. He might get a few points for style.

Mallon crawled along the top of the trailer on his belly. He found the skylight, a fixed bubble of Plexiglas, and brushed away a crust of snow. Below there were faint lights—some sort of lab equipment, and a faint amber glow he assumed was the computer screen. After determining that the skylight was riveted in place, he moved to the vent housing.

Machine screws. He could tell that much by touch alone. Mallon eased over on his side and freed the tool kit from his hip pocket. Inside was a battery-powered screwdriver and an assortment of tips. He clipped on the machine tip and set to work. The screws were frozen in place and he found a good deal of wrist action was necessary to free them.

Now that he was working, his heart settled into steady rhythm. He felt almost giddy from the action high. His Special Forces instructors had said there was nothing like the euphoria of a combat situation. The intense cold was an added stimulus. Get in, do the job, get out.

The steel metal vent housing was fairly pliable. He left one side secured and tipped it back. The aluminum made a soft booming noise like distant thunder. Warm lab air wafted up, making his eyes water. The opening was just large enough to accommodate his shoulders.

Mallon took a deep breath, exhaled all the way, and lowered himself through the opening. His feet encountered something solid halfway down. A table or workbench. Perfect. He retrieved the gym bag and ducked down, closing the vent housing as he went.

There were noises in the lab. Clicks and hums. A variety of medicinal odors permeated the warm atmosphere. He began to sweat. With all the equipment jammed into a small space, there was very little room to move, or to breathe. The stifling darkness began to press around him.

Easy, he thought. *Take it easy. The hard part is over. The rest will be a piece of cake.*

Then he heard the snoring. A soft, sibilant sound that seemed to originate in the far end of the lab, near the door. Mallon remained frozen in place, aware of his heart thumping against his ribs. The snoring continued. Did the lab have a guard he didn't know about? Impossible. Had to be Dr. Bitch or the nigger hunchback.

You could leave right now, he thought. *Tell Tony Faro the place is under guard.*

The scorn he would have to endure made that option impossible. Mallon tightened his grip on the gym bag and made his way toward the amber glow he'd seen through the skylight.

It was, as he'd guessed, the computer console. He opened the gym bag slowly, confident that the soft purr of the zipper would not disturb whoever was sleeping. As he lifted the magnet free he found himself hoping that Dr. Bitch was there, asleep and vulnerable. The softness of her throat.

By the light of the screen he was able to locate a file drawer jammed with floppy disks. He passed the magnet over them, as instructed, then ran the heavy magnet around the computer housing for good measure.

What Tony wants, Tony gets.

He returned the magnet to the gym bag and closed the zipper. The mission was concluded. What he should do was leave the way he'd come. No one would ever be the wiser.

The soft, nearly inaudible sound of someone sleeping drew him forward. Creepy-crawl time. He had to know if Dr. Bitch was there. Mallon bumped his hip into a lab table. A small metallic thump. Suddenly he was aware of a sharp, intoxicating odor. Vaguely familiar. His questing fingers encountered a canister, cold to the touch. He drew his fingers away, sniffed them. What was it? Some noxious chemical.

Ether.

Damn straight. They'd used ether on him when he was five or six, the only time he'd ever been hospitalized, to have his tonsils removed. His mother said, "They're going to put you to sleep," and he had struggled, recalling that what they did to cats and dogs was called putting them to sleep. He'd never forgotten the sensation of dread, or the terrible smell that made him sick.

He left the can of ether where it was and worked his way forward, taking great care. He found himself looking down at the nigger hunchback, who lay on his back, sound asleep on a small fold-out cot. He looked like a child, a harmless child, and Mallon felt a pang of disappointment.

He was just starting to back away when a shrill noise erupted.

An alarm.

Mallon ducked behind the filing cabinets. A moment later the lights came on and he heard the hunchback mutter, "The bastards. The bastards."

8:46 P.M.

Susan was sound asleep. She was lying on the warm sand at a beach, totally content, and then suddenly she was being rudely awakened.

"It's Ozzie," Tom said. "He just called. It went off, Susan! The damn thing *went off*."

She sat up, tried to clear her head. It was a hell of a lot more fun dozing on the warm beach. Couldn't it wait until morning? What was Ozzie being a pest about now?

"The radar detector just fired off," Tom said. He had the lights blazing and was hurriedly dressing. His eyes were an intense, startling shade of blue. He was excited. "The bastards are pulling an end run."

The bastards? Then it was all clear: the PULSE test had been moved up. Maybe they'd learned of her cable to DARPA, or maybe they were just taking advantage of Goddard's absence. The "why" didn't really matter.

She quickly got out of the bed and looked around for her clothes. Tom helped her. Bending over, they kept bumping into each other. Under any other circumstances her impulse would have been to embrace him, coax him back into bed. Now it would have to wait.

"What else did Ozzie say?" she wanted to know.

"That was it. I said we'd meet him at the lab."

Susan pulled up her pants, buttoned her blouse. She had been unable to locate her brassiere. The hell with it. "You go to the lab," she said. "I'm going straight over to the plant."

Tom was aghast. "Susan, you can't."

"I've got a security pass," she countered. "I'm cleared, thanks to Goddard. If I put up enough fuss, maybe they'll call it off."

Tom grasped her shoulders, turned her around. "Susan, please," he said. "I can't let you go in there alone."

She gently pulled free. "Don't be silly," she said. "I won't be in any danger. The worst that can happen is they'll refuse to abort the test."

"I'll come with you then."

She shook her head. "You'll never make it inside without a pass."

"Damn it, I'm coming."

"Tell you what," she said. "Go find Jack Webster.

He's the head of Security. I'll wait for you inside the gate.''

"Promise?"

"Sure," she said. They kissed.

The itch had moved inside his skull. There was no way to scratch it. As the Thorazine injection wore off it only got worse. Goddard clawed at his temples until the blood ran into his eyes, and when that didn't work he began to weep.

He was weeping when the lights dimmed.

The transformers are kicking, he thought.

He absentmindedly licked at his bloody fingers while he considered the significance. The transformers being activated. Only a full-scale warmup of the prototype would require activation of the transformers. Had the dimming of the lights been another hallucination? A taunt from inside his head?

Goddard sat up. *Concentrate*, he thought. *Think*.

He forgot about the itch.

Tony. The boy was going to run the final sequence without him. Goddard staggered into the bathroom. He turned on the shower and thrust his head under the icy stream of water.

Think.

PULSE, he thought.

PULSE.

A gust of wind rocked the trailer. Freaking snowstorms. How did they stand the weather up here? First it was just a snow squall, now it was a polar wind blowing down from Canada.

Ozzie shivered. The heating system in the lab was supposed to be more than adequate, but apparently the wind was too much for it. He could feel a distinct draft. Was the thermostat set too low, or had he spaced out, left the vent open?

He shrugged on a cardigan-style sweater, a Christmas gift from Susan. A real beauty, handmade in Ireland. Did she know that cool weather sometimes settled into the deformations of his spine? That he found it easier to don a cardigan than a pullover? Probably. Hard to keep secrets from Susan. Although it was going to be considerably easier now that she was distracted by Mr. L. L. Bean. Ozzie grinned to himself. He'd been playing cupid for some time, shooting imaginary arrows into any reasonably attractive and decent male who crossed her path. Until Tom Weston came along, nothing had taken, and a bad marriage to that condescending snob loomed as inevitable. Now Professor Eliot James was out of the picture for good, and Ozzie was content.

We'll settle this ugly business and get the hell out of here, he thought.

Cold air. He stood up, aware of a nagging ache between his shoulder blades, and shuffled toward the rear of the lab. Check the vent. The computer screen was on—he always left it on, to save the trouble of waiting for it to warm up—and the amber glow illuminated a gym bag left on the workable.

Now how had *that* gotten there? Was it something Tom Weston had left behind? Strange that he hadn't noticed it before.

Ozzie paused by the cryostat machine. The freezing unit clicked on, the compressor hummed. Something was out of place. The microtome unit, his pride and joy for paper-thin tissue preparation, was not exactly as he'd left it. He reached out and discovered that the knife was missing.

The enormity of the missing microtome knife was so compelling that he almost didn't hear the single footstep behind him.

Ozzie turned.

He tried to say *Oh, it's you,* but something thin and hot entered his throat and suddenly his chest was warm. He felt himself becoming light. Light enough to float away into the darkness.

Light enough to become the darkness.

The snow was coming in hard, grainy pellets, driven horizontally by the wind. Tom had the presence of mind to put the Jeep in four-wheel drive and leave it there. There was nothing he could do to improve the visibility. Not even the high beams could cut through the white veil of the storm.

Jack Webster had not been at home. Having called, and getting no answer, Tom had driven there to make absolutely sure that Jack hadn't fallen asleep in front of the TV. He should have known better: a career cop like Webster would be attuned to the ring of the phone, whether asleep or awake.

Tom headed for the main Security office, adjacent to the gated entrance to the village, less than a half mile from the complex where Webster lived. He was relieved to see the office lights on. Inside he found a young security guard warming his hands over an electric heater. The guard looked guilty; he was supposed to be outside in the shack, manning the gate.

"Where's Jack?" Tom demanded.

"Who, sir?"

"Jack Webster. Chief of Security. Your boss, I assume. Where the hell is he?"

The guard appeared tongue-tied.

"I'm not going to report you, for god's sake. Just tell me where I can find your boss."

The guard gulped. "Gone," he said.

"I can see that. Where'd he go?"

The guard shrugged. "He's out looking for Deputy Mallon. He just, you know, took off."

"Took off?"

The guard nodded miserably. "Chief Webster didn't tell me nothing, sir. Only I should remain on my post."

He finally found the chief at the clinic. Or rather he found Webster's cruiser, idling unattended outside the ER entrance. Tom got out of the Jeep, went to the cruiser, and leaned on the horn. Webster exited the ER almost instantly.

"Doc!" he called out. "What's the problem?"

Not wanting to waste time with lengthy explanations, Tom merely said that Susan was heading for the plant and that he believed her life was in danger.

Webster assumed the danger was Kurt Mallon.

"He's out here somewhere," the chief said. "I can't raise him on the radio, or else he won't respond. Suppose to make his circuit by here on the hour, but there's been no sign of him."

"You're talking about that crazy deputy?" Tom said. "Look, never mind him for the moment. Help me get through security at the plant."

Webster stepped back, shading his eyes from the blinding snow. "Maybe you better tell me what's going on, Doc."

"On the way," Tom said, urging him into the Jeep. "We'll take this; I've got better traction."

He intended to crash through the rear gate again, if necessary. Leaving the clinic, he turned, taking a shortcut through the parking lot.

"That's strange," he said. "Ozzie just called me from the lab."

"What's strange about that?" Webster was rapidly becoming irritated by the doctor's inexplicably manic behavior. What the hell was this about circumventing security at the plant?

"The lights are out," Tom said.

He stopped the Jeep and ran to the trailer. Webster, sighing, heaved himself out of the passenger seat and followed. He found Tom standing stock still just inside the darkened doorway of the lab. Snow blew in around his feet.

"It was unlocked," Tom said in a hushed voice. "Listen."

Webster listened. Something was thumping against the side of the trailer. "Just the wind," he said. "Tree branch came down."

"Ozzie?" Tom called. "Ozzie, where the hell are you?"

"He usually leave the door unlocked?" Webster asked.

Tom shook his head. "Not tonight he wouldn't."

"Shit."

The thumping continued, slow and steady. Webster felt the hairs rise on the back of his neck.

"Ozzie?"

Tom started toward the sound.

Webster drew out his service revolver and stepped in front of the doctor. Taking over. It was a question of correct procedure. He was the investigative officer. It was his duty to investigate, whether he wanted to or not.

"You find the goddamn light switch," he ordered, his voice husky with anxiety. He hated unexplained noises, bumps in the night. He hated mysteries of any kind. He hated what he was smelling: that distinct, coppery odor.

When the lights came on Webster immediately saw the trail of blood. He wrinkled his nose in disgust. A slaughterhouse smell. He advanced sideways, easing his bulk through the crowded lab, trying to keep his feet clear of the blood. It was impossible. There were long, arterial spurts of it everywhere.

In the rear of the lab he saw the dark, nappy head; the wet, crimson sweater. Chester Oswald had gotten as far as the back wall, and there he remained, striding slowly in place.

"You better come here, Doc," he said.

Tom squeezed by. When he saw the immense quantity of blood, the deep slash that had severed the jugular, he knew there was no hope.

"The poor little bugger is still trying to get away," Webster marveled, staring down at the plodding feet.

Tom knew better. He knew a deadwalker when he saw one.

9:21 P.M.

There was one bad moment when Susan was convinced she was being followed. The snow was nearly blinding, and it was all she could do to concentrate on peering through the smeared windshield. When a glint of headlights flashed in the rearview mirror she glanced up and saw, or *thought* she saw, a white Saab close behind.

In the next heartbeat the headlights disappeared and the mirror became a black hole full of swirling white dust. Just ahead of her, looming like an alien spacecraft, was a huge snowplow blazing with lights. Greatly relieved, she stayed within range. The truck was spraying a mixture of sand and salt that improved traction on the icy road.

Now and again she glanced into the mirror. Nothing. She decided that her anxiety had supplied an image to go with the flash of headlights. Simple trick of an overwrought mind.

The snowplow was excruciatingly slow, but Susan had calmed down enough to be sensible, keeping the pace. There was no point in going faster if it meant risking a skid into a snowbank. After a mile or so she parted company and turned into the brightly illuminated entrance to the Experimental Division.

As the bundled-up guard came out of the shack to greet

her, Susan decided not to wait for Tom. It had taken longer than she'd anticipated to reach the plant. There was no time. He would be angry, or worried, and she would make it up to him later. It might even be fun, the making-up part.

The gate was the first of three security stops, and each seemed to take longer than the previous. Inside the building, at the final checkpoint, a grim-looking guard walked away with her laminated pass, leaving her alone in the foyer. Susan paced. Who was the guard calling? Had she come this far only to be denied entry?

Three minutes later the guard reappeared, handing her the pass.

"Sorry, Dr. Cullen. We have to make sure the new passes are logged in the computer."

Susan hurried through the door. Goddard had driven her through the hangar in an electric cart, but there were no such carts in evidence now. No doubt they were all in use. She started to jog along the corridor, rehearsing her speech.

As director of Sprauken's Biohazard Lab, I am responsible for the well-being of all company employees. I demand that this test be aborted right now.

Forceful, but would they buy it? Maybe the Goddard gambit would sound more convincing.

I have reason to believe the Special Projects Director wants this test postponed.

If threats didn't work she would resort to begging.

You may be killing people. Please stop.

The corridor zagged to the left, through a fire door. Susan found herself in the rear of the hangar. The sudden dimness, in contrast to the brightly lit corridors, left her momentarily blind. All she could discern were lights in the distance and the skeletal steel structure surrounding the target area.

Susan put her hands to her eyes and blinked.

Something seized the hood of her parka, jerking her backward. She lost her balance and fell.

She opened her mouth to scream.

An evil-smelling rag was shoved between her teeth.

Then she was falling, falling, falling into the rabbit hole.

* * *

The impulse to act normal was a strange and powerful thing, Bernie Simms reflected. Here they were, two gravely ill gentlemen calmly playing cribbage in a fake hospital in the middle of a huge hangar, surrounded by video cameras. In a situation that was distorted and unreal, they were compelled to behave normally.

"You're not concentrating," Sam admonished him. "You got a fine mind, you should utilize it more."

"You feel anything?" Bernie asked.

Sam made a face. "Feel? What should I feel? Except I feel I'm going to skunk you again, if you don't focus on the cards."

"I don't know," Bernie said. He leaned forward, speaking in a lower voice. "I have this feeling all those little video cameras are turned on. You know, watching us."

"So?"

"So, if they're watching us, maybe the test has started. This psychological test."

Sam shook his head. "Never mind with the psychological. For this kind of money they'll put poison in our prune juice, come morning. Or they'll give us a disease, maybe. Forget psychological and try remembering what card I just played."

"But can you feel those cameras, Sam?"

"Yeah, sure." Sam glanced at the top of the partitions, where a number of small video cameras were mounted, covering the lounge area and each cubicle. "Television. There's one thing I've always wanted to do on television."

"What's that, Sam?"

"This," he said, holding up his middle finger to the cameras.

Bernie laughed. Sam looked twenty years younger giving the finger. Bernie tried it. It made him feel lightheaded. He'd never given the finger to anyone in his life, never, and here he was, onstage and performing. He wondered what the psychologists would make of two old men waving skinny, mottled knuckles at an unknown audience.

"They'll think we're crazy," he said.

"So what? Be a little crazy, you've got the right. You don't think you were a little crazy when you were all the time jumping out of airplanes?"

"That was different," Bernie said. "That was wartime. The world was crazy."

"Let me tell you something," Sam said. "The world is still crazy. Only a more dangerous crazy. Back in Germany that nutball Hitler started a new thing, this Big Lie idea. He used the Big Lie to go after the Jews. The idea was, you say a lie enough times to enough people, eventually it becomes true. Now *that's* crazy."

"That was Hitler," Bernie said. "Look where it got him."

"You think the Big Lie stopped with Hitler? All that happened is the public relations firms took it over. The advertising men. They knew a good thing when they saw it. The ad men control the world now. They choose the politicians. They put the spin on the news. Whatever they want us to believe, we end up believing."

Bernie laughed. "You know what you are, Sam? You're a paranoid."

"Again with the psychological!" Sam said, exasperated. "In this century, with all the terrible things that have happened, what sane man wouldn't be a paranoid?"

"Poison in the prune juice, Sam. That's a paranoid idea."

"Going to the showers and getting gassed to death, that was a paranoid idea also. But it happened."

Discussions with Sam Carnovitz were always stimulating, if sometimes irritating. He was a know-it-all; the trouble was, he *did* know a lot. He had theories. He liked big ideas. And the son of a bitch always won at cribbage.

"You should learn to concentrate," Sam suggested. "My ten-year-old granddaughter can play better than you."

Bernie threw his cards down in disgust. He happened to glance up. "Hey," he said. "We got company."

Another gurney was arriving, pushed by a young man with a dark mustache and dark, hooded eyes. He wore a gray Sprauken lab coat that was a little too short in the sleeves. The young man checked the cubicles until he found one empty, and pushed the gurney and the unconscious volunteer inside. He closed the door and started to stride away.

"Hey you," Bernie said. "Who is this new person you brought us? Does he have a name?"

The young man in the lab coat hesitated, undecided. When he turned to Bernie and Sam he was smiling. Bernie noticed the healthy tan, the strong white teeth, and felt a pang of jealousy.

"The patient is very ill," the young man said, indicating the closed door of the cubicle. "Please don't disturb her."

"Yeah, sure," Bernie said.

Apparently satisfied with the answer, the young man hurried away.

"Her?" Sam said, brightening. "I thought this was a bachelor party. A bunch of sick old men. And now we got a her? Maybe I should brush my teeth."

"She's sick," Bernie pointed out. "Unconscious."

"You never know," Sam said, eyeing the door. "At our age you always got to be ready."

Webster had to resort to threats before Dr. Weston was cleared to enter the plant perimeter.

"We're supposed to follow the regulations," the guard said, his voice quavering. "That's what you told us, sir."

"And now I'm telling you we have an emergency situation. Lift the gate."

The guard appeared to be in pain. He fidgeted. "I don't know what to do, Chief."

"Lift the gate, Jones. Don't forget I'm the guy signs your time card. You want to get paid this week, lift the goddamn gate, return to the shack, and keep your mouth shut."

The gate lifted. Tom drove through. "Which way?"

"Hang a right," Webster suggested. "We'll make a circuit until you spot her vehicle. Then we'll go from there."

They drove along in silence. The discovery of Ozzie's body had been stunning. It was an act of such incomprehensible violence that it left Tom feeling numb. His one thought was to find Susan. There was no longer any doubt that she was in great danger. What he would do when he found her was something he would have to figure out when the time came.

Tom Weston was terrified that Susan would be snatched from him, as Jeannie had been. At first he had tried to deny that fear, and in so doing he had kept his distance, convinced that love would inevitably end in disaster. Now, having seen Ozzie with his throat horribly slashed, he knew the fear was not irrational. There were forces beyond his control at work. Murder was the ultimate anarchy, and the realization filled him with dread.

"Take it easy, Doc," Webster said. "We'll find her."

What they found first was not Susan's rental car but Kurt Mallon's white Saab. It stood out from the other vehicles because much less snow had accumulated on the roof, trunk, and hood. Jack Webster got out of the Jeep with his revolver drawn. He circled the Saab, peering in the windows, and returned to the Jeep.

"No obvious bloodstains on the seats," he said. "Maybe it wasn't Kurt who broke into the lab. Whoever killed Ozzie had to have been covered with blood."

Tom said, "Let's just find Susan. You can deal with your deputy later."

"Patience, my son," Webster said. Inwardly he winced at the phrase "your deputy." It hurt to be reminded that Kurt Mallon was his responsibility. If he'd done a thorough job of vetting the boy's service record Chester Oswald might still be alive.

"I'm going to finish inspecting the vehicle," Webster announced. "Time I started doing this job by the book."

Using his spare set of keys, he unlocked the Saab and ran a flashlight over the floor mats and the seats. There were a few dark drops on the mats, but a mere visual examination couldn't determine the substance. Could have been blood, could have been motor oil or cough syrup. He put the mats aside for the State Police forensic unit.

Tom got out of the Jeep, agitated. "Hurry up, Jack! For god's sake, you can play detective tomorrow."

Webster ignored him and went to the trunk. He popped the lid. A small dome light came on. The trunk area looked clean.

"Fine," Tom shouted. "You stay here. I'm leaving."

Webster lifted the cover to the wheel well. The familiar coppery smell was suddenly sharp and distinct in the crisp air. Inside the wheel well, wedged against the spare tire, was a blood-soaked uniform shirt. He probed the shirt. Something glinted.

"Can you identify that?" he asked.

Tom, looking over his shoulder, grunted. "Yeah. I think it's a lab tool. A microtome knife. Used to slice tissue samples."

"Sharp?"

"Extremely," Tom said.

"Well," he said. "Now we know for sure he's started."

"What are you talking about?"

Webster removed a cigar from his pocket and clamped it unlit between his teeth. The cigar was ballast, something to steady him now that he knew the worst. "You know how the FBI is about statistics, Doc. They don't call it a bureau for nothing. We used to keep updating the profiles on psychopathic behavior. Got so we could predict how certain kinds of killers would react in certain situations. And once a man with Kurt Mallon's profile starts killing, he's compelled to *keep* killing."

"You're scaring the hell out of me, Jack."

The cigar waggled as Webster grinned. "I'm scaring the hell out of myself."

10:05 P.M.

When the ghost emerged from the elevator, conversation on the observation platform ceased. Tony Faro was the first to recognize him.

"Dr. Goddard!" he exclaimed. "We weren't expecting— that is, we had no idea . . ."

"Good evening, Tony. Colonel Bentley. Good evening to all of you."

Goddard limped from the elevator cage. Although his voice seemed firm and in control, his body was visibly devastated by the effects of amphetamine abuse. His complexion, always pale, had become virtually translucent; his bones appeared to be emerging through the taut flesh. His eyes were more drained of color than ever, and had sunk deep into his head.

He's a skull, Tony thought, fighting to hide his distress at Goddard's unexpected appearance. *A fucking skull.*

"Obviously the human test phase is going ahead without my authorization," Goddard said, addressing himself to Colonel Bentley. "Does this mean I've been terminated as Special Project Director?"

Bet your bony ass, Tony thought, smiling brightly as he waited for confirmation.

Colonel Bentley had lost none of his cool restraint. He ordered the team members to resume their positions on the platform, and then took Goddard aside. Tony followed. He wanted to be there when the ax fell. The king is dead, long live the king.

"I've been in consultation with my superiors," the colonel began. "The situation is as follows. You have been suspended as Project Director, retaining all pay, benefits, and stock options, pending your agreement to check into the company detox facility."

"I see," Goddard replied gravely.

Tony Faro didn't quite see. He didn't like the tone, the implication of "suspended." Suspended? The man had been fired; he was gone, dog meat.

Glancing at Tony to judge his reaction, Colonel Bentley continued explaining the situation to Goddard, who appeared to be in a trance. "After successfully completing the detox program, you will resume your post as acting Special Project Director."

"I assumed you had put Tony in charge," Goddard said.

The colonel smiled. "Tony has been helping out on a temporary basis. Isn't that right, Tony?"

Tony almost gagged. It was so goddamn unfair. "Anything you say, Colonel," he managed.

"There are new appropriations hearings coming up," Colonel Bentley continued. "We feel your testimony will be crucial, Dr. Goddard. The subcommittee members have great respect for you, for your accomplishments, your reputation."

So that was it, Tony thought. *The money thing.*

They wanted to use Goddard, the certified Apollo hero, to sell PULSE to Congress. It was simple, time-proven strategy. Tony Faro just didn't carry the weight.

"I made a formal request that the human test phase be delayed," Goddard said. He sounded like he had something stuck in his throat.

"Request noted," Colonel Bentley said, "and denied. We need the data, Kenneth. When you come out of detox you'll see it all more clearly."

Tony was seeing it now. He was seeing it all very clearly indeed. He had been set up. Bentley had made him the designated fall guy.

He thought, *Screw you, junior. I've got my own agenda.*

He said, "Good to have you back, sir," and shook Goddard's limp, sweating hand.

Tom spotted the green hood. It was from Jeannie's parka, the one he'd given to Susan. He snatched it up off the concrete. His eyes welled with tears.

"She was here," he said.

Webster crouched, running his hands over the floor. The hangar loomed over them. It was such a goddamn big place.

"We'll find her, Doc," he said. "Don't worry."

Sometimes it was necessary to lie, just to keep hope alive.

The pain was like a stainless steel gyroscope spinning in the precise center of her head. Opening her eyes only made it worse. She tried to breathe, but something covered her mouth, and her nostrils still reeked of that horrible, evil smell.

Ether.

Susan kept her eyes tightly shut and tried to bring her aching mind into focus. Ether, yes. She'd been knocked unconscious. With that realization came a spasm of anxiety.

Where am I? What happened?

Movement was impossible. She was in the grip of a giant hand, a hand that squeezed her, covered her mouth.

Susan forced her eyes open. Everything was blurry. She concentrated, and her vision cleared somewhat. There were stars overhead, stars glinting in a black sky. A strange sky, so close she could have reached out and touched it, almost. Had she been able to move.

As the minutes passed she forced air into her lungs, attempting to purge the dizzy stink of ether that seemed to be exuding from her body, from her very pores.

Her stomach began to rebel. It wanted to retch. She resisted. *You're my stomach. Obey.*

As her mind cleared, as she started to come out of the drug-induced dream state, Susan realized that she was not looking up at a night sky bright with stars but a fine black netting, with artificial lights twinkling through from above.

So she was not outside.

She flexed her fingers, encountered stiff canvas, the bristling surface of a Velcro strap.

Restraining jacket.

Her head was afforded some movement. An inch or so from side to side. She was able to discern the surrounding walls of the cubicle, the door, and a glass eye staring at her from atop the partition.

A video camera.

She rested, closed her eyes. She was inside the maze she'd seen under construction when Goddard took her on the tour. What did it all mean? The last fumes of ether reached out from her bloodstream, attempting to drag her back down into dreamland.

Why not? she thought groggily. *Why not?*

It was going to be one of those nights. First the human skull had emerged from the elevator, now it was two apparently deranged individuals, one of whom was waving a green flag. Tony went to confront them, eager to show off his leadership qualities. Make Colonel Bentley see his mistake.

"This is a restricted area," he said. "What the hell do you think you're doing here?"

The older individual, huffing and puffing as he tried to get his breath, was Jack Webster, Chief of Sprauken Security. The younger, wild-haired man, who had been waving the green flag, was Dr. Thomas Weston, the clinic director. Dr. Tom to the villagers. Tony would never have recognized him.

Not the way his eyes were bugging out and his jaw muscles were throbbing. He appeared to be in an acute state of anxiety.

"I don't care who you are," Tony said dismissively. "You can't just bust in here. You're in violation of a National Security ordinance, and subject to arrest."

To Tony's astonishment, Dr. Tom grabbed him by the shirt and lifted him off the platform.

"Where is she, you little snot! Tell me!"

Chief Webster intervened. "Take it easy, Doc. Put him down."

Weston lowered Tony, but failed to relinguish the grip on his shirt.

"We're looking for my deputy, Kurt Mallon," Webster explained. "We have reason to believe he may have abducted Dr. Cullen."

Now Dr. Tom was waving the green flag in Tony's face. He could see it was not a flag, but the detached hood of a parka.

"He already murdered an innocent man, and now he's snatched Susan," Tom said, loosening his fingers. "I figure you're mixed up in this somehow, Faro. Mallon was your spy."

Tony turned to Chief Webster. "What the hell is he talking about? He's crazy. Demented."

"Doc is concerned about the lady, Mr. Faro."

"Ah, you're both nuts. Colonel Bentley! Can we do something about this situation, sir? Have your men escort these two individuals out of the area."

The colonel had been holding back, observing the confrontation with undisguised curiosity. Now he came forward. "What seems to be the problem?"

"Deputy Mallon is wanted in connection with a murder," Webster explained. His eyes were bloodshot. He'd lost his cigar on the elevator. "He's somewhere in the building. We think he's abducted Dr. Cullen. We found part of her coat, and evidence of a struggle."

"Dr. Cullen?" the colonel said.

"The Biohazard Lab," Tom interjected. "She was on her way here to put a stop to the PULSE test."

"I see," the colonel said. He appeared to be faintly amused. "And how is it you happen to know about PULSE? I wasn't aware you'd been given security clearance. Was Dr. Weston given clearance, Tony?"

"Fuck no. I mean no, sir, of course not."

The colonel nodded. "You gentlemen will have to be detained, I'm afraid."

"Now just a goddamn minute," Jack Webster said, coming close enough to bump his belly against the colonel's starched uniform. "You can't arrest me, I'm the security chief. Damn it man, I was in the corps myself. Have a heart."

Colonel Bentley smiled. "I said *detain*, Chief. Not *arrest*. You're disrupting an activity crucial to the national security. If you were a marine you'll understand I have rank in this matter."

While the argument ensued, Tony slipped away, returning to the master control console. He decided to take precautions. He had one last shot at Goddard's job, provided the test sequence came off exactly as he'd planned. Operation mental meltdown. Drive Goddard around the bend, beyond the point of no return.

He touched the sequencing keys, activating the altered program.

Checkmate, he thought.

"We need to mobilize a search of the building," Chief Webster was saying when he returned. "A woman's life is at stake."

Tony almost chuckled. The dweeby old cop was so sincere it was sickening. And Dr. Tom, he looked like he needed to take a pill or something. Totally spazzed out.

"Look," Tony interrupted. "Kurt Mallon hasn't been up here. Neither has Dr. Cullen. We're doing very important work, and we really have to get on with it. Colonel Bentley, why not let these two do their thing, and we'll do our thing? Sound reasonable?"

The colonel gave him a withering glance. He addressed himself to Jack Webster. "We'll suspend operations here for exactly one hour, and assist in a search of the premises. Satisfied?"

"Thanks," Webster said.

Tony noted that Dr. Tom appeared to be holding back tears. What a wimp. "Excuse me, Colonel," he said. "We're into the fail-safe sequence, sir."

Colonel Bentley stared at him. "What's that supposed to mean?"

"Means the program is already up and running."

"Well, interrupt it," the colonel demanded.

"Can't, sir."

"What the hell are you saying, Tony? Of *course* the program can be interrupted."

"Not anymore, sir. If you recall, we had some trouble with glitches in the fail-safe sequence. Dr. Goddard altered the command structure. Once we hit the three-minute mark, the program locks in."

"And when do we hit this three-minute mark?" the colonel said.

Tony smiled. He glanced at his watch. "Right about . . . *now*, sir."

"Could be part of the test," Bernie said. "You know, to see how we'll react."

Sam gave him a puzzled look. "So what are you suggesting?"

"Just that we act normal," Bernie said. "In the hospice, they bring in a new guy, we'd go check him out, right?"

"Of course. But this is no guy. It's a girl. A woman."

"And we wouldn't check out a woman?"

Sam squinted. He came to a decision and pushed against his cane, rising from the chair. "We'll just go in there, pay our respects."

" 'Atta boy, Sam."

The two men shuffled to the cubicle door.

"So who goes first?" Sam asked.

"The Airborne," Bernie said. "We always went in first."

Webster stood at the rail of the observation platform. He had no idea what he was looking at down below. Beneath the net was some sort of construction, inhabited by a few elderly-looking men. Wearing bathrobes and pajamas. What the hell was going on?

The question vanished from his mind the instant he spotted Kurt Mallon. He was lurking in the shadows outside the illuminated area, wearing a gray lab coat, but it was definitely Mallon.

"Kurt!" he shouted.

Don't be a fool, he thought. *Just go after him.*

But Mallon had heard him. In a heartbeat he vanished.

Webster sprinted for the elevator.

Tom felt as if he was enclosed by thick glass. He couldn't seem to move or react. All he could think of was the unthinkable. Susan was already gone. Finding the torn-off hood of the parka he'd given her only confirmed his worst fear: when he loved a woman she was as good as dead.

He looked around. The observation platform was bustling with activity. Webster seemed to have disappeared. For the first time he really took in the PULSE prototype. The huge barrel was beginning to pivot, bringing itself in line over the target area.

Tom went to the rail. Tony Faro and the DARPA colonel were at the console, arguing heatedly. Dr. Goddard was slumped in a chair, covering his face with his hands.

Tom looked down.

It was hard to see through the black netting. He discerned men around a pool table, furniture, beds.

So these were the volunteers. Did they know what was about to happen?

Tom glanced behind him and saw a bank of video monitors. Now he had a close-up view of the pool table. He could see faces. Haggard, human faces. The monitors covered the target area from every conceivable angle.

Tom searched the screens hopelessly. It was useless. Susan would not be there.

Like Jeannie, she was gone. His love had killed her.

Jack Webster was seriously concerned for his heart.

He was too old for this shit. Running like a madman. Riding an open elevator. Chasing a young psychopath who was almost forty years his junior.

His pulse was booming in his ears. His eyes seemed to be affected. Everything was tinged with pink. Was that a sign of impending cardiac arrest?

He took a deep, shuddering breath. The pink tinge went away; his eyes focused better. Adrenaline. Use it or lose it.

He ran across the outer perimeter of the target area and arrived at the place where he'd spotted Mallon.

I'm a psychopath, he thought. *I've just killed one, maybe two people, and I've been found out. What do I do? Where do I go?*

"How the hell do I know?" Webster said aloud.

He spotted a door, ran to it, pushed through into an empty corridor. More doors.

"Shit," he whispered, his nose wrinkling in disgust.

What a night for unpleasant smells. The stink was awful. Bad enough to make his eyes water. Worse than the monkey house at any zoo he'd ever visited. He pushed through the next door and found himself in a room of cages. Now the smell was palpable, a physical presence.

Tears ran from his eyes.

There were things in the cages. Silent monkey-things that did not move. Dozens of dark, glistening eyes, staring at nothing.

Through the bars, on the other side of the cages, dark eyes blinked. Intelligent eyes. Human eyes.

"Kurt?" he said.

A bullet exploded just above his head.

"I still think it's part of the test," Bernie said.

He and Sam were inside the cubicle, staring at the young woman immobilized on the gurney.

"The poor thing is insane," Sam said. "That's what they do with insane people when they get violent. Put them in straitjackets."

"Look at her eyes," Bernie said. "She looks frightened, not crazy."

Sam shook his head. He leaned on his cane, catching his breath. "A person can be insane and frightened at the same time," he said.

The woman was blinking furiously at them, struggling against the canvas jacket.

"We better go," Sam said. "We're upsetting her. She'll maybe have a fit."

"It's not right, keeping a person confined like that," Bernie said. "How can she breathe with her mouth covered?"

"What are you doing?"

"I'm acting normal," Bernie said. "I'm letting a person breathe free."

Webster had his sight centered on Mallon's forehead.

"Put the weapon down on the floor, Kurt," he said. "Push it away from you."

"This is crazy, Chief. You're wrong about me."

Webster kept his revolver steady. All he could see through the bars was Mallon's head. There was a sound of something skidding across the concrete floor.

"Okay, Chief. I pushed it away. Check it out."

Checking it out would mean looking under the cages. Taking his eyes off Mallon. He couldn't risk it.

"Stand up," he ordered. "Real slow."

Webster blinked, fighting to keep the ammonia-induced tears from blinding him. Mallon's eyes were wet, too. *Here we are*, Webster thought. *The chief and his trusted deputy, crying in the monkey house.*

"Stand," he repeated.

Mallon got to his feet. Webster came around the side of the cage.

Tony watched the numbers unraveling on the screen.

"This should be a personal triumph for you," he said to Goddard. "The prototype is yours. The program is yours. The test sequence is yours. We couldn't have done it without you, sir."

Goddard frowned, troubled. "I don't remember altering the fail-safe program," he insisted. "It was an electrical malfunction."

"Must have slipped your mind, sir. You've been under a lot of pressure."

"How could I forget a thing like that?" Goddard said doubtfully. The itching had started up again, right against the inside of his skull, in the little space between bone and brain tissue.

"Ten seconds," Tony said cheerfully. "Keep an eye on the monitors, sir. Take credit where credit is due."

Tom was watching the bald spot. For some strange reason it had attracted his attention. Possibly because it was the only monitor screen that had an obscured view. It made him want to see what was beyond the blurry image of the bald man's head.

Not that he expected to see Susan. Why would he hope that? All of those in the target area were about to become statistics, objects of study. Impaired, maybe terribly injured. This was exactly what Susan had been trying to stop.

It was all his fault. He'd had the bright idea to set up his stupid little radar detector. If the detector hadn't fired off, Susan would still be in his bed. Safe and asleep.

You killed her, he thought. *You let her go.*

The bald head shifted out of the way and Tom found himself looking at the inside of a small cubicle. A woman was sitting up on a gurney, dressed all in white. Her face turned toward the camera.

Susan.

SUSAN.

Alive.

Tom ran.

He would get down the scaffold, take Susan in his arms, run from the target area.

"Five seconds!" Tony Faro announced. "Everybody look sharp!"

No time. No time to think. Time only to act.

He changed direction in mid-stride and headed for the rail. He vaulted over the rail, into the air.

Falling.

His fingers closed, gripping the vacuum housing that covered the base of the prototype. His body slammed into the counterweights. His feet kicked, trying for a foothold.

* * *

"Rock and roll," Tony said as the final digit expired into zero.

PULSE shifted. The counterweight cables spun, reacting to Tom's added mass. The long barrel began to tip upward, gaining momentum.

Colonel Benjamin E. Bentley, Jr., saw it coming. His reaction was immediate. He dropped his clipboard and sprinted.

The first burst of full-power pulses hit the scaffolding and dissipated. The blue glow of the field effect zagged upward, like reverse lightning.

The barrel tipped inside the gimbal, gathering speed. Tom clawed the slick, shifting surface for a handhold. He was slipping.

Tony Faro looked up from the console to see the lethal end of the prototype rise above the safety rail. The focusing horn was aimed right at the observation platform. Right at Goddard. Right at him.

Impossible. He stood up, trying to decide which way to run.

Not me, he thought.

And then he thought no more.

Falling, Tom thought.

He fell.

10:31 P.M.

"What you're going to do next," Webster said. "You're going to put your hands on top of your head."

He eased around the side of the cage, keeping the sight on Mallon. The boy had a strange look on his face. A sort of inner glow. Webster didn't trust that look. He wanted to get the cuffs on him soon, before his strength gave out. Before the ammoniated stink of the monkey cages blinded him with tears.

"Come on, Kurt," he urged gently. "I'll do what I can. Get you a lawyer. Get you help. Whatever I can do, I will."

"I didn't do anything bad."

"Fine," Webster said. "Then you won't mind putting your hands on your head."

He blinked away the tears.

Mallon's right hand was moving. Reaching for the bars of the cage. Reaching for the butt of the revolver he'd wedged between the bars.

"Stop!" Webster ordered.

Mallon's hand closed over the gun. He pulled it free of the bars. His lips lifted in a blinding smile as he raised the gun.

"Me," he said. "My turn."

Webster pulled the trigger. A small red hole opened in Kurt Mallon's forehead.

After the net came crashing down, and all the shouting commenced, Bernie helped the young woman get free of the restraining jacket. She slipped away, having said not a word, not even a thank-you, and he was beginning to think that she really was crazy, that the whole world was crazy, just like Sam always said.

"What happened?" he asked Sam after the woman rushed from the cubicle.

Sam was at the door, looking out at the mess of tangled netting, the collapsed pool table.

"Somebody fell," he said. "Who knows, maybe he jumped."

Bernie decided to follow the young woman. There was a crowd around the pool table. Veterans from the volunteer group, Sprauken technicians, everybody was getting into the act.

The young woman was fighting to get through.

"I'm a doctor!" she was shouting. "Out of my way!"

Red hair, Bernie thought. *She's got a temper.*

In the center of the crowd, caught like a fish in the great black net, was the body of a man.

The young woman screamed a name.

"Tom!"

The body came to life. The young woman scrambled over the torn netting.

"Let me near him! Get back! I'm a doctor!"

Bernie thought, *Red hair, a temper, and she knows what she wants. What a combination.*

He followed her, astonished at how alive he felt. Like after a jump, or making love to Louise, or the very first time he saw his very first grandchild.

Now the young woman was cradling the man's head in her arms.

The man groaned. "I won't be needing a pathologist," he said.

"What?"

He groaned again, then laughed. "Get me a good orthopedist, and a cigarette. My legs are broken."

For some reason that struck Bernie as funny, very funny. He started laughing. It did his heart good.

After several delays he finally got through on the priority line.

"Colonel Bentley here, sir," he said. "Sorry to pull you away from the Redskins game, but we've had an unfortunate accident. I'm afraid there have been fatalities. Yes, sir, that *is* too bad. What I recommend, sir, is you send me your best PR team. We need to get the right spin on this if we're going to save the project."

Bentley listened. He and the general went way back. They had an understanding.

"PULSE, sir?" he said. "No, the prototype wasn't damaged, quite the contrary, it functioned beautifully. I agree, General, that's the important thing."

GREAT BOOKS

E-BOOKS

AUDIOBOOKS

& MORE

Visit us today

www.speakingvolumes.us